Big Girl, Small Town

MICHELLE GALLEN

JOHN MURRAY

First published in Great Britain in 2020 by John Murray (Publishers)
An Hachette UK company

First published in paperback in 2021

1

A CIP catalogue record for this title is available from the British Library

Paperback ISBN 9781529304220
eBook ISBN 9781529304237

Typeset in Monotype Bembo by Manipal Technologies Limited

Printed and bound in Great Britain by Clays Ltd, Elcograf S.p.A.

John Murray policy is to use papers that are natural, renewable and recyclable products and made from wood grown in sustainable forests. The logging and manufacturing processes are expected to conform to the environmental regulations of the country of origin.

John Murray (Publishers)
Carmelite House
50 Victoria Embankment
London EC4Y 0DZ

www.johnmurraypress.co.uk

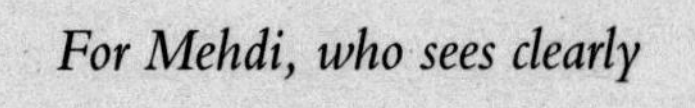
For Mehdi, who sees clearly

What if we accept these points of light, their translucence, their brightness; what if we let ourselves enjoy this, stop fearing it, get used to it; what if we come to believe in it, to expect it, to be impressed upon by it; what if we take hope and forgo our ancient heritage and instead, and infused, begin to entrain with it, with ourselves then to radiate it; what if we do that, get educated up to that, and then, just like that, the light goes off or is snatched away?

Milkman, Anna Burns

Majella kept a list of stuff in her head that she wasn't keen on. Her top ten hadn't changed in seven years:

1) Small talk, bullshit and gossip
2) Physical contact
3) Noise
4) Bright lights
5) Scented stuff
6) Cunter
7) Sweating
8) Jokes
9) Make-up
10) Fashion

The full list of things Majella wasn't keen on extended to ninety-seven items, with subcategories for each item. For example, make-up included nail polish, lipstick, foundation, mascara etc., and Majella had further itemised each subcategory:

Item 9.1. Make-up: nail polish:

- Is too heavy – weighing fingers down.
- Looks utterly unnatural when coloured – e.g. red, orange, black – giving people the appearance of wearing beetle carapaces on their finger ends.
- Difficult to apply, requiring practice, time and skill.
- Prone to smudging during drying period.
- Impermanent: cracks and flakes sometimes in hours, but always within days.
- Requires chemicals during the production process and for removal.
- Complete waste of money.

The list of things Majella *did* see the point in was much shorter:

1) Eating
2) *Dallas* (except for the 1985–86 season, also known as Bobby's Dream)
3) UK Gold
4) Her da
5) Her granny
6) Smithwicks
7) Painkillers
8) Cleaning
9) Sex
10) Hairdryers

Sometimes Majella thought that she should condense her whole list of things she wasn't keen on into a single item:

- Other People.

It was people who talked shit. It was people who made up rules that said you were cool or not because of what you wore. It was people who judged one half of the human race for not wearing make-up, and the other half for wearing it. It was people who switched on lights, made noise, sweated and fought, wept and shouted. Majella knew when she came down to it, she wasn't keen on Other People.

Monday

4.04 p.m.
Item 12.2: Conversation: Rhetorical questions

— Majella?

Her ma's voice was coming from the hallway. Majella pulled the duvet over her head, balled it in her ears and closed her eyes.

— Ma-jell-ah?

She could still hear her ma's oversized monster slippers slapping closer on the stairs. Joke slippers were item 10.4 on Majella's list.

— MAJELLAH? Are ye STILL lying in yer pit?

Majella took her hands from her ears and began to flick her fingers to distract herself. She flinched as her ma cracked her sharp knuckles on the bedroom door.

— Majella? D'ye not have work tae go til this evening?

Majella had work to go to, just as she had done every Monday for the past nine years. And Majella knew that her ma knew that, because her work schedule and weekly Mass were the only routines their lives revolved around. She didn't know why her ma was asking her a question that she already knew the answer to. So she didn't reply.

— Am ah standing here talking tae myself? Am ah just some eejit wasting her breath talking til her daughter's door? Is there nothing that—

Majella needed her ma's voice to stop. — Ah'll get up when ah'm ready. Ah'm not in tae six.

Majella lay stiffly in bed as her ma stood outside the door for a few moments. She slowly relaxed when she heard her shuffling away and flopping back down the stairs. Majella waited until she could hear the telly chittering, then she swung her feet to the ground and stood up. She unlocked her bedroom door and trudged to the bathroom and locked the door behind her. She sat on the plastic toilet seat and began to pish. She pished for thirteen seconds, which was a good long pish, made possible by the two litres of Coke she'd drunk before bed. She'd read in one of her ma's *Your Health!* magazines that Coke was a diuretic. The magazine highly recommended diuretics to its readership, to reduce bloating from excess water. But the *Your Health!* team weren't fans of Coke – they recommended an all-natural organic dandelion tea that readers could purchase from their magazine or website. Majella had been impressed that scientists had proved that dandelions were a diuretic. At school everyone'd called dandelions 'Pish-the-Beds' because they said when you picked one you'd wet your bed that night. Majella knew this wasn't true, but in school, she watched the big boys in the yard pick on the wee-er weans, forcing them to pick a dandelion, then jeering at the child for the rest of the day. Some children wet themselves in class before ever getting near their bed, earning a scolding from the teacher, who would then dress them in the classroom-accident pants. Majella didn't like the classroom-accident pants: the same washed-out pair had served both boys and girls for years unknown in St Jude's Primary School. Majella had only been got once by the dandelion gang. The big fellas had surrounded her in the school yard one break time. As soon as she'd understood they wanted her to pick a dandelion, she walked straight over to the nearest bunch, plucked the biggest bloom she could see and presented it to Charley Daly, the ringleader, with her blank face (the one she used when her ma and da or the teachers were shouting). Charley Daly had been pure raging. He'd knocked the dandelion to the ground and mashed it into the tarmac with his foot. Then he'd shoved Majella so hard she fell back on her arse. Majella had sat where she fell watching him and his gang walk off behind the prefab classroom, then she picked herself up and went back to sitting on the step of Mrs McHugh's classroom on her own, where she'd hidden her hands in the cradle of her skirt, flicking her fingers and humming until the bell rang.

Majella stood up and went to the mirror. It was spattered with flecks of toothpaste from where her ma'd brushed her teeth the night before. Majella couldn't brush her teeth with the mirror like that, so she turned on the electric shower and stripped off as she waited for the hot water to kick in. Her da had installed the shower in 1988. It was the last home improvement he'd done. The last home improvement that had been made in the house in fifteen years. The grouting was now black with mould, the shower head leaking from a warped seal. The white tiles around the bath clashed with the patterned tiles that had covered the rest of the room ever since the seventies. Her da'd promised to rip the old tiles down and fit the whole room with plain tiles – he'd even bought enough tiles to finish the job. But when his brother Bobby died, he'd lost all interest in the bathroom and had left the tiles sitting where they still sat, locked in his shed in the back yard. Majella remembered him that autumn after they'd got the news. The way he shrank into a dark place inside himself. Things were never the same after that.

Majella watched the steam rise and clot on the window, then she climbed into the green bathtub. The water was as hot as she could bear and she stood under it for a long time, until she felt sure that the smell of too many years of chip grease, fish batter, burger meat and sausage fat had been washed from her burning skin. Afterwards, when she was towelling herself dry, she thought she could catch the tang of incense from the funeral last week. She didn't know how to wash that away.

5.00 p.m.

Item 21, sub-items 1–4 (inclusive): The news

Majella listened to the creak of each stair as she made her way down them. Ever since she was wee she had loved these sounds. She loved how they sounded different depending on whether you were coming up or down the stairs, and the speed at which you were travelling. She did not love the way the fag smoke drifting from her ma in the living room clashed with the fresh after-shower smell of her skin. She went into the kitchen, where she flicked the kettle on before dropping four slices of white bread into the toaster. She grabbed her soup mug and spooned three sugars into it, then went to the fridge. There was frig-all in it, as usual: a carton of skimmed milk, a tub of spreadable margarine and twelve mini-bottles of her ma's probiotic yoghurt. She poured some of the anorexic milk into her mug, then closed the fridge. She dropped two round spoonfuls of SPAR Value instant-coffee granules on top of the milk, careful not to lose a single granule. Majella hated the way her ma scattered coffee around her when she made a cup. The kettle was grumbling its way to the boil. Majella checked the time on the kitchen clock: 5.05 p.m. Her shift started in fifty-five minutes, so she had plenty of time for breakfast and telly. The kettle switch flicked up and the toaster popped at the same time, sending a surge of pleasure through Majella, and she flicked her fingers to release the tension. Her da had liked it when the toaster and kettle stopped at the same time. Sometimes when she was wee he'd sing to her when the toast was near ready to pop and the kettle about to boil and, every now and then, he'd get the timing just right and the toaster and kettle and *pop* would happen simultaneously.

Half a pound of tuppenny rice
Half a pound of treacle,
That's the way the money goes
POP goes the weasel!

Majella spread an even layer of margarine over the top of her toast, then smeared each slice with MACE raspberry jam, which bore the claim of being 20% *real* fruit! Majella knew the other 80% included glucose-fructose syrup, citric acid, acidity regulator (sodium citrate), gelling agent (pectin) and that the sugar content of the jam was noted as being 65g per 100g. She did not know why the jam was not called sugar jam (65% *highly-processed* sugar!). They did not buy the jam based on its fruit or sugar content, nor for taste. They bought MACE raspberry jam because it was the cheapest jar on the shelf. Majella took a moment to survey her breakfast, then nodded to herself in satisfaction before carrying it through to the living room. The local news was coming on, so her ma turned the volume up. Majella did not like the local news, but her ma loved it. She sat up in her chair for the reports of car accidents wiping out four members of the same family on Christmas Eve, stared mournfully at the pictures of smiling children who'd drowned on their first foreign holiday, shook her head at the night-time footage of fishing boats searching for three generations of men for weeks, for months, while the fishes and crabs feasted. When a bride and groom crashed on their way to the airport for their honeymoon, Majella's ma first sucked up the misery on BBC Northern Ireland before switching to UTV for a slightly different angle and camera footage. If a tragedy was of sufficient magnitude to feature on the Free State news, she'd try to catch it on RTÉ too. Majella stared out through the grey net curtains to the drizzle outside. Throughout her childhood, the local news had been a litany of deaths, explosions and murder attempts. Things only got worse after peace broke out. Reporters who'd worked internationally on terrorist atrocities were now reduced to covering record-breaking attempts that usually featured children or vegetables.

Police in the small village of Ag-gee-Bow-gee . . .

The reporter's mispronunciation of her hometown caused a shot of pain to lick down Majella's back. She didn't understand why reporters from Belfast couldn't pronounce Aghybogey. They were as bad as the Brits.

. . . are calling for public cooperation in . . .

Majella's ma scrabbled at the + volume button. Majella braced herself before the TV boomed.

. . . reporting the latest developments in a story that has gripped and shocked this small, close-knit community . . .

Majella eyed the podgy reporter in a beige coat who was standing in the centre of Aghybogey to cover this *shocking and tragic* story.

The Police Service of Northern Ireland have made it clear that the DNA testing and fingerprinting of males aged between sixteen and sixty will be selective, that samples will only be used in connection with this case, and that all samples will be destroyed once the police have ruled out the suspect. Police have also confirmed that the death early last week of eighty-five-year-old Mrs Margaret O'Neill is being treated as murder. Local residents have given a cautious welcome to the new developments.

A series of people Majella knew flashed up on the screen.

. . . well on behalf of the local community and my constituents I would like to condemn this senseless act of violence that has resulted in the death of a well-respected elderly woman. The PSNI are doing their best to apprehend the assailant and I would ask for the cooperation of all local people . . .

. . . well you know I don't mind what they do so I don't as long as they catch him so they do cuz it's not easy so it isn't tae sleep in yer bed at night so it's not when that beast's out there so he is prowling

after weemen and childern and it could as well be yerself next other than anyone . . .

. . . well all ah can say is he'd better hand himself in like cuz ye know ah wouldn't like tae be him and get caught by someone else if ye know what ah mean cuz some a the local boys is wile angry and ah sort ah agree it's hard tae hold people responsible if things sort ah just happen like . . .

The reporter signed off, sending his audience back to the newsroom in Belfast. Majella held her breath as her ma pushed the – volume button on the remote control. She sat still, chewing her mouthful of toast to mush, unable to swallow. Her ma dropped back in her chair, shaking her head.

— Well now. Ah'm sure yer Aunt Marie had wind of this for long enough before the reporters got tae it. And she didn't break her neck running over tae us til warn us about it.

Majella said nothing, her toast lying thick on her tongue.

— Ye'd think maybe even a phone call. But naw. We had tae find out over the telly. PissNI doing DNA testing! And ah bet ye every frigger around us knew before they went to the telly. Bertie Daly and the Shinners and the whole fucken shower of them.

Majella let the wad of toast slide down her throat, then she took a mouthful of coffee.

— Ach poor, poor Maggie. Never wan for the limelight but her now thrown in tae it again at her age and her not out of it even now she's dead and buried. 'Twas the shame that kilt her in the end, not what that baste did tae her.

Majella eyed the rest of her soggy toast, her appetite dead. Her ma stared mournfully at the christening photograph above the mantelpiece, where she stood sulking in a miniskirt despite a biting November breeze, aged just seventeen. On one side stood her mother-in-law Maggie O'Neill, stiff-backed and formal in a navy suit, her steely hair pinned tight underneath her hat. Majella's aunt and godmother Marie looked decades older than Majella's ma, despite being a year younger. Only Majella's father looked happy, as he stood there, flanked by the three women in his life, cradling his baby girl. He looked cosy in his brown velvet suit with his extravagant flares. Her uncle and godfather Bobby wasn't in the photo. He hadn't been arsed to stand outside the chapel waiting for the photographer to get the camera set up, so he'd pissed off to the pub. You couldn't see Majella in the picture: she'd been half-smothered in the blankets her granny'd wrapped around her.

Majella got up and went to the kitchen, where she dumped her remaining toast into the pedal bin, then washed her plate and cup in scalding water before leaving them to dry on the draining board. She lifted the plastic bag that contained her overalls, walked down the hall and opened the front door. She could hear her ma on the phone in the living room, complaining to someone about the DNA testing.

— Ah'm away.

She shut the door without waiting to hear if her ma said goodbye.

5.38 p.m.

Item 3.3: Noise: Shutters in work

Majella let herself in the side entrance of the chipper. Marty stepped past her, whistling.

— Bit early the day, are ye not, Jelly?

Majella glanced at the clock, then shook her head. Only Marty was allowed to call Majella Jelly. Other people might roar it at her in the street or say it to her face, but only Marty was allowed. He'd started that craic in the early days of them working together. She'd hated the nickname in school and she'd hated being hefty. But Marty liked big girls so the way he said Jelly was different. She also let him off with the slaps on the arse he'd give her when she was rummaging about in the chest freezer for another batch of chicken burgers. The slaps didn't do much for Majella, mind, but they cracked Marty up, so Majella didn't see the harm in letting them by her.

— Ah seen that bit on the news about yer granny. Shower of fucken eejits them PissNI. Like that baste'll walk up tae the door of the barracks and open his gob for them tae have a wee scrape at it?

Majella was climbing into her light-green overalls in the darkness at the front of the takeaway. The interior walls were a light blue. Mr Hunter's wife (joint proprietor of A Salt n Battered! Traditional Fast Food Establishment) had sponge-stencilled luminous pink fish onto the takeaway walls. When the fluorescent lights were on and Majella was tired, she felt like she was swimming along with the fish.

— And who else will walk up there tae hand their DNA over tae the cops? Destroy the samples after identification my hole. We all know what went on with the fingerprints.

Majella tugged the zipper at the front of her overalls up and over the swell of her chest, wondering what had gone on with the fingerprints. Marty was watching her. She guessed by the set of him that she was supposed to react, so she shrugged. Shrugging, she'd learned, was a useful response to a lot of questions and statements. Marty pressed on.

— Y'see, they have tae be *seen* doing something. And what they're doing is making a meal of yer poor granny-God-rest-her. If they have their way, they'll soon have us all on wan big computer over there in London. The cunts.

Majella was silent, her mouth now full of hairpins. She watched her reflection in the shop window as she fixed her hair under a nylon hairnet. She wanted Marty to stop talking, so she tried saying nothing – another good trick. The silence stretched on until Marty broke it by slapping his hand on the counter in resignation.

— Ah frig them anyway. Ah'll stick these fryers on, eh, Jelly? We need tae be ready for them fuckers outside.

Marty jerked his head in the direction of the shutters: through the slits Majella could see the O'Donnell and O'Doherty weans already queuing up. Majella knew they'd been to the pub straight after school to scrounge or lift money from their parents so's they could get a bite to eat. Marty said they put themselves to bed, which in fairness Majella and Marty had done themselves from no age. But their parents were usually sitting downstairs watching telly, not off down the town drinking. Majella recognised several families celebrating dole day with a takeaway. She spotted the builders who'd made it back to the town early from their jobs in the Free State, starving. Majella pulled her hat down and fixed it to her hair with the last of the clips. She scratched her arse through the rough nylon of her overalls, then began to empty the bags of change into the till, enjoying the click-clack of coins dropping into place. When she was done she looked over at Marty.

— Are ye right there, Jelly?

Majella nodded, so Marty ducked under the counter and walked whistling to the chipper door. He unlocked the door and wedged it open with the rubber stopper, then ducked back behind the counter. He flicked the switch to raise the security shutters. Majella hated this bit. She braced herself as the shutters screeched, feeling the noise feed down from her ears and into her teeth. Before the shutters had ground a quarter of the way up, the wee O'Donnell cub scooted in under them and landed up to the counter with a proud look on his face. Majella looked down at him.

— What can ah get chew?

— Big bag a chips with salt ann vinegar ann red sauce please.

Majella tingled with satisfaction as she heard the crackle and spit of the first basket of chips going down.

6.30 p.m.
Item 1: Small talk, bullshit and gossip

Majella shook the chips in the fryer to make sure they would get cooked all the way through. She liked this bit. Marty wasn't as particular as her about the chips being done evenly, which bugged her. He shouted from the counter. — Three more chips for the McHughs there, Jelly.

A minute later, he sidled down with what she had learned was his gossipy head on him.

— Now don't turn and gawk, will ye, but take a look at who young Breda Farren's in with.

Marty dandered past Majella, and she waited ten seconds like he'd taught her before turning to glance into the takeaway. She guessed that the only girl in the shop, the wee thing with a man old enough to be her father, was young Breda Farren. Majella knew that after they were gone, Marty'd drop by to fill her in on the latest scandal. Majella wasn't like Marty. He knew everyone in the town. He knew who was fucking who, who had fucked who and who wanted to fuck who. He knew who was drinking, smoking, swallowing or injecting what, and he often knew the where and when. He always had an opinion on the why. Majella eyed the chips. They looked done, so she raised them up and shook the worst of the oil back into the fryer. She bagged up the order and brought it to Marty at the counter. He rang up the sale while keeping up a flow of chat, something Majella could never do.

After they left, Marty leaned on the counter, and put one hand on his hip. — Ye probably don't know yer man Duffy, now. Works out in the bank across the bridge?

Majella shook her head to allow Marty to continue.

— Course he *says* he's just dropping Miss Farren off home after babysitting and getting a takeaway for the wife . . . but did ye notice he got young Breda her supper too? Ah bet ye his wife's chips get coul while he's gettin hot in the back of that nice new Land Rover!

Majella didn't know how Marty could tell all of this from serving chips to two strangers standing in the shop for ten minutes. She didn't care if he was right or wrong, for what did those two people mean to her? But she wondered what he told other people about her. About her ma. Her da. She'd sometimes wondered if he knew where her da had gone. For all she knew, the whole town knew where he was, and it was just her and her ma who didn't. That was often the way of it.

Majella thought of wee Róisín Murphy. She'd always come into the chip shop after the bingo on a Thursday to get a battered sausage supper for her old mammy, Mary Murphy. Marty'd always try to slip a free sausage into their parcel. And after they left he'd comment yet again to Majella about what a shame it was that the child didn't know that her 'Mammy' was really her granny and her 'sister' Rose was actually her mammy (and the town prostitute), for Rose had had Róisín so young that her mother had stepped in to rear the baby as her own. The whole town knew about Mary and Róisín and Rose, except for Róisín. Majella didn't understand all this pseudo-secrecy, the stories people told. She liked things straight. But things weren't like that in Aghybogey. It was a town in which there was nowhere to hide, so people hid stuff in plain sight.

7.15 p.m.
Item 3.4: Noise: Shite singing

Majella was eyeing the Connolly cub. He was sitting on the bench beside the war memorial, hunched up inside his hoodie. She knew he was waiting until the chipper was empty to run over. He was funny like that. She served the McHugh woman standing in front of her.

— There you go. Three fish suppers, a battered sausage supper, anna extra portion of chips ann onion rings.

Mrs McHugh swung the plastic bag off the counter and walked out, leaving the chipper empty for the first time since opening. Majella caught a whiff of fag smoke over the fat fumes; Marty having a break out the back. Iggy Connolly seized his opportunity. He mooched over, hiding his face in his hoodie. He opened the door about thirty centimetres and slid himself in without triggering the buzzer. Majella had wiped the counter clean of the spills of salt and vinegar.

— What about ye, Iggy?

— Ah'm all right. What about you?

— Grand. Surviving.

Majella threw the J-cloth into the sink and put the tap on. She lifted it and rinsed it through several times and then wrung it out. She liked a clean cloth. When she turned back to the counter, Iggy was standing close to the till, his hands deep in his hoodie pouch.

— Was thinking of heading over tae the shop. You looking anything?

Majella nodded, reaching for her purse. She pulled out a list and a tenner. — Some sweets and crisps. And a bit of bread and stuff. That all right?

— Aye. Gimme it here, sure, and ah'll be back up in a minute.

Iggy slid himself out the door. Majella wondered if he knew she didn't like the buzzer, or it was something he avoided for himself.

Marty came in, rubbing his hands together to warm them up. — Fucken nippy out there these days. We'll have tae get the oul thermals on soon enough, eh Jelly?

Majella didn't wear thermals, but she nodded all the same.

Marty frowned. — Maybe this year I'll hibernate. Or move tae California!

Marty started into a song about California. He was a woeful singer and the noise went through Majella. She threw the wet J-cloth at him and he caught it just before it slapped him in the face.

— Fuck off. You're just jealous, Jelly. I could've been a fucken superstar, me.

— Aye. And instead you're that cunt Jamie Oliver.

It was rare enough that Majella cracked a joke, never mind a funny one, so Marty stared at her open-mouthed for a few seconds before laughing.

Majella glared at the floor. — Go away and earn yer keep will ye? Get into the back room and count out a dose a chicken nuggets, for they're getting scarce.

Marty plodded into the back room, humming. Majella didn't mind the humming so much, for it was absorbed by the bubbling fryers. Iggy had been gone four minutes, so Majella threw on a small portion of chips and a couple of battered sausages, then hauled herself up onto the food preparation counter to rest her feet. She would love to have a stool that'd make it easier for her to take the weight off her feet, but Mrs Hunter wouldn't allow it as she believed it would encourage idleness. What Cunter didn't realise was that a stool would make no difference to the fact that Marty was a worker and was only happy when he was buzzing around at something, while Majella had her own pace. She was no chef, but the chips never burned, the oil never caught fire and they never ran low in stock when she was on the ball. She liked to clean, so she kept the place gleaming. Marty didn't like to clean. He'd said that he could barely be bothered to wipe his own arse, never mind the counter.

The door opened again. Majella slid down from the counter and raised Iggy's chips out of the scalding fat. Done to a tee. Perfect timing.

— Salt ann vinegar on yer chips?

Iggy nodded from inside his hoodie. He pushed a plastic bag onto the counter along with Majella's change. She passed his parcel of food to him.

— Ah threw in a few extra ketchups. And a fork. Thanks a million for the shopping.

— No bother, Majella. Ah'm away.

He went out with his head down. When the door shut she opened the till and dropped in some coins to cover his supper. Majella didn't like people much, but she liked Iggy. She liked him the way she'd liked strays when she was wee. The cats or dogs that skulked lame about the estates for days or weeks, before ending up lying dead in the road. Behind her Marty emptied a batch of bread-crumbed chicken fillets onto the food-prep counter. Majella stared at the window. She couldn't see beyond her faint reflection in the window, but knew that somewhere out there, her granny's murderer was probably settling down to watch telly. She couldn't picture where her da was. Not any more.

8.23 p.m.

Item 1: Small talk, bullshit and gossip

— Course your grandmother was a lady and that's what makes this whole thing such a terrible disgrace. A *real* lady who only ever stepped out with Mickey-God-rest-his-soul and was loyal to him throughout their troubles with the police back in the day.

Biddy Doherty's voice wrecked Majella's head at the best of times. This was not the best of times.

— The oul baste, is what I say. The oul animal to attack a widow lady of her age, ann her the mother of a dead patriot. You'd like to think them that call themselves patriots that are still walking around would stir themselves to look in tae the whole affair.

Majella wondered where the fuck Marty had got himself to. He'd disappeared again. This wasn't on.

— And did she say much in the hospital when you were up visiting? Did she give ye any details on the attack?

Majella shook her head.

Biddy paused and gave Majella the eye. Majella stuck with her blank face, so after a few seconds, Biddy continued.

— Ye know the dogs on the street have more idea of why someone would attack yer poor granny than them eejits in PSNI. Them that's done this will be caught, wan way or another.

Majella lifted a J-cloth and began to wipe the counter.

— I tried to get in to see her you know. Was up in Omagh doing a few wee messages so I just thought I'd head out, but sure I shouldn't have bothered my head for they hardly let me in the door, let alone near her.

Majella went to the fryer and pulled the basket up. The chips looked half raw. She dunked the basket again. The fat spat, splashing her arm. She rubbed it to relieve the pain as she returned to the counter. Biddy Doherty leaned in close, lowering her voice to a more intimate pitch.

— It was a blessing she died really. For how would she have gone back to that caravan on her own, with no one to look out for her? She was left very vulnerable with Bobby-God-rest-him in his grave and yer da . . . well yer da *disappeared*.

Biddy gave Majella a significant look. Majella turned to the fryer. The chips would do. The fucken fish would be fine. And if they weren't, Majella wasn't going to break her heart over Biddy Mouth Almighty Doherty getting food poisoning.

— Salt ann vinegar on yer chips?

10.00 p.m.
Item 8.4: Jokes: Repeated jokes

It was already ten o'clock. Majella knew it was ten without looking at her watch because Jimmy Nine Pints was in. He worked in the chicken-rendering factory in Strabane. Marty had explained to Majella that it was Jimmy's job to put his hand up a chicken's hole, grab the guts, twist, wrench and release the innards into a plastic container for the gizzard harvesters. Every morning at six Jimmy'd be waiting for the factory bus. Every evening at seven he'd be into the Wulf Hound for the first of his nine pints of Guinness. Majella knew this because Marty'd told her. She had never met Jimmy outside of the chipper, even though he lived out her granny's direction. Six nights a week at ten on the dot, Jimmy left the pub and called into the chipper for his sausage supper before getting a lift out the road. Jimmy rolled in, well oiled by nine pints. Then he plodded over to the counter and laid down a grubby five pound note.

— A sausage supper, my good woman, a sausage supper.

Marty already had the basket down, with Jimmy's chips and sausage bubbling furiously in the golden fat.

— It's on its way, Jimmy.

Majella took Jimmy's five pound note in her hands and rang it in. There was no point asking Jimmy if he wanted anything extra – like a pint of milk or some red sauce – or anything different – like a chicken burger. Jimmy only wanted his sausage supper. Majella snapped the till shut, which was the trigger for Jimmy's joke.

Jimmy shifted his weight, then leaned in closer to the counter. — D'ye want a bit of my sausage?

He wheezed a bit, slapping his hand on the counter. Majella waited for the usual five seconds before replying with the line Marty'd given her six years ago.

— I'll batter yer sausage if you're not careful, now.

Then Marty joined in with the laughter for boysadear it was some joke now.

10.30 p.m.
Item 6: Cunter

Majella was out the back having a fag. She detested the smell of fags. Her da had always hated smoking. He'd tried everything to get her ma off the fags – hypnosis, patches, emotional blackmail, herbal fags, holy wells, nicotine gum and prayer bouquets – but nothing had worked. Her ma had continued to smoke.

. . . ah only started because of you anyway. Ah never smoked in me whole life, and then ah had you inside me belly. D'ye think ah wanted tae be split open having a lump of a wean and me hardly more than a girl myself? Ah HAD to start smoking. Fucken hated it at the start. The taste and the stink and the price of it. But it worked. You were a wee babby. About five pounds, ah think. Smallest in the ward. Thought ah'd stop smoking after you were born. But fuck me after that gas wore off, all ah wanted was a fag. And that's the way it's been ever since . . .

Majella took up smoking when she'd started in the chipper, because it was the only way of getting a break. Before she smoked she'd just nip outside for five minutes here and there, to knock back a Coke and pace up and down, flicking her fingers and rocking on the balls of her feet. It was a break from the heat and fryers and the stream of faces. But one evening Mrs Hunter had burst into the yard, wanting to know what the fuck did Majella think was she doing, itching and twitching out the back, wasting the time she was paid to be working. She'd ordered Majella inside, then stood close behind her back, causing her to muck up the orders. After Cunter left, Marty'd told Majella to bring a packet of fags in to work. The next time she fancied a break she was to go outside and light up a fag, and if Cunter came near her again, she could just say she was having a fag break. Everyone was allowed a fag break and there was nothing Cunter could do about it. So Majella had nicked a half-empty cigarette packet off her ma. In the start she didn't light any fags, instead rolling one between her fingers, pointing the tip to the sky. But one day she'd heard Cunter coming, so she fumbled for a lighter and lit up just as Cunter entered the alleyway. She had stood and stared at Majella for a good minute before she spoke.

— Don't be all night about it. There's work to be done.

Then she stalked off, leaving Majella with the cigarette. Majella watched it burn down to the butt. It took her ages to get the smell off her fingertips and out of her hair. But she'd found gazing at the burning cigarette soothing and out of curiosity, she started sucking on the butt, choking on the smoke but sort-of liking it. From there she'd ended up smoking. She never sucked on the cigarette like her ma did, never lit up one after another, and she never smoked at home. She smoked out the back of the chipper and occasionally at the pub. Because really the thing she liked best about smoking was blowing small clouds up at the stars.

11.07 p.m.

Item 4.1: Bright lights: Fluorescent bulbs

Majella closed her eyes against the flickering fluorescent lights. One of the strips was at death's door, jittering on and off, but Cunter had refused to replace it, saying as long as it lit up at all it would do them rightly. Majella's stomach was rumbling. She wondered if she could get away with a couple of wee chips before the pub run.

— Anyone dead the night, Marty?

— Naw, love. Oul Paddy Onions was the last death ah heard of.

— Found dead in his bed, wasn't he?

— Aye. Young Red Onions found him.

Majella nodded. Apart from the reek of his breath, she'd not minded Paddy Onions. He was an old neighbour of her granny's and she'd seen him from time to time throughout her childhood. He'd often cycle up to her granny, carrying messages, bringing her the odd wee thing that couldn't be got from the bread van or the milk van or the shop van. Sometimes Majella listened as her granny and Paddy spoke of the olden days. Paddy had been a friend of her grandfather's. If he'd a drop taken, he'd talk about their involvement in the border campaigns. About resistance. They didn't talk so much about internment. That topic seemed to shut down conversations. Marty interrupted Majella's thoughts.

— Oul Paddy Onions made it tae a right oul age, didn't he?

— Did he?

— Och aye, aye. Musta been in tae his late eighties. Great health he had too. Ye wouldnta have taken him for wan that'd be dead before Christmas.

Majella shrugged.

— Ye never know.

Marty winced and reddened. Majella wondered if he was worried he'd upset her. He hadn't, but she was terrified that he might try to make amends, so she turned away and attempted to shuffle the paper napkins under the counter into order. She only succeeded in squashing them while Marty blustered around behind her, whistling ferociously. Then the door opened and a rush of air hit Majella's sweaty face. She sucked it down into her lungs as she surveyed the customers who'd left the pub early to beat the rush. A Salt n Battered! closed at 1 a.m. Monday to Thursday, and Marty and Majella were always busy to the last second.

— What can ah get chew?

Daddyburgernonionringsanchipsngravy
sausagesupperneggfryrice
gissakissjellybaby. gwan. gwan. justaweewun . . .
ihope theygethefuck thatdidyourGrannylove
batterburgeranchipsanressauce
Ivetayworkthemarrafucksake
ihope theyfuckenbustizzballz. fuckenbastart.

12.00 a.m.
Item 29: The Daly brothers

Mr Hunter came at midnight on the dot to collect the bulk of the evening's takings. This was the only time of day that Majella and Marty saw him. Majella noted with approval that Mr Hunter was wearing a yellow shirt, blue tie and grey suit. Mr Hunter always wore a yellow shirt, blue tie and grey suit. And he always coughed nervously on entering through the side door in the alleyway, looking with distaste at the raw food piled up on the counter, flinching as the fryers foamed when Majella or Marty threw something in. Majella thought that Mr Hunter looked like he could do with a good feed and a ride. But Mr Hunter never ate anything that was made in A Salt and Battered! and by the look of him he ate damn all anywhere else. Majella couldn't imagine Mr Hunter eating or getting a ride. Hunter and Cunter didn't have weans despite the life sentence of their marriage being well into its second decade. Majella felt sorry for him. She reckoned it would do him the world of good if she took him home, fed him up a bit and rode him. When she handed him the strong box with the night's takings, she smiled at his left ear. — Here you go Mr Hunter.

Mr Hunter blinked and took the strong box with a convulsive movement of his arm and addressed Majella's right ear. — Errrrm. Thank you Majella. Ah-herrrrrm. Thank you.

Unlike PissNI, Majella did not have a list of suspects for the attack on her granny. But if she had, Mr Hunter would not be at the top of the list.

fivedubblechickenburgurzzanfivefuckenchipzanfivetubsofgarlicmayoannatwolitrebottleaCokewhenyourereadyjellybelly

The Daly brothers were in. Majella knew without turning who had shouted the order: Charley, the oldest. She also knew that all five of the Daly brothers were some place close to the top of quite a few PissNI lists, including those related to racketeering, drugs, traffic offences and domestic abuse. And yet nothing had ever been pinned to them. Majella waited until Mr Hunter had left by the side door before tugging her overalls loose from her hot oxters. She wiped her face blank and turned around to deal with the Daly brothers.

1.00 a.m.
Item 7: Sweating

Majella's feet were drowned in sweat. The walls of the chipper were wet with condensation and the air was thick with smoke from the fryers. Marty bagged up the last order of chips and passed it to Majella, who dropped it into a plastic bag and gave it to Joanne Keane, who slurred *thanksamillion*. Marty stood by Majella's side and together they stared at the collection of drunks that had piled up in the chippie. Marty pushed the first button, closing the window shutters.

Then he hit the second button and moved the door shutters a quarter of the way down. Some customers took the cue and left: the rest stayed put. This behaviour had confused Majella when she had started in the chipper. She knew that the lowering of the shutters was a clear signal that the chipper was closing, the same way as the final blessing in Mass was the signal that the end was near. But she'd learned that people didn't always notice signals or heed rules like opening and closing times. Marty looked at the stragglers, then heaved a sigh.

— Ah'll get them lot cleared out.

He lifted the counter and stepped into the shop. Majella watched as Marty woke Monkey Keane and Mickey the Stool, who had fallen asleep on the window ledge. They took a few seconds to cop on to where they were, but soon gathered up their food and cans and stumbled out the door. Then Terry McGocks came up to the counter and leaned over to Majella.

— Bag a chips ann red sauce, Jelly.

Majella looked past his bloodshot eyes and focused on his left ear.

— Sorry, Terry. We're done for the night.

Majella knew that Terry McGocks wasn't going to be impressed with them being done for the night. She'd seen him in action a few times in the pubs. She knew he'd a reputation for not taking no for an answer.

— What the fuck's this *shite* about being closed? Fucken fuckers fucken . . .

Majella stepped away from Terry McGocks and began to clear the buckets of mayonnaise and tubs of coleslaw to the back room. McGocks shouted and pounded the counter, but Majella kept on clearing up, ignoring his shouts for *wan more bag a chips g'wan for fuck's sake*. The best part of Majella's night was the clean-up. She'd always liked clean-ups.

Marty was struggling to get Terry McGocks out the door. Majella came to the counter and kept an eye on the pair of them, ready to help Marty if he needed a hand. But after a few seconds, Marty tossed Terry into the street and ducked back under the shutter. Majella hit the close button and the shutter screeched down towards the ground. Marty shut the inside door and they had the place to themselves. Outside, Terry McGocks was roaring. Majella's eyes were tired. The fish on the wall seemed to be moving in the fluorescent light. Then she noticed someone had drawn eyelashes, lipstick and a fanny on one of the fish. Someone else had drawn a big hairy cock on the other one. It was funny, but Majella didn't smile. She reached into the bag Iggy Connolly had brought and found a Dairy Milk bar. She unwrapped it, broke off a chunk and crammed it in her mouth. She waved the chocolate over at Marty, who shook his head.

— Naw, you're all right. Ah'll just get our suppers on.

Majella watched Marty lower a basket for the last fry of the night. Food was part of the deal. They were allowed to take home a supper of their choice – nothing extra. Majella shoved the last few chunks of Dairy Milk into her mouth and wiped her fingers down her overalls. She lifted the J-cloth and started to clean. Marty joined in. He only gave the place a cat's lick. It made Majella's fingers itch, but she had learned a long time ago to leave well alone, and not go over what he'd wiped, for it drove him mad because he didn't see the sense in doing more than would keep Cunter off their backs. Marty didn't understand that Majella didn't clean to please Cunter. She was pleasing herself. When she'd started, the takeaway had been crusty with the dirt of years. She'd spent a satisfying month scraping muck off the counters and digging it out of crevices and cracks. Now the shop gleamed. They worked in silence, both pausing from time to time to wipe sweat from their faces. When they were done, Majella cleared the till. It had taken three years for Cunter to trust Majella with the takings. Since then she no longer turned up last thing at night to collect them, which was a relief for both Marty and Majella. When she came back to the counter she saw that Marty was finished up. They stripped off their overalls beside the heat of the fryers. Then Majella pulled off the cap and loosened her hair from the net. In Majella's head, this marked the end of the night. She was off duty and could relax. Some nights Marty and Majella shagged in the storeroom. Majella never knew when the notion would take Marty. She never said no to a shag. She liked the way that they sometimes had sex just because they both happened to be there. She didn't fancy Marty, not really. It was different when she'd first started in the chipper, nine years ago. He'd been engaged to Philomena at the time, not yet married, and he wasn't one bit interested in Majella. She'd been at her skinniest ever – just after quitting her A levels, with no idea what to do with the bones and curves that had surfaced from underneath the layer of fat that had kept her warm from birth. So she hid herself under cardigans or in her overalls. But after a few months of chipper food, the fat started to fold around her limbs, thickening her legs and arms, widening her face and arse. She was relieved that this made her more invisible to most men, and interested that it was only then that Marty had wanted her. The first time he'd come after her she'd been in the storeroom checking the stock before they opened the chipper. She was squeezed into her second set of overalls but already needed a bigger size. She had heard Marty walk into the storeroom, then stop and stand behind her. Her chest had tightened and she'd turned around. Neither of them spoke. Marty'd fucked her in the storeroom, against the wall, under the fluorescent lights and beside the boxes of chicken nuggets, Daddy burgers and fish fillets, all the time telling her how much he liked big girls, real girls, girls you could get a hold of. Majella wasn't keen on all the talk – she'd trained him out of it eventually. After they'd come, he'd reached down and cupped his hand firmly between her legs. He'd pressed the heel of his hand into her pubic bone, into the afterheat, and brought his mouth close to her ear, his stubble grazing her wet neck.

— You've a cunt like a Hovis loaf. Ah could eat you alive.

From time to time in work, Majella remembered his words and hot waves would travel her through her body, making her face glow under the sweat.

2.03 a.m.
Good list
Item 2: Dallas

Majella's estate was silent. She let herself into the house and walked quietly to the kitchen. She closed her eyes before flicking the light switch. The bulb stuttered, then hummed into a harsh glare. Majella didn't understand why people used fluorescent lights. No matter where they were used, they over-lit rooms, making everything hurt. She shivered. Her ma had let the fire go out and not bothered about the heating. Majella set her food down on the counter and walked into the living room. QVC was chittering away, offering her snoring ma a ring with fabulous simulated semi-precious stones in gold-dipped claw settings for less than half retail price. The light flickered around the living room, reminding Majella of Christmas years ago, when she was allowed to sit up later than normal to watch a movie. The only other thing they'd watched as a family was *Dallas*. It had been on every Saturday night for what felt like decades. After her bath, she'd kneel down to say her prayers beside her daddy, their backs to the telly. Majella would be damp and warm in her nightie with the sleepy-eyed bears on it. She could always tell when *Dallas* was drawing close, as her daddy'd start to race through the last of the prayers.

. . . Angel a God,
my guardian dear,
to whom God's love
commits me here,
everthisday
beeatmyside
taelightannguard
taeruleannguide
Amen
Inthenameathefatherannatheson
Annatheholyspirit
Amen

On the Amen, her da would hit the volume control on the remote with his left hand, while blessing himself with his right hand, and the *Dallas* theme tune would burst into their living room.

Duh Duh, Duh Duh, Duh Duh Duh Di Duh . . .

For years afterwards, Majella could hear the theme tune every time she said her prayers, and could see J. R. Ewing's bright white teeth bared in a smile, the shine from his moist, alcoholic eyes, and she felt his searing disdain for most folks, but especially Barnes, who just got dumber and dumber every day. Majella realised that her fish and chips were getting cold. She went back to the kitchen, grabbed her plate from her cupboard and dumped the package on it. She tore the paper open and breathed in the sharp vinegary steam that rose up around her. She tasted a chip. It was lukewarm, so she shoved the plate into the microwave and hit the MIN button. She listened to the telly offer her snoring ma a diamonique, faux-titanium choker necklace while she followed the microwave countdown, opening the door just before the bell pinged. She got her timing from her da. He always caught glasses before they hit the floor, her ma before she passed out. He'd even once claimed to have caught a falling piano, when he was working in America. And Majella had believed him. She'd been really gullible as a child. Her da'd taken advantage, filling her head with lies and notions and stories that she'd repeated to teachers or other weans, only to be laughed at. He'd once told her that bald men lost their hair as a punishment from God for wearing ladies' knickers in bed. It had taken Majella years to understand why Baldy Bradley had gone mental on her when she'd told the class she knew he wore ladies' knickers. Majella grabbed the red sauce and squirted a farty squelch of it over her chips, then shook more vinegar and salt over the whole lot. She tucked the two-litre bottle of Coke under her oxter and picked up her plate. On her way past the living room she looked in at her mother. Majella considered throwing a blanket over her ma. But she knew there'd be a risk of waking her and having to hoosh her up the stairs to her bed, so she left her to it.

Majella locked her bedroom door, plugged in the fan heater, and then climbed into bed to eat. She liked to believe that if she lived on her own the house would be different. Cleaner. With sparkling windows. She'd have plump cushions that you could sink into instead of the foam things they had, squished flat as pancakes from years of arses. She'd pull out the fluorescent lights, tear off the wood-chip wallpaper and rip out the swirly eighties carpets. She'd paint the walls magnolia and varnish the floorboards. Majella's room hadn't been done up since the time her ma'd stopped eating for what seemed like months. She'd gone so thin that there was talk of her being sent to the T&F. The T&F wasn't like a normal hospital, where you were sent for broken bones and to have bits of you cut out. It was a special sort of hospital for people who were bad with their nerves. Nobody who went there seemed to get well. They just disappeared for a while, then came back like zombies.

When her ma heard the talk about the T&F, she started to drink the banana-flavoured nutrition shakes that Majella's da had bought. Majella remembered him spooning the powder out of a tin, like baby formula. Then he added milk and beat it with a fork until it looked fluffy and sweet, like the American milkshakes Majella had seen on the telly. But it had tasted like wet, perfumed chalk. Majella didn't know how her ma could prefer that shite to the real dinners her da cooked. Years later, when Majella first tasted a banana-flavoured condom, she'd been reminded of her mother's health drinks, and that special trip they'd taken to celebrate her eating again. Her da had driven them and her granny to Omagh and they visited Harry Corry to get Majella a treat. The four of them had walked around eyeing the matching curtain and duvet sets. That had been the big new thing back then: matching shit. You could match your curtains with your duvet with your pillowcases with your scatter cushions with your lamp shade with your wallpaper with your wallpaper border with your rug with your bin. You weren't supposed to just buy a pillowcase or a duvet cover any more – it had to be a whole room. But they couldn't afford all that. Majella was told to choose curtains and a duvet cover. But Majella's granny didn't approve of the red duvet cover she chose.

Get the cuddy something plain so ye get good washing out of it.

They drove home from Harry Corry's with a basic cream duvet and matching curtains. Majella hoped she could choose the carpet. But her da measured her room and went down on his own to Hector's Hardware and Household Goods and took the remnant that was the best fit. After her da nailed the carpet down, the room felt warmer and sounds from downstairs were muffled. But Majella hated the way the carpet scratched her knees and the swirls snagged on her eyes. The duvet cover was eventually ripped to dusters after thinning out in the wash. The curtains still hung there, skimming the warmth from the light outside.

Majella crushed several mashed chips into her mouth. When Majella was eleven, she'd weighed more than her ma. She guessed she weighed about twice her ma now – she wasn't sure as she didn't let her ma push her onto the scales every week any more. Her size didn't bother her. Didn't bother any of the men she met in the pub. And she seemed to have settled now. Not getting much bigger or smaller even when she ate less. Majella had reached the bottom of the pack, where the chips and fish were mushed up together. This was her favourite bit, with the salt and vinegar thick on each mouthful. She paused to sigh in contentment. Then she scraped at the paper with her fingers, before ramming wads of food into her mouth. Chip fat coated her fingers and smeared around her mouth. She dropped the plate on the carpet and lay back on the bed, wiping her fingers and mouth clean on a handful of napkins. It felt good lying there, the heater blowing hot air around the room, her belly, eyelids and diddies heavy and warm. She stretched out her hand and checked her mobile phone.

No New Messages

She lay back and closed her eyes, sucking on her finger. She tasted the sting of the salt crystals and the chip grease under her nails melting in the heat of her mouth. For a few minutes Majella sucked, then she took her finger out of her mouth and moved her hand down inside her jogging bottoms. She closed her thighs around her hand, her fingers kneading between her legs. As her breathing quickened, she stretched her legs long and taut until she felt the waves of heat surge up and down her entire body. Afterwards she lay still, her hand clamped between her legs, feeling the pulse of her heart beating through her pubic hair. When her heartbeat had slowed to its usual steady thump thump-thump she brought her hand to her nose and sniffed. She slipped her finger back into her mouth, wondering if there was a man in another house, maybe not a thousand miles from where she lived, lying awake trying to forget about what it felt like to break an elderly widow's ribs with his fist.

Tuesday

8.43 a.m.

Item 3.7: Noise: Stuff smashing

It was the sound of a cup or a plate smashing that woke Majella. It was her ma's gurning that kept her awake. Majella lifted her head out from under her duvet. The air was hot and dead because she'd forgotten to switch off the fan heater. Her skin was slick with sweat. She pushed her head back under the covers and closed her eyes. After five minutes of listening to her ma howling, Majella hauled herself out of bed and unlocked her bedroom door.

— Majellaaaahhhhh?

The cold sliced through Majella's T-shirt and joggers, tightening her nipples. Majella always wondered about this reflex. It was an odd one.

— MA-JELL-AH? Ah've cut meself!

— Ah need a pish.

— Ah'm bleeding real bad!

— Ah'll be down in a minute.

— Ah'll bleed tae death!

Majella often had to repeat things for her ma.

— Ah said ah'll be down in a minute.

After Majella flushed the loo and washed her hands, she opened the bathroom cabinet and took down her da's first-aid box. She had, over the years, replaced everything in the box apart from the scissors. But she still thought of it as her da's first-aid box. She carried it downstairs and into the kitchen. It was a right fucken mess. A plate was shattered across the floor and her ma was clutching the kitchen counter, bleeding onto the Lino. Majella took control.

— Will ye quit yer nyammen!

When her ma quietened down to a bearable level, Majella laid the first-aid box down on the kitchen table and oxtered her over to the chair. Her ma was still wearing yesterday's clothes.

— What did ye do til yerself?

Her ma snorted a noseful of snotters down her throat, then wiped her eyes. Majella controlled her revulsion by focusing on the floor.

— Ah dropped the plate and it smashed on me foot and ah think ah've cut a vein or something open. Will ye call us an amblelance?

Majella felt it was too early to commit to an ambulance.

— Show us yer foot there.

She bent over and took her ma's bony foot into her hand. Blood was pulsing out, but Majella didn't see the point in getting excited. Majella rarely saw the point in excitement.

— Ah'll clean ye up and then we'll see if ye could be doing with going down tae the surgery.

Majella handed her ma a tissue, then walked to the kitchen sink in her bare feet, over the shards and blood. She filled the washing-up basin with warm water and fired a dose of salt in. Her ma noticed Majella's bare feet.

— Oh fer the love-of-God mind yer feet there or we'll both end up bleeding til death here on the kitchen floor!

Majella said nothing. She knew she wouldn't get cut. She rarely hurt herself, except for the odd burn in the chipper. Cunter made her and Marty record those accidents in the Green Accident Report Book, which hung on the wall, although Cunter'd never bothered reading it in all the years it had been hanging there. Some days, when Marty was bored, he'd take his pen to the book and write detailed reports on how he'd bruised his cock on the chest freezer, or on how Majella'd bitten her tongue when talking to Mr Mastering from up the Forestry. Majella didn't need to record her ma's accidents in a book. They played on a cinema screen in Majella's head all hours: the time she'd slit her hand open with the Stanley blade trying to cut Sellotape on a parcel; the time she broke her ankle going out to the back yard in a pair of joke slippers; the time she fainted in the chapel and hit her head and didn't come round, so she had to be taken to hospital and held in for observation. She was a car crash of a woman, someone people said had no luck.

Majella went back over to her ma and placed her foot in the basin of water.

— It's stinging me! It's really sting-Eee.

Majella's ma sounded like an annoying wean when she whined. Majella restrained the impulse to give her a clip around the ear.

— It's only salt whatter. It'll clean it out for ye.

The water turned reddish as Majella held her ma's foot down. When she lifted it out she was surprised by how small it felt in her own meaty hand. She wondered what it would feel like to walk on such tiny feet. She saw that her ma's foot was cleanly sliced open on one side, and as she looked, the blood started to pump out again. Majella knew her ma wasn't good with blood. She glanced up and saw that she had her face turned towards the free calendar she'd got off Feely's meats the previous Christmas.

Pleased to Meat You with Meat to Please You!!!

— Am ah cut bad?

— Ye'll live. But ah'll call a taxi and get us down tae the surgery. The nurse'll prob'ly want tae take a look at ye.

— Oh ah'm not able for a taxi . . . ah'm wild faint.

Majella got to her feet, dried her hands on her joggers, then went to dial Bogey Taxis. When Pamela McHugh heard what had happened, she put them to the front of the queue. Majella thanked her, put the phone down and shivered.

— Ah'm away tae put on a jumper, then we'll get out tae this taxi.

Without waiting for an answer, Majella climbed the stairs to her bedroom. She hoked out a pair of socks. It was a thing she made sure of, to pair her socks, for Majella couldn't wear odd socks. They made her feel like her feet were quarrelling, and she could never forget that one foot was patterned, the other plain, or that one foot was grey, the other pink. She squashed her feet into her trainers and hauled on a fleece. Then she checked she had her purse before combing through her hair. She knew the accident would be all around town in no time: the O'Neill wan cut herself again. God knows what rumours would go flying off the back of that story. But for now she needed to get a tea towel tied around her ma's foot so they wouldn't make a mess of the taxi.

9.07 a.m.
Item 40: The political situation

Majella didn't have to oxter her ma out to the car – Spade Byrne jumped out of the taxi and helped. Majella liked Spade, for he was a nice gentle lump of a fella. Some of the Bogey taxi men would've sat tight and pretended not to notice that her ma could do with help. After the three-minute run to the surgery, Spade killed the car engine so he could help her ma in the whole way. Everyone had a gawk at them as her ma was taken straight in ahead of the ones waiting, because of the blood. Majella hated the surgery. It was the town's only practice, so the Prods from the bottom of the town and the Taigs from the top had to wait together. The Taigs kept to the left, the Prods to the right. There was no sign saying, CATHOLIC PATIENTS ARE REQUESTED TO PLEASE SIT TO THE LEFT, PROTESTANTS TO THE RIGHT. YOUR COOPERATION IS GREATLY APPRECIATED BY THE MANAGEMENT OF BOGEYDOC, It was one of those unwritten rules that everyone just seemed to know, like which pub to drink in, which streets to avoid walking down, which pharmacy to get your pills from, what religion to marry. Majella perched on one of the bench seats and tried to ignore the whispers from the deaf oul biddies around her.

. . . they said on the telly that no one's come forward yet with the DNA so that baste's still free . . . the police is out lifting wans off a list of suspects . . . sure she's as well dead anyway . . . them O'Neill women are left a lonely bunch now . . . sure ye'd never know who's gonna be next ah have the door locked all day . . . ah hear they reckon she knew who it was that attacked her . . .

Majella realised by the sideways stares that she was rocking on the bench. She got up and told the receptionist that she was heading out for a bit and that she'd be back for her ma. Once outside she glued her eyes to the ground and set off walking at her favourite rhythm. The stroll calmed her though everything felt strange at this hour. The light fell at a different angle. People she hadn't seen in years were going about their routines. Empty school buses nosed along the street. Delivery vans were double-parked outside shops and busy wee women were pulling tartan trolley bags behind them. It all smelt and felt like being younger, of being got up for school and eating cornflakes in front of the BBC News before the long walk out the road to St Christopher's High School. Majella'd been good at school. She usually came near the top of the class without trying. But that wasn't good enough for Majella's teachers. Many of them had taught both her ma and her da, and had formed the opinion that Majella had brains to burn from her da's O'Neill side, but was afflicted by the lazy, crazy Keenan streak from her ma's side. So Majella never had it easy at St Christopher's. Half the teachers needled her about her ma.

. . . It's not hard seeing where you got the love of your bed from, is it Majella? Your own mother so lazy she wouldn't even scratch herself when she itched . . .

The other half tried to goad her into doing more with her brains than her da.

Your father was a great scholar. Could've been the first of St Christopher's to go to university on the free place, but instead he ran off to the States. Then when he landed back home he went straight into the factory. What a waste. Your father had the brains to be a teacher. But he threw himself away on the factory.

Majella's da'd told her he'd gone to America after leaving school because he wanted to build skyscrapers up to the angels. Majella's ma said he went to America to escape internment after his involvement with something he called Civil Resistance, which, from what Majella understood, wasn't the Rah but something that led down the road to the Rah. Majella was hazy on the exact details as this stuff wasn't covered in history class and everyone spoke about it in mutters while looking sideways as if they were under surveillance. Her da only got one year at the skyscrapers business before Majella's grandad died after getting a hiding in internment. The Brits had released him from Long Kesh before he died. Majella had initially understood this to be an act of kindness, but had it explained to her that dying at home relieved the authorities of a whole lot of paperwork.

Majella's da returned to Aghybogey to help her granny rear Bobby and Marie.

Majella ducked into McQuaid's garage shop to pick up chocolate and fags before walking towards the bridge. It marked the halfway point of the town, connecting the Taig and Prod sides. In history class they'd learnt that the first bridges had been wooden and were repeatedly burnt down during battles. When the planters arrived, they built a fireproof stone bridge and an untossable castle. Majella stopped on the hump of the bridge to get the best view of the castle ruins. Phelim O'Neill had tossed the castle on one of his glorious but ultimately doomed missions to drive out the planters. The invaders retreated to the good land on the east side of the bridge, while the Catholics were left with the ruined castle and scraggy bogland to the west. They salvaged stone from the castle to build the houses and walls that gave the town its first real shape. When the town was handed a grant to restore the castle, the archaeologists achieved what US diplomats and millions of pounds of peace funding couldn't, temporarily uniting both Taigs and Prods against their mission to rescue 'original stonework' from the tumble-down walls in the fields around the ruin. Oul wans from both sides of the divide had stood about at street corners or in the shops complaining, wondering whether the archaeologists would be coming into their houses next, to rob the stones from around their heads?

Majella hadn't minded the archaeologists. She'd been sitting her GCSEs that summer, so she'd loads of study time. Her and Aideen would go to the castle to smoke or share a bottle of Coke and talk to the archaeologists. They weren't in uniform because of the exams, so they pretended to be A level students. Bored out of their minds with everything else in Aghybogey, they were happy listening to the archaeologists shite on about the local area, letting them hog the odd joint that Aideen robbed off her brothers. Majella had sunburned over and over again during those few months, sitting down by the river. It had been the hottest summer she'd ever known, the one time she'd got a tan on her arms and legs that had made the rest of her pale skin seem luminous in contrast. She remembered taking refuge under the bridge when it got really hot, near the wet smell of the river and the slippery stones. The archaeologists told them about the battles that had happened on the stone bridge in the olden times. Majella'd liked the sound of those days, when entire clans went hooring off into battle and the river ran red with blood. While she was at school there were only the riots around the Orange marches to look forward to in the run up to summer, or the odd bomb or gun attack for a bit of excitement. Every now and then an American newspaper or TV crew would come and stand on the bridge where Majella was now, the tossed castle in the background, one foot on the Prod side, one foot on the Taig side, *an ironic symbol of a town divided*, giving a monologue on the Troubles while people restrained the likes of Francie Kingh from diving into the shot to give the fingers. Before last week, Majella couldn't remember the last time she'd seen reporters in Aghybogey. It was the Muslim fellas who got all the publicity these days. Aghybogey had to make do with hosting the PhD students who'd come and spend days trying to get to know the 'post-conflict' community, trying to dig up the sort of memories that most people knew were best left buried.

Majella leaned over to look into the river. It ran slow and deep. She'd sometimes seen dead sheep in it as a child, which confused her as sheep didn't come across as natural swimmers. Her granny had explained that the sheep hadn't drowned swimming: farmers dumped diseased or dead sheep into the river to get rid of them. It was around that age that Majella realised that the world in her library books, in which children went rambling on moors and swimming in rivers, was different to her world. She couldn't imagine camping in the black boggy fields of Aghybogey without tripping over British soldiers or risking a landmine. She couldn't picture buying eggs from the shotgun-armed farmers or drinking tea made from river water polluted with diseased corpses. And there was only her on her own. Majella had no cousins. No dog. Her only 'chum' was Aideen, who drank Coke instead of ginger beer (whatever that was).

Majella took a last drag on her fag, then dropped it into the sluggish waters below. The weak sunshine was warm on her broad back. She stretched and yawned before ripping open her Lion bar for a bite of breakfast.

9.50 a.m.
Item 23: Dirt and disorder

Majella walked into the surgery just as her ma was hobbling out of the nurse's room on crutches. She felt a wee thrill at her timing despite the scowl on her ma's face. Majella told her she'd ring a taxi, then left her sitting in the surgery explaining to Minnie Spence – and by default the rest of the waiting room – how she'd come to smash a plate on her foot. Spade Byrne arrived after five minutes, but it took Majella another ten minutes to extricate her ma from the waiting room. She hated the way her ma did that, kept people hanging on for her. When she eventually did get her out the door, her ma scooted over to the taxi handily enough. Spade Byrne helped her in, then drove them through the town. Majella surveyed a pupil straggling along the footpath on his way to school while her ma, drunk on the attention she'd had in the surgery, told Spade the story of the plate and her foot. After he parked, he saw them both to the front door and then insisted on helping Majella settle her ma on the couch. As soon as her ma was sitting, Majella guided Spade back to the front door, hurrying him away from the mess of the living room, the dirty front hallway, the piled up junk mail. She thanked him again at the door, and paid him before closing the door with relief.

She paused at the bottom of the stairs and tried to get her nerve up to head into her ma's room. In the months after her da'd disappeared the smell of the room had slowly changed, and her ma's clutter had gradually taken over every surface. Now there was nothing left of him except for his clothes hanging in the wardrobe. Her ma's dirty clothes, magazines, half-empty make-up containers and perfume bottles were scattered everywhere. It smelt of perfume, nicotine and something like sadness that made Majella feel like someone heavy was sitting on her shoulders, sucking the life blood out of her. She ploughed up the stairs and into the room where she grabbed her ma's duvet and a couple of trashy magazines, before shutting the door on the mess. She plodded back down towards the sound of QVC. Majella threw the duvet over her ma where she lay, and put the magazines down. Her ma was very pale.

— Ye all right?

— Ah'm ok.

— What'd she do tae ye?

— Gimme a couple a stitches. Two tramadol for the pain four times a day. Said tae keep me weight off it fer a couple a days. Ah get the stitches out in a week.

Majella knew her ma'd be delighted with the Tramadol for the way it went with the whiskey.

— D'ye want me to fill the prescription?

Her ma nodded and handed it over to Majella.

— Ah'll put the kettle on.

Majella headed to the kitchen to put the kettle and some toast on. She hoped if she tempted her ma with the smell of toast before ambushing her with it, she could be tricked into taking at least a few bites. Majella turned her attention to the smashed plate. She found an old *Daily Mirror* and spread it out on the floor, then she got down and gathered up the bigger shards onto the paper. After she'd swept the remaining fragments into a small pile, she scooped them up and dropped them on top. She expertly wrapped the packet before dumping it in the bin. The kitchen floor – not clean to start with – was now sticky with blood. After her da had left, Majella's ma had let the place go to hell. She took to cleaning in fits and starts, taking sudden notions to wash floors, hoover curtains and wipe skirting boards. She'd dump magazines, post and papers and 'organise' the rest of the clutter. For weeks afterwards, Majella spent ages working out where things had gone, identifying what had been dumped and what had just been 'tidied'. In between these cleaning bouts, Majella kept the kitchen surfaces and bathroom clean, and saw to her own bedroom like she'd always done. But the overall condition of the house was somewhere between a midden and a disgrace.

The lovely smell of toasting bread set Majella's mouth watering. She wondered if her ma could smell it from where she was lying. Majella could remember a few times she was sick in bed and her da'd been down the stairs making her toast. The best of it, nearly, was her lying upstairs, smelling the toast before he brought it up to her on a wee tray, with a cup of sweet, milky tea. No matter how sick she'd been she'd feel better then, with her da sitting on the end of her bed watching her eat, telling her some wee thing about what was going on in the factory.

Majella turned to the toaster just before it popped, then watched the toast jump up. She washed her hands before going to work on her toast with the margarine and jam. Then she made a big mug of sweet black coffee. When she'd the tray ready, she went to the medicine cupboard and took down a couple of Tramadol from her ma's regular prescription and dropped them beside the coffee. She brought everything through to the living room and set the tray down on the coffee table. Her ma ignored the toast and reached for the Tramadol.

— Ach, ye're very good, Majella.

Majella went back to the kitchen and sat at the table, flicking her fingers and rocking back and forwards to try and slow her heart. Her head was buzzing from dealing with too many people so early in the day without the buffer of the shop counter between her and them. She felt done in. So she stood up and headed back to her bed, taking comfort in the stairs creaking their friendly little greetings at her all the way up.

12.51 p.m.
Item 24: Jewellery

Majella could tell by the dim light in her bedroom that the morning sunshine had faded and that another blank grey sky was pressing down on them from above, and would do until the unseen sun sank behind the mountains. She checked her mobile phone.

She lay back in bed again, listening to the chatter of the TV downstairs. The bite of the chill told her that her ma hadn't stirred to light the fire or put on the heating. The Tramadol kept her ma sluggish at times, which Majella knew had its benefits. She wondered if her ma would remember her birthday. She usually did, in fairness, on the day or near enough, presenting her with a card and jewellery in a painful rite that Majella endured every year. Majella hadn't worn jewellery since she turned sixteen.

. . . Sweet Sixteen and Never Been Kissed, eh? Well sure come here and ah'll sort ye out love . . .

She couldn't abide the jingle of jewellery, the way it tangled on her clothes and hair. She hated the clunky feel of rings, the way they cut into her flesh, rapped against surfaces. She had a jewellery box full of unworn necklaces, bracelets, rings and earrings, for as long as she admired and tried on whatever it was her ma bought for her when she was presented with it, her ma didn't notice if it was never worn again.

Majella wondered what to do with herself. She was due into the chipper at four, so she'd no time to head to Strabane or Omagh on the bus to get herself a wee something for her birthday. She couldn't shop locally for she knew she'd be the talk of the town if she were seen out in Biddy's Boutique with her granny not yet cold in the grave. She guessed she would fill her ma's prescription before work. But that left her with a good hour to kill. Then Majella realised what she wanted to do. She got up and ran her finger along her DVD collection on the shelf though she knew exactly where to find the disc she was looking for.

She pushed it into the player, grabbed the remote control and pressed play. She settled herself into bed to watch a red Mercedes drive from New Orleans to Dallas. A young couple, not twenty-four hours married, were heading home. Majella watched closely as Pamela Ewing turned to her new husband, Bobby, and voiced her concerns at the welcome she might expect on the ranch. Episode one, series one, had begun. Majella stuck her finger in her mouth and began to suck.

1.55 p.m.
Item 13: Sentiment

The hour flew by with *Dallas* on. When the closing credits rolled, Majella stretched herself out underneath her lumpy wee duvet and yawned, her feet straining against the bottom board of the bed. She had a notion that one of these days she'd push too hard and pop the foot board off. Majella'd spent years getting bigger while her room and everything in it stayed the same size. It felt like a bum deal. She sat up, threw the duvet off herself and swung her legs around onto the edge of the bed. The room was warm and dry from the fan heater. She flicked it off with her toe and sat for moment, letting the blood settle in her head.

She knew she'd have to check up on her ma before she headed on to work, to see if she'd eaten the toast. But first she had to get dressed. She lifted her arms and pulled her T-shirt off over her head and threw it in her laundry basket. Then she paused to have a sniff of her oxters before wiping herself with a roll-on deodorant. The product description always irritated Majella, for deodorants didn't actually de-odorise her armpits: they just made them smell different. Majella much preferred the natural tang of her pits to the fake ming of the deodorant, but she'd learned the hard way in school that Other People preferred perfumes and deodorants to their own smells and that anyone who smelt like their own self was in for a rough ride.

Rummaging through her chest of drawers Majella noticed she was running low in clean clothes. She found a worn-out T-shirt she wasn't keen on and pulled it over her head. When she sat down to pull on her trainers she noticed that there was a red sauce stain down her joggers. Even though her joggers would be hidden under her uniform, Majella couldn't endure the thought of having that stain on her for the rest of the day. She only had her oul navy joggers left, which she usually wore for a kip or lying about the house because they were pockmarked with cherry bomb craters, but they'd have to do: in Majella's spectrum of laundry sins, holes weren't as bad as stains and stains were worse than smells. After she pulled on her fleece, Majella gathered her dirty clothes up out of her laundry basket, recoiling from the smell of them. Majella thought it was strange the way clothes stopped smelling like you when you took them off and just smelt minging instead. She reckoned it was probably a question of temperature, like the smell of bread or meat. Even her granny had smelt different after she'd died, and that wasn't all the work of the undertaker who had leggared make-up on her in an attempt to camouflage the bruises.

Majella unlocked her bedroom door and lumbered down the thirteen stairs. Majella didn't believe in good luck or bad luck. As far as she could see, shit just happened. But she knew Other People cared about things like the number thirteen and so she'd always wondered why the builders had built that number of stairs into their house, and every other house in the estate. At the bottom of the stairs she turned and headed for the kitchen.

— Majellah?

Majella ploughed on into the kitchen. — Ah'm putting on a wash. Ah'll be in in a minute.

— Will ye put the kettle on?

— Aye.

Her ma was a wild one for coffee and tea. She drank it by the bucket all day long and then wondered why she had bother sleeping. Majella dropped her dirty clothes in front of the washing machine. She poured a dose of powder into the machine drawer, then shoved her clothes into the drum. There was too much for one wash really, it was tight going to get them all in, but Majella didn't have the patience for two washes. She turned the dial to *40º colourfast cotton* and pushed the ON button. Majella focused on the humming and gurgling – she loved the song of it, knew it off by heart.

— Ma-jell-ahhhhh?

Majella flinched and paused for a few seconds to rock and flick her fingers. Then she shouted back. — Just filling the kettle.

When she was done, Majella walked into the living room. Her ma was lying in the same place. She'd eaten a slice and a half of the toast Majella'd made earlier, which was both better than nothing and not good enough.

— Would ye bring in wan of me yogurts, Jellah? Ah have tae keep up with me regime even after me accident.

Majella went back to the kitchen. She opened the fridge and grabbed a tiny bottle of yogurt. It felt comedically small in her hand as she shook it. When she tore the thin foil top off, a sickly, fake orange smell filled her nostrils.

She held it away from her as she brought the bottle through to her ma.

— Och ye opened it and all. Ye're very good. Thanks.

Majella sat down on the armchair, her feet stretched out in front of her.

— Ye wouldn't do something else for me?

Majella nodded, her eyes on the telly.

— Pass me the wee bag that's in there in the cupboard under the telly would ye?

Majella worked extra hard to keep her blank face on. She heaved herself up and went over to the cupboard and looked in. It was a mess of old photographs, junk mail, prayer books, undeveloped films, memorial cards and unanswered wedding invitations. There was a fancy paper bag on top of everything with a card underneath. She recognised her birthday present.

— This what ye want?

— Aye. Well. Ah'm hoping it's what *you* want.

Her ma sat smiling over at her. Majella stared doggedly at the gift bag, feeling her ma's eyes on her. She left the package on her knee while she opened the card – her ma had literally beat it into her that for politeness you always opened and appreciated the card before tearing into the gift. Majella pulled a flowery pink card out of a lavender envelope. The writing read

For My Daughter

Majella opened it. It was one of those posh cards that cost more because the print wasn't just done on the inside of the card, but on a thin piece of paper glued to the middle. Majella controlled the urge to flick her fingers and kept her eyes glued to the card.

— Och that's lovely, Mammy. Thanks.

— Ah knew ye'd like that one. Ah just knew it the minute ah picked the card up in Kelly's. Now. Open that present up there till we see what ye make of it.

Majella picked up the paper bag and pulled out a blue plastic box. She paused to run her finger all around the thin gilt border on the edge before opening it. She stared at the gold heart that hung from a necklace. It was engraved in all caps, in a plain font:

MAJELLA

Majella's older jewellery had been hand engraved by William Smyth of the jewellers. But his son Robert hadn't inherited his father's talent for engraving, so he'd bought a machine to do the job. Pens, necklaces, glasses, crystal, watches and bracelets could all be popped into the machine and would come out perfect (spelling mistakes earned you a generous discount). Majella hated the heart.

— Och, now isn't that lovely? Lovely. Thanks Mammy. Thanks a million.

She hoped her ma wasn't going to go all soft and expect a kiss or that. From the corner of her eye she saw her ma frown.

— Are ye not going tae put yer necklace on?

— Och mammy ye know oul Hunter's rules about jewellery in the shop.

— Och that wan's as sour as last week's milk.

Majella understood this metaphor for she'd once tasted last week's milk by accident. The foul taste had coated her tongue and could only be removed with toothpaste.

— Can't enjoy herself so she'll not let anyone else enjoy themselves.

— Sure ah know.

Majella had a feeling that her ma was warming up on the subject of Cunter.

— Oh ho. There's not too many that dunno what she's like. Ann that odd being of a husband. God be thanked that they didn't breed, anyway.

As her ma shook her head, Majella got onto her feet and put her birthday card on the dusty mantelpiece.

— Ah forgot about the kettle. Is it tay or coffee you're looking?

— Just a wee cuppa black coffee. Put them sweeteners in, not the sugar.

Majella nodded and hid the heart deep in her pocket.

2.22 p.m.
Item 40.6: The political situation: Commemorations, marches and flag waving

Majella was stood in front of the perfume display cabinet in the pharmacy, waiting for Tracey O'Donnell to fill her ma's prescription. Majella had picked a spot as far away as possible from the poster that had a picture of her Uncle Bobby on it. She could tell at a glance from the shamrocks, tricolours and old-fashioned Irish text that some committee or other had taken it upon themselves to include Bobby in some sort of commemoration. Before he'd disappeared, her da had always dealt with this type of thing, stating the family's position or representing them at events. In his absence, no one came knocking at her granny's door or stopped to ask her Aunt Marie what they thought of Bobby's inclusion in the latest roll of honour, ceremony or gun salute. The poster didn't upset Majella, for although Bobby had been her godfather, he was dead this sixteen years now and she had never really known him to begin with. She could remember him calling at the door, looking for her da, and them heading on together. The line they gave the police over and over again was that they were going fishing across the border, though they never brought fish home. When she'd asked her da about that, he'd said they sold their catch to a shop in Donegal as her ma couldn't stand the smell of fish cooking in the house. Majella had heard that Bobby'd done well in school – he'd achieved some of the best O level results anyone had ever seen not just in Aghybogey, but in Northern Ireland. But nobody bothered to suggest teacher training to him. According to her ma, everyone knew where Bobby's ambitions lay from the minute he sauntered into St Christopher's wearing a camouflage schoolbag decorated with a tri-colour flag coloured in on top of a blob of Tippex, and IRA ALL THE WAY biro'd on his left forearm. Local legend had it that this was a phrase he drew on his arm every morning, despite being forced to wash it off by the headmaster each and every day, until he had it tattooed on at the age of fourteen. When Bobby left school at sixteen, he started a dual apprenticeship – working as a carpenter by day and volunteering with the IRA in his 'free' time. Majella remembered the talk of Bobby being 'lifted' after local gun attacks or explosions, an experience she'd imagined might be exhilarating until the day the Brits had burst into their house and rifle-butted her da in the living room before pulling him into the street and bundling him into an armoured vehicle. This explained to Majella some of the bruises both men nursed for weeks after they were released from interrogation. The best lesson Bobby ever taught Majella was that being book smart wasn't enough. For as bright as Bobby was in the classroom, he'd fucked up big time in a small field outside Aghybogey, when the booby-trap bomb he was planting exploded prematurely.

Majella had watched the funeral on the news with a neighbour, who had murmured 'Long Runs the Fox' as the camera closed in on her da and granny standing stunned by the graveside. She watched her granny flinch as masked men shot a volley over her uncle's coffin. It was years before Majella realised that not everyone got a volley of gunshots over their grave.

— Majella? Your script's ready.

Majella looked up from the perfume bottles and walked back to Tracey O'Donnell, all the time ignoring the poster. She picked up the medicine bag and nodded at Tracey. — Thanks a million.

Tracey smiled at Majella, ignoring the poster. — No bother. Hope your ma gets better soon!

Majella had rehearsed a stock reply. — Och, please God, she will now please God.

She wasn't sure if she was addressing Tracey O'Donnell or someone else.

3.55 p.m.

Item 14.4: Medical stuff: Incurable diseases

Majella had dropped the Tramadol in to her ma, and was now passing the chapel on her way back down town towards A Salt and Battered! As usual, she kept an eye on her pace, trying to make sure she walked just fast or slow enough to avoid conversation. Tuesday was Market Day, which meant Majella ran the risk of bumping into Agnes Ferguson. In what Majella thought of as the Olden Times, farmers from all over Donegal, Fermanagh and Leitrim had gathered in Aghybogey every first Tuesday to barter and spit over the top of cattle, boys, fruit and vegetables. This tradition was disrupted in the early seventies when the Brits undertook an operation to 'secure the area' without discussing their plans with anyone on either side of the border. First the army blew up nineteen of the twenty country roads and every single bridge that criss-crossed the border between Aghybogey and Donegal. They then dug a bunker and built a heavily fortified checkpoint on the last open road. It was manned by partially bullet-proofed soldiers who checked cars at gunpoint about fifty metres away from the tin shack that served as the official Irish customs checkpoint. Anyone who wanted to cross the border had to run the gauntlet of not one, but two international checkpoints within the space of fifty metres. Majella could remember spending hours held up at the Brit checkpoint, her da out of the car, being searched and challenged while the Guards on the Irish side played cards in their tin shack, or occasionally wandered about outside with a nice cup of tea. For a few months after the road closures, the market had struggled on, but in the end nobody had the patience to spend hours at an army checkpoint to get a trailer of scabby spuds or carrots to Aghybogey. The market withered and died while local people started a new tradition of filling in the cratered roads and digging shallow beds in the river so tractors and jeeps could cross. The Brits in turn cratered the repaired roads and dug out the river crossings under armed guard. And so it continued, until the Ceasefire, when a few roads were officially reopened. That was when Agnes Ferguson, who everyone knew was flaky because she'd left the town in a huff following the April Fool's Day bomb that had flattened her house but left the RUC station still standing, returned to Aghybogey. Agnes told everyone she spoke to that she was back to build bridges. Marty had explained to Majella that the bridges were not literal bridges – Agnes wanted to build bridges across community divisions. This struck Majella as a much more difficult engineering project, one complicated by the fact that although most people could see the need for rebuilding the literal bridges, no one had an eye for invisible bridges. Majella herself did wonder why no one had considered drawbridges in the whole scheme of things, which could serve as bridges when the need arose. But she suspected that was a rare thought and so she didn't share it with anyone, unlike Agnes, who seemed to have no hold on her thoughts. The first time Majella saw Agnes she was struck by the woman's deep suntan. She noted the silver rings on Agnes' fingers, toes, nose and ears. She listened to her funny accent and snuck glances at the three caramel-coloured children Agnes had brought home without a man. During their first months in Aghybogey, Agnes' children cut their long hair, lost their European accents, donned Nike trainers and Levi jeans and started smoking Players. Majella watched as their lovely skin faded to grey in the watery winter light. Agnes was different. Although she lost her tan, she didn't change her hippy ways to fit back into Aghybogey, even after she got the cancer. They found it first in her lungs

. . . they're saying it's from the joints, not the marijuana of course, but the raw tobacco. If I had to do over again I'd still smoke every single joint but I'd use a filter. But we were so innocent in those days. That's what was beautiful about us: our innocence . . .

then in her left breast

. . . I just told them to take it off, I mean, what's a breast anyway once you've weaned your children? It's just so much fat, isn't it really? . . .

then in her right breast

. . . if nothing else, it'll even things up a bit – I'll not be so lopsided . . . a ha ha hack . . . hack . . .

and then in her cervix

. . . the doctors did say that women who've slept with very few men have a smaller chance of getting cervical cancer. But I was always one for free love and this is a small price to pay for so many experiences. I wouldn't be the soul I am today if I hadn't given my body so freely . . .

During one remission period, Agnes had got Majella and most of the town to sign a petition supporting an application to the peace-money people for funding to restart the Tuesday market. Peace Money had been a new thing in the town. Instead of being asked to donate money to intense-looking strangers collecting for the Cause in the pub, they were now supposed to fill in forms so the government would give them, the community themselves, money for stuff that supported economic and social progress, community cohesion and shared spaces and services. It was always people like Agnes who won the money for 'initiatives' like Market Day. So the way Majella saw it, Peace Money was to blame for the fact that every first Tuesday in the past year she had to try to sneak past Agnes' rainbow-painted stall, which was laden with limp organic vegetables. The only vegetables Majella ate were deep-fried battered onion rings and chips. But once cornered by Agnes, she felt pressured to buy something. She usually bought a small bag of spuds that ended up rotting in the cupboard under the kitchen sink. Worse than that was having to listen to Agnes herself. Her cancer was back again, she'd been telling Majella only last month, this time in her throat.

. . . it's the good food I have to thank for the cancer being beat this four times. And I'll beat it again . . . hack . . . hack . . . hack . . . just need to keep taking my vitamins, eating organic and meditating . . .

On Market Day, Majella took the long way round to work, skirting the bridge area at the bottom of the town to avoid Agnes, for it wasn't just about the vegetables and the cancer. Agnes also dotted burning candles in coloured jars around a poster beside her stand. Each month she highlighted another tale of injustice in the world, and would ask her customers to write a letter of support, or at least sign a petition, for some poor frigger stuck in some shitty jail in some fucked-up wee country Majella had never heard of. But the worst thing was that Agnes seemed to see Majella as a project, someone she'd plaster onto a poster and start a petition for if she could. Majella had a notion that her granny's murder had raised her profile with Agnes, and she took extra care to avoid her gaze. She had almost reached the safety of A Salt and Battered! when she heard Agnes shout her name across the Diamond.

— Majell-AH! MA-JELL-AH?

Majella pictured Agnes' raw-looking eyelids blinking behind her. She shuddered, then pushed her way into the chip shop.

5.05 p.m.
Item 18.1: Periods: PMS

Majella's hairpins were sticking into her. No matter what she did, she couldn't sort them out. It was fucking her off. She knew by the all-over body aches and the itching and scratching feeling she had under her skin that her period was due.

Marty was in foul form too, having had a row with Philomena. This was not Majella's problem and she hoped Marty would not make it her problem.

The buzzer sounded and Red Onions walked into the chipper, his pasty freckled face streaked with dirt from work. Majella hadn't seen him since he'd found his da dead on the settee, and knew she should say something to him. She paused for what she knew was too long, searching for the right words. Then she spoke. — What canna get chew?

Red Onions took a long look at the fluorescent menu board above Majella's head, then turned his grey eyes towards her.

— Big sausage supper and a can a Coke, please.

— Coming up.

She wrote the order on her wee notebook, ripped the page out and spiked it onto the board, even though she could tell Marty'd heard the order as it came in, and already had the food bubbling in the fryer. Red Onions sat down on the window seat, put his toolbox at his feet, and rested his head in his hands. Majella watched him comb his fingers slowly through his glowing ginger hair. He looked tired. Majella hadn't seen him for a week. She'd taken six days off work (with no pay) for her granny's wake and funeral. After that Red Onions had his da's wake and funeral to attend to. Majella hated wakes. She spent three days trapped in her Aunt Marie's house greeting an unending stream of people who'd come to have a look at the corpse laid out in the only bedroom. It had been a big wake, almost as big as Brendy Hagan's after he'd been blown up by the Loyalists because his photo'd been in the paper for distributing shamrocks before Mass on Paddy's Day. Wakes for people killed in explosions usually featured closed coffins, but because the hospital staff did such a great job of patching Brendy back together during the seven days he'd survived after the explosion, the town had the novelty of a half-open coffin at his wake. Everyone with the faintest connection to the family dropped in for a gawk at Brendy's sewn-up face. Majella had been dragged along by her ma, who had pushed her into the crowded house. Majella spent the whole hour in a horror of embarrassment, crammed into close range with neighbours, people from school and strangers. It unnerved Majella to see they'd put Brendy in a full-size coffin, even though he'd lost both his legs. After she'd found a place to stand and been given a cup of tea, she'd stood there wondering if they'd refrigerated his legs when he'd first been brought into the hospital, in case he'd die and could be buried complete, or if they'd incinerated them when it became clear there wasn't enough to sew back on.

Majella didn't get wakes. Everyone at her granny's wake had blethered on about the brilliant tradition of wakes and how they were a power of good for the bereaved and how wakes kept the community together and how if it wasn't for wakes and funerals sure they'd hardly ever see each other any more because of the way the telly keeps everyone indoors. The wake didn't feel like a power of good to Majella, who was obliged by tradition to tramp around her Auntie Marie's damp wee house for hours offering a tray full of scones and sandwiches to a load of wet-eyed oul fellas who kept telling her what a great dancer her granny'd been in her day. Everyone told Majella what she already knew – that no one deserved that end: no one. Hour after hour Majella carried the tray, and all she could think was, I'm still at it – still serving food up to the greedy fuckers. She stared out over Red Onions' head to the Diamond, where Agnes Ferguson was bent over coughing while her son packed up her stall in the fading light.

6.00 p.m.
Item 1: Small talk, bullshit and gossip

Majella tried to catch the toll of the Angelus Bell over the foaming chip oil as she transcribed Declan Mulqueen's order onto her A Salt and Battered! pad. He was in for the family's monthly takeaway, which covered himself, his wife and his twelve kids. Marty always said Declan worked hard, was never at rest. Majella suspected that his wife worked harder, stuck at home all day managing twelve lumps of weans, even if four of them were teenagers. But Majella liked what she saw of Declan Mulqueen on his once-a-month visits to the chipper and once-a-week visits to the chapel, where his family took up two whole rows at the front. He always came in to Majella with a neatly written list that he simply passed to her, not wasting any breath on small talk. Declan's order was more complicated than the usual orders, on account of the Mulqueens not having individual suppers, but combining different dishes to make their money stretch further. So a regular fish supper and chips would do three smaller weans, but a large sausage supper could only stretch to two weans, and then for every three weans an extra bag of chips was ordered in case of running short. Declan and his wife each took their pick of a full order. As the kids got bigger, Majella'd seen the order grow, for none of the teenagers would share a meal. The trick with the Mulqueens was to try and make sure that all the dinners were ready more or less together, so they'd all still be hot when they opened them. Majella felt there was a bit of an art to it.

— That'll be about fifteen minutes, Declan.

Declan nodded in her direction. — Thanks Majella.

Then he left the shop and went next door to The Full Cup for a shot of Jameson's, no ice. Majella knew what he drank because Marty followed him one day, slipping out the side door of A Salt and Battered! and in through the side door of The Full Cup, pretending he needed a box of matches. Majella's ma once said that Marty was worse than a woman sometimes, with the nose on him. Majella wondered if that was why he got on with women so well.

6.49 p.m.
Item 20.1: The security forces: The Brits

Majella was sitting out the back of the chipper, taking a drag of her fag. She was thinking about the wrinkles each suck was crinkling into the skin around her lips. She knew that between sucking on fags and sucking on her finger she'd have a mouth like a cat's arse by the time she was forty. Just like her ma, who looked like she'd been sucking lemons for most of her life, except when she fell asleep and her mouth hung slack as an empty sack. Her ma had been a good-looking woman. A complete hoor according to her Aunt Marie, but a good-looking one. When Majella'd first gone drinking in the pubs in town, she'd had to put up with man after man shiting on about her ma, watching lazy grins curl across the faces of dirty oul men once they figured out who she was. Then she had to take the gobshite comparisons and agree that she wasn't her mother's daughter, she was her father's daughter. Not that her da had ever been hefty like her. He'd always kept himself trim, even after he gave up the GAA. He'd been a player for the Aghybogey Red Hands. They'd been a good wee team in her da's day. Lean hardy fuckers of men who played a dirty game when it was needed. They trained on a boggy pitch a few miles out of town, most of them walking there and back, stripping in the ditch before changing into green and gold jerseys. Despite not having sixpence behind them, the Aghybogey Red Hands came close to winning the championship a few times, kicking the arse of better financed teams from bigger clubs. They only ever came close though – the Red Hands never won. Her da'd been captain for a few glorious seasons. Majella remembered the hassle from the Brits increasing after the time they found the guns hidden in the GAA centre. Her da had been in a rage about that. He'd said that nobody should be hiding guns in the centre. That they were giving the Brits and the Loyalists an excuse for targeting the whole team. After that he was held up at checkpoints for hours on his way to work or on his way home. He was lifted and taken up to Castlereagh for days at a time. The whole team was once detained at a checkpoint so long they missed a game. Her da endured all this, but after Bobby died, his hunger went off him and he quit the game. When she was wee, before the worst of the hassle, her da had taken her to a few of the bigger matches. Majella remembered sitting on her ma's knee in the front of the wee Fiesta, with three big hallions of men crammed into the back. The games had always scared her – the jumping and pushing, the ball being fisted, the slap of leather in the muck, and the blood mixing with the rain and mud on the players' faces. She always remembered the tired but pumped-up men on the way back from the game, the strong sweaty smell of them and their anger and joy at the game, no matter which way it went. Majella had wanted to be a Gaelic footballer when she grew up, but her ma put her out of that notion before long. Majella knew she wasn't like the other girls who the boys liked to chase round the school yard in a game of Kisscatchers. She didn't like being chased. She learned early she was no catch.

Majella looked at the long ash tail that hung on the end of her fag. She flicked it into the air and watched it fall, before dropping the butt on the ground. She mashed it with her trainer and stepped back into the shop. Marty was leaning on the counter, chatting to Andrea Gurney, who was giggling at him. As Majella watched Andrea took a reddener. Majella knew Andrea liked few things better than a nice supper of a bag of chips and a giant battered sausage washed down with a can of Fanta from A Salt and Battered! Majella didn't bother to check the pinned order and instead went to the fryer, threw Andrea's food into the basket and dunked it into the boiling oil. From the counter she could hear Andrea squeal.

— Marty you're a wild fella altogether!

9.09 p.m.

Item 12.1: Conversation: Banter and the craic

It was quiet for nine oh nine. Marty'd taken charge of the shop counter for a while, leaving Majella to sit up on the prep counter to rest her feet. Her socks were wet with sweat and her face was pink. Marty said the heat of the lights and fryers made the cooking area feel like a sauna. Majella wondered why anyone would pay good money to go to a sauna to feel the way she did right now.

— Did ye get up tae much the day, Jellytot?

Majella wiped her face with the back of her hand. — Naw. Watched a DVD.

— Did I not hear you ann yer ma were in the surgery first thing this morning?

Majella thought it was as well for Marty that he wasn't a cat.

— Aye we were.

There was a silence as Marty rubbed the back of his head and Majella kept her blank face on.

— What happened anyway?

Majella tossed her head convulsively and hated herself for the betrayal. — She dropped a plate and it smashed on her foot.

— Jesus. She all right?

— Och aye. A few stitches. Spade Byrne was a great hand.

Marty scratched his arse absent-mindedly. — Is she on the crutches?

— Aye. Has tae keep the weight off it for a day or so.

Majella was pissed off with herself. He always did this, somehow. Started with a wee question about something you didn't want to talk about and then suddenly there you were telling him your fucken life story.

— Lucky, all the same.

Majella said nothing. She hoped one of the neighbours would drop by to tend to her ma, as they often did.

Marty turned to look out the window, then quickly turned back to Majella. — Oh ho. The Snake Connolly's on his way in. Wait til ye see this for a plaster.

Marty settled his face into a sociable grin as the buzzer announced the arrival of Jake the Snake Connolly. Majella sat where she was, just out of sight. She wasn't a fan of Jake. He liked to make out he got his name from his snake hips and quick tongue, or, if he'd enough drink in him, he'd tell you his nickname came from the length and girth of his cock. Majella, like the rest of Aghybogey, knew he was called the Snake because he was so fucken rare. He always wore all-black leather trousers and waistcoat. His shirts were royal blue and split as far down as his waistcoat would go, so he could swing a gold medallion that featured the Virgin Mary with her hands open in welcome.

He wore high-heeled clickety-clackety shoes and slicked-back dyed-black hair, which he always claimed was natural. The Snake Connolly was a right dose at the best of times. But when he came into the chipper, and started talking pure shite to Majella:

. . . my good lady, you deserve to be serenaded, to be swept away from this grease and stink and lain upon soft silk cushions and kissed with moist lips . . .

He really annoyed her.

Fuck off, Majella would think. Just Fuck Right Away Off.

— I'll just have a small portion of chicken nuggets and a small portion of chips, Martin my good fell-o. I must watch my figure!

Martin nodded and juked his head into the back towards Majella. — Jelly-tot! Fire on a Kiddie's Chicken Nugget Special Meal for Mr Connolly here.

Majella smiled, then slid down off the prep counter to throw Jake's dinner into the fryer.

10.00 p.m.
Item 8.4: Jokes: Repeated jokes

Majella watched Jimmy Nine Pints lay his five pound note on the counter.

— A sausage supper, my good woman, a sausage supper.

Majella knew that Jimmy's chips and sausage were bubbling in the background.

— On its way, Jimmy.

The till chimed as it opened. Majella tucked Jimmy's greasy fiver away, then closed the drawer and waited in silence. Jimmy shifted his weight, then leaned in closer to the counter.

— D'ye want a bit of my sausage?

He wheezed a bit, slapping his hand flat on the counter. Majella waited for the usual five seconds before replying.

— I'll batter yer sausage if you're not careful now.

Marty joined in with the laughter as the chip fat spat and frothed over Jimmy's Tuesday-night sausage supper.

10.30 p.m.

Item 34.3: Fighting: Pretending not to fight

Marty was out at the counter telling Majella about Dinny Teague, who was in a rage because some young wans had broken into his house and robbed a load of his porn and had posted it, page by page, through all the letterboxes in the estates. Dinny knew who'd robbed the magazines, but Marty explained to Majella that Dinny was caught between a rock and a hard place, for due to the nature of the stolen goods, he could ask neither the IRA nor Father Travers for an intervention. As Marty chatted, Majella kept an eye on young Iggy Connolly, who looked like he was working himself up to run into the chipper as soon as Marty went out back. But before Marty finished, the buzzer raged and Philomena walked in. Majella watched Marty jumping to attention.

— Hiya, Majella. Things ok with you?

— Hiya, Fill. Not a bother on me.

Majella pulled herself up from her leaning position on the counter.

— Going out back fer a fag, Marty. Shout if ye need me.

Marty didn't look over at Majella nor in Philomena's direction – he was doing what Majella liked to do: staring out at the empty benches in the middle of the Diamond.

— Work away.

Majella stepped outside into the cold alleyway. The light from the chipper spilled onto the concrete, warm and yellow as fryer fat. Shivering, Majella groped for her fags, which she'd crushed into her breast pocket. She pulled out a Marlboro and lit it with the lighter she'd got free (*The Bogey Inn for ceol agus crack*). She took a drag, wondering how Philomena and Marty's nicey-nicey-all-smiles-teeth-grinding-nails-digging-into-palms argument was going. If customers came in, they probably wouldn't even notice the row going on under their noses. Majella certainly hadn't noticed stuff like that in the start. It was Marty himself who'd educated her about this type of argument, so different from the spitting and shouting attacks her ma launched. And it was Marty who'd taught her to make herself scarce, instead of hanging around at the counter like she'd done in the start. Majella always knew when the coast was clear, because Phil would shout through to Majella that she was heading and Majella'd shout back —Safe Home, then wait a wee minute before going back in, where Marty'd be bulling. This was marriage. Majella wasn't too sure why anyone bothered with it. She particularly didn't understand Marty and Philomena, who didn't seem to have any craic at all. Philomena hadn't even been up the duff when they'd married – their weans only happened in the years afterwards. Majella thought by Marty's way of going on that he didn't give a flying fuck about Philomena any more, but he was forever telling Majella his heart was broke over his three wee girls, which meant Philomena had him by the balls. It was all too complicated for Majella, way more complicated than the goings on in *Dallas* that she'd been analysing repeatedly for years, still learning new stuff every time she watched.

The Full Cup side door opened, brightening the alleyway, and Majella braced herself against the imminent noise. Young Peader Devine rolled an empty keg out the back, then hit it a kick and watched it roll and batter off the far wall. When it stopped moving, he walked over, picked it up and swung it up on top of the other kegs. It wobbled before settling into place. Majella unclenched when the noise stopped. Peader turned to her.

— What about ye Majella?

Peader was old enough to know Majella's nickname, but too young to use it. She preferred it that way.

— Grand. Yerself?

— Top. Keeping rightly.

— Busy the night?

— Kept going. What about yer joint?

— Tide never goes out.

There was a long silence. Majella took another long drag of her fag. Her and Peader had fucked one night, in the alleyway, after a Sunday-night lock-in. She remembered holding him up afterwards until he recovered himself.

— Any chance of a free sausage supper?

— Not the night, Peader. Cunter's checkin up on us. Try us on Saturday.

— Ah'm off Saturday. Going tae the Purple Parrot in Donegal town. Big bus of us going. What about ye?

— Working Saturday. Off on Sunday. Might drop in fer a pint.

Peader nodded and smiled. He was a decent cub, Majella thought.

— Ah'd better head on here, or me da'll be out after me.

— See ya.

Majella thought it a pity Peader would grow up. In a few years he'd be like the rest, sitting sniggering at the bar, growing a beer belly, getting too drunk to get a decent hard-on. She dropped her fag butt and stared at it smouldering in the dark. Philomena's voice rang out from inside the chipper. — I'm away, Majella.

Majella flicked her fingers quietly, happily in the dark.

— Safe Home, Fill.

She counted to ten and then stepped back into the light. As soon as Marty saw her, he marched to the back of the shop where he grabbed the mop and bucket.

— Frigging shower a shites ann assholes . . .

Majella looked outside to the orange-lit Diamond. The benches by the war memorial were empty.

— Fuck. Basturd. Cunt. Hoor. Fucken. Usin. Bitch. Ball. Breakin. Cock. Sucken. Sow.

Young Iggy Connolly was gone. Majella knew she wouldn't see him again that night.

11.03 p.m.
Item 1: Small talk, bullshit and gossip

Out of the side of her eye, Majella watched Marty scrubbing at the prep counter with a scourer, which she knew was something he only did when annoyed. He wasn't talking to her, which was a bad sign, but he had stopped swearing, which was a good sign. Majella wanted him to relax and thought she'd maybe figured out how to do that. She flicked her fingers quietly under the counter before speaking.

— You all right?

Marty stopped scouring and stared at Majella, which made her feel like a torn-off order, pinned to the rack. — Now what d'ye think?

Majella tried raising an eyebrow at Marty. — Philomena still holding out on ye?

Marty looked away from her, scowling. — My conjugal relations with my wife are my own business, thanks very much.

Even though he wasn't looking at her, Majella tried a smile. — Still not getting any then?

She watched Marty frown again. Then he half smiled and tossed his head. — Nope. Bitch still holding out on me.

Majella felt some of the tension in the chipper ease. Her effort was worth it. Then the door opened and the buzzer rasped as Rose Murphy came into the takeaway wearing her trademark short black skirt, her stumpy but muscular legs blue-purple with the cold. At the sight of Rose, Marty dropped his scourer and wiped his hands on his apron as he came forward to the counter.

Majella greeted Rose. — What can ah get you?

— A chicken fillet burger anna wee bag a chips please.

Majella knew Marty'd ask her about salt and vinegar, even though he knew as well as she knew that Rose liked salt and vinegar on her chips.

— Salt ann vinegar on yer chips?

Rose looked at Marty like he was offering her a diamond ring and nodded.

— Aye.

Marty stood beside Majella as she ripped Rose's order and spiked it onto the notice board. She moved to the fryers to put the food on, while Marty had a quiet chat with Rose in the front. He had a soft spot for Rose. Majella couldn't figure out why – as far as she knew, he'd never fucked her, at least not after she'd had Róisín and went on the game. And she would've been a bit young for it before Róisín. Once, when Majella was practising the impossible art of small talk, she'd asked Marty who Róisín's da was. Marty had exploded and said that he was just some cunt who wanted to fuck up a wee girl who wasn't even out of school. This explanation hadn't helped Majella understand much more than she already knew, and the experience reinforced her dislike for small talk. She knew Rose and Marty had grown up in the same estate, and had been to school together from when they were four. But Majella herself wasn't best buddy pals with even one of the thirty-two people who'd been in her year at school. None of them had become prostitutes as far as she knew. And maybe that was the difference. After Majella lowered Rose's food into the oil, she stood in the glow of the fryers, watching Marty and Rose out of the corner of her eye. Rose's hair was dyed blonde, rough enough that even Majella could tell it was a home job. She was cleastered in make-up but still looked tired underneath it. Majella always thought Rose looked like one of the prostitutes she saw on *The Bill* from time to time – you kind of knew her story wasn't going to have a happy ending. Marty'd once said to Majella that Rose'd wanted to be a hairdresser when they were at school. He said it like it was a tragedy or something, how far she'd fallen from her dreams.

Majella flipped Rose's chicken-fillet burger. She'd learned in geography class at school that their local district had the highest unemployment rate in the Industrial World. When the teacher had them break down the figures inside their district, it turned out Aghybogey was the worst of the worst. In their weekly careers class, the teacher had chosen to ignore the 90 per cent unemployment rate among the Catholic population in the town, and did her best to promote Positive, Empowering Career Choices that would Challenge their Capabilities and help them Fulfil their Hopes and Dreams. Majella sensed that her careers teacher was disappointed by the fact that most of the girls in her class hoped and dreamed of being hairdressers. A couple of the more capable cuddies had nursing ambitions, and the two dolls with brains to burn wanted to be teachers. The farmers were just serving out their time in school before they could go full-time to the fields. The fellas with no trade or land dreamed of winning visas to Australia or America. Some of them had plans to join relatives in England or to enter the building trade in the south. Everyone wanted to escape the chicken-rendering factory in Strabane. Majella didn't know what she wanted to be, so she'd clung on to A levels as a way to stave off a career for few more years. Most of the A level students were like Majella – just treading water. And most of them – like Majella – dropped out before their final exams. Rose Murphy was different. After handing her baby daughter over to her ma . . . *no blood of MINE will be handed over tae strangers* . . . Rose had gone back to school. Despite trying her best, she failed all her O levels and didn't even get onto a hairdresser course. Majella didn't understand how Rose became the town hoor but, according to Marty, at least Rose was honest about her trade: if you asked him (and you didn't usually have to ask) he'd tell you that half the single mothers in Aghybogey were on the game – screwing the British government for a flat and benefits. Marty said that in Rose's defence, at least she made a few oul fuckers happy in the course of her day.

Rose's burger was nearly ready. Majella sliced a bun burger in half and pressed it onto the hot plate. Majella had never left Aghybogey, not even to do an NVQ in Food Hygiene in Strabane tech. She'd never gone further than Bundoran on holiday. She was now a Bogey face, someone people expected to see around the town. She knew her place. The fryer light switched from red to green and Majella raised Rose's chips and shook them dry. Then she scooped the fillet burger onto the bun. She could see the indentations of her finger from where she'd pressed the bun onto the hot plate. Majella knew Rose wouldn't notice.

— Mayo ann salad ann onions, Rose?

— Aye, thanks.

Majella squeezed a thick blob of mayo onto Rose's burger and heaped some limp, browning lettuce on top before crowning the whole lot with a raw onion ring. Majella didn't get people who liked salad. Then she placed the bun on top and dropped the whole heap into a polystyrene burger box. She shovelled the chips into a bag and shook them as she poured on the salt and vinegar to get a nice even finish. Finally she wrapped everything in sheets of paper before pushing the whole lot into a branded plastic bag.

A Salt and Battered! Food Worth Fighting For!

The bags were a new thing. Cunter had provided only the cheapest plain white plastic bags until their Prod rivals on the other side of the bridge started using branded bags.

The Cod Father – A Family Business since 1969

Majella knew that when The Cod Father opened in 1969, it hadn't actually been called The Cod Father. It got its name in the mid-nineties when Alistair, the oldest son, took over and refurbished old Phip's Chips. Majella had never been inside The Cod Father in her life and had also never knowingly tasted a Proddie chip. But she'd been told that A Salt and Battered!'s chips kicked the shit out of The Cod Father's chips any day of the week. From time to time she'd even seen the odd Prod sneak in during daylight hours to order one of their superior giant battered sausages and some onion rings. Prods never risked a visit after dark, however, in case the Daly boys were feeling frisky. Majella passed the bag of hot food over to Rose, who slid a fiver along the counter. Every time she took money off Rose, Majella wondered from out of whose warm pocket it had come before Rose took it. She knew where it was going next. As she rang in the sale and counted out Rose's change, a crowd of young wans came in. They'd been the wee weans running round the estates when Majella was a teenager but were now the town Goths. They all looked a bit stoned or monged, but then they all tried to look like that, pretending to be out of it even when they hadn't had shit in days, if ever.

— There we go.

— Thanks a million, Majella.

Rose kept talking to Marty, who was propped up on the counter by his left elbow. The Goths huddled together, counting out their change with nail-bitten fingers that they'd covered in fingerless black lace gloves. The thin black-haired lad that was with them was wearing make-up and giggling through his teeth. Marty'd told Majella he believed your man was as gay as a field of daffodils, but hadn't copped it himself yet, which was a mystery to Majella. How could you not know that you liked what you liked? She waited until the Goths had finished their furious whispers and giggles about what food they could order to get the maximum value for their shared money.

— What can ah get chews?

Behind the Goths the door opened again and the buzzer sounded. A crowd straight out of the pub landed in, drunk and laughing.

Rose looked at them sideways and then back at Marty. — Ah'll run on.

Marty put his hand on her arm. — You mind yerself.

Rose sidled out the door. Marty looked small and sad for a few seconds, but then straightened himself up and roared at the newcomers. — Right ladies and gentlemen! What can ah get chews?

Majella could tell that the Goths were ready to order. She picked up a pen and held it close to her order pad.

— Two veggie burgers ann a bag a onion rings ann three bags of chips, please.

Majella remembered noticing that the veggie burgers were well out of date. There just wasn't the demand for them. Hazy memories from Cookery Class at school surfaced, and she decided to fry them for a few minutes extra in the hope that might kill off the worst of any bacteria.

She ripped the order from the notepad and spiked it on the board.

— Want a knife ann fork with that?

— Can we have five?

Majella was sure Cunter wouldn't be impressed with that request, but she nodded anyway.

12.00 p.m.

Item 12.9: Conversation: Opinions

— It's not a bit wonder that monkeys ate their weans.

Majella's forehead creased in a frown. She was standing at the fryer with her head facing the wall, listening to Ruairí Kelly, who Marty said had never been the same since he got the Sky subscription and discovered the Discovery Channel.

— Ah don't blame them at all. Ah think there might be something in it.

Since then, Ruairí had become harder to listen to. Majella remembered the evening he'd spent a good ten minutes in the chipper explaining to the girl he was with that a certain species of octopus had a detachable penis, which could swim for up to two miles on the hunt for a female octopus (who apparently weren't happy to let their fannies swim off unaccompanied into the deep blue yonder and had instead evolved to give birth to hundreds of baby octopi simultaneously, in an explosive birth that caused their immediate death). Majella never saw Ruairí and the girl together after that, which was less mysterious than the evolutionary path the octopus family had taken.

— Ah mean, when ye think about it, when ye know what's ahead a ye, would ye really want tae bring another wee being in tae this life here, tae go through what ye've been trying tae get through?

— Och, ah dunno Ruairí.

Ruairí was talking with Proinsias Ó Néill. Majella had been to school with Proinsias when he was just plain oul Franci O'Neill, or Franci the Feel as he'd been called after their fourth-year school trip to the Jet Centre in Coleraine when Franci was seen down the back of the bus with Fionnuala Quinn, his hands rummaging around underneath her pink shellsuit. Majella hadn't been keen on pink shellsuits before then, and went right off them after that. In time, Franci had joined Sinn Féin, changed his name and started saying Gee A Ditch every time he met anyone. Majella's Irish had never got beyond learning the Hail Mary, Our Father and the lyrics of the national anthem, which Master

MacMickering had bate into them at primary school during his intermittent sober phases.

— What are ye sayin? Are ye sayin that it's all been worth it and sure isn't it all grand and let me have a shower a weans coz my life's been a fucken bed a roses?

— Och now Ruairí . . .

But Ruairí started up again, leaving Proinsias staring at the ground.

Marty was at the counter, listening. Majella watched him as he shifted from foot to foot, frowning, feeling one of his man diddies. After a few more seconds he waded in. — Houl on a minute now, Ruairí. Houl on. Ah'm a da now, ann no harm tae ye, but ah think what yer sayin's pure shite.

Ruairí turned around to face Marty, both eyebrows squashed together in confrontation. — Do ye now?

Marty shifted his position behind the counter and kept going. — Now, ah'm not saying this life's been a doss for me. Ah've had me hard times ann me good times like every other fucker. But what ah am saying is that ye have weans coz you kinda hope there's gonna be something better for them. That they'll maybe get the chance tae make a better fist of it than you got. Ye can only hope like.

Proinsias nodded in agreement. — Aye. You're right enough there, Marty, you're right enough.

Ruairí screwed up his face in disgust. — Marty, I bet ye had weans coz ye got yer Mrs knocked up one night when youse were both pished or ye gave in so she'd quit nyamming at ye about babbies. Ah well ann truly doubt that ye both sat down ann thought the process through.

Ruairi paused and looked at Marty, who said nothing.

— So what's yer three wee girls gonna come to? Far as ah can fucken see in this town, they've got the choice of harvesting chicken guts until they go on the sick, or getting knocked up ann lying around the town on benefits, taking shite off of whatever fella's still there. If they're lucky, they'll fuck off to Dublin or England ann you'll see them maybe once or twice'd a year, ann they'll be embarrassed tae see the cut of ye ann mortified at yer accent. Ah'm telling ye, Marty, the best fucken approach is tae make like a monkey and eat yer children when they're still tender.

There was a bit of silence in the chipper after that. Then Marty spoke. — What the fuck were you sucking the night, sir? Red diesel?

Proinsias burst out laughing. Then Marty started to laugh. Ruairí was left standing there frowning as Majella came over with their order.

— Salt ann vinegar on yer chips?

1.00 a.m.
Item 29: The Daly brothers

— Five double chicken burgers with chips, five tubs of garlic mayonnaise anna two-litre bottle a Coke when you're ready, JellyBelly.

Gerry, the youngest Daly brother, was at the counter. The others were still in the pub, having a lock-in. Gerry'd been sent to get food before the chipper closed. Majella knew they'd be steaming, for it was Paddy's birthday. Majella often wondered if her ma and the Dalys' ma had much to say to each other when they were lying up the hospital ward twenty-seven years ago. She doubted it somehow. She found it strange to think of her and Paddy Daly squirming side by side in the wee town hospital before it had closed. Marty was busy sweating over the fryers, trying to keep up with the orders that were being roared over the bubbling fat. Majella spiked order after order to the board. She found it easy to keep her face blank. It was harder to keep her voice even.

— What can ah get chew?

Fish supper ann two Cokes please
Battered sausage supper ann a curry chip when you're ready
Daddy burger n onion rings ann chips n gravy
Gwan giss a few eggstra chips Jellybaby. Gwan. Gwan will ye? Just a wee cuppla eggstra chips . . .
Cheesy ships peas ann gravy
Big bottla Coke anna curry chip ann peez
Garlick cheezy chipz pleeze
Double tub a garlic mayonaze
Wanna suck a my giant battered saussie, Jelly?
Fucken bastard I wuz here furst
Batterburger ann chips ann red sauce
Are ye on strike or what?
Gay uz a bagga chipz anna tubba garlick mayo, Jelly

After a twenty-minute wait during which Majella watched Gerry Daly chat up and then snog the face off some wee blonde doll wearing a belt bigger than her skirt, Majella packaged up the Daly brothers' order. Gerry squeezed the arse of the girl he'd been stuck to, then staggered off out the door clutching his brothers' food. The big steaming parcel tucked into the crook of his arm was as warm and heavy as a newborn baby.

1.23 a.m.
Good stuff
Item 9.2: Sex: Fucking

Majella relaxed when the grind and shriek of the shutters stopped. They were finished with the public for the night.

Marty was quiet, leaning on the yard brush. Majella wondered if he was reluctant to head home. It was a feeling she understood. She'd had her wee daydreams of being able to rent the flat above the chip shop, of living there in peace and quiet, not having to face the town twice a day, every day. But Gloria Loughran had rented it years back, and would most likely be carried out in a box decades from now.

Majella turned to Marty. — Tired?

He looked up at her. — Naw. 'Boutye?

Majella shrugged. — Starving as usual. Need to get me chips into the fryer.

Majella moved to the fryer and fired in her fish and two chips. Behind her, Marty clung on to the brush.

— Doing anything mad this weekend?

Majella turned to face Marty, but didn't meet his gaze. She shrugged again before answering. — Be quiet enough, I imagine. Might have a few birthday drinks.

Marty's eyes widened and his eyebrows climbed into his greasy fringe. — Is it yer birthday the weekend, Jelly?

Majella restrained the shrug that was itching in her shoulders. — Naw. Today. Well, yesterday now, I suppose.

Marty jumped up off the yard brush. — Fuck. Happy birthday, pet.

He grabbed her for a big hug, slapping her back. Majella stiffened and wondered if she should close her eyes for the experience or keep them open. By the time she'd decided to close them, he'd released her.

— Why didn't ye say earlier?

Majella had to shrug. It was a lot easier than explaining that her birthdays never much excited her – she didn't see the need for a big fuss. She didn't want to explain that she thought her new age – twenty-seven – was a good number.

— What d'ye want?

Marty considered his options. — Throw us on a batter burger there, cheers.

Majella rummaged around for a batter burger, then slapped it into the foaming oil. She watched it bob around in the scalding heat. Sometimes she wondered what it would be like to put her hand straight into the scalding oil. She'd watched a movie once where an undercover detective lady was finished off by a fella who'd plunged her head into a hot fryer. It had taken her ages to die. Behind Majella, Marty had just finished his last wipe of the food counter.

— Fancy a wee toke?

Majella turned around. Marty had a crumpled joint in his hand. It looked like it had been tucked away somewhere for quite a while, in case of emergency. He looked at Majella, then shrugged.

— Ah feel the need fer a wee lift.

Majella nodded and they both went to the door. Marty lit the joint and drew hard before handing it to Majella. They both stood in silence until the joint was sucked dry. Watching Marty stub the butt out on the ground, Majella knew the chips would be done just right. She went back in and switched the fryers off at the power socket. Then she raised the baskets and shook off the worst of the oil. Marty heaved himself up onto the preparation counter as Majella divided the food up into their separate servings. She didn't have to ask before shaking salt and vinegar over Marty's chips. Majella knew he was watching her arse. The thought of it made her want to twitch her arse cheeks to take the piss. It also gave her a tingle in her cunt. Majella noticed there was a bit of cheese left in the bottom of the cheese tub. She fired it onto her birthday chips before parcelling up both suppers, then she turned around to Marty and passed him his food.

— There ye go.

Marty sat with the food warming his lap and watched Majella as she pulled her hat from her head and removed the hair grips that had snagged in her hair. Marty'd already got out of his uniform. Majella unzipped the front of her overalls, enjoying the feeling of her tits spilling out under her T-shirt as they were freed of the green nylon. She felt the sweat marks at her back and on her chest grow cold in the air. She looked Marty straight in the eye. He was kind of stoned, she could tell. He slowly got down and stepped towards her. He slipped his arm around her waist and together they walked to the food storage room, where the boxes of chicken nuggets and Daddy burgers and buckets of garlic mayonnaise sat in the dark.

2.23 a.m.
Good stuff
Item 1.4: Eating: Fish and chips

On the walk home Majella tried to ignore the cold feel of her wet knickers between her legs. After the sex and the joint she felt like she was wading through water. The estates were lit only by the orange street lights, quiet and empty of anyone. It still felt strange to Majella, though it had been five years or more, to walk about Aghybogey without soldiers, or the chance of them. It felt like there was something missing. As she neared home she noticed a fox outside their door. Majella liked foxes, even town foxes. This one looked mangy and hungry, like it wasn't doing the best. It eyed her when she stopped to watch it, before loping into the shadows at the side of the house, where it paused on high alert. Majella reached into her plastic bag to grab a piece of fish for it, but when she moved the fox sank deeper into the dark alleyway. None of the wild foxes in the estate could be tamed. Even the tame cats weren't friendly. Majella knew it wasn't the worst strategy – it kept them alive longer, even if they missed the odd act of kindness. She left the fox, put her key into the lock and opened the door. She paused on the step. The house felt quiet and warm. She hoped that her ma had made it to bed with or without the help of a neighbour. On her way to the kitchen she took a gleek into the living room. It was dim, the only light coming from the dying embers of a fire. Majella decided to eat in there after she nuked her food. She didn't switch the kitchen light on, instead using the orange street lights to guide her as she opened the microwave and placed her fish and chips on the plate to heat up. She poured herself a pint of Coke before she remembered her wash. Yawning, she walked over and opened the machine. In the shadowy kitchen it looked empty. For several optimistic seconds, Majella wondered if a neighbour had pulled her clothes out and hung them up to dry. But when she put her hand in she realised the clothes had stuck to the drum. She pulled them loose and shook them out before dropping them into the plastic clothes basket. The microwave pinged behind her, so she turned her attention to her food.

In the living room she sat in what she still thought of as her da's chair. The one he always gave up to his ma when she came to visit. The glow of the fire softened the clutter of the room and soothed Majella. She sighed, then took her first mouthful of supper. Her birthday card was in a different position on the mantelpiece. The blue box containing the gold necklace was sitting on the other side of the armchair. A neighbour must've been in looking at them. Majella wondered what Philomena thought about Marty coming home late, or if she ever smelt the sex off him. Majella found it hard to miss the smell of sex off people, off clothes, off bed sheets. It was a powerful smell.

She heard the yip of a fox outside. Then a cat gurned. Her granny had been dismissive of town foxes in particular and cats in general. According to her, town foxes were always fighting, got diseases, and died young from eating shite out of bins. She thought the natural place for a fox was the countryside, where they lived by their wits and ate what they'd eaten for centuries. And her granny didn't understand why people kept cats as pets – she thought cats were little use for anything other than mousing. Dogs were a different story. She believed they were good companions, could be used for ratting, rabbiting or herding sheep. That they kept foxes in their rightful place. Majella'd never been allowed a dog and only ever had the one pet cat. Blackie had lasted a fair while – five years. But one summer day in 1990 one of the wee Doherty weans knocked at the door to say they'd found her up the back alleyway with a firework up her arse. Majella hadn't gone to look. Neither did her da, though she remembered how annoyed he'd been about the dead cat. A month later her granny's dog was found dead in the yard up in Garvaghy, his throat slit. That really upset her da. No one bothered about the death of a cat, but a dog was a different matter. Her da ruled the Brits out – they shot dogs as a rule. A local person was more likely to slit the throat of a dog suspected of sheep worrying. But oul Bessie was so old she was hardly fit to bark at the Brits, never mind chase sheep. So her death, those final few months before her da disappeared, remained a mystery.

Majella realised her fish and chips were finished. She hadn't got the good of them in the end. She found herself shivering, so she screwed the chip wrappers up into a ball, then heaved herself up out of the sagging armchair and onto her feet. She dumped the greasy wrappers onto the embers, where they sat and spat for a few seconds before bursting into flames. Majella turned her arse to the brief heat, watching the fire light up the room around her broad shadow.

Wednesday

9.45 a.m.
Item 17.1: Pain: Headaches

Majella's head woke her. It was bursting. She opened her eyes a crack, then reached out to her bedside cabinet, groping for some Kapake. She needed it to dull the pain and chill out a bit. She recognised the tablet package by touch and sat up to pop out two tablets. She swallowed them down with a mouthful of flat Coke. Majella liked knowing what tablets and medicine did to you and why. She liked knowing that aspirin thinned the blood and that a primitive form of aspirin could be brewed by boiling the bark of a willow tree. She liked knowing that if she took too many vitamin C tablets she could get a bad dose of the runs. She really loved the fact that codeine was made from the opium poppy, which was officially called *Papaver somniferum* – the word somniferum sounding to Majella like the noise a kind fat old man might make when falling asleep after lunch. Majella liked to focus on her body after she took codeine, waiting for the painkillers to hit. It felt like a big red flower slowly blooming inside her chest. She liked that feeling. In her head, co-codamol, Kapake and Tramadol were like the bowls, chairs and beds in the house of the Three Bears. Baby-sized co-codamol (8 mgs of codeine), Mammy-sized Kapake (30 mgs of codeine) and the big Daddy Bear, Tramadol (a not-to-be-fucked-with 40 mgs of codeine).

Majella felt her bare feet grow cold. She really could do with a bigger duvet. A throb of pain pulsed through her head so she pulled herself into the foetal position and put her finger in her mouth. She wondered if the headache was from eating cheesy chips before bed. She decided to lay off the cheese for a while and considered going down to the surgery to see about allergy testing. She quickly dropped the idea. Majella hated having to explain herself to the doctors. She hadn't minded nice Doctor Coulter, who'd been the only Protestant in the practice. He'd been a gentle soul with a bit of a drink problem. Like Majella he didn't enjoy eye- or physical contact, something that made appointments with him much easier to bear. Despite his booze breath, Doctor Coulter was well liked in the town, as he was quick with the pills and unquestioning about the sick lines. On his retirement Majella'd been switched to O'Hanlon, who was some wan up from Galway who'd married Doctor Conlon from Strabane. O'Hanlon was broadly thought of as a rare doll. First of all, she'd kept her own name after marriage. Second, she had continued to work while birthing and rearing eight children. Because O'Hanlon was an Irish speaker, they'd reared the weans half in English and half in Irish. Marty had gathered all sorts of reports on this carry on. He said that people said that one day'd you'd drop in to the family home, and they'd all be speaking in Irish, but the next it would be English. Then there was the matter of their names. All the cuddies took O'Hanlon for a surname while the cubs took Conlon. This meant that they were known around the town as the HanConLons, not that that bothered any of the children. You knew looking at them that they knew looking at you that they were going to grow up, go to university, and get as far away from Aghybogey as their fancy degrees would carry them. Marty said the HanCon-Lons added class to Aghybogey. They were the sort of weans who made a miserable teacher's day better. Nobody was allowed to rip the pish out of a HanConLon in school or out. And if anything was going – like a subsidised peace trip to America or a starring role in a local TV drama – the HanConLons were in on it. If some Irish news crew needed an interview with an authentic Irish-speaking child or an American news crew wanted to speak to a photogenic Northern Irish kid, the HanConLon weans could be relied upon to be eloquent in the required language. In her nine years in A Salt n Battered! Majella had never seen a HanConLon trigger the buzzer.

O'Hanlon was a different type of doctor to poor oul Coulter. She was a firm believer in sustained eye contact, had a thing against unwarranted prescriptions and an unhealthy interest in getting to the root cause of the patient's condition. So if in the course of O'Hanlon's interrogation Majella admitted she felt tired and lacking in energy, O'Hanlon would question her about her diet, push her up onto the scales and then print off a weight-loss and exercise programme suitable for her age and physical-fitness level. When Majella asked if there was anything she could do about her heavy periods, O'Hanlon pointed to Majella's age, explaining that the heavy periods were her body's way of asking for the fulfilment of pregnancy. Majella once made the mistake of saying that sometimes she found it hard to get out of bed in the morning. O'Hanlon asked her how she felt about her father's disappearance, and then recommended aerobics followed by a light salad before an early, regular bedtime. O'Hanlon and Majella did not get on.

Majella's finger had softened and wrinkled in her mouth. She had sucked all the salt and chip grease from it and now could taste her skin and her skin alone. Her headache was easing just a bit. As she lay there, savouring the opiates seeping into her blood stream, she thought again about the fox she'd seen on her doorstep the night before. Her da'd been kind to the foxes, leaving scraps out for them. Other people weren't so keen. She remembered the week before her da'd disappeared, the week the foxes were found dead around the estate. Poisoned, her da'd said – foxes were too fly to be trapped. He'd been disturbed by the dead foxes. Had gone out to help John Murphy gather them up for skinning. He wasn't around to see the fox population recover in the years after. Her ma'd put a stop to Majella feeding the foxes the way her da'd done. And she'd banned Majella from having another cat about the place.

Majella still missed Blackie. She had survived a diet of SPAR Value cat food (eight pence a tin ordinary, seven pence on offer) for six years, on top of popping out three litters of kittens a year. Majella remembered the first litter best. It'd seemed like a miracle when she'd gone to the shed and found the five tiny creatures squirming around Blackie. Majella had run inside to tell her da about the kittens. He'd been sitting in the living room watching the telly with the curtains closed because her ma was on the settee with one of her heads. Even though she was about to wet herself with excitement, Majella'd known better than to shout the news or even to say it out loud in front of her sleeping ma. Instead, she'd taken her da's hand and asked him to come outside for she'd something to show him. In the shed he'd got down on his hands and knees to count the wee kittens, pulling each one out into the daylight to have a better look. Looking back now, Majella could see that he'd been as excited as she'd been.

— What's goin on?

Her ma was standing in the back doorway, shading her eyes against the sun as she watched them. Majella went quiet and still. This problem was her daddy's problem. She knew that he would do the talking.

— Cat's had kittens.

Her ma cast her eyes up to heaven and sighed. — Fer fucksake. Didden ah know this would happen. How manya the wee friggers?

— Five. They're nicely marked wee things. Pretty.

Her ma had stood for a few seconds more. — We're not keepin them. I'll call in tae John Murphy once ma head settles.

Then she'd gone inside, leaving Majella and her da alone in the shed listening to the purr of the kittens.

11.30 a.m.
Good stuff
Item 9.1: Sex: Wanking

Majella woke up, blurry with codeine. It was a good feeling. She stretched her body out long and tense, making her hot feet poke out the end of the duvet. She loved stretching and yawning in private, though she felt the act of yawning in front of anyone else was sort of dirty. She hated the way people sometimes just opened their mouths and made a big *uh uh oaaaahhhh* noise and then maybe shivering a bit afterward. If the yawner was at Mass or in class or at a wake or something, then the next thing someone else and then another person would be at it. She'd read once in the paper that the Queen was never seen yawning in public. After that, out of curiosity, Majella had practised controlling her yawns. She could stop most before they started, and could stifle the rest inside her by keeping her mouth closed and pulling her ears back as the thrills ran over her back and around her tummy. She thought yawns were a bit like orgasms. Majella liked orgasms. She'd always liked them, ever since her first. It had taken her weeks of practice to get there, all on her own in her own bed. She'd been fifteen and had grown bored of almost everyone in her class obsessing over wanking. Everyone talked about it, and everyone denied doing it. She remembered Paddy Daly sidling up to her in the yard at break time in front of everyone.

— Jelly, did ye know that 50 per cent of people sing in the bath ann 50 per cent a people wank?

— Naw ah didn't know that.

— Aye it's a true fact. Ann d'ye know what song it is that they sing?

— Naw. What?

— Well you're obviously a wanker a hahaha haahaha haha aha hah wankerwanker a haha haha . . .

Majella's eventual conclusion had been that if wanking was such a big deal, she wanted a go of it. But it had been harder than she'd imagined to figure it out – she'd no idea what she was supposed to do. The magazines her ma bought for her in the shops had lots of tips on how to tell your boyfriend you Weren't Ready or how to put a condom on if you Were Ready. There was frig all about how to Do It Yourself if you weren't All That Interested in Fellas. So she'd just given it a go, night after night, after she'd finished her rosary.

After the sign of the cross, she'd push her rosary beads under her pillow and wait a few minutes to let the prayers waft away before moving her hands down to what her ma called her *bits*. Majella hated that description. Made her think of herself as broken – that she was in need of glue. When she learned that the word cunt wasn't just a synonym for a hateful fucker, she adopted the word, and spent night after night stroking and fiddling and rubbing and fingering and flicking and caressing and tickling and sliding until one night a hot rush of pleasure roared through her whole body making her stiffen up from head to toe before she arched her hot back up off the mattress, gasping. After she'd got her breath back she noted the faint connection between an orgasm and a yawn. And once she realised orgasms helped her get off to sleep, she added masturbation to the end of her nightly ritual, as wanking before the rosary seemed a bit sacrilegious.

Majella's feet were getting cold and she was tired of her feet getting cold. Suddenly she decided to buy a new duvet. She became a little breathless at the swiftness, the sureness of the decision. But she could see the new duvet in her head – a big fat fucker of a thing that she could burrow down into and lose herself in. Even the thought of the required trip down town to buy it didn't take away from the power of that vision. Majella frowned in concentration as she rehearsed each step of her journey in her head, planned the likely conversation, and pictured the ordeal ending when she once again reached the safety of her own wee room.

12.39 p.m.
Item 14.7: Medical stuff: Medical procedures

Majella was hot, pink and moist after her shower. The sound of the telly chittering downstairs indicated that her ma had managed to get herself up. Majella hoped her ma wasn't feeling whiny. She had PMS, and despite the Kapake, she felt on edge. Her period was due around Saturday, and while she hated this bloated PMS feeling, her painful and swollen diddies, she hated the stink and pain of her period more. She switched on the hairdryer and started to blast her hair. She hated having wet hair, especially at this time of year. It reminded her of walking home from St Christopher's in the rain. She'd be soaked and would have to change from her uniform as soon as she got in the door, even before she had a cup of tea or her baked beans on toast. That's when her ma'd bought Majella her first hairdryer, one of the few presents she'd truly appreciated receiving in her life. Majella's first discovery was that, despite the name, hairdryers weren't just good for drying hair. It turned out you could warm your bed or your clothes with them, or even dry your arse properly after a shower. She loved that all-over dry feeling that only lasted until she worked up a sweat on her walk to the chipper. She switched the hairdryer off and roughly brushed through her wavy hair. It had been dead curly when she was a wean. But the older she got and the longer and thicker her hair got, the more it had pulled itself down into waves. Majella liked having long hair. When she'd been a wean, she'd only been allowed short hair. Her ma couldn't be bothered with the hassle of keeping long hair – the plaiting and the combing and the ribbons – so she'd cut Majella's hair as short as any boy. Majella spent her childhood dreaming of curly hair, long enough to suck. She still remembered the slap she'd got in Primary Two from oul Master Bradley for sucking on Fionnuala Quinn's ponytail during Quiet Time. Though Majella had been tall for five, Master Bradley was tall for fifty-five, and it had stung.

Majella's stomach rumbled. She went to her bedroom door, unlocked and opened it, then listened. Her ma wasn't alone in the living room. A woman's voice, warm and clear, honeyed with wisdom, rang up the stairs. Majella paused to listen.

. . . this is YOUR life. YOUR responsibility. You need to do your best RIGHT NOW, this VERY SECOND so

you're in the best place for the next minute, the next hour, the next day . . .

An Oprah repeat. Majella had a suspicion her ma didn't really listen to the words of wisdom Oprah purred at her every day. But that was by-the-by because when Oprah was on, her ma was placid, so it was safe to go downstairs. On her way to the kitchen, she paused to pick up the pile of junk mail that had collected on the welcome mat.

— Jell-ah? You up?

She flicked through the envelopes. Only the one for her. From the doctor's surgery by the looks of it. One junk mail for her da. And loads of crap for her ma, who was forever signing up for offers.

— Aye.

Majella lifted the mail and took it towards the kitchen.

— Jell-ah?

Majella ignored her ma until after she'd dumped the junk mail in the fire bin.

— What?

There was no answer, just the sound of her ma coughing. So Majella took the kettle and turned to the sink, turning the tap on full blast. She couldn't hear whether or not her ma was talking over the sound of the water, but even if she was, she'd just be durning on and what it would boil down to was the fact she wanted a wee cup of tea. When Majella turned the tap off, she heard the tail end of what her ma was saying.

— . . . anna wee cuppa tay?

Majella put the kettle on to boil and then pulled four slices of white bread from the sliced pan that sat on the counter. The bread was from Monday and had hardened. Majella checked it for mould and could see nothing. She knew it would do grand for toast but might not stand up to the next day.

— Majel-lah?

Majella slotted the bread into the toaster, then plodded into the living room. The fire hadn't been laid and her ma lay on the settee under a blanket. Oprah was hugging a skinny white girl, who was crying behind bad glasses and baring what looked like too many teeth. Oprah looked well-fed, well-paid and content with herself. Majella liked Oprah.

— What d'ye want?

— Ah was just saying that ah'd love a wee slice a toast and a cuppa tay.

— I have it on for you. Jam on yer toast?

— Och naw. Ah'll just have it dry. Me stomach's not able.

Majella nodded, knowing she'd ignore that, and went back to the kitchen, where the smell of the toast was warming the air. She pulled the teapot off the hob and tipped the old teabags into the bin, then set the pot down. She took two mugs out of the cupboard and poured a drop of her ma's milk into the heel of each mug. Neither Majella nor her ma or her da took sugar, not after the Lent when Majella'd been eight. Her ma'd been dithering for weeks between giving up the drink or the sugar in her tea. In the end she'd gone for the sugar in her tea and on Ash Wednesday had forced Majella and her da to join in. Nobody could thole the taste of sugary tea after the forty days were up, and so it had persisted. It was funny how it was different with sweets – no matter how many Lents Majella had been forced to give them up, she never lost the taste.

Majella stared at the steam pluming over the kettle, trying to block out the angry sounds of the water thrashing against the white plastic. She sighed when the OFF switch popped and everything settled down. She threw a bit of hot water into the arse of the teapot and swirled it around to warm the pot. She emptied the water down the sink before dropping two teabags in and filling the pot to the stroop with water. Just as she set it on a low heat on the hob, the toast popped. She threw her mother's single slice of toast onto one plate, then spread butter and jam onto her three slices on another plate. When the tea was brewed, she poured it out into the two big mugs. She knew by the smell of it that it was good strong tea, with a bit of flavour. Majella thought it was strange how good a pot of tea tasted compared to tea from a bag in a mug. Not that you would be bothered with the fuss of a teapot the whole time, but it was nice on occasion. Breakfast was ready before Majella remembered the brown envelope that had been addressed to her.

— Ma-jell-ah? Is mah breakfast ready?

Majella lifted the envelope.

— Coming in a minute.

She took a clean knife and slit the envelope, then pulled out and scanned the letter. It was a smear-test reminder. She had a new appointment in two weeks. Majella's stomach turned over in revulsion. She dropped the letter into the fire bin on top of the junk mail, then carried breakfast through into the living room. She set everything down on the coffee table beside her ma.

— There's butter ann jam on yer toast. It's not Lough Derg you're at.

— Och, you're right. You're wild good til me, Jellah, wild good altogether.

Majella took her own tea and toast over to her chair and sat down. Oprah was on a break and Christmas ads twinkled on the dusty TV screen. Before Majella could take her first mouthful of tea, the doorbell rang. She and her ma looked at each other. Nobody local used the doorbell. Her ma was first to speak.

— PissNI.

Majella didn't reply. She knew the drill. She put her breakfast back on the coffee table and got up to answer the door.

2.02 p.m.
Item 19.1: Shopping: Going shopping

Majella joined the queue for the cash machine. She'd stupidly timed her duvet shopping trip with Aghybogey's lunch rush-hour, so there were three people in front of her. She knew none of them, which meant they were probably Prods. They usually used the ATM over the bridge, which was at the Ulster bank, but they were known to use the Bank of Ireland during daylight hours if they'd business over the Taig side of the bridge. Majella took a look at the shape of their necks and ears. Definitely Proddie. Satisfied, she glued her eyes to the ground so that she wouldn't have to speak to anyone. Majella knew that sometimes she had to work at reading faces for emotions, to identify if someone was angry or sad. But she could tell a Prod from a Taig from behind. After a few minutes, the queue cleared and Majella moved in close to the screen. She fed her cash card into the wee slot and entered her PIN. She requested cash with printed receipt, then paused. She wasn't sure how much a duvet and cover and all would cost, so she took out £80. Majella rarely withdrew more than £40 at a time, and that was nearly always for a night of drinking. £80 seemed like a wild amount of money to spend on something for kipping in. She felt a surge of boldness thrill through her as she folded the money and stuffed it into her jeans pocket. She moved away from the ATM and checked her bank balance.

Bank of Ireland

DATE:	*21/11/04*	*TIME 14:07*
903587	*395720*	*93725*
NSC:	*903587*	*A/C No: 13128729*

CARD No: 3857982

WITHDRAWAL	*£80*
BALANCE	*£5,679*

Thank you for Banking with us

The capital B in Banking upset Majella, as it always did. She screwed the receipt up in her fist, then pushed it into a pocket before walking off. Her balance wasn't too bad, even after the money'd gone for the duvet. And Thursday was payday, so she'd be able to put some of her wages in to bump it back up. Sometimes Majella imagined what her savings could buy her. Maybe a year travelling. A car. She could definitely afford a car and still have money left over. She knew it was even close to a deposit on a wee house. But she wasn't really saving up for anything. Since she bought the TV and DVD player she didn't really want anything else. Sometimes she thought she'd splurge when her savings hit £6,000. Majella was hoping that would happen in about a month or so. She got paid in cash on a Thursday and she tucked her fag and food money into her shopping purse and put the rest straight into the bank. When she went down the town for her Sunday night pints she'd take her empty drinking purse and she'd withdraw the money she needed for the night. That way she always knew where she stood with her spending, and she didn't go over no matter how plastered she got. Any other expenses – the notion for a new top down the town or a pair of trainers – was covered by the odd wee withdrawal here and there. So although she earned fuck all (she'd been on £1.50 an hour until six months after the minimum wage had come in, when her and Marty'd threatened strike action unless they got it, at which point Cunter was forced to double her wages) she never felt that badly off. She gave her ma nothing in the form of housekeeping or rent, for the wee mortgage on the house had been paid off before her da left, and Majella knew if she handed her ma anything it would end up in the till down in the off-licence. Majella remembered celebrating with a takeaway the day her da'd made the final mortgage payment that meant the house was theirs – all theirs. They were one of the few people in the estate at the time to own their house and there was sour grapes when her ma'd crowed about the mortgage being paid off. Some people asked how he could afford that on his factory wage. They pointed at Majella's ma, who'd never done a day's work in her life. No stint in the factory, not even a stretch at CostCutters or childminding. But Majella knew her da was careful with money and her ma never needed to work – she got more in benefits and disability than Majella earned from a week's work in the chipper. That's how the mortgage was sorted. Then her da started putting the mortgage money towards improvements. He put the electric shower in. He'd started at the retiling. He'd plans for the kitchen. Notions for the wee house out in Garvaghy. All of which came to a sudden stop when Bobby was blown to bits.

— What about ye Jellah?

Majella blinked and looked up at Peader Devine. She'd been standing still too long.

— Peader. Not a bother.

Peader walked past her towards the barracks and Majella headed the opposite direction. She wondered if the experts from the Serious Crime Unit were staying in the barracks or if they'd already made their escape and were booting up the motorway to Belfast. During their visit, she had spent some time mulling over the name of the unit. Were they a *Serious* Crime Unit or were they a *Serious Crime* Unit? She knew better than to ask, and let her ma do most of the talking. She found her heart racing and decided it was best to stop thinking about that visit. Flicking her fingers in her fleece pockets, she turned her attention to her destination. There was only the one place in town for duvets: Hector's Hardware and Household Goods. Majella hadn't visited the shop in years. She'd noticed building works earlier in the summer. The shop front was given a lick of fresh paint, but didn't look that different by the end of the whole business, so in Majella's head it was the same wooden-floored, dreary wee shop, with paint, lightbulbs, floral wallpaper and rollers stacked to the ceiling in the front of the shop, and floral duvets, damp cushions and curtains out the back. Majella pictured Hector hovering behind his counter wearing his shop overalls and Saved smile. Despite Hector being the Saved sort with a reputation for trying to Save others (Taigs mostly), Majella thought he was all right for a Prod. He had never tried to Save Majella, which suited her just fine, though she did wonder whether he was scared to Save her, or thought she was a Lost Cause. Majella stopped at the shop window and frowned. Bigger changes than a lick of paint had occurred. Blindingly bright lights shone on jewel-coloured scatter cushions and patterned duvets. Sheets were draped in fans, with colours graduating from dark to light. Thick blankets were stacked like in the pages of a fancy magazine. Worst of all, there were no prices to be seen. Majella took a deep breath, pushed the door open and stepped into the shop. Hector was gone. In his place was some big lump of a fella, with lovely blue eyes and bleached-blond hair who didn't look one bit Saved. He smiled at Majella.

— Hiya. Not a bad day.

Majella avoided his eyes. — Naw. Not the worst.

She felt her face burning up, so she shoved her hands deeper into her fleece pockets and quick-stepped deeper into the shop. It was lit like a football pitch, and felt much bigger than Majella remembered. The far wall was lined with packets of duvet covers. A burgundy duvet cover with a cream flower print splattered across it caught her eye, followed by a brown duvet with a blue wave pattern. She was impressed by the choice in the shop; though there were some dreary floral and lace affairs, most of the duvet covers were as nice as anything she'd seen in the Argos catalogue. Majella's eyes moved between the wave pattern and the flowers, even though she knew she wouldn't buy anything like that as patterns did her head in. She picked a packet up and slipped her fingers inside the plastic to have a feel of the material. It felt smooth, and thick enough to have a right bit of wear in it.

— Can ah help you there at all?

Majella flinched, then took another reddener. — Ah'm grand, grand. Just looking a duvet cover.

The nice young fella smiled at Majella. She felt one of her sweats breaking out.

— Well, them's all new stock. Pretty popular too. Worth the money.

— Are they dear?

— Not specially. The single's £20, the double's £30 and yer king-size'd be £40.

Majella pulled her hand out of the packet. — Dear enough.

Majella felt her sweat soak into her T-shirt where it was clinging to her back.

— Och well, ye get what you pay fer all the same. What size were you looking?

Majella cleared her throat. She would've been happy enough just taking her own time to find her own cover. Now she felt under pressure.

— Ah dunno. Ah need a new duvet as well. My one's too small. S'only a single.

Majella wished she could flick her fingers and rock right there in the centre of the shop.

— A single'd hardly cover a wean, never mind a full-grown woman. Get yerself a nice double or a king-size.

Majella liked the way he said full-grown woman. He made her size sound comfortable rather than cumbersome. Majella followed him over to the shelves and watched him pull several quilts down to the floor.

— There's different types. You've got yer duck down, eiderdown ann yer hollowfibre. Hollowfibre's cheapest, but there's no last innit. Goes flat in no time. Once the air's out, the heat's out.

— How much would they be?

— King-size or double?

— Ah dunno.

— Well, would yer bed be a single?

— Aye.

— Well, a double's probably yer best bet. King-size'd drown a single bed.

Majella nodded. She had a suspicion a king-size would drown her room, never mind the bed.

— A double duck down's £45. Yer cover'd be £30. But ah could give them both tae you fer £70.

Majella wanted to point out that he was not giving her the duvets for £70 – she was paying for them. But she held her tongue by narrowing her eyes.

— Now I can do you a hollowfibre duvet with a free pillow for just £20, so that'd be £50 altogether.

The young fella stood up to look at Majella.

— But if ye want my opinion, ah think there's no comparison between the two.

He laid the duvets on the ground and nodded his head at her.

— Come here a minute ann feel the difference between the duck ann the fibre.

Majella knelt down beside him and felt the duck down duvet. It felt like nights of deep, dark sleep. Then she felt the hollowfibre. It felt like hunger and emptiness and the flat as pancakes cushions defeated by her ma's bony wee arse.

— D'ye do feather pillows?

The young fella smiled. — A pair a duck down pillows is £20.

Majella didn't need him to do the sums for her. She could see her £80 blow away in a puff of feathers. — Ah don't have that on me. Ah couldn't get just the one, could ah?

The young buck's forehead furrowed as he thought. — They come in packs of two. But gimme a minute. Ah'll check out back fer ye.

He disappeared out the side door. Majella stayed kneeling on the ground for a minute, feeling her money dig into her hip through her jeans pockets. When she felt better, she got up and went back to the duvet covers. She hadn't picked one for definite yet. There was a plain burgundy one and a plain navy one. They were her favourites. She looked at them both again, comparing them. The blue seemed cold to Majella. She couldn't imagine it doing anything for her pokey wee bedroom. But the burgundy one promised warmth even in November. She picked up a double and tucked it under her oxter. Then she lifted the double duck down duvet and carried both towards the counter.

— Here! Let me carry that fer ye!

The young fella came up from behind her and took the duvet bag.

— I found a display pillow if ye don't mind. Special price of a fiver.

— Och naw. That's great, so it is. Thanks.

Majella watched the young fella from the far side of the counter as he rang in the sale. She passed her money to him and got a grubby fiver back in change. After he bagged up her duvet, pillows and cover he passed them to her, keeping his hand pressed firmly on top of the bag.

— There you go.

Majella nodded at him and put her hand on her stuff to lift it. But he didn't move his hand. So she tried a thanks. — Thanks.

Still he kept his hand on the bag. Then he leaned over the counter, speaking in a low voice. — Ah just wanted tae say that ah'm awful sorry about yer granny. Ah hope you ann yer family find solace and take comfort in our Lord Jesus Christ.

Majella pulled back. Again a reddener rushed up her back and neck, spreading over her face. She felt a trickle of sweat run down her back. She nodded at him.

— Right chew are.

Then she pulled the bag to her chest and stumbled towards the door. She caught sight of herself in a mirror and stopped. She turned back and looked him in the eye.

— Sorry. I meant thanks. Fer the duvet ann all.

Outside, the weight of the cotton and feathers Majella carried in her arms surprised her. The bag started off heavy and got heavier the further she walked. Like the weight of her granny's coffin on her shoulder.

3.33 p.m.
Item 34.2: Fighting: Shouting matches

Majella took a step back and looked around her room. It looked different now that the burgundy cover was on her new duvet: warmer, more welcoming. The duvet draped right to the floor, covering up the old bed, overwhelming the fat feather pillow underneath. The scuffed paint on the walls closest to the bed had a blush on it from the rich colour of the duvet cover, softening the room. Majella took off her trainers and climbed into her bed. She kicked the duvet up into a cave around herself before going still so she could feel the feathers settling back down. The heat quickly began to build up under the duvet, it being bigger, heavier and more solid than her oul duvet, which she now realised was a ragged, lumpy, long-dead excuse of a thing. Majella stretched out full length. She smiled when she felt her feet stay covered, tucked up warm at the foot of the bed. She came up for air and slowly dropped her head on her new pillow, enjoying the air whoosh out as her head sank down. She looked around her at the rest of her room. Her tatty plywood wardrobe. The mildewed curtains hanging over the filthy window. The rickety old chest of drawers standing on the swirly eighties carpet. Her old duvet lay limp on the floor. She couldn't do much about the rest of the room, but she could at least fuck the duvet out. She pulled herself out of bed and shoved her feet back into her trainers. She bundled the duvet into a loose roll and then left her bedroom, careful to close the door behind her. She'd managed to sneak her new stuff upstairs without her ma seeing and hoped she could get the old stuff down the stairs and out the back in the same way. At the sound of the first creak, her ma piped up.

— Ma-jell-ah?

Majella's fingers itched to flick. She continued downstairs and dropped the duvet at the front door, then went into the living room. Her ma was under a blanket. There was a collection of empty mugs building up on the coffee table and floor beside the settee. Majella stayed standing by the door and stared over at the telly.

— Hiya.

— Ah didn't hear ye come in there. Ye musta been quiet.

— Aye.

Majella balled her hands into fists inside her fleece, and pushed her thumbs in under the first finger and squeezed hard. Oprah was on again, which was a sign her ma was in need of more support than she could find in a rerun of *EastEnders*. Majella couldn't hear what was being said on Oprah, but she watched the screen closely, hoping her ma didn't want to talk about what the police had called in for.

— You workin the night?

— Aye. In at six.

— O right. Suppose ye won't be eating before ye head.

— Dunno. Might grab a toastie or something. What are you looking?

— Och, now, ah'm still not able really. The stomach's not right. The police put me in bad form.

Majella began to slowly move her thumbs between her fingers, backwards and forwards, backwards and forwards. She glanced down at her ma. She had her sad face on, the one that indicated suffering. Majella decided to try a bit of attention.

— How's yer fut?

Her ma looked pained and pulled up the blanket to show Majella. The skin on her foot looked bloodless and yellow. Most of her ma looked yellow these days – from her nicotine-stained teeth and skin, to her piss-coloured hair and eyeballs.

— Well. What d'ye think?

Majella knew better than to share what she thought, so she used a response she'd heard from the neighbours time and again.

— Well now, I'm no doctor, but it looks to me like you'll live. What time are ye heading til the surgery the morrow?

— She says tae drop in anytime between ten ann four. S'pose you'll be lying in yer bed.

That irritated Majella. — Ye could try walking.

— Aye. Ann ah could probably run the fucken Belfast Marathon ann all while ah'm at it.

Majella got up. She didn't have the patience for her ma's shite today, not after the police this morning. She went into the hall and gathered up the duvet as her ma guldered in the living room.

. . . ann me lying here crippled ann you there taken the hand laughing at yer oul mother well if yer father was here this day you wouldn't be so fucken smart ye wee trollop . . .

Majella opened the back door and walked out to the yard where the near-empty wheelie bin hulked in the corner. She ignored her feelings of revulsion and opened the bin, jamming the duvet in. She dropped the lid and shook her hands as if she could shake the contamination from her skin. When she turned around she jumped at the sight of her ma leaning against the doorframe, scowling. Panic rose in Majella's chest and she began to flick her fingers and rock on the balls of her feet where she stood.

— Ann what are you at?

— Nothing.

— Finger flicking again, eh? Thought you'd quit that carry on?

Majella knew her ma hated the finger flicking and the rocking. She always had. Majella wanted to stop but she couldn't, not with the panic pounding in her chest.

— Ye better not have been dumpin any a my property.

All seven stone of her ma stood there, barring the way into the house. Majella desperately wanted back inside, out of the bright light and huge space under the sky, away from the neighbours' eyes and the rev of cars.

— I was doing nothing. Now, will you get outta me road?

Her ma didn't move. Majella couldn't take it any longer so she stepped up into the doorway and pushed her way past her ma. As she passed, her ma went all wobbly and made out as if she was going to fall.

— Quit that shite. If ye go down, ye'll have only yerself tae help ye up.

Majella knew her ma had no interest in lying on the dirty kitchen floor – she'd much rather be back in the living room under her blanket, feeling sorry for herself, watching Oprah or QVC and necking Tesco Value whiskey to drink away the pain, waiting for one of the neighbours to come in and listen to her troubles. Majella tore out of the kitchen and rushed up the narrow staircase to her bedroom, where she paced the room over and over again – step-two-three-four-turn . . . step-two-three-four-turn . . . – not caring if her ma could hear. After a while she began to calm down, and she sat on the bed with a sigh. She hated fighting with her ma. Neither of them ever won.

Sometimes she wondered how her da had managed her ma, what with his own mother, her Aunt Marie and herself on top. But she knew by the end he hadn't been managing. After Bobby died, her da's visits to his ma up in Garvaghy dwindled. He hadn't visited his sister in Clonbogey for a year. He was spending less and less time at home and more and more time away. Those last few days when Majella came home from school, she'd find her ma lying upstairs in the bed. Some days Majella knew, by the tiny changes in the house from when she'd left, that her ma'd been up and about at least the once. Other times Majella knew she hadn't been up that day or the day before or the day before that. In those last days her da'd come in the door after a day of tinkering with machines, coaxing engines back to life and fixing broken stuff at the factory, and he'd drop his toolkit at the door and leave again before Majella could even say hello. Some days he didn't come home. People would call to the door to ask if he could fix something or give a hand at a car, and Majella would have to say she didn't know where he was.

She remembered the last time she knew where he was. It was coming up to Halloween. Majella had been sitting scratching at her homework in front of the telly when she'd heard his key in the door and then the sound of his toolkit hitting the floor. Her heart skipped a beat when she realised he hadn't turned on his heel and left immediately like in recent evenings. Instead he walked into the living room. She'd smiled up at him. Tried not to make a fuss.

— 'Lo, Daddy.

It was clear he was tired, but he gave her a wee smile.

— 'Lo, Jellytot.

Majella was delighted to have him to herself, no matter what humour he was in. She tried her best not to disturb him. She watched as he sat down in his armchair and turned up the volume on the telly. The news was just coming on. Majella remembered the coverage that day. The IRA had hit the media jackpot with a tactic they called proxy bombing. Reporters described how earlier that morning three families had been taken hostage in Derry, Armagh and Tyrone. The women and children were held at gunpoint in their homes while the man of the house was driven off by the IRA. They'd strapped the men into vehicles loaded with explosives and told them to drive to specific targets. All three bombs were remotely detonated at each destination. Two exploded, killing seven men. The security forces mentioned that but for a faulty detonator in the bomb at Omagh, the death toll would be much higher. Majella wondered about these faulty detonators. There seemed to be a run of them locally. The inquest into Bobby's death had stated that the detonator had prematurely triggered the bomb he'd been planting.

After watching the news on the BBC, UTV and RTÉ, Majella's da turned the telly off. It wasn't often that the telly was off, and Majella remembered the strange atmosphere in the room as she waited for her da to speak.

— Proxy bombs are nothing new, 'Jella. Don't be listening to what the media says. They've been used for years.

Majella had nodded. She was used to this. To watching the news and then getting the true story from her da or a neighbour. She knew the news wasn't to be trusted.

— But before, we always gave the proxy the chance to get away.

Majella stored the facts in her head, as if she was in class.

— This business is different. And if you ask me, it's a dirty business.

Majella nodded, to show she'd heard, even if she didn't really understand. To her, the whole business of bombs and guns and beatings was a dirty business. The attacks and the reprisals. The taking of sides and the waving of flags and the beating of drums. The statements and the refutements and the rumours and the verdicts. She remembered the silence stretching out between her and her da then, spreading and swelling until it filled up all the space in the room. Minutes that she wished every day she had over again. For it was then he got up and walked out the door.

Majella realised she was rocking backward and forward on the edge of the bed, making the frame creak. She took a deep breath and tried to get a grip on herself. She got up and opened her wardrobe. She bent down to her oul trainers on the floor of the wardrobe, and slipped her hand under the tongue of the shoe. Her face relaxed as she found what she was looking for: a small lump of plastic-wrapped hash. She straightened up, turned on the telly and then checked that her bedroom door was double-locked before slipping a DVD into the player slot. As the DVD auto-played, Majella turned up the sound.

It was snowing in Dallas, Texas. Lucy Ewing was riding on horseback to the post box. Majella rummaged in her bedside locker for the lighter, tobacco and skins that she kept with her codeine, tissues and loose change. She found the pouch and reached under the bed for the biscuit tin lid that she used as a tray. She pulled a wad of tobacco out and teased it along the length of a skin, then she unwrapped the hash and started to toast it. On the telly, Lucy had collected the mail and was burning a letter. The ashes fell onto the white snow, the flames pale in the early morning snowlight. Majella crumbled the hash onto the tobacco, then toasted the rock again. She could smell the sweet smoke of the hot hash drift towards her head. She crumbled one more layer onto the tobacco, then dropped the rock into the pouch and rolled the joint. She used the tip of her tongue to moisten the thin strip of adhesive without slabbering the frail paper. Then she tore a strip from the paper wrapper for a roach, and tapped it into place. As Pam Ewing befriended Lucy, Majella lit the joint and toked hard, her biscuit tin lid perched on her diddies, protecting her duvet from the cherry bombs she knew were going to fall.

5.04 p.m.
Item 23.1: Dirt and disorder: Clabber

Majella was deep underneath her new duvet, flexing her toes. The feeble high from the joint had worn off, and she'd worked her way through two episodes of *Dallas*. The stoical Miss Ellie had taken a head stagger and smashed up a few plates during dinner, having realised that her beloved Jock wasn't coming back. Everyone was sympathetic, because they understood that with no body, Miss Ellie could have no funeral, and therefore no closure. Majella liked this episode. When the closing credits flowed to a halt Majella flicked the TV onto standby, plunging the room into a streetlamp twilight. Majella wondered if she'd ever go a bit mad and do something mental like smashing up A Salt and Battered! She doubted it. She was more like her da, shrinking into herself, seeking silence. Her ma on the other hand wanted booze and people and noise to distract her from whatever was in her head. People and noise were the last thing Majella wanted when she felt bad. Like the week before, up in her Aunt Marie's wee house, at her granny's wake. The daytime hadn't been too bad, people dropping by in dribs and drabs. Majella'd been able to pass herself by acting as if she was in the chipper, only with trays of tea and coffee instead.

Milk ann sugar in yer tae?

But by five o'clock, just as it started to get really busy, Majella found herself exhausted by the platitudes, the tears, the ghoulish interest in the details of the assault and death. She wanted to get out for a walk to clear her head, but it was dark and there was nowhere safe to go. The road was lined on both sides with parked cars, yet the border hoppers were still hooring down the road at ninety. Her

Aunt Marie said they'd no respect for the dead, none at all. Majella wondered how you could respect the dead for doing the only thing the dead do – lying still. She thought it was strange that her granny'd spent her whole life complaining about the closure of the border roads, reminiscing about the good old days, when there'd been shops, and more houses, and traffic going between Tyrone and Donegal. But then when they'd reopened the roads only a few months before she died, she was even more upset. Majella had read the newspaper reports in which local politicians said there'd be big gains in local house prices, promising that journey times would be shortened, the town rejuvenated, and old traditions revived. Majella had wondered what her granny thought of the reports. She hadn't been out to visit her in months at that point. When she was wee, her and her da would head out several times a week in his wee red Fiesta. After he disappeared, Majella had to cycle the five miles there and back, which she'd done once a week for a while. During the winter that went down to once a month. The following year, special occasions. She hadn't been on her bike in years now. That day she'd taken a taxi out the road. And right enough, just as the papers had said, the road had been busy.

Majella got dropped off at the entrance to the muddy lane that led to her granny's caravan – it had never been tarmacked and taxi drivers refused to drive up it. She'd walked up the lane and stopped at the pile of concrete bricks that sat between the caravan and the old house. Her da's work, or the beginnings of it. He'd moved her granny into the caravan after he'd paid their mortgage off, so he could start doing up her wee house. But work ground to a halt when Bobby died.

Majella had turned to the caravan, hating the squelch of mud under her shoes. The muck, smells and bright, wide-open spaces of the countryside overwhelmed her, making her feel too small, sending panic fluttering around her chest. She remembered rapping on the frosted plastic panes of the caravan door, then the shuffle of her granny towards the door. When it opened, a wave of moist, gassy heat had poured over Majella. Her granny was wearing the navy cardigan that she'd got her for Christmas. She'd stared through narrowed eyes at Majella for a few seconds, then her mouth fell open in a smile. Majella immediately noticed that her granny hadn't got her false teeth in.

— Och, Majella darlin, how are ye?

Majella found herself smiling back at her granny. — Och, ah'm grand, grand. Yerself?

— Och, sure, ah'm top. Come in, come away in outta that. Come in to me here.

Majella stepped into the small caravan, which creaked as it took her weight. She turned to her granny, who held her arms out for a hug. Majella wasn't much into hugs, but it was different with her granny. When she finally let go, the old woman tottered to the left and put her hand on the table to anchor herself.

— Well, ye haven't lost any of yer strength, anyway!

Majella smiled. — Naw. Still a growing cuddy.

— We'll have tae get ye fed then.

Her granny stepped over to the sink and picked up the kettle. She filled it and plugged it in to boil, then turned back to Majella. — Ah have tae get me teeth in. Houl on a wee minute.

She hobbled to the tiny bathroom. Majella listened to the clink of the glass as her granny fished for her teeth. False teeth unsettled Majella. The baby pink of the gums. The shining whiter than white of the teeth. They reminded her of the perfect teeth she saw in *Dallas*. Teeth that didn't suit the ruined faces wearing them in Aghybogey. Her granny came out of the bathroom, smacking her lips together. Then she pushed her thumb up into her mouth and readjusted her top set. Majella quickly looked at the furious kettle that was spitting its way towards boiling point.

— Well, now. What's the news of the world?

— Och, there's not much now. Not much happening.

Her granny moved over to the sink again, and splashed some hot water into the pot, to warm it. — You'll have a slice a wheaten bread or a wee biccy?

— Slice a wheaten, if it's going.

— D'ye want jam on yer bread?

— Aye. Rhubarb.

Her granny's jam was the real deal. They'd made it together, when Majella was so small that the thick stalks of rhubarb grew as tall as her. She remembered her granny pulling the rhubarb out of the dung in which it grew and handing it to Majella, who had paraded around the yard under the canopy of the leaf, pretending she had a parasol. The jam itself was simple to make: half fruit, half sugar, with a wee rub of ginger. Once cooked, her granny poured it into scalded jam jars that she sealed and stored in the broken fridge in the yard. Majella wasn't mad about rhubarb jam itself – it was too slimy, too stringy. She preferred blackcurrant. But the jam wasn't just about the taste – it was the making of it.

— You sit yerself down there, Jellah.

Majella sat down without offering to help: the caravan was too small for two people to get anything done together. When she'd visited with her da, they'd both sat down while her granny moved about the place, buttering bread, footering with doilies and warming the pot. The telly was tuned in to RTÉ. Her granny only ever seemed to watch RTÉ. Majella didn't know how she did it. She'd die of boredom if her ma hadn't got Sky in and if she hadn't bought her

DVD player. She wondered how her ma would survive in the caravan, in this arsehole of a no place, with only RTÉ for company.

— There we go. There we go now. Cuppa tay anna slice a wheaten tae keep ye motoring fer a wee while more.

— Thanks a million.

The two of them sat supping at their tea. The blue flowery curtains on the window were clean but faded. The plastic tablecloth on the wee card table was scored with knife marks.

— D'ye remember the way yer daddy wanted tae do the wee house up fer me, d'ye, Jellah?

— Och, aye, ah do, aye.

— He was a great man with his hands, yer daddy.

— Och aye, he was, so he was.

The gas heater purred in the silence.

— Mind you, he wasn't as slow as he walked easy either, yer daddy. Coulda gone on tae college.

— Oh aye, he used tae talk about how he'd had the chance of college, all right.

— Aye. Was a great hand at the books. Terrible shame he didn't take himself on. Or get himself a trade. The factory's grand, but there's no hope of anything outside of it. Maybe if he'd been a plumber or that, things woulda been different for him.

— Oh sure, ye never know, do ye?

— Naw. Ye don't.

There was a long silence. Majella sat feeling her cup of tea growing cold in her hand.

— Ye know he promised tae come back out here to live once he had the house sorted?

Majella glanced over at her granny in surprise. Sometimes her granny did this. Veered from the set conversation they usually had and mentioned something Majella didn't know. Something that changed how Majella saw things in her world.

— Naw, ah didn't know that, now.

— Oh, aye. He'd had her all planned. Did me out wee drawings ann all. He was gonna put a wee bit of an extension on with a bathroom ann another bedroom, ann then ah would've had me own place ann youse were all tae come out here ann live with me.

Majella had known about the renovation. She hadn't known about her da's plans to move back out to Garvaghy.

— God, now sure that woulda been brilliant for ye.

— Oh aye. Company, y'see?

— Aye, company.

— Aye. Close enough tae see yeez, but with me own space too.

— Aye. Woulda been lovely.

A silence settled on her granny as she looked out the caravan window. She had a great view over the border road, right the way down the fields to the Bogey river that ran the whole way from the mountains to the town. Up here the river was thin, running rusty from the bogs. It grew fatter and darker, more bloody, as it rolled down the mountain, through the glen and into the town.

— Well it was a long time ago now he showed me those plans. Ann sure ye know yerself it didn't happen. Yer mother wasn't keen, ah know that much. But yer daddy was still going to fire ahead. Said he'd put in central heating ann tile the roof ann put a wee kitchen in jist fer me. Me own bathroom. Can ye picture it?

— Ah can. Sure, he was wild good at things like that.

— He was looking about a grant. Y'see, that was his head working. He wasn't sleeping, yer daddy.

— Naw he wasn't.

— But sure then Bobby-God-rest-him died and the wind went out of yer daddy.

— It did, right enough.

Sometimes when the river flooded and the sun shone, the fields below gleamed as though they were sheets of liquid gold.

— And then he disappeared.

Majella felt a lump rise in her throat.

— Ah can't say ah don't miss him, for he was the last of my boys. But ah like to think he's happy where he is.

Her granny was nodding as she spoke, like she knew where he was, and thought it was a good place.

— Sometimes ye shouldn't tie a man down.

— Naw, ye shouldn't.

Majella's da had fished that river with Bobby. They'd learned to swim in it.

— Naw. Ye shouldn't tie a man down. Ye have tae let them go.

— Aye. Go their own way.

Majella reached for the teapot and refilled her granny's cup, blinking furiously.

— Och, well now. What about you? Any word a you tying a man down?

Majella shifted on her seat as she selected the right answer from her bank of stock replies. — Ah would if there was anything worth tying down.

Her granny smiled at that. Majella liked making her granny smile. Four cars zipped down the road, leaving the hedges bouncing in their wake. Majella nodded towards the road.

— That new road is a power a good, ah hear.

Majella watched her granny's face crease up with contempt. — Power a good, me arse. Ah dunno what they were at when they opened that up. The traffic's wild.

There's gonna be someone kilt up here, that's for sure, the way them young wans drive. Lethal they are. Pure lethal.

A tractor chugged past with Foncey Logue in the driver seat and his five-year-old daughter at his side. He lifted his hand and saluted Majella's granny. She lifted her hand in recognition. Nobody in the line of cars behind waved.

— Ah thought youse were all dying tae have the roads open again?

Majella's granny tutted and shook her head. — Opening the road's not a pile of use tae us now. When they blew them up they left the shops tae die off ann the land fall tae nothin. They left us with nothing. Ann then didn't we get used tae the quiet of the place? The wee birds singing ann the emptiness. Only us up here. Now ye wouldn't know half the cars that be on the roads. Ann the speed of them! There'll be someone kilt up here before the year's out.

Majella turned her head from the road. The wee house was on its last legs. It would fall down if it was let go much further. But who was there to do it up? It started on the road to ruin the day her da disappeared. Another stream of cars streaked past them on the road. The cow in the wet field next to them began to bellow. Majella looked at its shite-clabbered arse, its mucky hooves and legs.

— Is yer man Maguire still renting the fields off ye?

— Aye. Aye he is. Ann he's always torturing me tae sell them tae him.

— Would ye?

— Ah would not. That land's been with us for years now. Yer grandfather God-rest-his-soul had it after his father and his father before him. It's poor enough soil, but it's ours ann it's always been ours.

Majella looked out at the boggy, rushy fields that surrounded them, dotted with small, gnarled trees. Her granny owned ten acres. When she'd been wee they'd walked the fields together, Majella carrying her granny's axe, to tackle the ivy. Her granny couldn't abide ivy choking the trees – she said they'd bother enough with the wind. When Majella spotted creepers sneaking up around a trunk, she'd hand her granny the axe, and watch her chop through the ivy as close to the ground as possible. Majella could see the ivy snarled around the trees closest to the caravan. She'd no idea where the axe had got to now.

— But ye know, ye could sell this place up ann get yerself wan a them nice warm wee houses in the fold in the town. A house with central heating ann someone tae check in on ye the whole time. Ann ah could be visiting ye every day. Marie has her car ann she'd be down tae see ye too.

Her granny tutted and threw her head back. — Ann what business does a country woman have in the town? Ah was born out in the townland of Garvaghy ann ah'm gonna die in the townland of Garvaghy.

Majella remembered checking the time on her mobile phone. She'd only been there for half an hour, but it had seemed longer. She had no reception. She remembered feeling irritated at the thought of walking back down the lane and maybe up the road to get a bar on her phone so she could call a taxi. Outside, a bank of clouds blew in over the mountains, swallowing the weak sunshine. A squall of rain followed, sweeping over the fields and splattering against the wee caravan. Majella itched to go home. That's the feeling she remembered about that last time she had sat with her granny in Garvaghy. Wanting to leave. She buried her face in the soft material of her new duvet until all she could see was a deep dark red.

5:29 p.m.
Item 34.2: Fighting: Shouting matches

Majella's mobile began to vibrate under her head. She turned away from it and into the darkness of the wall, but the handset buzzed until she grabbed it and hit the SELECT button. She groaned. She hadn't meant to fall asleep. It was going to leave her stupid for the rest of the evening. She had work in half an hour, so she heaved to her feet to get ready. She had just made it to the front door when she heard her ma calling.

— Ma-jell-ah?

Majella hesitated. — What?

— Where are ye away tae?

Majella took her hand off the door handle and quickly flicked her fingers. — Work.

— Are you running out the door leaving me lying here without a bite tae ate?

Majella dropped her hand to her side. She walked into the living room, where her ma lay up on the settee. She looked tired. There was a photo album by her side, one from their early years, before Majella was a teenager.

— What d'ye want?

Her ma lay back and shook her head. — Och ah dunno. Ah dunno what ah'm able fer.

Majella flexed her fingers around the plastic bag she held in her hand. — What about a bit a toast?

— Och, now ah'm tired a toast, so ah am. It's *always* toast so it is.

— Chicken curry?

— Och, ah dunno. Might be a bit much on me belly. It's not the best, y'know. Probably the painkillers fer me foot cutting the stomach off a me.

Majella felt the knife-flick of seconds ticking past her. — Mam, ah have tae get tae work here. Ah'm gonna be late. Ah'll do ye up a cottage pie.

— Well, now, if you're gonna be late fer work there's no point in you worrying about me lying up here alone without a bite tae ate all day long ann . . .

Majella walked out of the living room and went to the fridge freezer. A cottage pie box lay under a crust of frost. Majella pulled it out and ripped the cardboard packaging off, then stabbed a fork through the plastic several times. She stuck the container in the centre of the oven, set the timer to forty minutes and then closed the door. Then she remembered her wash, which was still lying in the washing basket. She went over and lifted a T-shirt. It had a ming from being left lying damp too long.

. . . fat useless lump of a daughter. Lazy clart that ah'd be better off without. It's no wonder yer father left when he did . . .

She opened out the clothes horse and threw her clothes over it. When she was done she shoved it up close to the radiator to get the good of the heating.

. . . greedy selfish bitch . . .

Then she threw a knife and fork onto a plate on a tray, and left it sitting ready for her ma. On her way past the living room she shouted at her ma without breaking her pace.

— Yer pie's ready in forty minutes.

She slammed the door. From outside she heard her ma shouting back at her. — MA-jell-AHHHH?

It was cold outside. A hard, fresh evening. Majella felt a sudden urge to go on a walk. But there was nowhere she wanted to go. No one who wanted to see her. Nobody except for Marty and their regulars. So she turned and plodded faster than usual towards A Salt and Battered!

6.02 p.m.

Item 15.1: Time-keeping: You being late

Despite hurrying, Majella was late in the door to work. Marty wasn't pleased.

— Sorry about the time, Marty. The ma needed me.

Marty tossed his head and scribbled down another order. — She's not the only wan. Git yerself ready ann get out here.

Majella walked past Marty to the storeroom. She shook her overalls out of the plastic bag and tugged them over her head. Because she was sweating with all the rushing, they bunched up and caught over her diddies. Majella hated being trapped half in and half out of her overalls. She struggled, hunching her back until she'd yanked the overalls over her chest. Panting, she pulled her hair back into a bun and dragged the hairnet over her head before securing her hat with a few hairpins. Majella hated the stress of being late, the way her head buzzed and everything seemed to go wrong. She couldn't face the counter the way she was, so she stood flicking her fingers and rocking backwards and forwards in the tiny room to calm down. When she felt better, she opened the storeroom door and went to the front counter.

She put her hand out to Marty. — Ah'll take that off ye now.

Marty dropped the pen and order book on the counter without saying a word and tramped to the fryer. Majella hoped she wasn't in for a whole evening of him sulking. Marty could make a shift really hard going when he was in bad humour. Majella considered hiding in the storeroom again, but instead she picked up the pen and order book and turned to Strawberry Donnelly. — What can ah get chew?

Strawberry furrowed his brow and cleared some phlegm from his throat. The snort and suck of him made Majella feel a bit bokey.

— Ye'll have tae gimme a minute. Ah haven't made me choice yet.

Majella breathed out as Strawberry slowly read out loud the menu board from Fish Supper right through to Choice of Beverages, then started all over again. The buzzer rasped as Damien Devine came into the chipper. Majella savoured the brief cold breeze on her sweaty brow. Damien stood patiently behind Strawberry until Majella spoke to him.

— Sure, ah'll put ye through if ye know what ye want?

Damien nodded and stepped up to the counter.

— A curry chip, tub a coleslaw ann a Daddy burger please, Majella.

— Right chew are.

Majella scribbled the order down, then spiked it to the board as she shouted out to Marty.

— A curry chip ann a tub a coleslaw ann a Daddy burger there, Marty.

— There's no coleslaw out. Ah don't have two pairs a hands.

Marty didn't look up when he spoke. Majella sucked her left cheek between her teeth and bit down, then she went to the prep counter and opened the mega bucket of coleslaw that had been delivered earlier. She set out ten polystyrene tubs and dolloped a helping of coleslaw into each. Then she pressed the plastic lids on top. It could be a footery job, as the lids were hard to fit onto the tub, and if you didn't get the coleslaw straight into the container, you'd be fiddling for ages with the tubs. But Majella managed it no bother. She went past Marty back to the counter, where Strawberry Donnelly was still having a think, making whistling noises as he pushed air through his rotten front teeth, and sucked it back through his hairy nostrils. Majella knew everyone thought of Strawberry as an odd being. He was a bachelor farmer from up the Meenkeeragh hills near her granny's place. He'd been called Strawberry on account of being born with a big birthmark on his left cheek, which he'd had removed by the NHS when he was five. He'd never seemed interested in anyone but himself and his wee sheep farm high up in the hills. Marty had once commented that he had everything a man needed up there, and nothing a woman wanted.

Strawberry cleared his throat again and came up to Majella.
— Ah'll take two a yer giant batthered sausages ann a big bagga chips.

The door opened as Majella was scribbling the order down, the buzzer sounding furiously loud in her head. She took a quick glance up to see who had come in and her stomach turned. Agnes Ferguson with her big watery eyes blinking in the fluorescent light. Majella hurriedly ripped the order from the book and went out the back to Marty.

— Please will ye take Agnes' order, for ah can't face her, Marty?

Marty looked up at the counter and then back down at the frothing chip oil. — Fuck off ann grow up.

Majella felt like she'd been slapped. She stood where she was, with her mouth hanging open for three seconds before she caught herself on.

— Fucken grow up yerself, ye sulky big babby, ye.

She dropped Strawberry's order on the floor beside Marty's trainers and then walked back up to the counter, her heart pounding, her blood hot in her ears. She couldn't believe the big thick head on Marty just because she was a few fucken minutes late. Agnes Ferguson was at the counter.

Just as she opened her mouth to speak, Marty shouted up from the fryer. — Fish supper fer Brenda McLaughlin.

Majella retreated back to the fryer and picked up the food, neatly wrapping it before dropping the package into a plastic bag. Brenda McLoughlin was waiting at the counter. Majella didn't like her. She was known as a chancey wee fuck, one of the McLoughlin clan from the top of the town who everyone said would steal the eye out of your head and you looking at them. Majella didn't know if Marty'd already charged Brenda, but she sure as hell wasn't going to check with him. She'd rather let Brenda get a free supper.

— Did he take for it?

Brenda's eyes never flickered. — Aye.

— There you go.

— Thanks, Majella.

Majella watched Brenda smile one of those smiles that doesn't reach your eyes before leaving with her food. Agnes stepped back towards Majella. Majella knew Agnes wasn't there for a nice piece of battered cod.

— Hiya, Majella.

— What can ah get chew, Agnes?

— Well, now, I'm not here for a nice piece of battered cod. You know me and my commitment to an organic diet from sustainable food sources. That's not just for the cancer.

— Aye.

Majella lifted the J-cloth and began to wipe down the counter, forcing Agnes to lift her elbows and move back. Agnes waited until every last inch of the counter had been wiped scrupulously clean, then she came in close to the till again. Majella threw the cloth in the sink and rinsed it out with the cold tap, her hands burning under the gushing water. When she'd wrung every last drop out of the cloth she turned back to Agnes. — What are ye looking, then?

— I'm not looking for anything, Majella. I'm just in to pay my respects, you know, for your granny and that. I wasn't able to make it up to the wake or the funeral what with my hospital appointments and my immune system.

Majella suddenly had an awful itch in her left oxter. She dug her right hand in and scratched hard. — Thanks.

— And you know, if there's anything I can do for you or your family, you know, if you ever need anyone to talk to, or maybe a bit of therapy, well you know I'm there for you all.

Majella hated the dry rasping friction of her nylon uniform under her fingernails. — Thanks. Ah'll let ye know.

She stopped scratching.

— I mean, I'm not looking paid or anything. Just if you need a chat.

Majella wished she could rock and flick while Agnes durned on. — Dead on.

— How's your mother coping with it all, Majella? She's always been a fragile sort of a woman, I've heard.

Majella shrugged. — She's grand. Lyin up in the house as usual. Not a bother on her.

— Hmmmm. I see. Could be delayed shock there. For all of you I mean. The trauma could be so great that . . .

— Curry chip ann a Daddy burger ready here, Jellah.

— Houl on.

Majella turned away from Agnes and went to the fryer to wrap Damien Devine's order. She dropped it into a plastic bag and placed a tub of coleslaw on top. When she turned back, Damien was waiting at the counter.

— Ah didn't take fer this, sure ah didn't?

— Naw. Can ye get us a can a Coke there as well?

Majella nodded and went over to the fridge, where she grabbed a can of Coke. — Six pound ninety there please Damien.

Damien dug about in his pockets and brought out a load of coins. — D'ye mind a bit of shrapnel?

— Not a bother.

He counted out the exact money and dropped the warm coins into Majella's hand. She checked it and nodded. — Thanks a million. See ya.

— Bye.

Majella had barely closed the till drawer when Agnes was back up at the counter.

— I was just thinking Majella, you all have to be careful of yourselves – you and your mother and your auntie. You know, you've all been through so much already, and now this. You have to watch yourselves. And remember I'm here for all of you.

Majella kept her face blank. She really didn't know what Agnes wanted from her. And Agnes clearly didn't know what Majella wanted from Agnes: for her to fuck off and leave her in peace. Behind Agnes the door opened and the buzzer sizzled. A load of young wans up from the parks arrived into the chipper, all sparkly make-up and sullen lips.

Behind Majella, Marty roared up. — Two giant battered sausages ann a big bag a chips there.

Majella looked at Agnes. She fought the frown that was settling into her forehead.

Agnes blinked, then sighed. — Look Majella. I can see you're busy. I'll leave you in peace.

Majella said nothing in reply. Agnes went towards the door and Majella turned away and went to the fryer to bag up Strawberry's battered sausages and chips. The rasp of the buzzer told her that Agnes had finally gone. She brought

Strawberry's food to the counter and rang in the sale. She hadn't seen Strawberry at the wake or funeral, which was unusual for such a close neighbour. But then Marty said Strawberry was as odd as two left feet, a configuration of anatomy that Majella had often pictured and had always found not just odd, but disturbing. She watched Strawberry walk through the crowd of young wans as if they were a flock of sheep, swinging his bag of food. She was glad he was gone. She picked up her pen, straightened her order book and spoke to the nearest teen.

— What can ah get chew?

6.47 p.m.
Item 7: Sweating

Majella watched one of the youngest Devlin weans head out the door, already eating his feed of chips. For the first time since she'd come in, the chipper was quiet. She leaned on the counter and used a napkin to wipe the sweat from her face and neck. The thin tissue tore, leaving a strip stuck to her face. Majella pulled it off, then screwed it and the napkin up, and tossed the ball into the bin.

— You all right?

Majella opened her eyes. Marty was at the far end of the counter, looking at her. She closed her eyes again. — Grand.

There was an awkward silence between them. Majella wished he'd slink away back to the fryers and leave her alone.

— Yer ma ok?

Majella stood up straight, sighed and shrugged. — Same old.

Majella found her fingers trembling. She took another breath. — Ah'm away for a fag.

She opened the fridge and grabbed a Coke, then walked out the side door into the alleyway. She sat down heavily on a beer keg. The cold metal burned through her nylon overalls and joggers. She opened the Coke and balanced it on the ground while she lit a fag, then she picked the can up in one hand and drank down three deep gulps. She felt the cold of Coke hit her stomach, the fizz prickling in her nose. Then she opened her throat and put the tin to her head again. She poured it into her mouth, draining the rest of the tin in one go. She dropped the can and put her foot on it, crushing it flat. The tip of her cigarette glowed in the dark and she stared at it, watching the white ash build flake by flake. Then her guts rumbled and Majella lifted her head to the skies and let out a long, deep burp that shivered the ash of her fag to the ground.

7.15 p.m.

Item 26: Wakes, weddings, christenings, funerals

Cabbage McAteer was outside the chipper, tying his five dogs to his rickety old bike. Majella wasn't keen on Cabbage. He was a dirty wee croil of a man, who lived out the bog road in a thatched cottage whose roof was more rot than rush. His house had no running water or electricity, and was under siege from a barrage of social workers who wanted to move him to more comfortable, modern accommodation. But Cabbage would not be moved. Marty said he got his name by telling stories of how he'd outwitted the latest social worker assigned to his case, stories that always ended with the words:

Ould Mickey here's not as green as he is cabbage-looking . . .

Marty had explained to Majella that this meant he wasn't as slow as he walked easy, which meant he was smarter than he looked. Majella never understood why people described things the way they did in Aghybogey, using codes and riddles. It was hard work figuring it all out. Cabbage always came in of a Wednesday evening for a fish supper. Marty reckoned it was the only hot meal the man had each week. Majella tried not to think about what he ate the rest of the time. She watched him limp to the middle of the floor, where he stopped to squint in the direction of the menu board. Marty had told her that not only was Cabbage half-blind and mostly deaf, he also couldn't read, having only been to school briefly for a few months here and there during the thirties. Yet during his every visit he'd stand back to have a gawk at the menu board, a display of vanity that interested Majella. When Cabbage tilted his head back, whatever was inside his nose flowed backwards. Majella turned her head away as he quit staring at the board to suck a stream of snotters down his throat.

— Evening.

Cabbage spoke generally. He never knew who was behind the counter on account of his bad eyesight.

— What can ah get chew, Mickey?

— Ah'll have a fish supper ann a pinta fresh milk.

— On its way, Mickey. On its way.

Majella scribbled the order out and pinned it to the board, then shouted it to Marty, who'd gone out back for a smoke. She turned to the fridge and pulled a pint of milk out and handed it to Cabbage, who took it and hobbled over to the window. Cabbage had a habit of staring out at the small town of Aghybogey in a way that made Majella feel like he was awed by the wonder of it all. The bright electric lights. The good tarmacked road. The government-funded iron benches. The tall three-storey houses with their slate roofs and wide doors. The motorcars whizzing past and the young people with their modern fashions. He'd stand and stare for a good five minutes, and then shake his head. Majella sometimes considered that maybe it wasn't wonder – maybe he was like her, sick at the fucken sight of the place.

9.09 p.m.
Item 20.2: The security forces: PissNI

Majella was on her knees refilling the fridge with drinks. For no reason she could figure out there'd been a run on them. She didn't like refilling the fridge, for it was a damp and cold job. She'd much rather be at the double tubs. She sat back on her hunkers to have a break and caught Marty staring down at her with an odd look on his face.

— So d'ye think anyone's actually gone up tae PissNI for the DNA thing?

Majella shrugged, which made Marty frown.

— Are ye not curious?

Majella put her head back inside the fridge. — Don't give a fuck.

— What d'ye mean ye don't give a fuck?

Majella kept her head down, stacking the milk shelf with pint cartons. There was a mould growing from the milk carton that had leaked a few weeks before. Majella was itching to clean it out, but she didn't have the time to do it right.

— Ah mean ah don't give a fuck. She's dead ann buried ann what good's a court case tae her?

Majella could feel Marty's disapproval staring into her back. She knew she should've kept her mouth shut and her opinion to herself as usual. She had learned a long time ago that it was a bad idea to tell people what she was really thinking.

— But if ye leave that baste on the loose, he'll only be looking fer someone else. Ye dunno who'll be next!

Majella scrunched up the empty cardboard packing that was heaped around her, then slowly got up off her knees. She closed the fridge door and turned around to Marty. He had hidden his eyebrows in his fringe.

— So here's something you might not know. We had PissNI in tae see us earlier today. Told us they were going to start lifting suspects. Said it like they were doing a favour for us.

— Jesus Christ! D'ye know who they're lifting?

— I haven't a clue. All I know is, they know nothing and when they start lifting people, me and the ma are gonna get it in the neck.

Marty took a step towards her, his hand out in front of him, as if he was a statue in the church. — Ah now Jelly that's not true . . . PissNI will be—

— End a the fucken story, Marty. Ah don't want tae talk about it no more.

Majella felt her breast pocket.

— Ah'm away out fer a fag.

She walked outside into the dark. It had got colder as the night had cleared. The stars shone bright in the gap above her head. She pulled her cigarettes out of her pocket and crammed a fag into her mouth. She was annoyed to see that her hands were shaking, again. She lit the fag and sucked hard, her eyes watering. Majella hadn't cried in years. She hadn't cried when her da disappeared, for she never knew whether or not she should. Then she just kept not crying. It had started off at days, then it was weeks, months and before she knew it, years. She tilted her head up and blew smoke at the stars, and kept looking. Tears didn't fall if you looked up for long enough. Her brain whirled as she looked at the stars above her, racing to count them. She'd never believed there were more stars in the sky than sand on a beach. She'd once been to the beach at Bundoran as a wean and she'd a far harder time counting sand than she ever did counting stars. The best place for seeing stars was deep out in the country. She remembered star gazing when she was wee, and was let stay in her granny's for the night. That happened a few times every year, always in the summer holidays. They did the exact same things every time she stayed over, in the exact same order, so now all the days she'd stayed there over the years had mashed up into one long day in her mind. Being taken up the road by her daddy. The three of them going for a dander up to the border, walking past the dead-end signs. Her da'd tell her the names of the blown-up bridges and the dug-out rivers and count out how many times they'd filled in the road and rivers, and how many times the Brits blew them back up. Her granny'd talk about the good meat and vegetables they used to sell in the closed-down shops. She'd rhyme off the names of the people who'd left for England, Australia or America, good neighbours she'd lost, who had little choice but to leave and let their houses to fall to ruin. After that the three of them would go back and have a feed of cabbage and bacon and sausages and good new spuds before her da headed on across the border to join Bobby at the fishing. Majella would play cards with her granny until it was time for Father Dowling on the telly. After Father Dowling they drank cocoa, said their prayers and went to bed. It was hard to fall asleep in the bright long evenings. Sometimes Majella stayed awake until it got dark, and she'd lie there staring out the window at the stars, listening to her granny snoring.

Majella tipped her head back down and stared at the ground. Her eyes were clear again, her fag almost finished. She took a last drag, then dropped it and ground it out with the heel of her trainer. She took in a deep breath, then walked through to the counter without saying a word to Marty. He was fidgeting with the hairs on the back of his neck. He always did that when he was awkward with Majella, something she hated. She leaned down onto the counter and stuck her arse out.

— Cold out there the night.

— Aye. Felt it earlier.

Then the door opened and the buzzer rasped. Iggy Connolly came in. His face, half-hidden in by his hood, looked swollen and tear-streaked. Majella turned to Marty and jerked her head to the fryers. — You wouldn't stick us on a big sausage supper, Marty?

Marty nodded and walked to the fryers.

— 'Bout ye, Iggy?

— Ah'm ok. 'Bout ye, Jellah?

— Struggling. But sure, who isn't?

— Want anything from the shop?

— Aye, surely. Have a bitty an order the night though. Will ye wait while ah write it down?

Iggy nodded and Majella began to write out a list, starting with sweets, fags, milk, bread and toilet roll. As she wrote, she took a sneaky gleek at wee Iggy's face in the fluorescent light. He looked like he'd been given a right slap.

— Y'all right there, Iggy?

Iggy turned away. — Ah'm grand.

Majella finished the list and passed it to him with a twenty pound note. — There's a pile of stuff there, Iggy. If ye manage the whole lot ye can keep the change.

Iggy nodded, then moved to the door and slid his way out and down the town. Marty came back to the counter when he'd gone.

— Is he OK?

— Dunno. Poor wee fucker looks like he got a slap.

Marty stood there tutting. — That mother of his isn't fit tae rare dogs, never mind weans.

Majella knew the stock response and delivered it bang on time. — Ye need a licence fer a dog.

Marty shook his head in agreement, then went back to frying Iggy's dinner. Majella put her back to the cold tiles of the wall and stared at the fish so long that they began to swim and swirl around her. It was only half-past nine. Marty bagged up Iggy's sausage and chips. He slipped a few extra ketchups and a wee tub of garlic mayo in on top of the steaming package and went to the front counter to wait with Majella. Before long, Iggy slipped back in, holding two full carrier bags. She lifted the counter and grabbed the bags from him.

— D'ye want the receipt?

— Naw. Ye're grand.

She dropped the counter again. Marty passed Iggy's food over to him.

— There ye go, bucko. Ah put in a wee taste of garlic mayo. Watch ye don't get fat now.

Iggy's face cracked into a quick little smile, then he turned away and slipped out the door, holding the hot parcel close to his chest. Majella watched him pad across the Diamond like a fox, glancing around him as he went.

10.00 p.m.
Item 8.4: Jokes: Repeated jokes

Majella watched Jimmy Nine Pints lay his five pound note on the counter.

— A sausage supper, my good woman, a sausage supper.

Majella knew that Jimmy's chips and sausage were bubbling in the background.

— On its way, Jimmy.

The till chimed as it opened. Majella tucked Jimmy's greasy fiver away, then closed the drawer and waited in silence. Jimmy shifted his weight, then leaned in closer to the counter.

— D'ye want a bit of my sausage?

He wheezed a bit, slapping his hand flat on the counter.

Majella waited for the usual five seconds before replying.

— I'll batter yer sausage if you're not careful, now.

Marty joined in with the laughter as the chip fat spat and frothed over Jimmy's Wednesday-night sausage supper.

11.11 p.m.
Item 12.10: Conversation: Flirting

Marty and Majella were both at the counter watching the drifts of oul wans shuffling their way out from the bingo in the parish hall. Majella didn't mind the bingo crowd. They were usually in good humour, win or lose, for they seemed to enjoy the outing as much as anything.

— Suppose it'll not be long now before ye'll be at the bingo, eh Jelly?

Majella kicked Marty in response. She wished her own ma would take to the bingo instead of the booze. The buzzer screeched as Mrs Rankin and her husband Charlie came in. They stood, as usual, near the door, while Mrs Rankin scrutinised the board and Charlie counted out the change in his pocket. Then Mrs Rankin came up to the counter, Charlie following a few seconds behind. Marty stayed slouched by the counter, so Majella took up the order book and pen.

— What can ah get chews?

— Fish supper with ann extra chip there, please, Majella.

— Coming up.

Majella scribbled the order and spiked it on the board, while Charlie continued to count his coins. Mrs Rankin never paid for the food. Though sometimes, if Charlie was caught short, she'd make up the price of the food from her own wee black purse.

— That'll be four ninety.

There was an anxious pause as Charlie recounted his change just to make sure he had it right.

Then he frowned and handed over the exact amount. Though Majella had already counted the money as he counted it and knew he'd got it right, she took a few seconds to make a show of counting it herself.

— Four ninety there, all right. Thanks, Charlie.

Charlie smiled and the old couple shuffled over to the window bench, where they sat down, almost touching each other, staring at the glowing board above them. The bingo crowd were not adventurous with their food. They were pensioners, the most of them. Oul married couples who usually shared a fish or sausage supper between them. The buzzer went and the three McQuaid sisters came in through the open door one after another, stepping in time to the counter. Majella knew they preferred Marty to take their order, so she passed the book and pen to him and went to the fryer to start on the Rankin supper.

— Hello, Martin.

— Hello, ladies. A sausage supper for Bridie, a half fish supper for Bernie and a nice chicken breast for Mary, is it?

— It is! Ye have us pinned, Marty, ye have us pinned.

Marty smiled his big warm smile and the three spinster ladies beamed back.

— So how is it youse are this evening, ladies? Any luck at the bingo?

— Och now, is there ever any luck at the bingo? And if there was, wouldn't Marian Lynch have the best of it?

The women chatted on at the counter, each vying for just a second more of Marty's attention than the other. Majella wondered what it would've been like to have had sisters. And to grow old with them. It had dawned on Majella fairly recently that she was a spinster. Not even a spinster lady like Miss Deeny who'd taught the recorder and the special class in St Christopher's. Just a spinster. Majella didn't like the word. She'd heard it from when she was a wee thing, first about her Aunt Marie, then about other single women dotted around the hills and houses of Aghybogey. To her it had meant a woman living on her own. But then Miss Deeny had taught her the meaning of the word.

. . . a woman who is not married, and beyond the usual age for it . . .

Spinster was a word that squeezed a lot of meaning into the spit of its few letters. A skinny, spare word, unlike the word *bachelor*, with its rich round sounds and slurring letters. Majella found herself staring into the sizzling chip fat, watching the bright lights from above glimmer in the golden froth.

— JELLAH?

Majella flinched.

— Sorry?

— Ah was asking if ye've got the McQuaid ladies' suppers on yet?

— Aye. Naw. Sorry. Getting tae it now.

Majella measured three generous portions of chips into the basket, then dunked them deep into the seething oil. The McQuaid sisters, she reckoned, could do with some feeding.

12.00 a.m.
Item 42: Hypocrisy

Majella stared out the window at the rain that had swept down from the hills. It hopped off the pavement and benches, splattering against the window. The chipper was quiet for a Wednesday, the rain keeping everyone away. A white HiAce van pulled up outside. A man jumped out and dashed into the chipper. Paddy FitzSimon. The striplight flashed crazily for a few seconds, then died, then hummed and relit itself, shakily.

Majella never knew how to chat to Paddy FitzSimon. As a child he'd been a bogeyman, someone she'd been bundled past in the street, someone who was tortured by the gangs from the estates, even though the weans had no idea what they were torturing him for, only that if their mams and dads were mean to Paddy then they'd get away with being mean to him. It turned out Paddy was one of Them Queers. How people treated Paddy had slowly changed as time went on. Majella noticed it first after *Queer as Folk* became a big hit on the telly. Then that squeaky gay fella had appeared in *Corrie*. The next thing was that film with the bent cowboys in it, which hadn't been shown in the Derry cinemas, so everyone had to go to Lifford in the Free State to get a look at it before they could report on the holy show it'd been. In recent years, Majella had noticed that more and more fellas were coming out in Aghybogey. They could be seen hanging around Paddy FitzSimon's flat, sometimes even getting the balls up to head out to the pub for a drink. But sooner or later even the most popular of the gay fellas would get a hiding off the Daly brothers and then they'd leave Aghybogey for the brighter, kinder lights of the Kremlin in Belfast. Paddy FitzSimon was still Aghybogey's only official Queer Fella. He wasn't welcome at any function or do on either the

Taig or Prod sides of town. But Majella rarely saw him on his own. And Majella had never known Paddy to buy a single fish supper – there were always chicken nuggets, a double daddy burger or a giant battered sausage supper in his order.

— All right there. Majella, love?

Majella blinked and grabbed her notebook. — What can ah get chew?

— Two sausage suppers and a large tub of garlic mayo, please, my darling.

— Right chew are.

12.59 a.m.
Good list
Item 8: Cleaning

It was nearly closing and it didn't look like the Daly brothers were out on the tear. Majella hoped that the feed of drink from the night before had flattened them and that they were taking it handy. She did not want to consider the alternative. The chipper'd been so dead that her and Marty'd cleaned the whole place already. They propped themselves up at the counter, both watching the clock tick down the last few seconds before closing, their suppers foaming in the hot oil behind them. The clock hands moved to 1 a.m. and Marty flicked the shutter switch. The steel curtain ground down and wiped out Majella's view of the rain-swept streets of Aghybogey.

01.22 a.m.
Item 28.2: Death: Pets

Majella stood on the *Fáilte* mat at the doorstep of her house, looking for the fox from the night before. It wasn't around so she let herself in. The house was fucken freezing, which meant Majella's wash would be as wet as it was when she hung it out. She could hear her ma snoring from the living room over the murmur of a TV show. Majella walked to the door and peeked in. Her ma was lying under a duvet, her mouth hanging open. It took Majella's eyes a few seconds to adjust to the blue light of the telly flickering around the wreckage of the room. She noted the half-eaten cottage pie lying on the coffee table, the fork still stuck in it, the empty whiskey bottle by the ma's side, and a glass cowped over in the middle of the cups and mugs. She sighed and went over to check her ma's position. Her rule was to leave her ma lying wherever she fell as long as she was reasonably well covered up, or at least in the recovery position. Majella decided her ma was stocious but stable for now. As she turned to leave the room she clocked her old duvet, the one she'd shoved into the wheelie bin. Her ma had only gone and fished it out and wrapped herself in it. Majella stood there disgusted, her hand wrapping the plastic bag tighter and tighter around her fingers. She could see no course of action that was worth taking, so she walked to the kitchen and grabbed a plate and a pint glass before climbing the stairs to bed.

Majella was warming up nicely under her new covers when she realised she hadn't checked her ma for pills. It wasn't unlike her ma to take a feed of drink and pills when she was in need of attention. Majella squished a chip into her garlic mayonnaise and then rammed it into her mouth. She debated getting up to check on the ma. She remembered what J. R. Ewing did when he found Sue-Ellen in a similar state. He simply left her to her own fate, assigning her to the care of the good Lord above. Majella considered all the signs from the days and weeks before, before arriving at the conclusion that her ma'd probably just wanted to get out of her box and wouldn't thank Majella for a trip to A&E. Their family trips to A&E were at an historic low, which was in part because Majella didn't drive, and so her ma had to pay for a taxi, and in part because Majella wouldn't call an ambulance as quickly as her da had done. Majella didn't always believe that the pills from the empty bottle dropped by her ma's bed were in her ma's stomach. She tuned out the shite-talking about drowning in the Bogey river because she knew damn rightly her ma'd never throw herself into cold water. She understood what her ma meant when she said she wished she was dead. And she understood that neither of them were likely to do anything about that wish, one way or another. The NHS wasn't going to fix whatever it was that was wrong with her ma.

After Majella ate the last of the squished chips she dumped the empty chip wrappers and her half-eaten fish onto the floor. She wondered if a pet would help her ma. Something like a cat – warm and gentle, quiet of itself. But her ma'd not been mad about Blackie. Had never let the cat in the house when she was there. She was the one who called John Murphy to see to Blackie's kittens. Her da had made sure Majella was up in her bedroom the first time John came. Majella hadn't understood what was happening, and had sat upstairs listening to the men's voices. She could hear almost nothing – just the low rumbles of her da and John's conversation. She heard them walk through the kitchen, and then, minutes later, the kittens mewing. She could smell the smoke from John's pipe and hear the clink of the coins her father slipped him at the door. When the door closed, she got up and went to the window and watched John carrying a cardboard box across the grass towards his own house. Majella had cried, even though her daddy had asked her not to. She kept crying even when her ma had got mad with her gurning and belted her. Then she'd run out to the shed and cried and cried and cried, sitting rocking in the half-light with Blackie.

The next time Blackie had kittens, Majella had run away before John had come. She'd waited at his house for him to bring the box over. John had been a big quiet man, grubby from his hunting and shooting. The weans in the estate never bothered him. He wasn't the kind of fella anyone fucked with, even in later years, when he had a stoop and was half blind. Marty said John still gave him the feeling that he could string him up by the heels and hang him out to dry.

That day John wasn't shocked to find Majella sitting on his doorstep.

— Looking yer kittens back?

Majella had shook her head. John's forehead twitched, an expression that Majella thought might be surprise.

— What are ye looking?

— Ah wanna know what you're gonna do til them.

John had been silent for a bit. — Ah'm going tae dip them.

Majella still sat there, on John's warm front door step, waiting. John eventually spoke again.

— Want tae watch?

Majella nodded. She followed him into his dark, strange-smelling house that was the structural twin of her own home, but utterly different. Dead rabbits hung in the kitchen. Bits of fox fur draped over chairs. There was a goat skull leering at her from the mantelpiece, its powerful horns curving back from empty eye sockets. The house stank of fish and blood and piss. He opened his back door and fresh air flooded in.

Majella crept onto the back door step, and watched as John put the box of mewing kittens on the concrete ground outside, before turning to an outside tap to fill a big yellow bucket full of water. Majella remembered that bucket clearly. It looked brand new, and stood out – so clean and bright – against the litter of rusty traps, dirty bones, cloth sacks and bits of broken things around it.

— Ah make sure the water level's right with this here saucepan lid.

John pushed a dirty saucepan lid down into the bucket. It went below the water level and wedged in the bucket. The holes in the lid allowed the bubbles of air to escape and pop on the surface.

— That's dead on. Next thing ah do is fire the kittens in.

He paused and looked at Majella, his head on one side.

— Ye sure ye want tae see this?

Majella was sure she was sure, so she nodded. John shrugged and opened the box. Blackie's kittens mewed loudly in the sudden daylight. John rubbed a rough hand over the kittens.

— Poor wee basturds.

Then he scooped up the five kittens and dropped them into the bucket. They sank to the bottom, squirming. John jammed the saucepan lid into the bucket and balanced a stone on top. Majella watched streams of air bubbles floating out of the air vent in the saucepan lid and popping on the surface of the water. She listened to the soft claws of the kittens scratching on the bright yellow bucket, imagined their tiny pink mouths opening and closing in the water. After a while, the stream of bubbles trickled to a standstill. John nodded at the bucket of still water.

— Well that's that.

Majella nodded. John looked at a loss.

— Ye have tae leave them for long enough. Tae be sure.

Majella nodded again but didn't move. John rubbed a dirty hand across his heavy, wrinkled face.

— D'ye want a lemonade?

Majella nodded one last time, then followed John into his kitchen. She watched him hunt for a glass. The first ones he found were filthy. He eventually found a pint glass that wasn't the worst, and he rinsed it out under the tap in the sink. After wiping the wet glass with a dirty tea towel, he filled it to the brim with cream soda and passed it to Majella. She had never had so much cream soda in all her life. She sat on a kitchen chair drinking silently. John had poured himself something that her ma would describe as medicinal. They sat there for what seemed like ages, long after Majella had finished her pint of cream soda. She was trying to swallow her burps when John stood up.

— Should be finished now.

He eased himself to his feet, then strode outside. Majella followed. The sunshine was blinding after the dim kitchen. She watched John lift the heavy wet stone from the saucepan lid. Then he pulled the lid up from the bucket, the movement setting the kittens bobbing around on top of the water. Majella wondered why the living kittens had sunk, but the dead ones were floating. John scooped them out two at a time, and put them in a plastic bag. Majella asked to see the plastic bag, she remembered, to look inside. They were so small, the wee drowned kittens, much smaller than they'd been before they died. Not like the bloated sheep down in the river that looked bigger in death. It made her feel sad.

— What d'ye do with them now?

John shrugged. — Fire them in a ditch. Best thing for it. Something'll ate them or they'll rot in tae fertiliser.

Majella had a feeling that her face betrayed her at this point, for John snapped at her.

— Animals like that, they're more use dead than alive.

Majella could remember nodding, though she knew she didn't agree.

Thursday

9.33 a.m.

Item 31.1: Telephone calls: The phone ringing

Majella shoved her head under the pillow and stuffed it around her ears to muffle the rippling bleep from the telephone downstairs. She noticed with satisfaction that her new pillow did a better job of blocking out noise than her old one. After fifteen cycles, the phone rang out, and in the after-silence Majella sighed and relaxed into her duvet again. She wondered who would be calling them at that hour, or indeed who would be calling them at all. The telephone rarely rang in their house and when it did, she let her ma do the answering, for Majella hated speaking on the phone. But there was no hope of that this morning after the feed of whiskey her ma'd taken. Majella closed her eyes and snuggled down into the centre of the bed. After a minute, she could feel herself falling asleep, trying to remember what her da's voice had sounded like.

9.47 a.m.

Item 31.1: Telephone calls: The phone ringing

The phone echoed through the house again, jerking Majella from the shallow sleep she'd been in. Now she was raging and wanted whoever was ringing to Fuck Right Off. Groaning, she shoved her head under the pillow and held it over her ears even after the phone stopped ringing, watching black spots dance behind her tightly shut eyes. It took her much longer to relax this time, and her forehead felt knotted right up to the moment she fell sleep.

10.03 a.m.

Item 31.2: Telephone calls: Having to pick up and talk to a stranger

When the phone rang for the third time, Majella sat up in bed.

— Fucken Basturds!

She threw the duvet roughly from her and swung her feet to the ground. After opening her bedroom door to the chill of the landing, she thundered down the stairs towards the phone. At the last second before picking up the handset she hesitated, then took a deep breath.

— Hello?

— Hello. Am I speaking to Nuala O'Neill?

Of course the call was for her ma.

— Naw ye're not. She's lying up in her bed.

— Am I speaking to Majella O'Neill?

— Ye are.

— Hello Majella. This is Mary McGrory from McConville's solicitors in the town.

The secretary paused. Majella was scratching her neck but realised by the protracted pause that she was required to acknowledge Mary.

— Hiya Mary.

— Majella, I'm just ringing to ask if both you and your mother would be available to come to an appointment tomorrow at a half twelve?

— What fer?

— It's the reading of your grandmother's will. You're both among the named beneficiaries, and it would be in your interest to attend.

Majella frowned. She'd no idea her granny'd made a will. She'd no need for a will: everyone knew the farm would go to her Aunt Marie.

— Right.

— Ok. Well, can I confirm your attendance, Majella?

Majella couldn't be sure, but she thought she detected impatience in Mary's voice.

— Aye, surely. Ah'll be there.

— And your mother?

Majella could hear the impatience for sure now. Mary was using a pretend patient voice, the sort of tone teachers had used with Majella in class, a tone that had focused everyone's attention and derision on her. Majella didn't like that voice.

— Ah'll make sure she goes ann all.

— OK. So that's a half past twelve tomorrow in our offices in the town here.

Majella wanted the voice out of her ear. — Grand. Thanks Mary.

— OK Majella. Thanks for—

A thought struck Majella. — Who else is going?

There was a bit of a pause on the phone. Majella wondered if Mary was irritated by the interruption or if she was considering what information she was allowed to share with Majella.

— Well, we've been unable to contact your father. However, your Aunt Marie has agreed to attend. So it's just yourselves and your Auntie Marie.

Majella took in the information and nodded to herself. — Grand. Thanksamillion.

— Don't mention it. Bye.

— Bye.

Majella dropped the receiver back into its cradle. She held her breath and stood listening for ten seconds, to see if her ma'd been woken by the ringing and the chat, but there was no sound from upstairs or downstairs. Majella took a breath and pushed the living room door open. Her ma wasn't on the settee, which was a relief. She turned and headed back up the stairs and into the bathroom. She locked the door behind her and sat on the clammy toilet seat. As she pished, she began to think about the phone call. Her granny'd never made any mention of a will nor had she ever discussed inheritance, but somehow Majella and everyone else in Aghybogey understood that with her da and Bobby both gone, Marie'd get the farm. So she couldn't figure out what her granny had decided to leave to her ma and herself. Majella knew her granny's belongings inside out, could catalogue them for PissNI without going as far as the caravan. She had her collections of navy cardigans and holy magazines, her squat wee telly, a clatter of holy medals and an old photograph album. Majella would love the photos, but doubted that she'd get any – Marie'd probably lifted them. Majella felt exhausted, so she went straight to her bedroom and switched on the wee fan heater before collapsing into her still-warm bed. She decided that she'd give her ma the news when she got up later in the day. Right now, all Majella wanted was sleep.

1.43 p.m.

Item 26: Wakes, weddings, christenings, funerals

Majella'd given herself a faceache with the strain of keeping her eyes closed. She gave up and let them twang open. She stared at the hatch to the attic above her head. Her da'd stored stuff like the Christmas decorations up there. Nobody but the police had been up there in years as it was such a pain in the arse to get up. Majella eyed the flaking paint and wondered if she should hoover the ceiling. She'd a suspicion she might bring down the ceiling.

It didn't feel like it was a whole week since they'd put her granny into the ground. Majella remembered sitting in the GAA centre afterwards, everyone around her digging into a feed. Majella hadn't been able to eat. She'd sat there listening to Blister McGovern the gravedigger shite on about how the clay of Meenkeeragh graveyard had a way of preserving the wood of coffins and flesh of corpses, which made his job a real handling. Majella thought of the bog bodies that she'd seen on a documentary on telly. People who looked like they'd been carved from wet peat, with squashed foetus faces and slit throats. She remembered the coarse rope still tied around the hands of a girl they'd found, rough against her slippery skin. Majella wondered if one day people would find beautifully preserved bodies in Meenkeeragh graveyard, and marvel over fingers laced with rosary beads. She turned over on her lumpy mattress. The funeral played in her head, over and over. The last day of the wake, Majella hadn't been herself after the evening rosary, when Father Travers had called her, her ma and Marie together. He said that word had come back to him that her da was not to be found. They'd initiated a call for him as soon as her granny'd been found after the assault, and put out their highest alert after her death, but he was sorry to report that no one had seen or heard of him since the night he'd disappeared. Majella hadn't known the Catholic Church had feelers stretching into every home that hung a crucifix on its wall, a reach wider, deeper, creepier than the police. Despite Father Travers' sorrowful gaze, Majella knew it was possible that the Church just hadn't found him. She pictured her da hearing the news somehow, in a hot, faraway place. She saw him leaving whatever life he'd built, whatever name he was using, to jump into a tiny plane. She imagined him transferring onto a crowded jumbo jet destined for Dublin airport. She knew he'd shiver in the cold weather as he made his way north, gearing himself up to face the rumours. That thought kept her going. But darkness fell and he didn't arrive. The last night of the wake – the long night of waiting up with her granny – was hazy. Majella'd sat and knocked the tea and Jameson's into her. She was well-oiled when she took a taxi home early the next day to dress for the funeral. Her head had started to hurt by the time she returned. She walked behind her ma as they made their way towards the house. Her ma had been glamorous in her black coat, wearing the best of her thick gold jewellery, her dark eyes heavily ringed with kohl. She greeted a few waiting mourners with a lingering hand clasp and a murmured word as she passed them on the path. She was a woman born to play the role of a beautiful young widow. But Majella's ma was stuck in limbo. Not a widow and yet no husband. She had nothing but his clothes hanging limp in the wardrobe, his work shoes mouldering in the shed, the fading photos and news clippings, the rumours murmured behind her back. Once inside the house, Majella sat down at the kitchen table and let people with things to do eddy and flow around her.

At ten o'clock she was called into her Aunt Marie's wee front bedroom to say goodbye to her granny before the undertakers 'fixed' the coffin lid. Majella knew there was nothing to fix – that they were going to screw the lid down. But she didn't understand why that was something they wouldn't do in front of them. She could imagine banging nails into a coffin would be a painful experience, with the noise, the violence of it. But screws were a different story. Majella felt there was something satisfying about screwing in screws. She liked the feel of the thread catching when turning a screw by hand. She loved inserting the screwdriver into the head of the screw, then rhythmically turning the nub of metal until it closed up tight. Majella'd far rather screw down her granny's coffin than do what she was expected to do before they closed it. She watched her Aunt Marie go to the coffin and kiss the corpse's forehead, touching the bruised cheeks with her hand, before stepping back, tears streaming down her face. Her ma was next in the hierarchy. Majella could tell by the step of her that she was conscious of all the eyes in the room on her. She watched her ma let a few tears slip before she too kissed the corpse's forehead. Then it was Majella's turn. She'd felt huge and awkward in the small room, and when she stepped towards the coffin, she took a reddener. She didn't want to kiss her granny's waxy forehead. She couldn't look at her sunken cheeks and sealed-tight-shut eyes, the bruise-stained face under the cleaster of make-up. Instead she'd stretched out her hand and touched her granny's hands, which were wrapped in her second-best pair of rosary beads. When she touched the cold flesh her stomach turned. All the same, she'd kept her hand there, counting to ten with her eyes closed to make it look like there was something – anything – happening in her head. Then she'd taken her hand back and blessed herself lightly, trying not to touch any part of her body with the feeling of the cold flesh.

When she'd followed her ma and aunt to the front door of the wee house, the crowd outside rustled and readied itself. Smokers took a last drag on their fags before dropping the butts into the mud. Someone blew their nose noisily. A few people straightened ties, others tightened scarves. The BBC camera crew moved in for a better angle as the murmur died to a hush. This was what everyone had been waiting for. Majella blinked in the cold sunlight. She hadn't been to many funerals. She wasn't really sure of what she was supposed to do and felt like an amateur surrounded by seasoned pros. A flail of wind whipped through the crowd, causing people to pull their coats around them and push collars up around their cheeks.

There was a movement from inside and Majella caught sight of the coffin being manoeuvred around the tight corner at the front door of the house. The undertakers, awkward but sure of themselves, got the coffin out without scuffing the paintwork. At the doorstep, four men – neighbours they were – came forward and hoisted her granny onto their shoulders. They clasped their hands around each other's shoulders and steadied themselves, waiting for the priest's last blessing. Father Travers started into the prayers, sprinkling holy water over the coffin and mourners as he went. A splatter of holy water hit Majella in the face, and she wiped it away quickly, for fear that anyone would think she was crying. Father Travers moved off, and the men shouldered the coffin down the garden path. Her aunt and ma set off after the slow-moving coffin. She followed, feeling the heat of the crowd closing in behind her.

About halfway down the path Majella's ma took a big snivel, stopped and slipped her arm into Majella's elbow for support. Majella stiffened, wanting to shrug her mother off, but she was conscious of the camera crews, felt everyone's eyes on her. They walked to the crossroads, where the pall bearers stopped at the waiting black hearse and lowered the coffin onto a sort of trolley that allowed them to slide it into place. Once the hearse closed, everyone scattered for their cars. Majella trembled in relief as her ma unhooked her arm and click-clacked over to the car they were sharing with Marie. She followed and climbed in the empty front passenger seat. The driver signalled to the undertaker, who made a signal to the hearse driver, who set off at a steady speed. The driver of their car waited five seconds, then moved off. Behind them car after car choked into life, then joined the cortege that slowly covered the road to Meenkeeragh church.

Majella lay still and straight in her bed, staring at the ceiling above her, wondering if the flaking paint might one night fall on her face like snow.

2.30 p.m.

Item 32.2: Boking: Retching

Majella woke to the sound of her ma boking up in the toilet. Her ma'd never been a quiet puker. She'd cough and choke and retch so hard you'd hear her from the street. The bathroom went silent for a few seconds. Majella knew her ma would have her head on the toilet seat, feeling sorry for herself, and that a fit of gurning was probable. She heard the toilet flush, and then the gurning started. Majella heaved herself out of bed, pulled on her fleece and trainers, then went out to the landing. The bathroom door was wide open. The toilet was still gushing and her ma was hugging the toilet bowl, snivelling. Majella reckoned she'd be there for another while yet, so she trudged down the stairs and into the kitchen. She filled the kettle and eyed her limp washing. It was still damp. Majella sighed, then grabbed a plastic bag from under the kitchen sink and jerked it through the air to check for holes. It seemed airtight, so she went through to the living room, where she pulled the curtains open to let the sunlight into the room. Then she got down on her knees and began to shovel the ashes from the fireplace into the bag. When she was done, she took the grate brush and gave the fireplace a rough brush-down, raising a cloud of dust that hovered briefly, before being sucked up the chimney by the backdraught. It was a thing Majella saw to, the sweeping of the chimney. Not doing it herself as her da once did, but paying Tommy the Coalman to call in when a sweep was needed. Majella lifted the bag of ashes and the coal bucket and walked out through the kitchen to the wheelie bin in the yard. She dropped the ashes into the bin and watched as a small cloud of dust rose and blew around the yard.

She went to the bunker and shovelled coal into the black bucket until it was piled high. Then she carried it back through the house and into the living room. Upstairs she could hear the sound of running water and the whine of the electric shower. It was a good sign that her ma was having a shower, but no guarantee that she'd come round. Majella laid three firelighters in the centre of the grate and put a match to them, then she shook three shovels of coal onto the flames before pulling the fireguard in front. They burned the cheapest coal, the kind that spat and stank when it was first lit. Majella looked at her hands. They were black with soot and coal dust. She went through to the kitchen to wash them off, loving how they went from dusty black to white pink and wet clean while her ma yelped in the shower as the hot water ran cold. The kettle had boiled and steamed up the window, turning the blue sky outside into a lovely mist. Majella dried her hands in the towel and went back into the living room. The sunlight had lit up the wreckage of the room – the whiskey bottle, the dirty glasses, the coffee and tea cups that were beginning to moulder. Her ma's magazines lay where she'd dropped them, and Majella's stinking ould duvet was crumpled on the floor. Majella picked up a tea tray and loaded it with dirty cups and glasses, and brought them to the kitchen. Then she went back and gathered up all the magazines and put them in one pile. She wrung out a dishcloth and wiped the coffee and tea stains, the hardened toast crumbs from the coffee table. She pulled the settee back from the fire and folded her old duvet into a square. The room looked a hell of a lot better. Upstairs the sound of the shower stopped, and the water trickled to a standstill. There was a crash as her ma dropped something in the bathroom. Majella listened as her mother's cracked voice swore and the bathroom door slammed.

3.31 p.m.

Item 32.3: Boking: Vomit

The fire had taken, orange flames were licking over the black coals. But Majella's ma hadn't appeared downstairs. Majella sighed, then got up and left the fire for the kitchen. She knew that a bit of breakfast would do her ma a world of good. She lifted a single slice of bread from the toaster and put it on the tray beside a mug of sweet black coffee, a bottle of her ma's health yogurt and four Kapake. She carried the tray up the stairs, slopping coffee around. Majella knew she wasn't cut out for tray carrying, which was one of the reasons she'd ruled out a career in waitressing (the other more intractable reason being that there was only one restaurant in Aghybogey, and it hired only the youngest, skinniest and bustiest of girls). She turned around at her ma's bedroom door and slid her elbow down on top of the door handle. The door swung open and a fug of whiskey breath, fags and boke hit Majella. Her ma moved under the duvet and groaned. Majella put the tea tray on the ground and then half-opened the curtains to the blue skies outside. She looked at the bedside locker, which was loaded with more dirty mugs and empty pill bottles. The ashtray was overflowing. Majella lifted it and emptied it into a mouldy mug, then gathered the mugs and piled them up outside the bedroom door. Taking a magazine, she opened it and swept the pill bottles and trash onto the pages and then laid them on the floor. As she lifted the tea tray to the locker, she caught the sweet black smell of the coffee before the whiskey and boke reek swept in again. There really was a right ming in the room. Majella opened a window and gulped down the fresh cold air that streamed in.

— Ah brought ye up some coffee ann toast.

Her ma groaned again and poked her head out of the top of the duvet. She looked rough.

— There's painkillers there, ann yer yogurt stuff.

Her ma opened her eyes a crack and then closed them and sighed. — Ah'm not feeling the best.

Majella raised an eyebrow but said nothing. The smell of boke was now stronger than the smell of whiskey. Her ma's wet hair had made a damp patch on her pillow. Her curls were thick and shaggy from not being combed out. Her ma'd got awful grey at her roots, Majella noticed.

— Ah'm wondering if ah'm not coming down with something.

Majella moved around the bed to tidy up her da's side of the room. Her stomach heaved as she realised that her ma'd boked down that side of the bed. Watery whiskey puke stained the valance sheet and carpet below. She retreated back to the doorway.

— Coffee ann toast there. Don't be letting it get coul.

Her ma groaned again and struggled to sit up straight in her bed, holding her head stiff. Majella knew there was nothing to be done about the puke while her ma was in the room.

— Gwan. Get that coffee down ye. It'll do ye a power a good.

Her ma stretched a shaky hand out towards the half-full mug. She lifted it and brought it to her lips, where she first took a sip, then a greedy swallow of the scalding coffee.

— D'ye think it's the flu ah have on me, Jellah?

Majella had been taught this game by her da – *Let's pretend your ma isn't hungover!*

— Maybe.

Her mother nodded weakly and took another big gulp of coffee.

— What time is it?

— Quarter tae four. Ah'm gonna head on, fer ah'm in at four.

Her ma took another swallow of coffee and then put the mug back on the tray. She groped on the bedside cabinet for her fags, lit one, then lay back on her pillows, her eyes closed.

— Mary McGrory of McConville's solicitors rang earlier.

Her ma opened her eyes fairly sharpish. — What fer?

— She's looking us down tae the office the morrow at a half twelve. They're reading Granny's will.

— Yer granny did not leave a will, did she?

Majella wondered at the point of this habit of her ma's, where she'd hear something and then say the opposite, but ask Majella to confirm the original statement. Like Majella would say — It's raining out, and her ma would answer — It is not raining, is it? Majella knew she was supposed to state the original fact again, only amplified, saying for example — It is surely raining outside, before her ma would accept the fact and say something like — Oh, Lord, now the rain.

— Mary McGrory says she did.

Majella paused to allow her ma time to answer. — Oh Lord now, a will!

Majella nodded patiently. — You, me ann Marie are all named. We're tae be down in the office the morrow at a half twelve.

Majella's ma had perked up, her face crinkling in interest. Deep purple circles ran under her eyes. Her skin hung around her mouth, dragging the corners of her lips down.

She took a long drag on her fag, nodding. — God now ah'd need to get back on my feet for that. Wonder what that business is all about? Maybe Maggie left us a quid or two, d'ye think, Jellah?

Majella pictured her granny sitting alone in her wee caravan, remembered the smell of the chemical toilet, the biting cold of a winter's night. — Ah doubt that.

— Ye never know with them oul wans. They can surprise ye with what they tuck away in their mattresses.

Majella shrugged. If there had been anything in her granny's mattress, it was long gone, probably spent by whoever'd booted her in the head before they left her for dead.

— Right. Ah'll run on here now. You're OK?

— Och, well, ah'll just have to sleep through this bug, won't ah?

Majella nodded and moved towards the door. — Bye.

Her ma reached for the coffee cup, coughed and then waved her fag at Majella. — Cheerio.

Majella stepped over the stacked-up mugs in the doorway and went to her bedroom. She put her purse in her pocket and stuck her uniform, hair grips and hairnet in a plastic bag. She was ready. Then she sat down heavily on her wee bed, both hands gripping the mattress, her head slumped on her chest. She didn't know what had come over her. She didn't want to go to work. It wasn't like she ever *wanted* to go to work. But today she felt she couldn't face it. Her stomach was turned and her legs were weak. She felt something hot crushing her chest. She closed her eyes and sat back in the bed. She'd never missed a day of work in her life, not until her granny's death. She'd never taken a day off on her own account – no matter how sick, tired or hungover she'd been. Just like at school she'd never ever missed a day all the way through St Christopher's, even after her da disappeared. Majella stood up and rubbed her eyes. Then she stood rocking and flicking for as long as it took to make things easier. When she felt better, she left her bedroom and trudged down the stairs. Outside the sky was clear and blue, with streaks of pink hanging in the west. She turned her eyes to the pavement and headed towards the town centre, some heavy raw thing frying in her chest.

3.55 p.m.
Item 28.1: Death: People

Majella was walking down town when she realised her head had gone again. Caught between Tara's Tanning Salon and Get the Snip, Majella ran for cover in the chapel. She blundered through the side door and sat down on one of the benches at the back, her heart pounding and her head dizzy. She gulped in the still air, tasting the tang of incense and flicking her fingers in her pockets. The silence settled into her, and after a while she came round. When her head stopped spinning she tried to stand, but her legs went from under her again. Majella trembled in frustration. She pulled her phone from her fleece pocket and texted Marty.

Gonna b late4work cu soon sorry Majella

She felt guilty for leaving Marty in the lurch again, but it was Thursday so there'd be no rush on just yet, and on Thursdays young Johann-Pol was there to give them both a hand. She stared at the single message in her text inbox. It was from Aideen. She hadn't heard from Aideen in years before this text.

Saw yr Gran's fnrl on tv. V sad. Hope u ok. Will send mss crd. ⋆lol⋆ Aideen x

Majella thought ⋆lol⋆ looked like a cheerleader punching the air with a pair of pompoms, which didn't fit the message. She knew she was supposed to choose between Laugh out Loud and Lots of Love for the ⋆lol⋆ bit. Majella had a fair notion that Aideen meant ⋆lol⋆ and wished she'd just typed Love, which was not only one character less than ⋆lol⋆, but was a lot less confusing. Aideen's Mass card still hadn't arrived. Majella didn't think it would. Aideen was full of good intentions, but always busy. Too busy to come home even at Christmas these days. It was three years since Majella had seen her last, her and her English fella, him so posh and ill at ease in the Bogey Inn, slabbered after four pints while Majella went her usual eight without it taking a flinch out of her.

Majella deleted Aideen's message and put the phone back in her pocket. The chapel was cool and quiet, with a couple of oul wans on their knees here and there on the benches. Bridget Dolan was doing the Stations of the Cross, her rosary beads in hand. Majella stared up into the steel girders above her head. Sometimes when she was wee a bird would fly in during Mass and the whole place would get excited and distracted at it flying around, ducking at the danger of shit splatters. The priest would always carry on with the Mass as if the bird wasn't there, but you could tell he was thick with the bird for invading the chapel, which was another part of the craic.

Majella didn't really like the church. It was a modern build – all concrete and glass. It'd been built with compensation money after the April Fool's Day bomb had flattened the old chapel but left its intended target – the RUC barracks next door – intact. The new chapel was in many ways an improvement. It didn't leak. It had effective heating and amplification systems. Everyone had a seat. There was wheelchair access and soft kneelers. But everyone missed the old chapel the same way oul fellas missed the smell of fags and pish and the tobacco-stained fittings of the Bogey Inn after it'd been done up.

After the new chapel was opened, Majella'd always looked forward to the occasional visits to Meenkeeragh chapel, out near her granny. Meenkeeragh was the real thing – stuffed full of brass candlesticks and life-size white marble saints and doll-sized angels. Every surface was covered in a painting or a cloth or a clutch of rosary beads. The windows glowed with jewel colours: ruby, sapphire and emerald, the church warm with real candles, the walls soft with creeping mould. When her and her granny went up to light a candle, Majella would slip her sticky coin into a slot and listen to the clink of it falling onto the little pile of coins hidden inside the box. She'd pick a candle from the open shelf, unfold the wick for lighting and choose a flame from which to light it. She always held the lit candle in her hand for a wee minute, imagining that she could somehow imprint her prayer on it before putting it in the most important place. People liked to put their candles on the top row. Closer to God, Majella'd once thought, as if your prayers would skip to the head of the queue.

But what Majella had liked best about the candle box was that her granny told her that if Majella ever needed a candle to burn for her and she was lost somewhere far away or even if she was at home and she didn't have the two pennies to rub together, that she could come in and just light one. God would understand she didn't have the money, that she would put it in later, when things were better. The electric candle machine in the new chapel didn't let you do that. If you'd no coins, you couldn't press a button to make an electric candle shine for a pre-set 20 minutes.

Majella sighed and dropped to her knees on the faux-leather kneelers, as if she was about to pray. She didn't really know what she was doing in the chapel. She hadn't prayed in years, not properly anyway, as she had a fair idea that having a wank after the rosary had probably cancelled her prayers out. She hid her head in her hands, closing her eyes. Her head was full of the funeral. It wouldn't leave her. Over and over it played. She remembered sitting there at the end of the funeral Mass, watching the undertaker organise the last lifting of the coffin. It was then that she realised that she'd been waiting. Waiting for her da to show up so he could carry his ma to her rest. But he didn't. And Majella knew there and then that her da was dead. For if he'd been alive – if he'd been anywhere on the face of the planet – he would've heard about his ma and he would've found some way of making it home. She knew that. But she didn't know why she'd got to her feet, causing a stir throughout the chapel. She didn't know why she went up to Oisín McGlinchey, feeling the burn on her back of all the eyes behind her. She remembered touching Oisín's sleeve to get his attention. He turned to her, calm and sombre, not a bit like his usual self in the pub.

She'd whispered at him. — Ah want tae carry the coffin.

Oisín was shocked, but he hid it well enough to pass. — Well now . . . are ye sure Majella? Ah've the men all sorted.

— Ah want tae carry her.

Oisín paused to take the measure of her height with his eye, then nodded. — OK. Give me a minute.

He went over to the waiting men and had a quiet word with one of them. He nodded and slipped back to his seat, then Oisín came back over to Majella.

— You take the front with Gerry Doherty. He's of a height with ye.

Majella nodded. Oisín put his hand on her sleeve, let the weight of his arm rest on her.

— If you're not feeling up tae it or if you want tae swap out, just give me or Seán the eye.

Majella nodded again. She kept her back to the mourners packed into the church behind her until the last moment. Then she took her place by the coffin. When it was lifted she stepped forward and took the weight on her shoulder and locked her arm around Gerry. They steadied themselves and as the choir began to sing, they started the slow walk down the aisle. Majella didn't see anything around her. She just felt the comfort of the solid coffin against her cheek, the tension in Gerry's arm as he dug his fingers into her shoulder. She heard the rustles and clacks of mourners filing down the aisle behind her. Outside a skift of rain had passed over, leaving the ground soaked. They walked slowly, firmly through the muck. Majella felt her wet trousers slop around her ankles as she walked in step with the men, carrying her granny to the lip of the hole that had been dug for her at the back of Meenkeeragh graveyard.

4.41 p.m.

Item 4.1: Bright lights: Fluorescent bulbs

Majella opened the chipper door and walked into the heat. She thought it was funny how the buzzer sounded quieter when she triggered it herself. Perhaps it was because she was prepared for the noise. Marty was behind the counter. She checked the time on the fish clock on the wall that had come free with the cod pieces they'd once tried out. It was after twenty to. The fluorescent light was still flickering away to itself. Majella squeezed past the customers who were standing waiting to get their order filled, and paused as Marty unsnibbed and lifted the counter to let her in.

— Thanks Marty.

— No bother, Mrs. You all right?

— Am grand.

Majella tried to stretch away the frown that had dug itself into her forehead. She plodded to the back storeroom, passing young Johann-Pol, who gave her a big grin.

— I see you are late, Miss O'Neill. I think perhaps you have to be careful, or your job will be at risk.

Majella smiled at Johann-Pol. He said his name funny. Yawn-pawl. Claimed that's how they said it in Poland.

— Suppose you've a sister or a brother or a cousin looking work, Yawn?

Johann-Pol grinned at Majella again. Majella gave a toss of her head in order to stop the interaction, then stepped past Johann-Pol into the storeroom. She closed the door and switched the light on, keeping her eyes closed until the flickering had settled down. The frown dug itself back into her forehead as she pulled her overalls out from her bag and squashed herself into them. She held her breath as she tugged the zip up the front, then let it out slowly, feeling her flesh press against the seams. Her hair was the last thing to fix up. It was greasy, which made it easier to pin back. When she was ready she smoothed the backs of her still-trembling hands over her body until she felt calm. She could remember doing that in primary school, until the teachers had knocked the habit out of her. She knew now to do shit like this only behind closed doors.

She took a deep breath, then lifted a bucket of garlic mayo and opened the door. At the food-prep counter there was a stack of tubs sitting waiting. Majella enjoyed measuring out double tubs, so she lined sixteen of them along the counter, then passed back along the line, dolloping a helping into each tub. She didn't miss a single tub or slop any mayo over any of the tub sides. Then she picked up lids and put them on each tub, savouring the little click as she snapped each lid on tight. She reckoned she'd do fifty or so double tubs before the singles, and then she'd look about the coleslaw. From the front of the chipper she could hear the Devlin wean in again.

— Ann a big bag a chips.

— No bother. Five minutes.

Majella started into the double tubs.

6.09 p.m.
Item 27: Nicknames

Majella was stacking up the freshly-filled tubs of mayonnaise. The double tubs to the left, the single tubs to the right. Majella knew from filling them that you actually got better value if you bought two single tubs. But hardly anyone bought the single portions – they were all after the double tubs. Marty slapped Majella on the arse. She dropped the last tub and it rolled to the edge of the counter. Majella caught it just as it was about to fall.

— Fuck off Marty. Ye nearly made me drop that!

Marty laughed. — Sure you always catch stuff. Haven't seen ye drop anything in here yet.

Majella quickly searched for the right answer. She knew that it was a clever thing to take something someone had said, and twist it a little in return, so that their words were now used against them. The answer clicked with her.

— Aye, well, if ye keep harassing me ah might drop you. On yer fucken head.

Majella left Marty laughing and went to lean at the counter. There was a bit of a lull, but she knew it wouldn't last. It was dark outside, the wind getting up. A gang of weans raced around the war memorial, scooshing water bottles at each other. Marty joined her, and started giving out about their 'anti-social behaviour'. Privately, Majella felt that firing water around was a much healthier pastime than doing drugs, but Marty's tone would have her believe it was a close call.

The weans settled themselves when the water ran out, some standing there, some sitting down on the benches, laughing and shaking their clothes under the orange light. It was far too cold for that sort of business. Majella watched as they stared over at the chippie. She knew that shortly they'd harass whoever had a few quid to head on over and get a bag of chips for sharing out between them. Not that they needed feeding, for like most of the young wans going about these days, they were a pack of fat bastards. After a few moments of wrangling, three of them detached from the gang and headed towards the shop. Without shifting her weight, Majella slid the order pad in front of her and picked up the pen. The buzzer rasped as the young fellas entered, sly looks on their heads. They came up to the counter, stood awkwardly, stared up at the menu board, then the biggest one shoved the younger two and they stood in front of her, half-singing, half-roaring

Jelly on the plate,
Jelly on the plate.
Wibble wobble
Wibble wobble
Jelly on the plate

Marty had fired up the counter hatch by the time they'd got to the second wibble wobble. He raced them out of the shop, calling them a shower of fat hoors and fucken basturds. Majella leaned on at the counter, watching as the young fellas ran across the street and then sat laughing. Marty roared on for a wee while from the door, then he came back in, still swearing. He slammed the hatch down, and squeezed Majella's arm in passing. Majella had already moved to the second verse of the rhyme in her head.

Sausages in the pan
Sausages in the pan
Sizzle Sizzle
Sizzle Sizzle
Sausages in the pan.

Behind her the fryer hissed and spat in protest against the latest batch of raw chips.

7.07 p.m.
Item 12.12: Conversation: Same old shite

It'd gone quiet again. There'd been a mad rush on before seven – one of the oul dolls in *Coronation Street* was being killed off, and everyone from up the estates wanted to get their food in before the episode started. Majella took advantage of the lull to have a stretch to herself. She couldn't take the full stretch she needed as she wasn't sure the seams on her uniform could take the strain. She reckoned she'd maybe put on a few pounds with the PMS. Her diddies were definitely swollen. She pulled herself out of the stretch and reached for her fags, then walked to the back of the shop. Yawn-Paul didn't smoke. So when he needed a break he did stuff like wiping down the worktops. He was a great wee cleaner and left them hardly anything to be done by the end of the night. And he always had a big cheerful head on him – he spent half the shift singing. Weird Polish shit, but he'd a lovely deep voice for such a wee fella, so Majella kind of liked hearing him in the background. Majella found Marty rooting around in the storeroom.

— Marty?

— Whah?

— Fag break?

— Aye. In a minute.

Majella opened the back door and stepped outside. Her nipples tightened and her skin goosebumped. How those wee friggers had stood about outside in the cold after soaking each other she didn't know. She pulled out a fag and lit it. The door behind her opened and Marty came out, fag already in his mouth.

— Baltic, eh?

— Not the warmest anyway.

Marty struck a match and puffed on his cigarette until it glowed. Majella sat down on a beer keg, feeling the cold of it burn through her uniform and joggers.

— Yawn-Paul's at the cleaning again, ah see.

Majella recognised this conversation and knew the reply off by heart. — Aye. He's a great wee cleaner.

It was a conversation Majella had seen evolve over the past few years, since the Poles had landed. People weren't sure of them at first, and feared they were after their jobs. But before long they'd won local respect for not being choosey about what work they'd take on. And also their drinking.

— He is, aye. Leave ye with hardly anything tae do at the end a the night.

— Aye. He'd have it nearly done for ye.

— He would. He'd nearly put ye outtay a job.

— Aye. He nearly would. Very good workers, the Poles.

— They are. Hard workers. Big drinkers too.

— Aye. Drinking and driving. No wonder so many've them are kilt on the roads.

— Aye. The drinking and then the driving on the wrong side.

— Aye. Well as long as they only kill themselves.

— Aye. Leave us outtay it.

— Aye.

— Great workers, though.

— They are, aye.

Majella thought it was interesting the way everyone had worked out a wee story about who the Poles were, and what they were like. It was kind of like with the Prods – a list of stereotypes and clichés. Nobody talked about what Majella thought was pretty obvious: the Poles were welcomed because they were Not Prods. Every Pole who came over to Northern Ireland tipped the scales another wee bit lower in favour of the Catholic side. Majella reckoned it'd be a different story if the Poles were Muslim.

She sucked on the last of her fag, dropped it to the ground and crushed it out. She wondered if Cunter would take it into her head to ban the backyard smokes. She could see it happening: anything to make their lives just that wee bit more miserable. As she stared, Johann-Pol opened the back door.

— Martin and Majella, we have customers!

Majella walked back into the chipper. Behind her Marty was staring at her crushed cigarette on the ground, the last of his fag burning between his fingers.

8.27 p.m.

Item 4.1: Bright lights: Fluorescent bulbs

The flickery light strip was getting worse. There was a loud buzzing noise coming off it now, and it flickered: *Onnnnnn off-on off-onnnnnnnn offonoffonoffon offffffffff* . . .

And just when Majella felt relieved that the fucken thing had finally died and left her in peace it would buzz again, then flicker back onnnnnnnnn. It was wrecking Majella's head. The buzzer went as a few more customers came in. Fat Suzy Loughlin and her skinny wee boyfriend whose name Majella could never remember.

— Well, Majella.

Suzy always greeted Majella while keeping her eyes on the menu board.

— Well, Suzy.

Majella always greeted Suzy while keeping her eyes on the street.

Suzy stood reading the board hungrily from Chicken Nuggets to Beverages, her eyes darting in the fat of her face. Her boyfriend came up and leaned on the counter, uncomfortably close to Majella. She didn't move.

There was a long silence, unbroken until Suzy waddled over to the counter. Her boyfriend pressed himself against her. — What are we having pet?

Suzy ignored her boyfriend and spoke to Majella. — A fish supper, a chicken fillet burger supper, a daddy burger, a curry pea ann chip ann a two-litre bottle a Coke. Extra salt on the chips.

Majella wrote the order down quickly. — Rightcheware.

— Gwan throw us in a couple a tubs a that garlic mayo too.

— No bother.

Majella passed the order to Marty and moved back to the counter where Suzy and What'sHisName were still standing. Suzy was frowning up at the ceiling. — Ah see thon light's on its last legs.

Majella nodded.

— Can ye not do something about it? It's wrecking my head.

9.29 p.m.

Item 3.4: Noise: Shite singing

Majella looked up as the buzzer went. Arlene, Darlene and Jolene Logue trooped into the takeaway. Jolene had her wee cub by the hand. The whole lot of them were all dollied up in their country and western gear.

— Jellah.

— 'Lo Majella.

— Hiya, Mrs.

Majella nodded at the sisters. — Hiyas.

The girls stopped to check out the menu board and Majella threw her eye over them. The sequins on their outfits sparkled under the flickery light. Majella always wondered where the Logues got their clothes. Maybe on eBay. She was pretty sure that they weren't getting them in Patterson's Patterns in the town or New Look in Strabane. The wee denim skirts with the spangly bits. The glittery belly tops. The cowgirl hats. And the fancy leather boots. Like something you'd see on some daft American TV show. They even had the wee fella dickied up like a miniature cowboy, for he was part of their act. Marty had explained that country and western was in their blood, for their father had been a big man at the singing before he'd had the accident and took to the pain-killers. Majella picked up her pen as Arlene came over to the counter.

— What can ah get chews?

— Can ah get a fish supper with a can a Coke?

— Daddy burger ann a can a Fanta ann a Kiddie's Chicken Nugget Special Meal for the wee man here.

— No bother.

— Onion rings ann garlic mushrooms ann chips for me, Jellah, thanks.

Jolene was the vegetarian in the family and knew better than to order veggie burgers.

— Coming up.

Majella straightened up and headed to the back to pass the order to Johann-Paul. Marty came out of the storeroom. — Busy?

— Naw. Just the Logue cuddies in.

— The Logue Ladies, ye say? Yee-har.

Marty pulled out his imaginary lasso and circled it in the air. He lassoed Majella and started tugging her towards him. Majella knew she was supposed to let herself be tugged along for a few steps and then they would have a laugh, but she just stood there awkwardly, feeling like a heifer.

— Ah, you're no craic at all the night, Jellah.

Majella wanted to explain, but instead she shrugged and walked back out to the counter. The three Logue girls were sat at the window seat, practising their harmonies and vocal twangs while the wee fella nodded along under his Stetson, seeming to agree that sometimes it is hard to be a woman.

The light flickered *onnnnnn-off-onnnnnnnn-offffffffffffffff.*

10.00 p.m.

Item 4.1: Bright lights: Fluorescent bulbs

Majella watched Jimmy Nine Pints lay his five pound note on the counter.

— A sausage supper, my good woman, a sausage supper.

Majella knew that Jimmy's chips and sausage were bubbling in the background. The broken light flickered *on-off-on-off-on-off-on.*

— On its way, Jimmy.

The till chimed as it opened. Majella tucked Jimmy's greasy fiver away, then closed the drawer and waited in silence. The light buzzed furiously, building to a crescendo, then flicked off.

Jimmy shifted his weight, then leaned in closer to the counter. — D'ye want a bit of my sausage?

He wheezed a bit, slapping his hand flat on the counter. Majella waited for the usual ten seconds before replying.

— I'll batter yer sausage if you're not careful, now.

Then they all had a laugh while the light flickered *on-off-onnnnnn* and chip fat spat and frothed over Jimmy's Thursday-night sausage supper before the light died again.

11.00 p.m.

Item 4.1: Bright lights: Fluorescent bulbs

The Puke McCanny was in for his usual (*bag a chips, no salt no vinegar*). He was standing staring out the window at fuck all, for there was fuck all happening outside apart from the rain drizzling down. Marty was staring at the light that was flickering furiously *onoffonfoofofnfofofnsaonfofnfonnnoffonoffonfooffff*

— Well, fúck me if ah don't take a hammer tae that light the night.

Majella knew Marty didn't have a hammer and so wasn't likely to attack the light. She was not sure of the relationship between him not hammering the light and her having to fuck him. It seemed a very complicated way of communicating that he found the light to be an irritation.

— Fucken head wreck.

Majella closed her eyes against the flicker and Marty. But she could still hear the *buzzzzzzupffffbuzzzzzzzz* of the light stuttering on and off and she knew Marty wasn't done yet.

— Should just hit it a fucken slap ann have done wi it.

Marty stood up and threw his cloth on the counter.

— Fuck this. Am away for a fag.

He headed out the back alleyway, slamming the door behind him. At that moment the lightbulb fizzed and then popped. The chipper seemed silent and dim. Majella held her breath for as long as she could. The light stayed off. Then Johann-Pol shouted from the back.

— Ready!

Majella breathed out long and slow, then fetched the Puke's chips and brought them to him. He'd already paid.

— Yer order.

— Thanks. The Puke hesitated at the counter. — Ah see yer light's gone.

— It is, aye.

— Ye'll need to change that now.

— We will, aye.

The Puke coughed, then leaned in towards Majella. — Tell me this, ann tell me no more. How many Sinn Féiners does it take til change a lightbulb?

Majella shrugged.

— None. Irish lightbulbs have the right tae govern their own future. The Puke started up with his wheezy oul laugh. — What d'ye make a that then? Irish lightbulbs have the right tae govern their own future!

Majella smiled at the Puke, though she didn't get the joke. The lightbulb was finally dead, and that really was something to smile about.

12.12 a.m.

Item 12.1: Conversation: Banter and the craic

Majella was at the back, operating the fryers. She'd had enough of the slabbering going on out the front counter. Johann-Paul was taking a turn at trying to understand the food orders. He wasn't half bad at it for someone who'd only landed in the country six months ago. Though he'd studied English at school, Majella doubted that the English he'd learned in the classroom was anything like the speech he was trying to understand now.

— Battured sausage supper ann chips ann gravy.

— That is one battered sausage supper with chips and gravy. Would you like anything to drink with that, please?

— Mulk.

— A carton of milk. That is everything, yes?

— Aye. That'll do rightly.

— Majella! A new order!

Majella took the order from Johann-Paul, who quickly stepped back to the counter.

— Next please?

Majella could see two of the younger cuddies eyeing up Johann-Paul. They were bollixed drunk and egging each other on.

— Hi. Yawn-Paul. She fancies you, y'know.

— Shuddup Sinéad! Shuddup! Don't mind her Yawn-Paul. She's blootered.

Majella knew that Johann-Paul's forehead would be crinkled in confusion and his eyes big with curiosity. He loved learning new words.

— Blue-toured? What is this word blue-toured?

— Blootered! Y'know, like plastered?

— Plastered? Like a wall?

There were laughs at the counter.

Marty stepped in. — Means drunk. Like this lot. Lamped. Mowldy. Ossified.

Johann-Paul had turned to Marty, smiling, with his head cocked on the side like one of the smarter breeds of dog. — All these words for drunk?

— Who are you calling pished?

Marty slowly turned to face Seamus Dunne. — Aw now. Ah wouldn't say you're pished. Or lashed. You're not even stoven. But you'd be more half-tore.

— Peeshed? Lashed? Stoven?

— Sure that's hardly the half a them. Ye can be langered too. Or locked. Then there's polluted.

— Lang-hurred?

Sabrina Carr joined in at the counter. — Well I'm scuttered.

— At least you're not shit-faced or stocious.

— Stow-shuss?

The whole place was listening now. Ciara Maguire piped up. — Horse drunk.

Her friend piped up. — Piss drunk.

Franci Boyle raised his head up from what had looked like a deep sleep. — Full drunk.

Marty took a look at him and nudged Johann-Pol. — Blind drunk. Or pure twisted.

— Well last week ah was put sideways. Ah was full as a sheugh.

Majella was stood at the fryers when the side door opened and cool air poured in. Mr Hunter slid in the door.

— Slaughtered.

He looked in Majella's direction. — The takings?

Majella looked in his direction. — Coming up.

— Steaming.

— Full as a bingo bus.

Majella handed over the takings. — There you go.

— Full as a Catholic school.

Mr Hunter cleared his throat awkwardly. — Thanks, Majella. Thank you and goodnight.

— Goothered.

Majella threw a smile at Mr Hunter's left ear. — Night Mr Hunter.

— Gee-eyed.

He turned and left.

1.52 a.m.

Item 12.4: Conversation: Reminiscing

Majella came into the estate and walked across the green to her house. It looked like every light in the house was on, a sign that her ma was pissed and that a neighbour had called over. She put her key in the lock and opened the door. The hall was warm.

— That you, Majella?

Majella closed the door behind her. — Aye.

Her ma said no more, so Majella walked into the kitchen. The dishes she'd piled up earlier had been washed and put away. A neighbour had definitely been in. Majella grabbed a plate and put her food in the microwave, then poured her Coke and sat down at the kitchen table. It was then she found the ming off her trainers. She pulled her feet from under the table and looked at the soles. She'd tramped in dog shite. Majella cursed and kicked her shoes off. She checked the lino in the kitchen. Smudge after smudge of dog shite where she'd walked, each print growing fainter. Majella pulled on a pair of rubber gloves, grabbed a J-cloth, doused it in bleach and began to wipe the floor. The microwave pinged but she kept on wiping, right through to the hallway, right up to the door. When the whole place had been cleared of the shite, she went back and fired the cloth in the bin and pulled off the gloves, then washed her hands for a long time at the sink to get the rubbery smell off them. When her stomach had settled, she took a big swallow of Coke, lifted her fish and chips and went into the living room. Her ma was sitting on the settee under Majella's dirty old duvet, her face wet and swollen from crying. She had every last one of the family photo albums out.

— Hiya.

Her ma didn't reply, she just looked away, wiping her hand across her face to rub away the tears. *The Biggest Love Songs from the Eighties* were belting out of VH1. Her ma lifted a damp tissue and blew into it, dropped it on the floor and then lifted her glass with a trembly hand. — D'ye want a drink, Jell-ah?

— Nawww. You're all right thanks.

Majella's ma sniffed and turned a stiff page in the photo album. — Ye never drink much with me, Jell-ah. Sometimes ah could be doing with some company.

Majella mashed the chips in her mouth with her tongue and teeth, then swallowed. — Ah'm not much for drinking in the house.

— Aye. Suppose not. You're like yer da. He never drank much at home. He'd be out after the company.

Majella pulled a piece of fish out and eyed it. She knew looking at it that it was a perfect combination of salt, vinegar, batter and cod. She let her mouth water for a few seconds before cramming the fish into her mouth. She chewed slowly, enjoying the tang of the salt and vinegar against the creamy soggy inside of the batter and the firm flesh of the cod.

— Aye. He was a man for the company. One time ah would have been wan for the company too. Course that all changed with you.

Majella nodded and dunked a chip into a splodge of ketchup. She wondered what had changed when her ma had had her. For things must have been very social altogether before Majella was born, if the fights she remembered right from when she was wee were an improvement on 'before'. She remembered the roars of her da at her ma when she'd come in from being out in the town all night. The weddings they'd gone to where Majella'd be left to sleep in the car outside the hotel, while her da tried to prise her ma loose of whatever company she'd fallen into. Majella's chip broke, one half falling into the sauce. She retrieved it and put the whole thing into her mouth.

— Never get married, Majella. Never get married.

Majella watched as her ma took a big swallow of whiskey. The quarter bottle under the coffee table was empty. There wouldn't be much left in her now, for the drink the previous night would've knocked the wind out of her. Majella popped the last bit of batter that had fallen from the cod into her mouth and chewed slowly.

— There's no happiness in marriage, Majella. No happiness. Ye loss yourself. Ye loss everything. You're right tae be a spinster. Take the road of yer Aunt Marie. Have yer own place ann yer own stuff ann tae hell with everyone else.

Her ma dropped the tumbler into the flat folds of the dirty duvet and gazed over at Majella.

— D'ye know what it's like tae get tae my age ann only tae've loved wan person?

Majella understood that the question was rhetorical, so she said nothing and instead watched her ma collapse back onto the settee, weeping. Majella looked back at her food. There were only a few chips left. She scraped them together with her fingers and pushed them into her mouth. Her ma lay with her eyes closed, weeping. Normally Majella couldn't stand her ma crying, for it was usually a messy, noisy performance. But sometimes, like tonight, her ma just wept – no snivelling, no sniffling – just the tears rolling down her cheeks. Majella watched her ma reflectively for a minute, then pulled herself to her feet.

— Right. Time fer bed.

Her ma didn't move. Majella went to the kitchen and dumped her food wrappers. The floor had dried from where she'd wiped the shit up. Now she could see the clean patches shining out against the dirt. Majella knew that the whole place could do with a really good scrub. She walked back into the living room.

— Right. C'mon. Time for bed. Ah'll give ye a hand.

Her ma turned her tear-filled eyes towards Majella. She gently lifted the duvet from her ma and put out her hand. Her ma pushed her hand away.

— Ah'm all right. Ah'll get up on me own. Ah'll be grand.

She pulled herself to her feet and then hobbled out of the room. She was unsteady, but not in any wild danger of cowping over. Majella stood in the living room, waiting to hear whether her ma'd go straight to bed or was sober enough to go to the bathroom to see about the toilet. Then there was a creak on the bathroom floor above her head, so Majella sat on the settee to wait until her ma was done. She looked at the photo albums lying in front of her. Majella hadn't gone through them in a long time. Her favourite albums were the old ones from the seventies, where everyone was young and wore mad clothes. She hadn't seen the last photo album in years now. Her ma had hoarded it for a long time. She'd gone through a phase of carrying it around with her – to bed, out shopping, just sitting with it in the house. That album covered the longest period, the time after Majella's First Holy Communion. She opened it up. There they were, the three of them at Majella's eighth birthday. Her granny'd taken that photo, which was why they were all in it, but the cake was cut out. Her da'd liked to take pictures with the cake in the frame, making it easy to date the photo later on. She flicked through the album, seeing her da and ma and wee Jella in various poses until her eleventh birthday. Her ma'd taken that photo. There was no cake in this picture either – her da hadn't been there to make it. Majella looked fat and unhappy under an atrocious head of hair. Her ma'd given her a home perm for her birthday and Majella had hated how the curls gave her the air of a sulky poodle. Then the photos stopped and the newspaper cuttings started, the earliest from 1990. They were old now, Majella noticed, going yellow. She began to read. They were just text reports at first. The RUC appealing for help in finding a local missing man. The stories took up more and more space as time went on, starting when the RUC revealed that they were worried about the man's safety. When the reporters got wind of some of the rumours that were flying around, the articles started to include photos. Majella skimmed the tabloid stories that made allegations about her da's involvement with another woman. She read the political articles, which shone a spotlight on the family's Republican connections, dredging up old, soft-focused photos of her Uncle Bobby 'the fox' O'Neill, speculating on how such an experienced member of the IRA fell victim to a premature explosion, mooting the possibility of sabotage by an informer. She puzzled over the anonymous sources who said cryptic things about her da, like 'you can't run with the foxes and hunt with the hounds'. She frowned at the link a reporter made between her da's disappearance and the proxy bombs, insinuating he'd gone on the run before he was himself strapped to one of his own bombs. Then there was the awful article published around the ten-year anniversary of his disappearance, on Majella's twenty-first birthday.

Mother and Daughter Appeal for News

The article featured a photo of her and her ma sat together on the settee. Her ma was dolled up to the nines, clutching a framed photo of her husband. In the photo, Majella's da wore a GAA jersey that was ten years out of date, and he wore a moustache you'd only see now on UK Gold. Majella flipped past to the last pages. Her heart pounded as she found the latest entry into the album – fresh from this month's papers.

Elderly Widow Beaten in Remote Caravan – Police Consider Motives

Majella was too tired to consider motives. She folded the cutting and closed the album. She got up, switched off the living room light and climbed the stairs to bed.

Friday

9.30 a.m.
Item 3.6: Noise: Alarms and sirens

Majella's phone vibrated under her right ear. She groped under her head and found it, then hit the SELECT button to silence the alarm. Nine fucken thirty. A totally uncivilised hour of the day. Majella humped under her duvet and burrowed deeper into the bed, wondering what state her ma'd be in. She had a fair notion it wouldn't be the best, so decided to get her own bathroom business out of the road before wakening ma. She threw back the covers and went into the bathroom. While she sat on the toilet she wondered what she was supposed to wear to the solicitors. Her only good clothes were her going-out clothes, which she'd worn for the funeral. She knew it wouldn't feel right wearing something she got stocious in, but she didn't really have a choice. She sighed as she got up off the toilet, then looked at herself in the mirror. Her eyes were bloodshot and she looked pasty. She thought a splash of water might do her a bit of good, so she ran the tap and threw a couple of scoops of cold water around her face and neck. She stretched into a yawn, then opened the bathroom door and stepped over to her ma's bedroom door. She paused, then gave it a good batter.

— Geddup now, will ye, for we've the solicitors tae go tae!

She stood and listened to hear if her ma was awake. There wasn't a sound. Majella pounded the door again.

This time her ma responded. — Achhhh. Leave me be for a wee minute more! Ah'll be up soon enough!

Majella rolled her eyes. This meant she had a job on her hands. — Ah'm away tae put the kettle on. When ah'm back up, ye'd better be looking about yerself!

Majella turned and tramped downstairs to see about breakfast.

The kitchen was cold, and a cool blue light from the north had lit the whole place up. Majella went over to her washing and had a quick feel of it. It was dry, and the stale ming had gone off it a bit. She filled the kettle and stuck it on. She decided against coffee. It would be a big pot of tay that she'd make, enough to do both her and her ma. She knew her ma wouldn't be fit for food, but Majella fancied her toast. She paused when she heard the unsteady tread of her mother's feet across her bedroom floor towards the bathroom. The toilet flushed after a while, then there was silence. Majella's heart sank, but she dropped the bread into the toaster and got the crockery she needed together. And just as the toast popped, the shower whined into action. Majella buttered her toast and spread the scrapings of the raspberry jam on top. Then she brought her plate and mug into the living room before going back to the kitchen for her ma's mug, the teapot and painkillers. Majella stopped to consider the painkiller options. Clearly her ma was on the move, so she wasn't dying. But she'd still have a head on her. Majella needed her ma to have some fuel in her tank, but for her not to be too mouthy, so she picked Solpadeine. It was pricey stuff, the Solpadeine, and her ma got the Kapake for free, but Majella knew the mix of caffeine and codeine in the Solpadeine made it worth the price. She brought everything in to the coffee table and then settled herself into her da's armchair. She switched on the telly and sat back with her plate of toast in her hand. She heard her ma treading across the bathroom floor. When the door opened, Majella guldered up the stairs.

— There's a pot a tay sitting down here waiting fer ye.

Majella heard her ma shuffle down the stairs. She came into the living room huddled in her grey dressing gown, her hair twisted up in a faded pink hand towel. She perched on the edge of the settee and reached out her two hands for the teapot. From the corner of her eye, Majella watched the pot shake, her ma spilling tea onto the coffee table and the magazines. Her ma picked up the Solpadeine and squeezed out two tablets. She threw them into her mouth and swallowed them down with her tea. Even after all these years, Majella admired her ma's way with tablets. She watched her sat there trembling, her hands clamped tight around the mug, staring at the TV, where Phillip Schofield and Fern Britton were collapsing into giggles over a suggestively shaped root vegetable.

10.27 a.m.
Good list
Item 2: Dallas

Majella'd put on her black trousers and a black top. After staring at her reflection in the mirror, she threw on her grey fleece in the hope that it made her look less like she was ready for a funeral. She had a notion that you should bring a handbag to go see a solicitor, so she hoked out her only one. Majella was ready, which was good – she wasn't anxious about being late. She wasn't worried about her ma getting ready either, for between her greed for what might be coming her way and her love of dolling herself up, Majella knew she'd pull herself together in good time for the appointment. So Majella had time to kill. She lifted her wage packet, pulled the notes out and counted the cash. It was correct to the last penny. Majella had to give Cunter her due – in all years she'd been making up the pay packets, she'd never once done Majella short. Never done her long either, mind you, but never done her short. Majella folded up the money and stuck it in her handbag. She decided to lodge it down the town before heading to the solicitors. But it was too early for that, even. Her ma was still curled up in front of the telly in her dressing gown, nursing her tea and hangover. Majella couldn't face sitting down there across from her. But she was going to go mad sitting in her own room staring at the frigging ceiling. She threw herself down on the bed and grabbed the TV and DVD controls. The *Dallas* theme tune kicked in and Majella lay back. Pam Ewing, she knew, had a date with a tanker.

12.01 p.m.

Item 3.8: Noise: Babies/weans wailing

Majella was stood in the bank feeling very self conscious with her handbag and good black trousers on. She hoped no one would notice how she was decked out. The fella directly in front of her was not decked out. He was a farmer in from the hills, clabbered to his thighs in muck. He was holding the hand of his wee cub, who was dressed the same as his da, though he was barely the height of his da's wellies. Majella didn't like farmers. She didn't like the way they were always whinging in the pub about having no money, but could be seen lodging stacks of cash in the bank. And she didn't like the way they seemed sort of bigger, tougher than town people, as if they were made of something hardier. But mostly she just didn't like the way they smelt, especially after toasting their shite-covered wellies at a radiator for fifteen minutes. Caitriona Meehan finished up her business and moved away from the counter, so Majella swallowed her thoughts and moved up with the queue. She wanted to lodge the most of her wages, to fill the hole left in her account from the duvet. There was just the farmer fella in front of her now. His wee boy had got loose and was standing at the toy corner, watching some wee blonde cuddie talking in an American accent to the plastic bricks she was building with. Majella'd noticed the weans in the estate doing that sometimes. Talking with Brit or Yank accents instead of their own. And then the teenagers talking with that *Friends* accent. All No Ways and Seriouslys and Whatevers. The boy reached his hand out for a brick.

The girl shot her hand out quick as a cat and snatched it away from him. — Excuse me, but I'm playing with these toys?

She spoke like she was asking a question when she was really saying fuck off. Majella was impressed at the cut of her, despite her age. The wee farmer fella took a long look at her and the house she was building, summing up the situation. Then he raised his fist and brought it crashing down on the plastic brick house, shattering it. Everyone turned to gawk as she started to wail. The wee girl's mother finished up at the counter and rushed over to rescue her. The boy was just standing there, quietly. Not smiling, not looking scared, just watching the crying girl and her raging mother.

— Gerard?

He turned around and looked at his father.

— C'mon. S'our turn now.

Gerard followed his father up to the counter. Majella let the mother pass, carrying her snottery daughter, then she moved to the front of the queue. Majella took a gleek at young Gerard, who was standing beside his daddy, his cheeks glowing red. He stared up at Majella for a second. She winked at him. He frowned, looked puzzled, then turned quickly away. Majella felt like smiling.

12.39 p.m.
Item 30.1: Legal stuff: Lawyers

Majella, her ma and her Aunt Marie were all in Paddy McConville's office. The reading of the will had been due at half twelve, but Paddy, staying true to form, was late. Majella was holding out hope that his fine-looking lump of a son would also attend. She figured he would participate, as her granny's death was the first notorious death in the town since the Ceasefire was declared in 1994, and it'd be something he'd be able to talk about back in Belfast with his fancy mates. Majella's ma was sat on her left-hand side, scratching at the dry patches of skin on her bare arms. She was dolled up for the occasion, wearing her good grey trousers with a black top. She'd the best of her gold jewellery on and had taken time over her face. Her crutches were leaning to the side of her chair. She looked well and smelt grand considering the feed of whiskey she'd horsed into herself the night before.

— Well he's takin his frigging time, isn't he?

Majella's ma looked around at both Majella and her Aunt Marie for a reaction. Her Aunt Marie just sat still, staring into space. Her watery blue eyes were red-rimmed and she was in black from head to foot.

— Anyone'd think we'd time tae waste.

Majella's Aunt Marie fired a dirty look at her ma and then turned back to the wall again. Marie took after Majella's granddad. She had his beaky nose, squat wee body and muscular shoulders and arms. She was a shape of woman that wasn't in wild demand in Aghybogey even before the internet had brought the Filipino girls within reach of the more tech-savvy bachelors. She'd never married, although she'd had a few belated offers after Bobby died and her brother'd disappeared and it was thought that the land might fall to her. But she'd turned her nose up at them all, and in the end she'd rented a wee house a few miles from her mother, and seemed happy living on her own up there. Marie and Majella's ma had never got on. Majella's ma said that Marie'd never forgiven her for marrying her big brother and moving him off the mountain and into town. Majella's Aunt Marie said it was because her ma was a trollop. Majella felt like she could understand both points of view. After Majella's da'd disappeared, Marie had stood for Majella at her Confirmation, and then dropped her godmotherly duties. Majella'd never felt any loss on the relationship, for she always thought Marie was more bother than she was worth. Majella turned her head and stared out the window. There was a great view of Aghybogey Diamond from up in McConville's offices. She wouldn't mind a job sitting up there, looking out at everyone with nobody staring back in at you, only dealing with folk through a computer screen. The door opened and they all turned around to see Paddy McConville shuffling in.

— I'm sorry for keeping you waiting ladies. Awful sorry. I had . . .

He paused. They all waited.

— I had . . . business to attend to. Business.

Paddy nodded gravely to himself.

— You're all right, Paddy. Don't you worry yerself.

Majella's ma was smiling her shiny public smile. Majella remembered how it had worked years ago, in shops and pubs. At Mass and out down the town. The men all tripping over themselves to help her and the women half-hating her, half-falling for it at the same time.

— Aherm. We're here to read over the last will and testament of Margaret Anne O'Neill, whose untimely death was a crime! A *terrible* crime.

Paddy held a silence for a few moments. Majella watched as Marie's forehead crumpled and her jowls trembled. Her ma nodded and tutted.

— Och, shockin. Wild thing tae happen tae a widow woman. Wild.

Paddy nodded at her ma. Then there was a silence as he worked his way through the papers on his desk.

— You ladies have been called here as named beneficiaries of Margaret O'Neill's will.

Paddy put his glasses on and peered at the sheet in front of him. Then there was a soft knock at the door and the door handle turned. Paddy's son Michael came in.

— Sorry for keeping you waiting ladies. I was just finishing up a phone call there.

Majella found herself shifting in her seat. Her ma beamed at young Michael McConville.

— You're all right, son.

Michael McConville flashed a professional smile in the direction of Majella's ma while Majella cringed. Then he stepped over to the left-hand side of his father's desk. Paddy McConville looked up from his papers and over at the women.

— Will we begin?

Majella's ma and aunt nodded and Paddy turned his eyes back to the will.

— Margaret made her will some time ago with me. It's a simple will and I'll deal with it as quickly as I might. The first named beneficiary is Nuala O'Neill of seven, Dreggish Park.

Out of the corner of her eye, Majella saw her ma grow more nervous, twisting at her gold wedding band.

— It is stated here that Nuala O'Neill is the daughter-in-law of the deceased, and has been bequeathed the sum of £500 to erect a handsome headstone in the memory of her husband.

Majella blinked, then slowly turned to her ma, who had gone white as a clean sheet.

— Have you any questions about your inheritance Mrs O'Neill?

Majella's ma shook her head.

— The money is held in a trust administered by this firm. When you are ready to access the fund, you can make application to ourselves.

There was a silence, the three women sitting strained and unblinking.

— The second named beneficiary of the will is Marie O'Neill of forty-nine Drumcarney road, Drumcarney. It is stated here that Marie O'Neill is the only daughter of the deceased, and has been bequeathed the sum of £3,000 to spend as she sees fit.

Marie's pudgy cheeks flushed pink. Majella blinked. £3,000? She never suspected that her granny ever had more than was in her purse from one pension day to the next. How in hell had she ever gathered up £3,000? Paddy nodded gravely at Marie, who gripped her handbag tightly to try and hide the tremble that ran through her entire body.

— I will release the money into your possession at your convenience, Miss O'Neill. Have you any questions about your inheritance?

Marie just shook her head. Majella noticed that Marie was struggling to control her shake. She wanted to reach out and put her hand on her to steady her, but she sat still, paralysed by twenty-seven years of rejection. Paddy returned to the will.

— The last named beneficiary is Majella O'Neill of seven, Dreggish Park.

Majella started at the mention of her name. She'd forgotten about her own part in this.

— It is stated here that Majella O'Neill is the only grandchild of the deceased, and has been bequeathed the lands and properties of the deceased. These include ten acres of farmland, on which stands a house in need of substantial repair and a small caravan, which is in sound condition. A rental income of £1,200 per annum is currently generated by the property.

Everything around Majella went black for a moment. Then she found Paddy and his son staring kindly at her. She looked away from them, over at her aunt and ma, who sat open-mouthed. Majella tried to say sorry, but no words came out. Her Aunt Marie turned her burning eyes on Majella and then back to Paddy McConville.

— *She* gets the farm? *She* gets *my* land?

Majella's ma was still staring at her in shock.

— Jellah? Are ye all right?

— That useless lump there that'll take it ann sell it or let the land run tae loss? *She* gets the farm?

Majella caught herself on. — Are there any conditions?

Paddy didn't seem to have heard Majella over her aunt.

— PADDY!

The room went quiet and everyone stared at Majella. She took a reddener, but pressed on.

— Ah was asking, are there any conditions on me getting the farm?

Paddy shook his grey head. — No Majella. It states here that you can do what you will with the farm. It's yours.

Majella could feel her aunt's eyes sizzling on her again. Her ma was staring at Paddy McConville. Majella hoped she wasn't going to ask the question Majella knew she wanted to ask. Not in front of Marie.

— Paddy. Tell us this. What d'ye think the worth a the land would be? Sale value.

Majella stood up awkwardly. Everyone looked at her again. She could feel herself take another reddener.

— Ah'm away out fer a fag.

She grabbed her bag, stumbled past her ma and aunt and clattered down the uncarpeted stairs into the street below. She turned away from the blinding winter sunshine and groped in her bag for her fags. She lit one with trembling hands. The first drag went deep down into her lungs and filled her head with an emptiness she wished she could fall face first into.

1.23 p.m.
Item 16: Booze

After clearing up some paperwork in the solicitor's, Majella'd ended up in Hey Good Cooking with her ma. It didn't seem right to be sat in a restaurant after the news. She knew that it'd look like a celebration to anyone with the gumption to put two and two together. But it was better than them heading to a pub where all the nosey friggers sitting there would get the news out of her ma after a few drinks had oiled her throat.

— Anna wee glass a house red please, Theresa.

Majella groaned internally. She hadn't clicked that there'd be booze on the menu.

— Anything for you tae drink, Majella?

— Just a whaatter, thanks.

— No bother.

The waitress headed off to the bar with the order. Majella watched her ma's gold jewellery flash in the light as she lit a cigarette.

— Well now that was a bitty a surprise, was it not? Eh? Anna pleasant surprise fer a change.

Majella shrugged.

— Well at least ye got some payback for all them cycles ye took up the road when ye were a cuddy.

Majella lifted her napkin and began to twist it in her hands.

— Ann that Marie wan was raging. Pure raging – ready tae spit nails.

— Well she was expecting the farm.

— Ye're dead right, she was expecting the farm. About the only thing that woman's ever expected, that fucken farm.

Her ma leaned in to Majella, tapping her temple with her forefinger.

— There's a wee want there if ye ask me.

Majella shrugged even though she agreed with her ma. There was something different about her Aunt Marie, something odd. She began to smooth the twisted napkin flat on her thigh.

— What about what Granny left you?

Her ma frowned and shook her head. — Money for a headstone? I'm sure Maggie was having a laugh with that.

Majella was sure her granny had taken her will seriously. That the headstone was a message for her ma. A message that hadn't got through.

— I dunno what yer granny was playing at, but I've enough going on right now to keep me occupied. I don't have the health tae be running around erecting gravestones.

Majella had a mental image of her ma running around Aghybogey, erecting gravestones left, right and centre. This image was far from the single headstone she herself had pictured in her head, shadowing her granny's fresh grave, the names of her husband and both sons carved into it.

Theresa returned with her ma's wine in a big glass, and a jug of water for them both. Majella doubted that her ma'd be doing the heavy lifting with the water.

— Och thanks now, Theresa. You're a great girl altogether.

— No bother Mrs O'Neill. No bother.

Theresa headed off towards the kitchen.

— She's a great girl, that. Always helping her ma out. Vera was telling me she brings money back in tae the house ann all too.

Majella shrugged. — Good for her.

There was a silence as her ma lifted the glass of wine to her lips and tasted it. She held the glass in her hand while she swallowed and assessed the taste.

— S'all right suppose. Not as good as thon Tesco stuff Monica brought me for Christmas last.

Her ma lifted the glass to her mouth again and took a slurp. She swallowed, then thrust the glass out to Majella.

— Ye'll have a taste?

Majella shook her head. — Work later. Can't be having any.

— You ann the fucken work. Can ye not take her handy for the day now after news like that? Take a bitty time tae think about things or have a wee celebration tae yerself?

Majella shrugged. Her ma took another swallow of the wine. The glass still hadn't touched the table. They sat in silence until Theresa brought out their starters.

— Gar-lick bread ann a mushroom soup?

— Soup here. Hers is the bread.

Theresa slopped the soup over the side of the bowl as she put it down in front of Majella's ma. Majella tore into her garlic bread as her ma shooed Theresa away from cleaning her soup bowl. When she'd gone back to the kitchen her ma sighed.

— Aye. She's a great girl. Great help tae her whole family.

2.30 p.m.

Item 23: Dirt and disorder

Majella was back in the house, sitting on the armchair in the living room. She didn't know how it'd happened. Although she'd tried to drag the arse out of the meal, she'd finished by quarter past two. It wasn't like her ma'd actually eaten that much. She'd spooned at the soup, eating less than Theresa had spilled, then she'd picked at her chicken and chips. She hadn't taken a dessert, although Majella'd gone to work on the chocolate fudge cake and even ordered a coffee. Still and all, by 2.20 p.m. her ma was scratching at her arms and staring at her empty wine glass. Her second glass. Majella'd sat there in silence. They hadn't spoken since Theresa'd taken the dinner dishes away and brought over the bill, which Majella had paid. Then her ma had said she was thinking of heading to the pub, for a wee wan, just for the day that was in it. Majella'd shrugged and they'd gone their separate ways. She knew the whole town'd be talking by the time she'd get into work. At least she was on at four. And she could even head in a bit early, make it up to Marty for being late the other days. Although it was a Friday, so it was a plenty long enough day anyway.

Majella stretched out into the chair and opened her mouth for a big yawn. She sucked up the shivers that ran through her, then got onto her feet and went into the kitchen. She was tired of it being bogging. She lifted the kettle and put it back down and flicked the ON switch. Then she went to the sink and put on the tap and let it run hot. She squeezed out the dishcloth under the hot water and put a squirt of washing-up liquid on it and started to wipe down the sink. But it was crusty with dirt, and after a while Majella had to admit that the cloth and the liquid weren't up to the job. What she needed was some of that industrial stuff Cunter bought in by the gallon for A Salt and Battered! And a decent scrubber. And a few clear days at the job, with her ma out of the way. As the kettle flicked itself off behind her, Majella dropped the cloth back into the sink, rinsed a mug and turned to make herself a nice cup of tea.

3.32 p.m.
Item 26: Wakes, weddings, christenings, funerals

Majella took a wee nosey into the window of Get the Snip as she was walking past. On a Friday it was usually full of fellas getting their hair done for the night out, so Majella had the chance of seeing a bit of talent. But today it was half empty. Before she was over her disappointment, Majella was startled by the beeping and blaring of car horns from a queue of cars following a Land Rover and trailer around the Diamond with their hazard lights flashing. A man was tied up in the trailer, covered in cow shite, straw and flour, with his head down. Majella continued plodding down the town, listening to all the young fellas and some of the young cuddies roaring as the Land Rover lapped the Diamond a few times, before it headed off up towards the estates. Majella got a second look at the trailer, but the fella in it was too cleastered for her to make him out properly. She knew Marty'd know. She arrived at the door of the chipper, and braced herself for the buzzer as she pushed her way in. Johann-Paul was behind the counter, frowning. Marty obviously wasn't in, and Johann-Paul had set up the takeaway on his own.

— Bout you, Yawn?

— Bout you, Majella? How are you doing?

— Not a bother.

Johann-Paul flipped the counter open for Majella.

— What is happening the man outside? Why is he being punished?

Majella looked outside, but she couldn't figure out what Johann-Paul was talking about.

— Who?

— The man who is going around the town behind the Land Rover. Are they going to kill him?

— Och him? He's just getting a doing for getting married!

— A doing?

Yawn looked at Majella, still concerned.

— Aye. He's getting married, so his mates have tied him up in a trailer and covered him in crap. Now they're trailing him around the town for a laugh.

Johann-Paul looked out the window and frowned. The Land Rover thumped over a speed bump and the fella in the trailer fell over.

— For a laugh?

— Aye.

Majella felt awkward. She supposed it would look a bit cruel to Johann-Paul, so she said what she'd heard other people saying in situations like this.

— Sure it's only a bitta craic.

Johann-Paul put a smile on his face, but his forehead was still creased. — Yes.

Majella scratched her thigh. She wasn't the best at this inter-cultural stuff, though she herself had learned a lot about the world of Aghybogey since Johann-Paul had started in the chipper. He asked all the questions a wean would ask, and Marty took great pleasure in explaining things to him in loud, slow, plain English.

— Ah better get me kit on.

— Yes, Majella. I will stay here.

As Majella walked to the back of the chipper, the buzzer sounded and she could hear the beeps and roars much more clearly until the door swung shut.

— Oh, ho! Did youse see the doing Jimmy Kelly's getting? Young Kerry McCoy'll not be wan bit pleased about that! He'll have tae make sure he washes behind his ears before he stands at the altar the morrow!

Marty was in.

— Clabbered tae the eyeballs! He's got a wile doing altogether.

Marty sounded delighted. Majella turned to see him standing at the window, staring out at the Land Rover and trailer, and young Johann-Paul staring at Marty. She reached into her bag for her overalls.

4.30 p.m.
Item 46: Snobs

Majella watched as the first of the school buses stopped at the head of the Diamond, dropping off the pupils who attended the grammar schools out of town. Majella thought it was weird how everyone went to the same primary schools, but after the Eleven-plus exam they were all divided up. The ones who didn't pass had to stay in the town and go to Saint Christopher's, and the ones who passed chose to buy an expensive uniform, get up for school nearly two hours earlier than everyone else, and then spend over an hour sitting on a rattling bus with a shower of other teenagers to reach whatever grammar school their mas and das wanted them to attend. Majella had passed the Eleven-plus, but she'd refused point blank to be sent miles away to the convent grammar to be sat in a classroom full of girls, being taught by a pile of women and nuns for the next five years of her life. She'd got her way and went to Saint Christopher's. She thought it was strange the way a uniform turned people's heads. Weans who were normal in P7, playing games with everyone else out in the estate, stopped speaking to the St Christopher's kids by Christmas. Even their accents changed, from plain old Aghybogey to poshy-woshy Omagh. The buzzer went off, and Majella turned her eye on the group of girls who slouched in the door. Snobby fuckers, she knew, looking at them. But they still came into A Salt and Battered! for a bite to eat some evenings. Bags of chips mostly, or a curry chip pea, shared out between them. She waited while they stared at the board. Anorexic Annies, the four of them – they'd hardly make one of Majella between them.

— Can we have a large chip, with salt and vinegar?

— Coming up.

Majella shouted the order back to Johann-Paul, though she could tell by the hiss of the fryers he'd thrown it in the minute he'd heard the order. The girls went over and sat on the window with their skinny stick legs poking out from the convent uniform. Aideen had been a convent girl. She'd lasted one whole year there, and then refused to go back. Her ma'd had to place her in Saint Christopher's in the end. She was the odd one out when she joined in second year. All the girls except Majella were paired off into desk mates or best friends. Majella was more friendly with a few of the lads in her year than the cuddies, as she found the lads more straightforward. The teachers had put Aideen and Majella together at the start of second year, and then somehow they'd fallen into step together. Majella liked Aideen's stories of the lesbian PE teacher in the convent, the psycho science teacher and the mad oul nun who was the last of the nuns left alive, so she was let off with anything she did because her actions were considered to be between her and God. It all made Majella glad she'd chosen Saint Christopher's.

— Ready!

Majella plodded down to where Johann-Paul was parcelling up the girls' chips.

— Thanks, Yawn.

She took them to the counter. The girls were still sitting down on the window seat, ignoring her. Majella dumped the chips on the counter.

— Yer chips.

They all looked up at Majella, then looked away. The leader girl got up and lifted the chips.

— Thanks.

She didn't look at Majella when she spoke or when she paid, or when Majella passed her change back. It wasn't that Majella wanted her to look, but she knew the girl's behaviour was designed to be an insult. She watched them dander over to the Diamond. They sat down on an empty bench and then shared out the chips. They ate slowly, like they weren't hungry, before dumping the wrappers in the bin and walking on up the street. Majella was pretty sure it wouldn't be long before one of them would have the chips boked up again behind a locked bathroom door. Waste of good food.

5.10 p.m.
Item 18.1: Periods: PMS

Majella was out from behind the counter, cleaning the big window. It wasn't a job she normally took on, but her back and belly were aching and she wanted to distract herself from it. She knew she'd her period coming on, but she wasn't sure when. Sometimes she was sore for days before she actually started to bleed. She stopped wiping the window, reached back and rubbed herself for a wee minute. It was hard to rub through the nylon of the uniform. Then she started wiping again, watching a couple of oul fellas wander from the bookies to the bar. Majella knew they'd won by the walk of them. All slow and taking their time, savouring the money in their pockets, having a good laugh. The losers were always quick out of the bookies, scurrying home if they were stung, or skiting in for a few jars if they had anything at all left in their pockets. Majella wondered where her ma would be by now, then sighed.

— What's up wi ye, Jelly? Tired or what?

Majella turned around to see Marty propped up on the counter.

— Nothing. Fed up's all.

— Aye. Tell me about it.

They both stood there for a minute, saying nothing. Then Majella went back to wiping the window.

6.01 p.m.
Item 1: Small talk, bullshit, gossip

Majella was leaning at the counter picking the dirt out from under her nails. It wasn't as satisfying as flicking her fingers, but it did. Marty shouted up from the back of the shop.

— Did ah see yerself ann yer ma going in tae Paddy McConville's earlier the day, Jell-ah?

Majella screwed her eyes shut. — Ah dunno. Did ye?

Marty sidled up to the counter beside her. — Well. Maybe ah didn't see youse myself. But maybe ah heard it said that youse were up tae see Paddy McConville today.

Majella opened her eyes and studied the fat-splattered ceiling. — Well, then you should've a brave notion of where I was.

— So youse were up with him?

Majella dug a wodge of salt out from under her index fingernail, then nodded. Marty leaned in against the counter, propping himself up casually on his left arm.

— So youse had a bit a legal business then?

— Aye.

— Like a will or something?

— Aye.

— Yer granny's will?

Majella nodded and moved onto her right-hand fingernails.

— So yer granny'd a will then?

— Aye.

— Well now a will's a great business. Cuts out any rowing. There's no arguing wi a will.

— Ah dunno about that.

Majella could've clipped her own lug. Marty was straight in.

— Oh right. Was there a disagreement over who got what then?

— Not really.

Marty was quiet for a moment, as he figured out his new angle.

— Well, ah suppose you ann yer mother'd hardly argue Marie's right til the farm, would youse?

— Naw, we wouldn't.

— So what did yer granny leave ye?

— Not a wile pile. Few photos ann stuff.

— Och, that's lovely. It's nice tae have the photos fer the memories, like.

Majella had cleaned out all the dirt from under her nails. She splayed her fingers in front of her, then swept the little pile of dirt onto the floor.

— Aye. Photos are great.

— Did she mention yer da at all in the will?

Majella turned to look at the fish with the cock. Someone had added pubic hair and a spurt of cum.

— Sure, what's tae mention?

Majella left the counter and went to the back storeroom to count the chicken nuggets.

7.14 p.m.
Item 6: Cunter

Majella passed Patsy Mulherne the squeezy ketchup bottle so she could add her own measure of sauce to her chicken burger. Patsy shook the sauce down to the squeezy lid and then took aim. She squirted out a big blob of red sauce right in the centre of the burger, and then circled the perimeter of the meat twice. Majella wondered if Patsy ever had the urge to write her own name. Sometimes Majella put an M on the inside of a burger, then squished the bun down tight on top before anyone could see. Patsy gave Majella back the sauce.

— Thanks for that, Majella.

— No bother, Patsy.

Patsy placed the bun carefully back on top of the burger meat, and then closed the polystyrene lid over. She carried the burger to the door in her hands, careful to keep it level. Majella didn't understand how the woman was so particular with the sauce and the box and the carrying, but still ate the shite that was inside the bun. Majella knew that the chicken burgers were described as *Chicken Fillet Burgers – Best of Breast* on the board, but she also knew that the boxes they got delivered to their storeroom were labelled *Economy Chicken Burgers*. She'd once read an article on mechanically recovered meat and had never touched it since. She stuck to her fish. She stood back from the counter and stretched, feeling the cloth strain against the seams. Then she felt a spurt of wet soak into her knickers. She restrained a groan.

— Ah'm away til the bogs, Marty. Mind the front, will ye?

Marty nodded so Majella went out the back door of the chipper and into the dark alleyway, where she groped for the toilet door. She opened it and pulled the light cord. A naked lightbulb lit up close to her head. She closed and locked the toilet door, then pulled her overalls up so she could tug down her joggers and knickers. She sat down on the freezing toilet seat and glanced at her knickers. She was on the rag. As she sat there, the water in the toilet plopped as more blood trickled from her. She sat for a few seconds, pishing and letting the first bit of blood flow, then she reached for the tampon in her jogger pocket. Majella had never been fond of tampons. They'd never seemed all that natural. At school, the girls had shared whispered stories about the evils of tampons.

Well my mammy says that when she was at school there was this girl who used tampons ann then she went in tae a faint ann she just died ann that was because a the tampon . . . my mam says that Father McAteer says that girls who use tampons are only half a virgin so they are ann men won't want them . . . my sister says that there was this girl in her class that used one ann it got lost up inside her ann they had tae take her tae hospital tae do a big operation tae get it out again ann it was men what did the operation . . . there was this girl in the convent ann she used this tampon that this woman lent her when she was over in England ann then she got AIDs . . .

It'd taken Majella years to get one up her. None of the advice she'd read on the instructions leaflets or teenage magazines about being relaxed and putting one foot up on the bath in a warm bathroom and gently inserting the tampon had ever worked for her. Instead, she'd got lamped with Aideen one night before heading to Donegal town, and then had a go. That had worked, though getting drunk every time she needed to insert a tampon was not a sustainable tactic.

Majella stood up and rubbed her arse to bring a bit of warmth back to the skin before pulling her knickers and joggers up. She washed her hands and shook them dry. Cunter never bothered about a towel for the outside toilet. She'd installed a hand dryer in the inside toilet. There was even soap. And she kept the door locked except for when herself, her husband or Environmental Health were around. Majella hurried back into the chipper. Young Johann-Paul was at the fryer. Majella looked up at the counter – Marty was chatting to Serena Lynch who was giving Majella a funny look. Majella hated 'looks'. As hard as it was to figure out what people meant from the actual words they used, she found figuring looks out near impossible. She ignored Serena and grabbed a napkin to wipe her hands dry. Marty pushed Serena's food over at her. — Well sure now, ye'd better take yer chips or they'll be getting coul.

There was an odd tone to Marty's voice, that Majella couldn't place. It was like he was an actor starting a new role on *Coronation Street* that he hadn't right settled into.

— Thanks Marty. Oul Billy'd be roarin at me if ah don't run! See ya, Majella.

— Bye.

Majella watched Serena run out of the chipper, setting the buzzer off again.

— What's her problem?

— What d'ye mean what's her problem?

— Why was she looking at me like that?

To Majella's eye, Marty now looked shifty. — Ah didn't see no look.

Majella stood there impassively, staring at Marty. She could do that for as long as she liked. Marty usually cracked under her stare and would start gabbling.

— Well I'm glad to see you two are keeping yourselves busy.

Majella sighed. Cunter was at her back.

— Hiya Mrs Hunter.

— Majella. Marty. Looks like young Johann-Paul here's the only person doing any work.

Majella said nothing. Cunter'd find fault no matter. But Marty couldn't hold his tongue.

— Och now, Mrs Hunter, sure we've everything done for the minute. She's ticking over rightly.

Majella closed her eyes, thinking red rag to a bull. Cunter's voice started up again, several painful octaves higher.

— Really? Nothing to be done?

Cunter started to look around the chipper.

— That floor could do with a proper good clean. And when's the last time the counters were stripped and wiped? Has the storeroom been swept this week? Has anyone cleaned the toilet since I was last in?

Nothing was ever clean enough, nothing was ever good enough. Majella moved to the counter and put her blank face on and stared at Cunter's left ear. Majella knew Cunter hated that. She watched Cunter's gaze flicker over and past her, then saw her eyes widen and her face flush pink.

— And *WHAT* is *THAT*?

Majella turned around. She'd forgotten about the fish cocks and cunts. She tried to contain the smile that welled up from somewhere deep in her belly. Marty jumped in.

— Och just some young wans in the other night when it was busy ann we didn't see what they were at.

— Well you can see it now! And what were you going to do about it?

Marty looked at Majella. Majella shrugged so it was Marty who had to reply. — We were gonna let ye know so you could paint over them?

Cunter was still pink-faced, frowning her skin into deep angry wrinkles. — Well I'll tell you what you're going to do about it. You are going to get a cloth and a bucket and you are going to clean that muck off my good walls, that's what you're going to do.

Cunter stared at them both, her pale blue eyes bulging. Majella's smile had drowned in the acid bath of her belly. Cunter turned on her heel and left.

Marty looked at Majella, frowning. — Ah'll get the bucket.

Majella didn't argue.

8.11 p.m.
Item 1: Small talk, bullshit and gossip

Marty and Majella were outside in the alley. Young Johann-Paul was in charge of the shop floor. Marty described this as a process of delegation and a valuable opportunity for a junior employee to acquire experience. Majella called it dossing. Marty leaned in to Majella and lit her fag, then lit his own from the same match. Marty was old-fashioned about some things. Using matches instead of lighters was one of them. Majella loved the smell of a struck match. Marty sat back on a beer keg and took a quick series of puffs into his lungs, then exhaled. Majella shivered in the cold.

— So what's this ah hear about you being an heiress, then?

Majella frowned. — What d'ye mean?

— Och, now, Jelly, ah just heard ye had a bit a good fortune.

Majella took a deep slow drag of her cigarette. — Did ye now?

— Ah did.

— Ann who toul ye that?

— Och now. Just the word is you came in tae a bit a land.

— Was it Andrea Gurney?

Marty shifted on his beer keg.

Majella snorted. — It was Andrea Gurney.

— Well now, she might've said tae me, but ah've been hearing all sorts all day.

— Granny left the farm tae me. You already know that. I don't know what else you're fishing for.

Majella dropped her half-smoked fag on the ground and walked back into the chipper, letting the door slam behind her.

8.30 p.m.
Item 43: The English

There was a bit of a rush on. A dose of people had piled into the chipper and everyone was getting narky about waiting – Majella had learned long ago that hungry people weren't patient. She'd been scribbling orders down at a fierce rate, keeping things moving along so that at least people felt that they were being seen to. But now she had Fidelma O'Brien at the head of the queue humming and hawing over whether to have onion rings or garlic mushrooms. Majella knew Fidelma would end up ordering the garlic mushrooms for onions repeated on her. She knew Sean McCormick was standing starving behind Fidelma, ready to order his usual curry chip onions and peas, and she could see Mary Byrne after him, who only ever came in for a fish supper. Majella knew that because there was a queue, everyone expected her to take their orders in order, a practice that did not always make sense. Later in the night, when people were more drunk she'd be able to give Sean McCormick the eye, and say 'the usual?' and he'd nod back and she'd slip his order in before Fidelma. But if she tried that now there'd be murder. Outside a gang of fellas started roaring, singing Hay Baby. Nearly everyone in the chipper turned around to have a gawk at Jimmy Kelly boozing it up before his wedding in the morning. Marty'd explained to Majella that Jimmy'd already had the proper stag do over in Newcastle, but now his English cousins were over for the wedding and he'd taken them out to crawl Aghybogey.

Majella watched a gang of fellas dressed almost identically in checked shirts and blue jeans stumble past the window shouting — Oo! Ah! They were lashed out of their heads, with Jimmy Kelly in the middle of them. He looked rightly cleaned up from his earlier doing. One of the English lads stopped at the window, gave it a batter, then lifted his shirt up and shook his beer gut before staggering after his mates. Majella was pretty sure that she – and the other females in the chipper – did not want to be his girl.

— Gar-lick mushrooms. Ah'll take the gar-lick mushrooms.

Majella could sense the relief steaming off Sean McCormick. She scribbled Fidelma's order down, the whole time picturing the English lad's belly wobbling in the window.

9.39 p.m.

Item 11.2: Bad smells: Bad breath

Marty'd done a great job on the fish cocks and cunts. He'd rubbed so hard that now all you could see was a pale glow of genitalia where the thick black lines had been. Majella jerked as the buzzer went. Fat Suzy Loughlin hefted her way into the shop. For once she didn't stop to stare at the menu. She came straight up to Majella, breathing heavily. Majella caught a powerful ming off Suzy's breath, a sick sort of a stench that made Majella straighten up and move out of the range of Suzy's breath.

— Well Suzy.

— Majella.

Suzy didn't look well. She turned her head and rifted loudly. The smell from her guts wafted over to Majella again.

— You well, Suzy?

— Ah'm not well. Ah've been dying all day with the skitter ann the boking. Fucken dying.

— Awright.

— Ann the only thing ah ate yesterday was the shite ah bought from this place.

— Awright.

— Fucken dying all day ah was. Boking. Running tae the toilet.

Majella had never seen Suzy running. She tried not to picture her boking. — Mmmmmm.

— Ann poor Eamonn. He's lying yit. Not able tae rise outta his bed.

Eamonn. That was his name. Eamonn What-dye-may-call-him.

— Och, God now.

— Him the same way as me. The skitter ann the boking.

— Mmmmmm.

Suzy paused, the sweat gleaming on her forehead. She wiped her face, then rifted again. Majella took a quick side step over to the napkins and gave them a shuffle.

— Well. What are ye gonna do about my food poisoning?

One of the few employee-training sessions Cunter had arranged for Majella and Marty had been around alleged cases of food poisoning, so Majella was prepared.

— I'm afraid A Salt and Battered! can't take responsibility for your food poisoning. But as a gesture in recognition of your distress, the establishment can offer you and Eamonn a free meal.

— Wan free meal?

Majella nodded.

Suzy looked raging, but soon paled. She went to the window and squished herself onto the sill for a rest. — Ah'll have a think about what ah want.

— Grand.

Majella let her eyes focus out the door as Suzy let another big rift out of her, then stared up at the menu hungrily. Majella suspected Suzy hadn't even noticed that they'd got the light fixed.

10.05 p.m.
Item 47: Shiftiness and double dealing

Majella watched the clock. It was after ten and yet Jimmy Nine Pints had not been in to lay his five pound note on the counter for his sausage supper.

Majella turned to Marty. — No sign of Jimmy Nine Pints the night.

Marty shifted on his feet and kept his eyes on the fryers. — Naw no sign.

The chipper was crowded and it was hard to follow the conversation with Marty, but Majella tried. — Not like him to miss his supper.

Marty snatched another order off the board and read it closely. — Naw. Must be something up.

Marty worked on. Majella was sure she could hear the ghost of Jimmy and Marty's laughter over the spit and froth of chip fat.

11.01 p.m.
Item 3.4: Noise: Shutters in work

Majella and Marty were at the counter. It'd been busy enough for the last hour. There was a lock of young wans standing in the chipper. Half of them were getting food before they got plastered, the other half were just in out of the cold. Outside a load of fellas were gathering up in the Diamond, waiting for their buses to open. The buses never let anyone on early, no matter how cold it was. Majella knew it was a wise enough policy, for the longer they were all on the bus, the bigger the clean-up would be at the end of the night. There were only a few cuddies in the Diamond – most of them had the wit to stay in the bars away out of the cold. Julie-Anne Peoples cleared her throat at the counter to let Majella know she was finally ready to give her order.

— What can ah get chew?

— Plain chip.

Majella scribbled the order down. Julie-Anne Peoples was hardly fifteen. And her wee friends weren't much above that. Majella reckoned they'd share the chips between them to save their money for drink. Majella stared out the window. The lads outside were drinking and squaring up to a few of the Prods who were standing outside the Duke Inn, drinking their beers. The English fellas were in the thick of it, jeering and throwing shapes. Majella thought they'd better watch themselves, for once a fight started, there'd be more than one side happy to kick an English head in.

Julie-Anne Peoples stared out with one eyebrow raised. — Them'uns are just looking a fight.

Majella nodded while Marty piped up from behind the fryers.

— Who's looking a fight?

— Them'uns outside.

Marty came up to the counter, and stood by Majella watching the craic outside. Majella kept her eye on what was happening as she took down a few more orders. When things happened, they happened fast. Someone threw a bottle at the Prods and when it shattered against the wall everyone went buck mad. Majella and Marty watched the fight with detachment until one of the English fellas bounced off the window and fell to the ground roaring and clutching his face. Marty jumped into action.

— Ah'll get the door. You get the shutters, Jelly.

Majella hit the shutter buttons as Marty threw the counter up and raced over to the door and locked it. The shutters squealed as they were grinding their way down. She watched the bottles flying outside. A gang of fellas had another fella on the ground and they were laying into him.

Johann-Paul had come up from the fryers. — There is some trouble, yes?

— Aye.

Majella watched a few cuddies screeching and hanging onto their fellas, trying to hold them back from the fight. The last they saw before the shutters closed down was an English fella lying on the ground with a couple of Prods laying into him with their boots. Once the shutters were secured, Marty unlocked the door and propped it open. Julie-Anne Peoples was upset.

— How are we gonna get out? Ah've a bus tae Letterkenny the night!

— Ah'll let youse out the side once youse get your food.

Johann-Paul went back to the fryers while Marty moved up close to the letter and parcel slot in the door shutter.

— Ah'll take the orders, Jelly.

Majella knew that Marty didn't want to miss a thing – taking the orders at the door meant he'd keep a good eye on what was happening outside. Oul Brendy O'Donnell moved away from gawking out the slits in the shutters and came up and leaned on the counter in front of Majella. Majella tensed up. She wasn't a fan of Brendy O'Donnell.

— Suppose there's worse places tae be stuck, eh? We'll not starve any roads.

Majella moved back from Brendy O'Donnell's garlic breath. — Naw.

There was a rattling at the door shutter.

— Hi! Hi! Are youse open?

Marty leaned into the parcel slot. — What canna get you?

— Daddy burger ann onion rings ann chips ann gravy.

— No bother.

Majella'd already written the order down. The window shutters rattled again as someone bounced off them. Majella went down to pass the new order to Johann-Paul. She was tired and she was sweaty. And she wanted a drink.

11.59 p.m.
Item 5.6: Scented stuff: Aftershave

Majella stepped out into the yard. It was now freezing and she shivered in the cold. She lit her fag, then stepped in against the wall out of the breeze. She clamped her free arm around herself and took a quick drag of her fag before slowly exhaling. The cold had curtailed the action in the street outside. Everyone had fucked off to wherever, leaving the police lurking in their armoured cars. Majella turned as the back door of The Full Cup opened. She hoped it was Peader changing a barrel but instead it was Damien Devine, who sometimes worked there. He was leading some cuddy in a miniskirt by the hand. Majella had noted that miniskirts were back in after a relatively short run of hot pants. Majella caught the reek of Damien's aftershave from where she stood. She watched him push the young wan up against the back wall, near the walls of kegs, where they started snogging the face off each other. Majella watched on, taking quiet puffs on her fag every now and then. It wasn't long before Damien had pulled your one's skirt up and she'd pulled her knickers down. Majella could hear the clunk of Damien's belt as he loosed it. Majella wondered that they weren't foundered with the cold. She had another suck on her fag while they worked away. Then quite quickly, to Majella's surprise, it was over. She dropped her spent fag and rubbed it out with her foot. The two at the far end of the alley didn't hear her. Majella heard the rasp of Damien's zip and the slap of his leather belt tightening. The wee doll was fixing at her skirt and hair, a somewhat sulky air about her. Damien headed in the door without looking back, and she went after him. Majella shivered with cold and hurried back indoors. It took longer than usual for her nipples to soften in the oily heat of the chipper.

12.20 a.m.

Item 9.7: Make-up: Fake tan

Majella was sweeping out the back of the chipper. She'd a bad belly on her with the cramps and she couldn't be doing with facing the ones out front, even if it was quiet. She'd already swept the storeroom and left the door open to air it out a bit. Johann-Paul was at the fryers while Marty was holding the fort at the counter, admiring Breda McElvaney's tan.

— That's some colour ye have on ye the night!

— S'not bad, is it?

— 'Tis not indeed. Ann that didn't come outtay a bottle now, did it?

Majella always wondered how Marty knew the difference between the ones who'd plastered on the Fake Bake and the ones who'd gone away to the sun.

— Did not. Not unless ye can squeeze two weeks in Bang Cock in tae a bottle!

— Jesus Christ. Ah wouldn't imagine they can!

Marty and Breda stood, cackling together. Majella was curious about Bangkok. She thought it had an unfortunate name, like Muff outside of Derry. But then they probably made the most of it, like Muff with its Muff festival and Muff diving club. Muff wasn't blessed with the weather however. Majella reckoned Bangkok was sunny enough if the colour of Breda McElvaney was anything to go by. Holidays had gone mad in recent years, with everyone flying off to all arts and parts at all times of the year. When she was wee they did little beyond get the odd day at Bundoran during the two weeks when everyone who worked for the factory got given their holidays. She remembered the proper holiday they'd had that once, after her da'd fixed up Brian Carey's oul Ford so it could manage a trip to England and back. In return Brian had offered her da the loan of his caravan at Bundoran. Majella remembered him landing home with a red bucket and blue spade in either hand, which he'd raised triumphantly in front of them both.

— We're going on our holidays.

Her ma'd been sitting at the kitchen table, drinking a mug of coffee. — Holidays? Like we can afford tae be gallivanting off on holidays?

— Brian Carey's given me the keys tae his caravan for factory week. We'll have the whole place tae ourselves.

— His caravan up in Bundoran?

— Aye.

Majella remembered the thrill that had gone through her. A caravan at the beach.

— Hardly Tenerife, is it?

Majella saw the sparkle fade in her da's eyes. Her ma cracked on, regardless.

— Where's he off tae that he doesn't need his keys?

— Taking Caroline ann the weans tae see his brother who has the cancer over in Dagenham.

Her ma'd sniffed at that and taken a gulp of coffee. That was when her da'd given her the red bucket and blue spade. Majella had taken them outside to the concrete back yard, where she'd practised digging sand, just so's she could be ready. In the end even her ma'd warmed up to the trip, and had taken herself off down the town and bought some new clothes. Majella remembered her laying out a collection of short shorts, pretty T-shirts and miniskirts. By the time they climbed into her da's wee car ready to start the drive to Bundoran, her ma was in great form, all smiles and lipstick, blinking behind her new sunglasses, waving at the neighbours. Majella was sitting in the back of the car with her red bucket and blue spade, feeling self-conscious in a pair of tight pink shorts her ma'd forced her into. They played the radio up loud the whole way down, her ma singing, the windows open, the sun shining fit to split the stones. They'd stopped for ice cream in some wee town and dandered around, licking their cones. When they arrived in Bundoran, Majella's da parked the car outside the caravan. They all stood by as he opened the door. Then Majella's ma had rushed in, pulling off her sunglasses. Majella'd followed, clutching her bucket and spade. The caravan had smelt funny. Damp. Fishy. There was a tang of gas in the air that caught at the back of Majella's throat. But none of that mattered. They were on holiday with the sun shining and the soft fiss of the sea all around.

— Ann the lady boys. Ye wouldn't believe the cut a them! They were all over the shop at Pat Pong's. Put ye tae shame with how gorgeous they are!

— Ah now, Breda. Us Irish fellas want the real thing. The real thing.

Majella glanced up at Marty and Breda, still carrying on at the counter, then back down to the pile of dirt in front of her brush.

— Ah'm told them fellas is even better than the real thing!

1.27 a.m.
Item 16: Booze

The chipper was bunged. Majella had long stopped asking people what she could get them. She was just trying to take the orders down and get them out, trying not to fuck things up, making sure that she only took one order from everyone, for some people were so plastered they couldn't remember if or what they'd ordered.

sausagesupperneggfryrice
Daddyburgerannonionringsannchipsanngravy

cheesyshippeassanngravy
pintamilkannacurrychipannpeez
doubletubbagarlicmayonaze
ferfucksakehowlongammawaiting?
fishsupperanntwoCokespleez
batterburgerannchipsannressauce
keepyerhandstilyerselfyoufucker

The free clock on the wall kept on ticking.

2.23 a.m.

Item 34.1: Fighting: Physical fights

Majella opened the door. She could tell straight away her ma was still down the town on the lock. She kept her guard up all the same, for her ma could land back at any minute. Majella hurried to the kitchen and stuck her food in the microwave. Then she headed up the stairs to her room, where she threw on the fan heater for a bit of heat and took her trainers and bra off. Her boobs felt sore now they were loose, so she gave them a wee rub to ease them. She heard the microwave ping down in the kitchen and itched to run down to her food. But she knew it was best to have everything organised so she could just get into bed with her food and stay there. So she headed to the loo and changed her tampon for a night-time pad and gave her hands and face a quick rub. She found a couple of co-codamol and swallowed them down. She knew she should give her teeth a rub, but she didn't want to ruin the taste of her supper. She nipped down the stairs and grabbed her plate and food from the microwave. The thick steam wafted right up her nose, making her mouth water, so she took the stairs two at a time. The stairs sounded a protest against this break in routine, but Majella bulled on. She locked the bedroom door behind her and sighed in relief.

Her bedroom had warmed up, so she flicked the heater off with her toe and settled herself into bed. It still didn't feel right to be in the new duvet and sheets with her fish and chips, but she felt safe and warm. She began to eat, pushing the chips and fish into her mouth, swallowing the hot food quickly, enjoying the feeling of it filling her belly. She wanted to be thinking about nothing. But she kept coming back to that wee caravan, her ma drinking only tea, her da reading the *Mirror*. She could see the three of them on the beach, her ma lying on a towel, with her tiny bikini and big sunglasses, ignoring yet savouring the fellas gawping at her. She remembered the way her da stripped to his swimming trunks even on the cloudy days, how the white of his back went red while his brown neck and arms went darker. They'd eaten out every day, catching snatches of the news on the Irish radio stations that made the North sound like one of those distant, war-torn countries you'd hear of from time to time, and for which you'd feel momentary sympathy, then try to forget. She remembered watching the rain bate down while they sheltered in a café, and them heading to the arcades to feed two penny pieces into the slot machines. They'd played poker for matchsticks in the caravan and ate ice cream every day. Their wee holiday had been boring and brilliant until it all went tits up the day a man who said he was her Uncle Paddy had come up to them in the Sea Shell Café when they were having their tea. Majella remembered that her da'd not been wild pleased to see the man and that her ma had barely spoke to him. But he'd hung on around them like a fly around shite, dirning on about nothing Majella could understand, droning on when everyone else at the table and all around them had gone silent. He'd asked Majella which caravan were they staying in, and she'd told. She knew from her ma's face that she'd done the wrong thing. Uncle Paddy had smiled at Majella and said he'd drop into them, and then her ma'd told him to Fuck Right Off and he'd looked all offended, and her da'd said — Easy now Nuala, easy. Her Uncle Paddy'd left the café, all the time asking, generally, to everyone sitting there, what had he ever done to offend anyone? After he'd left, Majella's ma lit up a cigarette. Normally she gave out yards when she was upset. But that day she'd just sat there smoking, saying nothing. She came around again later on in the amusements after winning the £5 jackpot on the slots. She bought a huge wad of candyfloss and shared it with Majella. And things were grand until the next day when the three of them were down at the beach. Majella'd needed to pish. She didn't like the smelly public toilets near the beach because she'd heard her ma say that someone had once given birth to a baby in there and left it to die on the toilet floor. Majella felt the ghost of that baby lick around her every time she went in, so she preferred to race up to the caravan to pee on her own. It was unlocked, for nobody ever locked anything in the caravan park over the summer. Majella'd opened the flimsy door and stepped in. The curtains were pulled over against the light, so she smelt him before she saw him.

— Well, Majella. Are ye not coming over tae say hello tae yer oul Uncle Paddy?

He was sat in her da's chair, smoking a fag. Majella hesitated, then stepped over to her uncle. She stopped when she met with the reek of beer. He'd a blue plastic bag full of tins on the floor beside him.

— Have ye not gotta kiss fer yer Uncle Paddy?

Majella shook her head. Paddy leaned over, picked up his beer tin and supped from it.

— Ye're not much like yer ma.

Majella stood on, watching his bloodshot eyes slide over her body.

— Not like how ah pictured a daughter a hers at all.

Majella didn't move. She didn't like Uncle Paddy. And it wasn't just the smell off him. She watched him watching her, but pretending he wasn't. Pretending he was interested in his beer. She'd seen her ma do that. Pretend to be drinking her tay or reading a magazine, but really watching whatever Majella was doing, ready to pounce on her. And then her Uncle Paddy pounced. But Majella'd been ready. She scarted back out of reach and he fell back into his chair.

— Well that's not wile nice, is it? Running away from yer uncle when he wants tae give ye a hug.

Majella said nothing and stood where she was. She didn't like the way she was up near the sink, with her uncle between her and the door.

— Naw. Ye're not a nice wee cuddy. Probably spoilt rotten by yer ma ann da.

Her Uncle Paddy swallowed the last of his beer, then crushed the can in his hand and tossed it on the floor. That annoyed Majella. It wasn't his caravan. It wasn't even their caravan. And they'd been keeping it real nice.

— You should pick that up.

Her uncle stared at her. — What did you say?

— You should pick that up. S'not your caravan.

Her uncle sat there looking at her with his mouth open.

— Ann s'not your caravan either from what ah've heard, ye wee trollop. Ann ah'll do what ah like innit.

Majella watched as her uncle pulled at his zip and opened it. Then he pulled his cock out.

— Ah'll do whatever the fuck ah like in it.

He stood up and took a step over towards Majella, his cock in his hand. He stopped halfway, staring at her, then he began to pish all over the caravan floor. The smell of it sickened Majella. He'd just dribbled to a stop when the caravan door opened. Majella's ma stepped in, her da coming behind. It took a few seconds for her ma's eyes to adjust to the light. Majella took a step backwards away from the soggy carpet.

— You dirty basturd. What the fuck are you doing in mah caravan? What the fuck are you doing with mah wean? You fucken dirty basturd.

Her Uncle Paddy stood there, slowly pushing his cock back into his trousers. Before he could zip himself up, Majella's ma threw herself at him, scratching at his face. Her uncle whacked into her ma with his fist and then his foot. But that was as far as he got for Majella's da was suddenly on top of him. Majella backed away as far as she could and watched the two men fighting, feeling the caravan shake. Eventually her da bucked her uncle out the door and down the steps. He landed on his arse in the grass outside and started scrambling backwards. Her da jumped out the door and chased him out of the caravan park. Majella watched her ma sitting crying on the wet carpet. Later that night, her ma'd opened the rest of her Uncle Paddy's beers and put them to her mouth one after another, until they were gone.

The next day Majella remembered, her ma'd been lying in bed. So her da'd taken her to the beach. Just the two of them. They'd paddled in the water and he'd got her an ice cream. He'd made a real pet of her that day. He checked over and over again that her Uncle Paddy'd not hugged or kissed Majella. Kept saying her uncle'd not be back in a hurry, that he'd seen to that. When they returned to the caravan for lunch, they found her ma'd gone. Her da had fixed Majella a quick jam sandwich, then taken her back over to the beach. He started digging a hole with her. And when he thought she was all into it, he said he had to go up the town to find her ma, that he'd only be gone a minute and then he'd come for her. Majella had kept digging the hole while he was walking off, in case he'd look back at her. And she'd kept digging for a good bit after that in case he came to get her as fast as he said he would. When the hole was deep enough for her to sit in, she put down her blue spade and stepped into it, and sat there waiting. She'd waited until her hunger got the better of her. Then she'd picked up her bucket and spade and walked to the caravan, where she made another jam sandwich and put herself to bed.

Saturday

10.07 a.m.
Item 18.4: Periods: Blood

Majella jerked awake. She was pretty sure the crash she heard had come from the kitchen. She lay still, waiting to hear what would happen next. After a moment, she recognised the sound of her ma treading on the first step at the bottom of the stairs. Majella closed her eyes and stretched into her bed, face down in her pillow. A thump came from next door when her ma fell into bed. Majella sighed and turned her face to the wall. Turning over was a mistake, for it set the blood flowing. She wedged her right hand between her legs, then got up, keeping her legs tight together in the hope she could hold back the gush of blood until she got to the loo. She shuffled to the bathroom and over to the toilet, then pulled down her pants and sat with relief. She checked the pad. It had held through the night so her pants and joggers weren't destroyed. But she was lucky she'd got up when she did. She sat until the last of the blood trickled, then dripped to a halt, then she cleaned herself up so she could grab another few hours in bed.

11.11 a.m.
Item 16.2: Booze: Other people's hangovers

Majella blinked, listening to the gulders of the weans playing on the grass outside. She wondered what it would be like to have a few weans about her. She tried to picture herself with maybe five or six, or even a dozen. She knew she wasn't likely to even get to five weans unless she met someone and swung into action within the next year or so. Long ago, Majella had decided that if she was ever to have weans, she'd have more than one. One child was such a miserable frigging number. She'd liked having her own bed, her own room growing up. She'd been told she was lucky never having to share her toys or books or parents with anyone else. But Majella hadn't liked being an only child. She'd been an oddity at school, where most people had at least three or four brothers and sisters.

Spoilt rotten you are . . . yer mammy ann daddy have you spoilt rotten coz there's only you.

For a long time Majella had believed what she'd been told and had seen herself as a spoilt brat, but she took comfort in the idea that she had it better than all the other weans in her class. When she was old enough to understand some of what was going on in other people's houses, she realised that she wasn't spoilt. There'd never been room for a spoilt child in their family with her ma sucking up all the air in every room. Later on, she understood her ma's monologues in the kitchen about Majella's difficult birth, her pointed references to things 'Gone Wrong Down There'. She understood only too well when her ma described her da's disappointment at being left without the wee boy he'd been wanting. Majella's ma would say it was sad to think that with Bobby dying childless and Marie mouldering away as a spinster up in the hills, the family name was going to go to loss, ending with Majella. Majella didn't understand why her da's name would have to end when she married. In her early teens Majella'd decided that she'd only marry the sort of fella who'd take her name and give the weans her name. She reckoned that, for the right fella, she'd consider letting him keep his name and she'd keep her own name, and the weans could take her name. Majella smiled to herself. She'd had her notions back then, all right. She sighed and turned over. She was restless. Waking early meant that the day stretched out even longer in front of her. Hours and hours of boredom, of lying about the house listening to her ma whine about her hangover. Majella's belly rumbled, so she figured she might as well get up and have breakfast before her ma'd stir. That way she might get a bit of peace.

11.21 a.m.
Item 33: Ornaments

Majella walked into the kitchen and stepped on something crunchy. She knelt down to have a look. There was a tiny china head in one place, and a lump of frilly pink skirt in another. She realised it was the dancing posh people ornament that her granny'd got for her ma and da one Christmas. It had embodied two aristocrats from olden times, the fella in a wig and knickerbockers, the woman in ringlets and a hooped skirt, both cleastered in lipstick and rouge. Her ma must've taken it down from the mantelpiece before dropping it in the kitchen. It was smashed into wee bits. Not even her da, who'd been so good at fixing things, could've fixed this mess. Majella stepped over the broken bits, grabbed the dustpan and brush, and began to sweep the fragments into a pile.

1.28 p.m.
Item 23: Dirt and disorder

Having eaten her breakfast in the living room, Majella went out to the kitchen and dumped her plate and mug in the sink. She would see to them later. She hoked in the second drawer down until she found a pair of scissors. They were an old but good pair of dressmaker's scissors that her da'd got out of the factory when they'd ordered a new load in. Nearly everyone in the estate had the same pair, still doing rightly, though the factory itself was shut up and derelict. Majella went into the living room and sat down on the settee. She pulled her old duvet onto her lap and started cutting into it.

2.31 p.m.
Good list
Item 8: Cleaning

Majella gathered up the slices of duvet that were scattered around her and shoved them into a couple of blue plastic bags. The duvet didn't amount to much now that it was cut up. Wee bits of filling scattered around everywhere and stuck to her clothes. Her hand had blistered from where she'd held the scissors. She carried the bag through the kitchen and opened the back door. She flipped the wheelie bin lid back, dropped the bags in and then let the lid fall. Majella headed back inside and went to the cupboard under the stairs for the hoover. She plugged it into the hall socket, then hesitated a moment. She pictured her ma sleeping up the stairs in her bed and she paused to flick her fingers, rocking on the balls of her feet. Then she came to a decision. She pressed the ON button and began to hum in tune with the hoover as she moved into the living room.

2.39 p.m.
Item 23: Dirt and disorder

The hoover was fucked, spewing out more through the filter end than it was picking up through the nozzle end. Majella hit the OFF button and listened to the whine dying down. There was still no noise off her ma upstairs. She knelt down and opened the hoover up. The bag was full as a tick, ready to burst. Majella wasn't surprised – she couldn't remember the last time she'd seen it changed. She went out to the bottom drawer in the kitchen to hoke out a new hoover bag. The drawer was damp and stuck as usual. When she eventually forced it open, she pulled out an empty bag of hoover bags. Majella sighed, then jammed the empty bag into the pedal bin and went back to the hoover. She pulled out the full bag and threw it in the bin as well. Then she shoved the hoover back under the stairs with the nozzle off so her ma might notice there was something the matter with it before starting it up and making an even bigger mess of the place. After all that, Majella went into the living room and stood there flicking her fingers. The place was still a tip for she'd only managed to redd the worst of the duvet up and had made no inroads into the underlying mess. She couldn't face sitting there staring at the shite for the whole day so she went out to the hall and picked up the phone.

— Bogey Taxis, where d'ye want tae go?

Majella hesitated, then spoke louder than she wanted. — Garvaghy. Up the border road.

3.05 p.m.
Item 1: Small talk, bullshit, gossip

Majella sat by the window waiting for the taxi, watching mothers and oul wans heading home out of the town with their shopping, greeting the teenagers and young wans who were only heading in. Majella remembered when her and Aideen would do that. They'd take hours over spending their pocket money on some useless shite they didn't really need. A dose of wee weans were running about on the green, squabbling. Majella wondered where everyone got their energy from. She closed her eyes until she heard the blast of a horn. She checked out the window to see if it was her taxi, then grabbed her bag and headed for the door.

— Ma-jell-ah?

For fucksake. Her ma roaring from the bed. Majella hesitated at the foot of the stairs.

— Ma-jellah?

Majella listened to the screams of the weans outside. Then she opened the front door and stepped outside.

— MAH-JELL-AHHHHH?

She slammed the door behind her and pounded up the street, passing her neighbours without a word.

Kevvy Breen was smirking when she climbed into the taxi. — Where's the fire?

Majella didn't like Kevvy Breen. — No fire. Just didn't want tae keep ye waiting.

— Right. Where tay, Mrs?

— Garvaghy. Up the border road.

Majella didn't have to look at Kevvy's face to see the flicker in his eyes.

— Right you are.

He pulled off from the kerb and soon they were driving through the town, Kevvy held up the first two fingers of his right hand and stiffened his neck at the drivers of all the Catholic cars they met. That way of going on reminded Majella of dogs sniffing around each other's arses.

Majella didn't want to talk to Kevvy, but she knew the drill. — Busy the day?

Kevvy didn't want to talk to Majella, but he too knew the drill. — Aye. Kept going, all right.

Majella flicked her fingers for the final push. — Sure it'd be worse if ye'd nothing on.

Kevvy jerked his head in agreement. — Far worse. Can't complain.

Majella reckoned that that conversation would do them the length of the journey, so she settled back into her seat. She'd always liked being driven around. On the way out of the town they got stuck behind a tractor. Kevvy started cursing and revving, pulling out like he would overtake, before being forced back in. Majella didn't mind going slow. They were passing St Christopher's and it gave her the chance to have a good gawk in at the buildings. The front had all changed. It now had big heavy security gates and a fancy sign – *Ardscoil Naomh Críostóir.* On the way past the PE pitch Majella got a shock. Half the school grounds were a housing development now. She'd heard the new Head had sold half the pitch off to raise funds for the school, but she hadn't been out to see the result. Tommy Baxter, who'd been a few years above her in school, had done the buying and the building. Tommy Baxter who could hardly write his own name when he was at the school and had been reared with a dose of brothers and sisters in some shithole the Council ended up condemning. The houses were all big posh things. Detached. Identical. Majella reckoned there'd be far too much cleaning in a house that size. The tractor in front turned off up the Kilcleen Road just as Eminem came on the radio. Kevvy turned the volume up, put his foot flat to the mat and hoored off out of the town. Majella knew the road like the back of her hand. She tilted her head to the left and stared out at the fields that stretched towards the mountains, green and brown and yellow.

3.20 p.m.
Item 28.1: Death: People

Kevvy pulled up outside her granny's caravan.

— How much'll a return be?

— Six pounds.

Majella pulled a fiver and a few coins from her pocket. — There you go. Thanks a million.

— No bother.

— Can ye get me back here in about an hour?

— Ah can indeed. If you've any bother ring me on the number.

— Fuck all reception out here, Kev. Just get me in an hour or so. Ah don't fancy walking through the clabber tae get a bar on me phone.

— No bother. An hour it is then.

Majella opened the car door and stepped into the mud. — Cheerio.

— Bye.

Kev reversed out of the lane with a skid, then spun away up the road. Majella shivered in the wet wind that whipped around the caravan and derelict house. She hadn't a clue what she was at. But she figured for now the best thing would be to get in out of the fucken cold. She plodded over to the door of the caravan. The broken window had been boarded up by someone. She fumbled for the key that she'd taken from home. It was for emergencies, her da had said years ago, when he'd had it copied. She opened the door and stepped inside. The thing she noticed first was the emptiness, then the cold. Never once in all her life had Majella entered the caravan without her granny. She moved to the heater and picked up the box of long matches and switched the gas on. She struck a match and lit the gas. Blue flames licked across the three faces of the heater, then grew strong and orange, throwing out a hissy warmth into the thin air of the caravan. Majella moved close to the flame, toasting her shins. She stayed there until she could bear the heat no more, then she moved away. For the first time, she looked around the little caravan. The whole place was wrong. The bed had been made, but with the quilt folded at the bottom instead of pulled up to the pillows, which she suspected was a Protestant way of folding a quilt. The crockery had been washed and left on the draining board, not dried and stacked away as it should have been. Traces of white fingerprint powder lingered on the shelves. The newspapers and holy magazines were tidied into a single pile, instead of being separated. There was a stack of post sitting on the table by the window seat. Majella sat down and began to sort through the letters. Her heart began to race as she recognised her da's writing on the outside of a large envelope addressed to her granny. It was already open, so Majella felt it was OK for her to look inside. She pulled out a sheaf of papers. They seemed to be plans of some sort. It took her a few moments to recognise that they were her da's sketches of what he'd planned to do to the old house. The kitchen and living room. Her granny's wee annexe. A nice big main bedroom. Then she saw her own name beside an arrow that pointed to a wee room that she knew had the fine view facing down towards the river. A skift of rain blew in from the north and battered off the wee caravan, the water running down the dirty front window. Majella shivered in her coat. She owned the land she could see to the front of her. The land to the back. She owned hedges and stones and grass. She owned the ruined house and the empty caravan. She owned the reflection of the grey clouds on the water in the ditch. She owned the mice and birds and rabbits and rats that crawled and shivered in the land around her. She owned worms and earth and trees and bushes and in the summer, she might own flowers. When Kevvy Breen pulled up in his taxi over an hour later, Majella was still sitting in front of the plans, the gas heater cold and quiet.

4.40 p.m.
Good list
Item 1.1: Eating: Sweeties

Majella was walking back up from the town, her mouth watering. She'd got Kevvy to drop her off at McHugh's shop, and she'd gone in and got a packet of hoover bags, a new toothbrush and a pile of sweets. Chewits. Wham bars. Lollipops. A load of sweet fizzy crap. When she got home, she was going to head to her bed and pig out.

5.05 p.m.
Item 26: Wakes, weddings, christenings, funerals

Majella was lying under her duvet. She'd eaten half the shite in the bag and had only stopped because her tongue had started to bleed. She wasn't really full, but her stomach felt inflated. Eating sweeties wasn't as bad as drugs, but Majella reckoned that the sugar still put you mad in the head. She wondered that St Christopher's hadn't banned its tuck shop. There'd been no tuck shop at primary school. Majella'd liked primary school well enough. It was different from the shite you had to go through at secondary. P1 was supposed to have been about learning how to do the alphabet, colours and a few numbers, but really it was mostly about learning how not to pish or shite yourself. P2 had been harder. The teacher had already decided who needed to be in the 'special' group, who was in the 'good' group, and who was 'mainstream'. Majella'd had been put into the 'good' group and had to work harder than the kids in the other groups. She knew she was supposed to be delighted with herself about being in the 'good' group – her da and her granny were all chuffed. But she hated the extra attention, not to mention the work, and was relieved when she landed into P3, which had only one group, because P3 was First Holy Communion year. All the reading and writing and sums went out the window because they had to learn how to eat Jesus. Their teacher, Mrs McGlinchey, talked a lot about God and angels. About how God was Everywhere (yes, even in the toilet – priests in Italy had checked) and your Guardian Angel was there to help you always, even if you just didn't know how to tie your laces (tying your laces was a P2 lesson, but Francie Kingh, Orla Mooney and Charlie Daly still hadn't mastered it yet and were sent back into the practice boot in P2 every break time to try and get it right). Mrs McGlinchey was preparing them for their First Holy Communion. She had to make sure everyone knew how to bless themselves so they wouldn't make a show of themselves in front of the priest. Blessing yourself was taught in P1, way before tying laces, but there was still a few of the class who did it backwards. Every now and then, Father McAteer would come in to see the whole school. Because they were having their First Holy Communion and the P7s were having their Confirmation they got special attention. First Father McAteer would knock gently, then he'd open the door. Mrs McGlinchey would get up quickly or stop what she was doing and say —Oh, come in, Father. Then she'd turn around and stare at them with big wide eyes. That was the signal for them to scrape their chairs back and stand up and say — Hello, Father McAteer. He'd look all delighted and say back — Hello, children. Then they all sat down again while he went over to Mrs McGlinchey to have a few quiet words. The next minute he'd turn around to them and say — Now, children, a prayer. So they'd all have to scrape back their chairs again and stand up and get their right hand ready for the sign of the cross. Someone always got the sign of the cross wrong. In P1 and P2 that was the teacher's fault, and the priest would say to Mrs McCanny or Mrs Kearny in a disappointed sort of way — Oh, I see Francie Kingh hasn't managed the sign of the cross yet, and then the teacher would get all red and mortified, and then after the priest was gone Francie Kingh would get a battering with the metre ruler. But in P3, if you didn't know how to bless yourself, it was your fault, and the priest would pick on you as well as the teacher. Majella didn't like any of that. And she wasn't fond of the First Confession business either, where they talked a lot about Sin and had to practise what they were going to say and rehearse their penance. Mrs McGlinchey made sure Francie Kingh was fit to say — Bless me Father, for I have sinned, these are my sins: I took the name of the Lord my God in vain, I told lies to my mammy and I stole sweets, but she didn't worry so much about the penance part of the confession. She said that whether or not Francie could say the Our Father and a Hail Mary was between himself and God. Majella was particularly unhappy at the whole dressing-up part of Holy Communion. The fellas had it easy – they just had to wear suits. But cuddies had to wear miniature wedding dresses. The mammies and daughters talked about dresses and bags and shoes for months before the day. Majella and her ma had little to say on the subject. Majella was the biggest child in the class and she hadn't fitted into any of the nice dresses her ma'd seen in the window of McAnea's shop. Her ma had to ask Donna Murphy the dressmaker to make a dress specially to fit, which Majella knew was an embarrassment. The only bit of First Holy Communion Majella liked was when they turned the classroom into a pretend chapel, with desks on both sides and an aisle up the middle. Then Mrs McGlinchey would say — Come up now to receive, and they would wait for a moment to show their manners before standing – front row first – to go up and receive. When they got to where Mrs McGlinchey was standing, they had to form a line in front of her. If there was no space, they had to line up behind and wait for a space, and they weren't allowed to squeeze into a small space because that would be ignorant. Then Mrs McGlinchey would come along the line saying — Body of Christ, and you had to look holy and say — Amen, and stick your tongue out so she could pop a flying saucer onto it. Then you had to bless yourself and go back to your desk. That was the best bit, the flying saucer. Majella loved flying saucers. Mrs McGlinchey practised Holy Communion with flying saucers because they were about the same size and taste as the Blessed Wafer, except the Blessed Wafer didn't have fizz in it. She explained to them the fizz in the flying saucer was kind of like Jesus in the Blessed Wafer. Majella would sit at her desk, with the flying saucer melting on her tongue, trying to keep the little parcel of fizz dry for as long as possible. When it melted, she'd spread the deadly fizzing sour sweet flavour all over her tongue to taste as much of it as possible, imagining she could taste Jesus. It wasn't much wonder, Majella thought, that she'd been disappointed by the Real Thing. Because although the Blessed Wafer really did taste like the outside of a flying saucer, there was no fizz. On her First Holy Communion, Majella could remember sitting in the chapel for a long time, with Jesus stuck to the roof of her mouth, and her trying to peel him off with her tongue. Somehow she knew picking him off with her finger was all wrong.

5.55 p.m.

Item 3: Pain: Other people's pain

Majella was walking down through the town when something gave her the smell of apples. She loved that smell. It made her think of the apple fair when the big trucks of the Armagh apple men shuddered into town the last Friday before Halloween. Majella didn't think the fair was much of a fair – for years it had just been the trucks and apples and the big hardy fucks of apple men. But her da'd said that in the olden days it'd been a bigger deal, with dancing and games and plenty of drinking. Agnes Ferguson had recently wangled a few quid off the peace fund so now there were some jugglers and Irish dancers, and Agnes' own stall. It still wasn't much of a deal, but Majella loved it. Her da'd had a fondness for the apple fair, for he'd once spent an autumn working the orchards in Armagh, and he knew some of the fellas on the trucks. She could remember being wee, her da holding her hand, leading her past the fellas with caps, them all hauling cardboard boxes brimming with green apples down from the trucks, then throwing them up on the wooden stalls. Back then, Francie Kingh would be down nicking apples. Majella'd found it weird, seeing Francie eating an apple. She usually only saw him eat what they gave out in school – a stubby bottle of milk in the morning, with a short blue straw for sucking on, and the canteen food.

She remembered that day staring at his shaved head that showed off a hairless zig-zag from the time his ma'd split him with the frying pan and there was all the bother with the social workers. She remembered Francie staring right back at her until her da pulled her past. He stopped to chat to an apple man, and Majella stood watching a Protestant feeling her way through the apples sitting on display on top of a box.

The apple man spoke to her. — Picked them wans meself. No oul machines or youngsters doing the work. Ah picked them and laid them down. There's no bruising in them, Mrs. Open the box and have a look.

Even Majella could tell that the apple man didn't want the Prod opening the box for a look. But she opened it anyway. The box was crammed with hard green cookers – the odd rosy one shining through in the fading light. The apple man laid a hand on the box flap as if to close it again. Before he could, the woman bent down and lifted the top apples off. Underneath were smaller apples. Then misshapen ones. And finally, some bruised windfalls. With a raised eyebrow, the woman picked one and held it out. There was a spreading brown stain on the apple, like a map of the world gone wrong. Majella heard Francie Kingh burst out laughing. The apple man pulled the apple from the woman's hand. Majella turned to look at Francie, watching his white teeth shine in the lovely dark of his skin. Then the rotten apple exploded in his face. She watched as sticky brown lumps dripped onto his jumper. Francie howled and jumped off the wall. He ran to the nearest stall and began to toss whole apple boxes onto the ground, throwing apples at the man. Majella was impressed at his aim. But the apple men weren't. They went mad and chased after Francie, who ran off, still howling. When things had settled down, her da'd bought some apples off a man he knew. He'd carried them home and stored them on a shelf in the shed, out of the road of Blackie. Majella'd loved the way the apples filled the shed with their smell, and she liked to go out there alone, to breathe in the sweet smell and to keep an eye out for rot.

Early that winter, she saw the first apple turn – a spot of soft brown on the skin. For days she watched the slow spread of the rot, counting the spots of white mould that sprang up like buds of icing sugar. Even though that apple rotted, the others stayed hard, clean and green. But then, overnight it seemed, they too turned – and every touching apple had a blotch of rot. It was then Majella ran and told her da, who'd headed out to the shed. He'd gathered the good apples into a bucket and brought them inside. The rotten ones were dumped in the bin. He made pastry, rolling it out, then fitting it over the saved slices of apple. After he'd thumbed the pastry into place, he wet it with water, and let

Majella sprinkle sugar on and make the fork pricks on top for the steam to escape. Later on, they ate the pie burning hot from the oven. Even her ma liked apple pie. The crisp pastry cracked cleanly under their forks, and the apples mixed with the pouring cream. After they'd all finished, her da loosened his belt, paused, then went in for a second slice. She always wondered if Francie Kingh ever had a good apple tart made for him. She doubted it, knowing the house he'd been born into. She'd never know for sure now, for Francie'd gone and hung himself on his twenty-first birthday, just weeks before his second baby was due.

Majella pushed the door of A Salt and Battered! open and the buzzer rasped.

— Bout ye, Jell-ah.

— Bout ye, Marty.

The warm smell of fish and chips filled her nose and made her mouth water.

6.42 p.m.
Item 1: Bullshit, small talk, gossip

Shauna Baird was in the chipper with her young fella.

— Shauna.

— All right, Majella?

Majella didn't answer. No one ever really expected her to answer. Sometimes she did. Most times she didn't.

— Fish supper fer me ann chicken nuggets fer the wee man.

— Cumminup.

Majella scribbled the order down and shouted back to Marty. She stood on at the counter while Shauna went over to the window and sat down. The wee fella stood at the amusement machine, trying to reach up to the controls. She looked tired, Shauna did. The buzzer went and a couple of oul dolls shoved their way into the chipper.

— Hello, Majella.

— 'Lo.

The two biddies stood staring at the menu board for a while, until one of them cast her eye around to see Shauna and the wee fella.

— Och, who's this now? Who's this wee man?

Majella watched as Shauna Baird took a reddener.

— My name's Sean.

— Sean is it now? And aren't you lovely? What age are you?

— Four. I'm four anna half.

Sean stood beaming at the two oul biddies, who smiled at him and looked up and down at Shauna.

— Och, he's lovely, so he is. Couldn't you just ate him alive?

— The wee dote. Is he yer wee brother?

— Naw. He's mine.

There was a silence as all three women smiled at wee Sean.

— Ach look at him, would you? The wee pet. He'll break hearts wan day, eh?

Marty passed Shauna's order through to Majella. Shauna saw it and hurried to the counter to pay. She grabbed her food and the wean's hand and disappeared out the door. The wee fella smiled and waved on their way past the window. The two women inside waved back.

— Och, bye! Bye now!

When Shauna went out of view the two oul dolls turned to Majella. — What age would that wan be now? Hardly out of her teens, ah'd say!

Majella shrugged. She didn't know and didn't care.

Marty sidled up to the counter. — Young Shauna, you're asking about?

— Is that her name? Who'd she be now?

— Och. She'd be a McSorley from up the head of the town. Her ma'd be Carr from Black Bridge direction.

— Och, right, right. She's not a big age, that wee doll.

— Och, naw. Maybe nineteen now, she is.

— Still a wean herself.

— Och, well. They're starting early, these days. Starting young.

Majella scratched her oxter. The oul dolls were giving her an itch.

— Ah'm away out the back.

Marty nodded, then leaned in on the counter. — The word is, she was seeing two a the Dolans at the same time, ann there was a big blow-up over it, but when she got herself in the family way, there was no fighting then. The two a the Dolans thick as thieves again, ann her stuck wi the DNA testing fer the maintenance and sure that's a whole other handling when it's brothers they're after.

Majella closed the door on the sound of Marty's voice and breathed in the fresh air. Toilet first, she reckoned, then a fag.

7.50 p.m.

Item 41.1: The weather: Rain

Marty and Majella were standing at the front of the chipper. It was pishing down outside. One of those long, miserable evenings that you just wanted to spend on your back in bed or on your arse in the pub.

— Wild night.

— Tis, aye.

Marty sighed beside Majella. Then Rose Murphy went past the window and ducked in half drowned.

— God, Rose, that's a wild night. You're half drowned!

— Och, ah'm all right. A few chips'll warm me up.

— Well you're in the right place. We'll get you sorted.

Majella said nothing and plodded to the back of the shop to let them get on with their wee moment.

— Wild weather for November. What's it like at all?

— Och, ah know. Wild.

Majella headed into the storeroom and let the door close behind her. She couldn't hear anyone properly when she was in the store. From here, the fryers sounded a bit like the sea. She pulled herself up on top of the chest freezer and let her feet dangle over the edge. She closed her eyes and just sat there, feeling herself breathe in the too-tight envelope of her overalls.

8.32 p.m.
Good list
Item 1.5: Eating: School dinners

Lizzie Breen came in the chipper. Majella always felt a bit flustered when Lizzie Breen was in. She remembered Lizzie from school days, when she was the head cook in the canteen. She'd been a giant of a woman back then, armed with a monstrous ladle. Now she was a croil of a thing, shrunken down and curled over on herself.

— 'Lo Mrs Breen.

— Hello.

Lizzie glanced sideways at Majella, and then up at the board. Majella knew Lizzie didn't remember her. Majella hadn't been a canteen regular because her da had had a factory job, which meant Majella either had to bring in dinner money or a packed lunch. She'd have a packed lunch the times her ma was grand and they had the chance of a good cooked meal in the evenings. She'd be given dinner money the times her ma had took to her bed or was under blankets in the living room.

— What can ah get chew?

— A triple-sausage supper please.

Majella wrote down the order and passed it back. Lizzie sat down on the window sill, and placed her substantial handbag on her knee. Majella liked how Lizzie always ordered a good supper when she was in. She didn't look like she subsisted off packed lunches, which Majella'd always thought were shite. Her lunches were usually a couple of slices of pan with sandwich spread or jam or a bit of cheese and pickle, then a Penguin biscuit or a fun-sized Mars bar for afters. She could remember the way she'd have her lunch finished off in under a minute and would have to sit there, trying not to eye what everyone else was eating. She was always half starved when she was on the packed lunches. The school dinner was a far better thing, except for the prayers. The master would herd everyone into their seats in the big canteen where Lizzie'd be glowering at them, her arms folded over her diddies, ready to strike with a ladle. All the other dinner ladies would be kept cackling and shouting at each other in the kitchen behind the big counter. Only Lizzie was allowed out, to keep order along with the master. The windows would be running wet from the steam, and the master would be racing around, going red in the face as he tried to get everyone quietened down

In the name of the John Murphy I'll kill you if you don't sit down. In the name of Fionnuala O'Neill, put down your knife and fork and sit like a Christian for once in your life! In the name of the Father and of the Meehan! Meehan! I'll swing for ye if ye don't shut up and sit down!

They'd hardly finish blessing themselves before everyone tore into their food. It wasn't that it was ever wild tasty, but the portions were generous – a load of spuds and a good dollop of stew or whatever. And they always got a dessert. You had no say over what you got, the food was just put down in front of you – doughy apple crumble with a wallop of custard or a bowl of half-melted ice cream with watery jelly. The only beverage was water from the tap that came to the table in giant metal jugs. Majella loved a good school dinner: solid food served up by a solid woman. You might fuck with the master, but you never fucked with Lizzie Breen, for you could end up in a pot.

— Triple-sausage supper.

Lizzie got up from the window. Majella could nearly feel the stiffness in her bones. She walked to the counter and paid for her food.

— Thank you.

Majella watched her walk out, her head bowed against the rain. When she was little, Majella had never thought of dinner ladies as people who were doing a job. In her head, the dinner ladies were creatures who cooked, ate and slept in the kitchen. Now she knew that, although the wages were shite, being a school dinner lady was a good steady job with a pension. There'd been the odd vacancy up in St Christopher's that Majella had seen going, but she wasn't up for it. It wasn't the thought of peeling spuds that put her off, as, from what she'd heard, the school food these days was basically chipper food anyway – they only needed a couple of women these days to fry up the chicken nuggets and frozen chips and to warm up huge vats of baked beans. Majella was well able for that. But she knew she wasn't able for all the weans, the noise, the shite talking she'd have to do with the other dinner ladies and staff. The chipper was where she belonged.

9.09 p.m.
Item 44: Dryshites

Hairy Feely was in the chipper for a fish supper. Majella felt sorry for poor oul Hairy. He was a wee baldy fella, who'd taken his name in the seventies, when he'd been blessed by a big curly head of hair. Hairy'd a wild taste for the drink. Ended up in Alcoholics Anonymous.

— Yer fish supper.

Hairy shuffled to the counter and picked up his food. Then he went over to the window to sit down and eat it. Cunter didn't like anyone to do that. Kept saying it was no café she was running. But half the drunk fuckers later on would be eating and dropping food round them, so Majella didn't see the harm in letting Hairy have his bite to eat on the window. Hairy was the only person Majella knew who'd been cured by AA. He'd been off the booze this years and years, which was great, but now he was a dryshite, which was bad. Majella remembered him drunk when she was wee. He'd be all smiles and curls and laughs, giving away whatever change he had on him after the pub. Following the AA he hardly spoke to anyone. Wasn't like he'd gone off and got married or got a job or that either after he'd got dry. He just lived on with his mother in their wee house. Majella reckoned his mother was probably relieved he was dry. There was probably a few more quid in the house. But it was a shame he was fuck all craic now. Doctor O'Hanlon had made Majella's ma go to AA once, after her da'd gone. Said she'd get no more counselling until she'd sorted her drinking out. They'd told her she could bring someone with her, for support. Of course Majella had got landed with the job and had to sit with her ma on the bus the whole way to the T&F – a hospital her granny'd still referred to as Omagh District Lunatic Asylum. Before Care in the Community had come in, her ma was no stranger to the T&F. But to be going there for AA was a different story, so her ma was acting up, playing doddery and acting childish, as if she wasn't able to buy her own bus ticket, or put her hand in her purse to pay for the taxi out to the hospital. They arrived late, and Majella had to ask where the meeting was being held and then find the way there. She didn't like wandering about the T&F. The sight of the doting oul wans and the mad young ones and the fucked-up ones lost in between unsettled her. She was glad when they reached the room. The door was open but it didn't look like there was a meeting on. There was just a load of men sitting on plastic chairs in a circle, most of them drinking tea, chatting. Majella stood in the doorway for a few seconds, waiting to be noticed.

Eventually, someone who seemed to be in charge looked up. — What are ye looking?

— AA.

— You're in the right place.

— Dead on.

Majella lumbered into the room. She felt the need to pish or have a fag. There was a big *No Smoking* sign. Half of the plastic seats were empty, the other half full of hardened-looking men who looked like they'd been left out in the rain and wind too long. Her ma tottered into the room, looking helpless. Majella didn't know what she was supposed to do, but she sat down on a plastic seat. She hated plastic seats, for sometimes her over-heated arse would leave a sweaty butt-crack mark when she got up. Her ma stood on, blinking and swaying.

The possibly-in-charge person took charge again. — You all right there, love?

— Aye. Naw. Och, ah dunno.

— Sure, find yourself a seat there ann sit yourself down.

Majella's ma collapsed into the nearest chair, crossing her legs, flicking out her hair and clacking at her bangles. Majella could see some of the more lively-looking characters checking her ma out. She folded her arms.

— A wee cuppa tay?

— Aye o God aye that'd be great, thanks.

— Yerself?

Majella thought a cup of tea would be great. Something warm to hold in her hands, to dry the sweat off them.

— Ah'm all right, thanks.

— You sure?

A nice hot cup of tea with a splash of milk.

— Naw, thanks. Ah'm grand.

Majella blinked.

— Well if ye're sure.

Majella watched the fella go over to the kettle in the corner to brew up, irritated with herself for not being able to say aye to a cup of tea. She took a quick gleek over at her ma. She was hunting through her handbag in a focused but pointless kind of a way. Majella reckoned she didn't know what she was after. Eventually, she brought out a compact and started to apply lipstick with a shakey hand. Then she took a deep breath and put her bag down by her side just as your man landed back with a cup of tea.

— There's yer tay.

— Och, lovely, thanks a million.

The possibly-in-charge fella took his seat again and sat up looking around him. Everyone else quietened in expectation. He said nothing. A few people shifted in their seats. Then one of the oldest men spoke.

— Right. Will we just get her going?

The possibly-in-charge fella nodded for a long time before speaking. — Conal, maybe you'd tell us how you're doing now on the probation?

Conal leaned forward in his chair and began to speak. Majella looked over at the still-open door behind her ma.

As Conal began to list off the things he'd done or were done to him while he was on the tear (which included misplacing his wife and weans), Majella realised she'd a raging thirst for a pint a Smithwicks.

Later, on the way home on the bus, her ma was in miserable form. When they got home she lay down on the settee and started gurning on about how she wasn't like that – she wasn't an alkie like those men. That she'd never hurt anyone or went missing or went to prison or went homeless. She was just sociable. She just liked a drink. It took Majella's ma a few weeks to get over the meeting. Then, after that, her ma just lied when asked about her alcohol intake. Fourteen units, spread out evenly over the week. Everyone knew she was lying. Nobody, least of all Majella, could do a thing about it.

— Me wrappers, Majella.

Hairy pushed his neatly folded empty chip wrappers onto the counter. Majella took them in her hand. Hairy never said aye or naw or cheerio, he just took himself away into the rain outside. Majella scrunched the papers up, then chucked them in the bin.

10.05 p.m.
Item 45: Change

Majella watched the clock. It was after ten and yet again Jimmy Nine Pints had not been in to lay his five pound note on the counter for his sausage supper.

Majella turned to Marty. — No sign of Jimmy Nine Pints the night either.

Marty shifted on his feet and kept his eyes on the fryers. — Naw no sign.

The chipper wasn't too crowded and they had the orders in hand, so Majella took a long look at Marty. — Not like him to miss two suppers, never mind wan.

Marty glanced at her and coloured up. Then he scrutinised the last order Majella had pinned to the board. — Naw. Must be something up.

Majella frowned. There was something up, all right. And she needed to know what.

11.11 p.m.
Item 41.2: The weather: The cold

Majella was sat on the toilet shivering, trying to smoke a fag. It was fucken freezing, but her belly was knotted with cramps and she needed to sit for a bit. She sucked on the fag until she ran it down to the butt, then she dropped it in the sink and turned on the tap. The fag hissed as the water hit it. Majella hugged herself and rocked. The cramps weren't easing. Time for the co-codamol. She tidied herself up, washed her hands and went back into the chipper. Marty was out at the counter, keeping everyone going.

— You all right, Jelly?

Majella nodded at Marty and went to the fridge. She grabbed herself a Coke and went out the back to where her plastic bag lay. She lifted a blister of co-codamol, pushed out four tablets and popped them in her mouth, one by one, before swallowing them down with Coke. She turned around and saw Johann-Paul looking at her.

— You are taking pain pills, I see.

— Aye ah am.

— What is wrong with you?

— Me belly hurts.

— Ah. I understand. It is women's problems, yes?

Majella crumpled her brow, then nodded at Johann-Paul.

— Don't worry. I understand. But you will be sleepy after those pills. Very sleepy.

— Och. I'll be grand. The Coke'll wake me up.

Johann-Paul nodded at her. — Yes. Coke will help.

When he turned back to the fryers Majella smiled at his back, savouring the oddness of him. She hadn't had a ride off Johann-Paul yet, but she'd an interest. She felt a burp rise up out of her, so she rifted, then put the can to her mouth to finish it off. The pills weren't working yet, but she knew in twenty minutes they'd hit and she'd be wrapped up in a blanket of codeine. She sighed, and headed out to the counter.

— Batter burger ann chips ann red sauce.

Majella picked up the pen and began to write.

12.00 a.m.
Good list
Item 7: Painkillers

The codeine and caffeine were working their magic. Majella stood at the counter in a haze, notebook in hand, watching the clock tick down the seconds until midnight. The women coming in the door of A Salt and Battered! were long past the Cinderella stage of the night. They were scuffed about the edges, mouths smeared with lipstick, eyes bleary. The whole lot of them were turning into Ugly Sisters while Majella continued to play the skivvy.

— What canna get chew?

— Cheesy chip peas ann gravy.

Fairytales had always fascinated Majella. Transformation. Frogs into princes, beggars into queens, straw into gold. One tale might be about a talking cat, another about magic beans and the next about a man on a horse skewering a dragon, but they were all really about the same thing: about whatever you had in the start not being good enough and someone waving a wand or performing a trick so that everything turns out all right in the end.

— What canna get chew?

— Battered sausage supper ann a chip.

When she'd been wee she'd been mad into the frogspawn. It was the nearest thing she got to magic. She'd dip a jam jar in the pond up near her granny's to catch some frogspawn. She'd take it home and keep it in the yard, watching the inky dots in the middle of the slime turn into wee wiggling things that eventually grew legs and ended up as tiny green creatures that moved around by jumping. Weird.

— What canna get chew?

— Curry chip ann onion rings anna Coke.

Butterflies really were magical, going from yellow eggs on a leaf to brown furry or bright green tubes with millions of legs to a hopeless-looking curled up dead leaf, to a powdery paper-winged creature that flew.

— What canna get chew?

— Fish supper ann a can a Sprite

Majella had yet to see the magic in the human journey. Mini-adults were born red and squashed. A few turned out cute, but most stayed ugly. Shit happens. Nobody seems happy. Everyone gets wrinkly and bits stop working. In the end, everyone dies. The buzzer rasped again and again as the hungry Saturday-night crowd piled in. Majella glanced at Marty. He was frowning and looked tired-out. She wondered if he ever wondered how she was doing, then looked at the next face in the queue.

— What canna get chew?

1.25 a.m.

Item 3.12: Noise: Disorganised crowds

It was hectic. Majella still felt stoned, though the raw edges of the chipper were coming back in focus. The customers were a confusing tangle of faces and noise in front of her, but she could tell the Daly brothers weren't in the thick of it. She knew that was a bad sign, that the only thing likely to be keeping them from their booze and food would be a death or being lifted. Neither were great options. Majella and Marty were both frowning and scribbling orders while Johann-Paul was flat out by the fryers. Majella had a notion it wasn't going to be easy to get the shutters down.

2.33 a.m.
Item 12.13: Conversation: Tackling someone

Majella stood back on the street as Marty locked up. They were both wrecked. The chipper had been destroyed with dropped food and rubbish. Even with Johann-Paul on the job it had taken them ages to redd up. The town was still lively. Bogey taxis and minibuses zipped past and young wans were standing about the place, shouting and cursing, squaring up to and pairing off with each other. The older generations were still in the pubs, drinking long past last orders. Majella and Marty waved Johann-Paul on his way, then they set off walking up the road, trudging along in silence. They didn't normally walk together – Marty usually had the car, but Philomena had taken it that day for a bit of early Santy shopping. Majella wasn't going to make small talk. She had a question for Marty.

— So what's the craic with Jimmy Nine Pints?

She noticed that Marty started to walk faster after she asked her question. Majella wasn't up for increasing her pace, so she held her ground.

— Jimmy?

Majella noted with satisfaction that Marty slowed down again.

— Aye. Jimmy Nine Pints. He's not been in. Did you hear anything?

Majella could tell by the way Marty glanced at her and then looked up the road that he'd heard something. She watched him nod.

— Aye. Ah heard something.

Majella let the silence stretch out for a few seconds, to see if he'd tell her. But he didn't. So she fired on.

— Was he lifted?

Marty looked down at the road as they continued to walk.

— He was, aye.

Majella looked straight ahead. They were coming up to the roundabout, where Marty would take the Dunree road to his estate, while Majella would turn in at the chapel for her house. There were only a few seconds before they'd part. Majella thought about Jimmy's sausage supper, his wheezy laugh, the joke they'd repeated six nights a week for seven years running. She stopped at the roundabout and turned to Marty and eyeballed him. He shifted from foot to foot. She figured it could be the cold.

— Safe home.

She watched him sag with relief. — Right Majella. Safe home yourself. Safe home.

Majella nodded, then walked off, shivering despite the heat of her takeaway, which she hugged close to her chest.

2.42 a.m.

Item 34.1: Fighting: Physical fights

As soon as she turned the corner into their estate Majella saw that their house lights were on both upstairs and downstairs. She stopped outside the front door and listened. It was quiet, which was a good sign. All the same, she gently pushed her key into the lock and slowly opened the door. Instantly, the heat of the house and the smell of fags hit her. There was another smell too. Beer. This was a bad sign. She closed the door behind her and sneaked into the kitchen. The striplight was on and the kitchen was a mess of Chinese takeaway boxes and wrappers. Her ma must've had company then. Majella opened a cupboard and took down a plate. She dumped her food onto it and tore a hole in the wrappers before slapping it in the microwave. Upstairs the toilet flushed and someone stepped heavily to the sink. Majella knew by the creak of the floorboards that it wasn't her ma. Whoever was up there was as heavy as her da had been. Majella hoped that her ma hadn't gone and shagged whatever loser she'd invited in.

The man in the bathroom opened the door and stepped onto the landing. Majella moved quickly and quietly to the microwave and caught it just before it pinged. She held her breath and listened to him move a few steps away from the bathroom, stopping outside her room. There was a pause, then he banged loudly on the door. Majella flinched. He quit for a few seconds, then started up again, banging and banging and banging.

— Come out tae fuck, Nuala. Come out a there ann fucken talk tae me.

Majella gently closed the microwave door on her food. She took down a pint glass and opened her can of Coke during the next battering session.

— Fuck aff Tony ann leave me alone. Fuck aff!

Her ma's voice sounded small and muffled. Majella resented her drunken ma being near her good new duvet. She hoped she wasn't smoking in her room. The man kept banging at the door. Majella didn't recognise his voice.

— Ah'll kick the fucken door in, Nuala, if ye don't come out a there.

Majella started counting to ten. She had got to seven when he started kicking her door. Majella didn't want her door kicked in. She liked having her locks, her privacy. She left the kitchen and carefully climbed the stairs, stepping in all the quietest places. At the top, she moved so her back was against her ma's bedroom door.

— Ann what the fuck d'ye think you're at, Anthony Cannon?

Anthony Cannon turned around and faced Majella. He was well langered by the look of him. He was standing with his fly open and a can of Tennants in his hand. He was so drunk that he could barely focus.

— Fuck you.

Majella eyeballed him. — Go home til yer bed.

Anthony staggered forward slightly, then back.

Majella sighed. — Go home til yer bed ann lie down before ah call the cops.

Anthony dropped his can of Tennants. Majella watched it land on its side. She heard the beer sizzling into the carpet.

— You gonna make me?

She looked Anthony Cannon straight in the eye again. She didn't know why, but she found it easy to look drunk people in the eye. Maybe it was because they themselves struggled to keep eye contact.

— If ah have tae.

She sized him up. He wasn't a big fella; she had the height of him. He was strong enough, but he wasn't fit – his years of boozing had grown him a slab of a gut that hung over his belt. And he was bollixed drunk. Majella fancied her odds. Anthony took a step towards her, suddenly looking steadier on his feet. Majella stood still. Then he cleared his throat with a long hack and spat at Majella. She turned her head just in time and the gob splattered into her hair. She turned again quickly as he stepped towards her. She gave him a quick shove and sent him bouncing off the far wall. Majella didn't like being spat at. Anthony staggered and leaned up against the wall, shocked.

— Ah said get the *fuck* out a mah house.

— Fucken fat cunt ye . . .

Anthony levered himself up from the wall and went for Majella again. She side-stepped him and when he lurched past, she grabbed him and turned him around to face the staircase. He missed his step and fell heavily on his arse, then slithered to the bottom of the stairs, where he crumpled into a heap. Majella could smell the booze and cheap aftershave of him on her hands. She quickly went down the stairs and jumped over him at the bottom. As he tried to get to his feet, she opened the front door. She looked around. There wasn't a being about she could call on. Behind her Anthony had managed to pull himself up by the banister. Majella left the door wide open and moved back, leaving the exit clear for him. But he just stayed there, clutching the banister.

— Out.

Anthony tried to focus on her.

— Ah said *out*.

Majella was freezing in the cold air. Her temper finally snapped. She reached in and grabbed Anthony by the collars and roared into his face while pulling him to the door.

— Ah said get out. Get the fuck out! Get the fuck out a my house ye ugly drunken hoor!

She found herself kicking and slapping at him, screaming and shouting. She knew she'd lost it but she didn't care who heard. She got him to the doorstep and pushed him out of the house. He staggered in the orange lights outside and then fell with an awful slap to the ground. Majella closed the door. Her heart was thumping and her body shaking. Her eyes burned with tears. She blinked quickly and then climbed the stairs to the bathroom. Her hair was sticky from where he'd gobbed at her. It made her feel sick. She stuck her head down into the sink and turned on the cold tap, letting the water gush through her hair. But the gob of thick spittle wouldn't wash off with just the water, and her stomach was turned with the slimy feel of it on her fingers, so she pulled her head up from the sink and went over to the shower. She grabbed the shower head and hit the ON button. As soon as the water was warm, she jumped in and soaked her whole head and lathered up with a fat blob of shampoo. Then she rinsed her hair until the water ran clean of suds and then scrubbed the whole of her until she was pink. Finally she turned the shower off and squeezed the long tail of her hair to get the worst of the water out. She grabbed the only towel she could see and rubbed herself dry before catching her hair up in a turban. She sat naked on the loo and she yanked out the tampon that had bloated up inside her. She sat for a while, her eyes burning, trying to catch her breath. When she felt calm, she stuck a night-time pad onto her pants, wiped herself and stood up. She dressed in her clothes, then checked her reflection in the mirror as she rinsed her hands. Her cheeks were flushed and her eyes sparkling. But the bags under her eyes showed up almost bruise-purple. Majella wanted her bed. She opened the door and went over to her bedroom.

— He's out the door now. Ye can open up ann go on tae yer own bed.

Her ma made no answer. Majella put her key into her lock and tried to open the door. But her ma had put on the snib.

— Open the door Ma.

Her ma just gurned a bit more.

— Please Mammy?

There was a silence.

— Ma, if ye don't open the door, ah'm gonna have tae bust her down.

Majella knew that she could sleep in her ma's bed and that her ma'd get up eventually the next day. But she just couldn't thole the thought of her ma smoking or maybe puking up in her nice new covers. She knew she would have to bust the door down.

— Ah'm gonna bust her down Ma.

Majella pictured her ma lying there, feeling sorry for herself, wanting someone to charge in and rescue her. She put her shoulder to the door and gave it a few strong, slow shoves, before the shitty lock gave way. Her ma was hiding under the covers, still gurning. Majella pulled them off. Her ma was curled up, her wee thin arms all scratched red from her long nails, her face a mess of tears and snotters, swollen from the slap Majella presumed Anthony Cannon had given her.

— You'd be better getting til yer own bed.

Her ma lay on, bawling and shivering. Majella noted she'd made an effort that night – she was wearing a black lacy top and a pair of jeans with a big shiny belt. A cheap necklace sparkled around her neck, which matched an earring in one ear – the other ear was naked.

— C'mon. Ah need tae get tae mah own bed. Get up.

Her ma didn't get up, so Majella pulled her up by the arm. She tried to fight Majella off, but then gave in, letting Majella help her to her own bed. Majella pulled off her ma's belt, earring and necklace, then covered her with the duvet. Her ma was still crying when she turned out the light and closed the door. Majella's belly rumbled again. She trudged down the stairs and set the microwave to two minutes and hit the START button. She sat down at the kitchen table and took a few big gulps of Coke, then she stared at the congealed remains of her ma's barely touched Chinese. The ping of the microwave woke her up. She grabbed her plate and glass of Coke, and headed to bed, switching off each light she passed until the house was quiet and dark. In her bedroom, she went to the window and pulled the damp curtains open. She rubbed a wet, orange-lit hole in the condensation and stared out at the garden below. Cannon was gone.

Sunday

11:27 a.m.
Item 14.5: Medical stuff: Hospitals, clinics, surgeries

Majella woke up with her finger in her mouth. She pulled it out and took a look at it. The skin was wrinkled and tooth bitten. She stretched her legs out long and stiff under the warmth of her duvet, and blinked the gluey clumps out of her eyes. She put her hand out to her mobile phone to check the time.

11:27
No New Messages

She'd time enough to make it to the late Mass if she got up now – she could even squeeze in a coffee beforehand. But Majella couldn't be arsed. She'd been to Mass already this month anyway with the funeral and that – she'd do for another while. Majella noticed that the light in the bedroom was brighter than normal. She looked at the window and saw she'd left a gap in the curtains where she'd gleeked out to make sure Cannon was gone. She pushed her phone under her pillow and pulled the duvet tight around her, relaxing as the feathers puffed up and then settled down all over her body. She didn't feel like getting up. She probably hadn't got to bed before four and she still felt wrecked. But she'd nothing to do and her ma'd be sleeping off the whiskey all day if she knew her. She heaved herself out of bed and went over to her telly. She picked out a DVD, shoved it into the player and closed the tray. She switched the telly on and the disc auto-played. She climbed back into bed and patted the duvet flat in front of her face so she could see the screen. Pam Ewing was in hospital. Majella loved it when a Ewing was in hospital because *Dallas* hospitals were clean, antiseptic buildings, full of wholesome nurses and doctors and kind clergy who always seemed both concerned and knowledgeable about the Ewings' conditions. Majella liked that the Ewings were a bunch of hardy fuckers – they usually pulled through cancer, and survived shootings and car crashes without cosmetic injury. She particularly enjoyed the funerals of the minor characters who were killed off from time to time. They were solemn, flower-filled occasions, the women glamorous in mourning black with big hair and spiky heels, clutching their serious-looking men, who held their cowboy hats over their crotches as a mark of respect. Majella snuggled back down into the warmth of the duvet. She humped over and resisted the urge to slip the first finger of her right hand into her mouth. Majella never did learn which finger was her index finger. All she knew was that she had a first finger, middle finger, ring finger and wee finger. And ever since she was a wee babby, she'd sucked on her first finger, spitting out each and every dummy tit her ma had pushed into her mouth. The day she'd started at St Brigid's, she'd sucked on her first finger so long and hard that she'd broken through the skin and bled into her mouth. Catriona Meehan had told on her and Majella remembered the teacher scolding as she disinfected, then bandaged the split flesh.

And what sort of a girl comes to school to suck on her finger making it bleed? You're not a baby any more, you're not sitting at home with your mammy watching TV. You're a big girl in school and you shouldn't be sucking your finger.

Majella had wanted to tell the teacher that she never sat at home watching TV with her mammy. Her mammy liked Majella best when she was away out of her road: outside someplace, or sitting quiet in her bedroom. Instead, Majella started sucking on the bandage, because although she had nine other fingers to suck on, and most of the other weans around her were sucking on their thumbs, she only wanted her own first finger on her own right hand. Majella was proud that she'd developed the self-control she had now. Rocking, finger flicking and sucking were under control and out of sight. Her ma wasn't one for the self-control. Fags. Booze. Men. Majella wondered what the story had been with Anthony Cannon the night before. Majella knew he'd been sniffing around her ma, but she'd never seen him all worked up before. She couldn't figure out how her ma'd ended up locked in her room with your man trying to kick the door down. Majella thought of the busted lock and grunted in annoyance. She'd have to fix that and tidy up the splintered door. But she had all day to see to it – she'd nothing to do until nine or so, when she would head down to the Bogey Inn for her usual Sunday pints. She hadn't made it into the bar the last few weeks, what with her granny and that. It'd been a Sunday when she'd died. Majella'd been on the bus when she'd got the word. Her ma'd rung her bawling. Majella'd listened for as long as she could, then hung up. She would blame the shitey mobile reception for a failed call. Then the whole way home from Strabane, Majella'd sat on the bus looking out the window at the rain, flicking her fingers in her fleece pockets, flexing her toes over and over again in her trainers, trying to contain the roar that she felt trying to bust out of her chest. She'd only just left her granny in the hospital, had just walked out the door, leaving her granny on her own. She wished she'd been there for her dying, but she hated hospitals, was no use at them. Her granny'd been in Omagh at first, which wasn't too bad. Her and her ma'd visited her there the day after she'd been found. Her granny'd been out of it when they'd seen her. Sedated, they'd called it, but stoned stupid was what Majella'd thought. Funny how she couldn't remember much about her granny from that visit, for she had spent her time trying to manage her ma, stopping her from torturing the staff, getting her a cup of coffee when she went all light-headed, listening to her whinge on about her da and how he should be there for herself and Maggie, poor oul Maggie. Majella hadn't touched her granny that visit. She'd been repulsed by the bruises and drooling and couldn't make herself reach out to fix her granny's hair or pat her hand or kiss her goodbye. The next thing Majella's ma told her that the hospital had called and that her granny had gone downhill and had been moved to Altnagelvin. Majella had pictured her granny freewheeling in a hospital bed down a big hill into Derry when her ma told her the news. On her next visit, Majella had gone on her own. It was a long journey on the bus from Aghybogey to the tenth floor of the hospital, and Majella felt exhausted when she arrived. She had stopped to catch her breath at the window. The view swept over the city and the whole way across to Donegal. Majella thought it was funny the way Aghybogey was right on the border with Donegal, but you couldn't see the Free State from anywhere in the town. It sat down in the glen, shut in by the mountains. A university fella'd once come to investigate the high cancer rates in Aghybogey. Everyone was hoping he'd pin the blame for cancer on the radiation leaking from the British surveillance towers and PissNI station, and were hoping for compensation. But the academic later released a widely publicised report stating that the unusually high rates of particular cancers were due to low population mobility and inter-marriage. He received special academic acclaim for pinpointing the cancers Catholics were more likely to get than Protestants. The report wasn't well received in Aghybogey.

Majella turned and headed down the corridor to her granny's room. She knocked before pushing the door open. The room had felt empty, the blinds tilted half open, the faded floral curtains pulled wide apart. Her granny lay on the bed under a blanket. Majella walked to her side and then stood and stared for a while. She wanted to feel something or do something. To say hello and comb her hair and put a neat navy cardigan on her. But the lump of swollen, battered flesh in the bed didn't feel like her granny. Majella'd seen the spectacular bruises on old people before on the telly. It was always the poor oul fucks, who'd opened their doors to some young wans who'd charged in and give them a hiding with an iron bar for the sake of a few quid or a battered wedding ring or a frigging war medal. You'd see the oul wan lying up in hospital after, eyes purple-swollen to the size of golf balls, their face a mess of spilt wine bruises. Majella hated those news reports, the ones her ma'd turn up real loud and then get outraged over. It was easy to believe it wasn't her granny in the bed. When Majella eventually reached out and took her granny's hand, it felt cold. The old woman didn't stir. And because Majella didn't believe she was sitting by her granny, she was able to spend what was left of visiting time holding that one cold hand between her sweating palms, staring out at the rain clouds blowing in over Inishowen. Before she left she was able to put her hand out to smooth this poor old woman's hair back from her swollen, broken face, to pull her nightie close around her cut neck, to tug the blanket right up to her face to keep the heat in, before she walked out of the hospital doors towards the bus. Majella turned over in her bed, buried her head deep into her pillow and breathed long and slow, long and slow, long and slow until sleep came back.

3.33 p.m.
Item 35.3. Lies: Obvious lies

Majella was sitting downstairs at the kitchen table. She didn't usually eat her breakfast there, but this morning she'd just ended up at the table. Her coffee was near finished and only lukewarm. She stared with narrowed eyes at her mobile phone, restraining the urge to fling it at the wall. For some reason, she'd sent Aideen a text telling her she could ring if she wanted, despite knowing that Aideen was no more going to ring her than Majella was going to go visit London like she used to promise every year. Majella shoved her phone deep into her fleece pocket, gathered up her mug and plate, dumped them in the sink and went upstairs to get dressed.

4.04 p.m.
Item 39.1. The neighbours: Watching you

Majella stepped into the yard, then plodded over to the garden shed. The ring of keys she held in her hand felt cold. The padlock was the same bronze lump of metal she remembered from years ago. Majella took a breath and selected the smallest key and fitted it into the padlock. It didn't fit, so she kept going, working her way up in size to the seventh key. It slid in and Majella felt the tiny spring of the lock move inside the padlock when she turned the key, but the hinge remained rusted tight and stuck. She let go of the padlock and returned to the kitchen, dropping the keys into the drawer. Then she took out the hammer and went back to the shed. She took another breath at the shed, then raised the hammer and brought it down again and again and again on the hinge of the padlock. Above and behind her she could hear her ma roaring out the window at her, and she knew that the Meehans next door would be gawking out their back windows, but she kept on going until the lock was smashed off the door.

— What are ye doing til the good padlock? Breaking the whole place in around our ears!

Majella turned around, her hands on her hips, and squinted up at her ma, who was hanging out of the bedroom window, face wrinkled up in the sun.

— Ah'm getting tools tae fix me door.

Majella knew the Meehans would've heard the drama the night before, so she felt like she was addressing them as much as her ma. She didn't wait for her ma's answer, and instead turned back and opened the shed door. Daylight flooded into the damp interior, and a smell of rot rose up. It hadn't been opened in ten years, when Majella'd fitted the lock to her bedroom door. Before that the detectives had poked around in the shed and the house, looking for 'evidence' that would help them 'resolve' the 'issue' of her da's 'disappearance'. They'd lifted some of his tools from the shed for forensic analysis, and never brought them back. Majella eyed the carpet remnant her da'd laid on the bottom of the shed. It was black with rot. The windows were a gauze of cobwebs studded with dead flies. Majella could see her da's drill at the back of the shed, in its plastic box. She stepped forward and grabbed it. The solid weight of it pleased her. As she walked back into the house she knew without looking that her ma had put her head back in the window, but that the Meehans were still staring out from behind their curtains. She put the drill box down on the kitchen table and opened it. The drill was set into its holder, the cord neatly folded beside it and all the drill bits in their little notches – nothing missing, nothing rusted, for her da had always maintained his tools, protecting them with a sheen of oil. But she wasn't sure if the motor would work after so many years. She pulled the drill from the holder and plugged it in, then pressed the ON button.

She felt a thrill as the drill whined and the bit spun around. She released the button, then went upstairs smiling, to fix her lock.

4.34 p.m.
Good list
Item 8: Cleaning

Majella had finished up with the lock. She hadn't done a bad job. Her da would've done a better job, but her attempt wasn't a dead loss. She packed away his tools and brought them back out to the shed, then closed the door. It took a good hard shove from her shoulder to get it to jam shut. The bust lock on the shed was useless now. She hoped she'd remember to call into Hector's Hardware to get a new one before some wee friggers got in to steal stuff or shit in it. She went back into the house and got the hoover out from under the stairs. She put one of the new hoover bags in and carried it up to her bedroom. She switched it on and put her hand to the tube to test it. The suck near took the hand off her. It was amazing what a new bag could do to an old machine. Majella began to hoover up the dust and shavings, humming at the same pitch of the hoover. When she was little, she'd followed her da around when he was vacuuming, and she'd hum along with the hoover. He'd never minded her doing that, though her ma had told her it was an odd thing to do. When Majella was finished, she could see the difference between the clean patch of carpet outside her room and the dustier patch inside her room, so she decided to hoover that too. After that she pulled the machine out onto the landing again, where she could see the difference between the clean patch and the rest of the carpet. She had a head of steam worked up, so she fired ahead and hoovered the landing. Then she bumped the hoover down the stairs one by one, cleaning as she went. When she landed at the bottom of the stairs, there was just about enough lead to give her the slack she needed to give the hallway a quick scart. When she came to the radiator under the hall mirror she saw something shining. She paused and picked it up. It was her ma's earring from the night before. Majella pocketed it. When she was finished, she took a look into the living room. It was in desperate need of a hoover. But Majella was tired. She put the hoover away and went out to the kitchen. She pulled her ma's earring out of her pocket and held it in the light, where it dangled, sparkling. Majella could see it was pretty, but she herself stuck to small silver hoops that required no attention. She left the earring out for her ma, then went into the living room and switched on the telly. *Antiques Roadshow* was on. A posh oul doll was sitting with her grandson and a load of teapots, which even Majella could tell were probably worth a fortune. The young grandson was a plummy wee fuck, all self-confidence and 'well actuallys' to the expert fella.

Well . . . how much do you think it's worth?

Majella liked this bit the best. She liked the way the poor folk always guessed high – probably about the amount they owed on credit cards and loans with a bit of a holiday thrown in – and the posh folk always came in low, or worse again, pretended they hadn't a clue, even though you could tell by the shiftiness of them that they'd already got whatever it was valued years before coming on camera. In this episode, the posh oul grandmother wittered on about sentimental value, while the youngster asked directly how much it was worth.

— Well.

Majella jumped. Her ma was up.

6.55 p.m.
Item 5.7: Scented stuff: Toiletries

Majella spat a mouthful of toothpaste and slabber into the sink. She scooped up some cold water in her hand, sucked it up and rinsed it around her mouth, then checked her teeth in the mirror. She could see right into the small gaps between her teeth, that were sometimes gummy with old food. Pleased, Majella closed her mouth and looked at her face. It was clearly about time she did something about her 'tache. She opened the bathroom cabinet. A selection of her ma's pills, creams, safety pins and razors cluttered the shelves. She lifted out a tube of Veet and closed the cabinet. She squirted a thick blob of the cream onto her finger and then smeared it onto her top lip, almost immediately choking on the ming of it. After a few seconds, it began to burn her skin. She held her nerve and put the tube away. Majella hated depilatory creams, but she'd been trained by her ma and Aideen to remove all facial hair below her cheekbones, to thin out anything above her eyelashes, and to plump up the eyelashes in between. She checked the time on her phone. The cream needed five minutes to do its work, five minutes that would feel like five hours to Majella between the smell and burning sensation. To distract herself, she picked up one of her ma's celebrity gossip mags and flicked through to the hall of shame section to gawk at the photos of sweaty, bleary, unhappy and monged celebrity losers. A few of them wouldn't look out of place in A Salt and Battered! She checked her phone obsessively until the five minutes were up, then pulled a whack of bog roll off and wiped the cream off her lip, dropping each soggy wedge into the toilet bowl until she was done. She splashed her face with water, then hunted for a fresh towel to dry her face. Majella loved a fresh towel, the only drawback being that a good clean towel highlighted the muck of the rest of the bathroom. She sighed and turned on the shower, then stripped off her clothes. She stood by the shower, waiting for the water to run hot, rubbing her hand under her diddies while she pictured a pint of cold Smithwicks.

7.37 p.m.
Good list
Item 10: Hairdryers

Majella locked her bedroom door and turned on both the overhead light and the wee bedside lamp. Then she dropped her towel and began to pull a comb through her long, wet hair. Droplets of water showered off the comb and onto her damp flesh. She mopped herself dry and then blow-dried her hair, humming at the same frequency as the motor. When her hair was silky dry she turned the hairdryer onto the folds of her skin. She loved that all-over clean, dry feeling, her hair smelling like conditioner, her body like soap. She decided to smooth on a posh moisturiser sample she'd robbed from one of her ma's magazines. It was ylang-ylang scented and promised extra elasticity in her skin. Majella imagined being able to grab a handful of her skin and pull it out to arm's length before letting go to watch it ping back onto her bones again, like knicker elastic. She doubted the sachet would deliver this vision, but she ripped it open, squeezed as much of the moisturiser out as she could and smoothed it on. Majella didn't know what ylang-ylang was – whether it was a fruit, flower or animal – and had no idea how to pronounce the word. But she loved the way it smelt like baby bubble bath. She wondered what it would be like to have the sort of lad who'd rub that stuff on for you. She'd learned, by reading her ma and Aideen's magazines, all the various sex positions and strategies she was supposed to adopt in order to attract and retain a fella. The magazines advised Majella that she should be engaged in a non-stop campaign to improve herself sexually, emotionally and physically, and that in return she could only expect the man in her life to provide sensual massage if she lit candles, put on music, dressed in fancy knickers and promised to 'reward' him afterwards. The main problem Majella had found in Aghybogey was that the lads weren't reading the same magazines as the girls, so they weren't engaged in any self-improvement programme and thought you were lucky to get the car radio tuned to the station you liked when they were after a blow job. She thought it would be nice to get a lad who'd be into rubbing stuff on you. That American tourist she'd shagged the once had been into things she'd read about in magazines. He was a bit gay, but nice all the same. She still remembered his name – Fontaine de la Cruz. He'd said the Fontaine bit meant Source of Water. The de la Cruz was something to do with the Cross or Crucifix. Majella had thought he was messing, but he seemed serious in the end. He'd asked her what Majella meant of course, which was an embarrassment. She'd hated her name since the very start of P7, when the teacher had told them all to go home and find out why they were called what they were called. Majella had waited til her da had come home and had his dinner. He came into the living room after and sat down with his cup of tea and his *Mirror*. Her ma'd been lying on the settee watching *Coronation Street*.

— Da? Why was ah called Majella Priscilla O'Neill?

Her ma had snorted at that. —Jesus. Here it comes Gerard, here it comes.

Majella hadn't liked her ma's voice. That bitter scratchy noise.

— Why ye asking, Jelly tot?

He was playing for time. She'd seen him do that with her ma often enough to know what it meant. It meant Majella wasn't going to like the answer.

— It's for homework. The teacher says we have tae find out for Confirmation. Ah have tae pick ma Confirmation name.

Her da had taken a big gulp of tea and shifted in his armchair.

— Ah didn't think ye picked yer Confirmation name. In our day ye had til take the name of yer godparent in respect a them.

— Teacher said that. Most of the wans in class are going tae do that.

— So your confirmation name'll be Marie after our Marie then, won't it?

Majella had nodded reluctantly. She'd a fair notion that Marie wasn't really all that fond of her. That the times Marie visited Majella for her birthday and Christmas she just wanted Majella to open her card and present, tell her thanks a million, and get away out of her sight. Her da'd gone back to his paper. Her ma was still watching, smiling slyly.

— Da? You didn't tell me about mah name. Where'd it come from?

Her da had lowered the paper again and cleared his throat. — Ah'll tell ye first where yer surname comes from, will ah?

Majella'd nodded.

— You're an O'Neill. Part of the noblest clan in Ireland. We were once the kings ann queens a Ulster. Ann Ulster was the best province in Ireland.

Her father seemed bigger when he spoke like this, frowning and serious.

— Ah thought we didn't like the Queen?

— Ach, thon oul English bitch is a different story. Ah'm talking about Irish royalty. That spoke til their people ann looked out fer them. That looked after our language ann our land ann our poets ann the animals.

Majella's skin tingled with a sense of pride at the royal blood that flowed through her veins. On the settee her ma sat up and raised her eyebrow at her da.

— Aye. Kings ann queens who've ended up lying the rest of their days in Aghybogey.

— Fuck up, will ye? Ah'm telling the child something about her people.

— Her people? Your people ye mean. It's always your fucken lot.

— Well ah'm hardly gonna tell her the fairy story of your folks, am ah?

Majella sat quietly between them, willing them to go easy.

— What happened to them Daddy?

Her ma turned her face from her da, picked up the remote control and flicked through the channels. Her da closed his eyes and took a breath, rubbed at his forehead with the heel of his hand.

— They left. The English drove them out of it. They flew away til Spain. It was called the Flight of the Earls. The Wild Geese flying. Our kings ann queens gone.

Her da was quiet then, his newspaper limp in his left hand, his right hand closing and opening in empty air. Majella felt something like a flutter of feathers fall down her back, a shiver blowing through her.

— Now we're known as the Foxy O'Neills.

Majella blinked. She'd heard her Uncle Bobby being called Bobby the Fox. She hadn't known why.

— Why are we the Foxy O'Neills?

— We can't be sure. Some say it's because red hair runs in the family. Some say it's because we're so smart. Some say it's coz we're hard to catch.

Majella nodded. Bobby'd been a redhead. And she knew the O'Neills had brains to burn. She'd heard bits and pieces about her family's history of smuggling, the way they'd dodged the law on both sides of the border.

Then her ma spoke up. — Ann some say it's coz yeez might run long, but yeez get caught in the end.

Majella's da narrowed his eyes at that, and there was a long silence between him and her ma. Majella watched her ma colour up before shrinking back into her seat and turning her head to the TV.

— Will ye tell the child how she got her name, anyway?

Her da'd turned to Majella and softened his voice. — You're named after me. And ah was named after Saint Gerard Majella. So your first name is my middle name.

Majella was a bit confused. She had a boy's name? But she knew of plenty of other Majellas about the place, and all of them were girls.

— Have ah got a cub's name?

— Naw, ye haven't. It's wan a them names – like Mary or Gabriel or Hilary – that can be a cub's or a cuddy's name.

Majella's ma giggled on the settee. Her da fired her a dirty look. Majella thought of something.

— Why's mah middle name Priscilla?

— Ah can answer that wan fer ye love. Yer da there had a wild notion a Priscilla Presley, ann that's why you're Priscilla.

Majella looked at her da. He'd taken a reddener, though it was hard to make out if it was in anger or embarrassment. But then he smirked. — Lucky for you ye weren't a cub, for yer ma would've had ye named Elvis.

Her ma started laughing then. — Elvis. Och aye! Elvis O'Neill!

Her da looked at her ma laughing on the settee. He started chuckling.

— Could ye picture some poor wee red-headed basturd running round the estates called Elvis 'the fox' O'Neill. Poor wee fucker.

Her ma's laughter rang out again, and her da started cracking up too. Majella smiled, wanting to get the joke. But she couldn't.

— Ye had a lucky escape, Majella, a lucky, lucky escape.

Majella had one more question for her daddy.

— Did ye want me tae be a boy?

Her da stopped laughing. Even her ma stopped a few moments later.

— Not at all, not at all. Ah just wanted whatever God sent us.

Majella remembered how she'd sat back on the settee and turned her face to *Coronation Street*. She'd watched the screen blankly, all the time wondering what the fuck she was going to write in her homework book for the teacher the next day. Fontaine de la Cruz had found it a bit difficult to understand that Majella'd been named after her da who'd been named after an Irish saint. Patron saint of childbirth and pregnancy, Majella had explained, though that didn't make things any clearer for Fontaine, who was an agnostic. Majella knew what an agnostic was from fourth-year religion class, but had never before – nor since – met a real live one.

Majella shivered violently as her body lotion cooled in the bedroom air. She pulled her towel around her and lifted her wee fan heater up onto the chest of drawers so she'd feel the heat around her body. Then she opened her wardrobe to decide which black top she was going to wear that night. She put her hand to her long-sleeved black top, with the deep scoop at the neck. She had learned that her diddies looked good in that top and it hid the fryer burn scars on her arms. Trousers were much of a muchness, so she just pulled out the first clean pair she could find. Then she rummaged for a bra. As she rooted around in the drawer she enjoyed the hot air of the fan heater on her face and chest.

When she found her good bra, she pulled it around her trunk, leaning forward so her diddies would drop into the cups like she'd seen in a magazine. Then she fastened the bra and stood up for a look in the mirror. She liked what she saw. She reached for her good black knickers, pulled them on, and made sure the string of her tampon was tucked inside before putting on her top and trousers. She took a quick check of her front and arse view. Majella reckoned she'd do rightly, even though Aideen had taught her that all black was bad, and that she should always use a splash of colour. Aideen had tried to get Majella to wear accessories, fiddly shit like necklaces and belts. But Majella never took to it. Nail polish was her compromise. She didn't like the feel of it, nor the waste of it, but she did like the colours, and the teeny tiny bottles with their little stiff brushes. She had collected thirty-six bottles of nail polish over the years, all impulse purchases in the chemist. Sunday was the only day she wore nail polish, for Cunter didn't allow painted nails. So Majella always painted her nails on a Sunday and stripped them on the Monday. She searched methodically through the tin before she found what she was looking for – a deep, dark red that matched her new duvet. It was a sombre colour, nothing too bright or glittery, for it would be thought of by some people that it was bad enough that she was out before her granny's month's mind without her being all tarted up. When she finished painting, she held both hands in front of her. Majella liked her hands. They were well-shaped and strong, the skin criss-crossed with the snail trails of silvery-pink scars from fryer burns. She'd been told she had big hands for a girl by Dermie McDaid, whose real problem was he'd a tiny cock for a full-grown fella. A rush of energy coursed through Majella at the thought of heading into the pub, and she closed her eyes and flicked her fingers.

8.17 p.m.
Item 9: Make-up

Majella didn't like make-up, but she'd been taught that she needed it. It was her skin that was the problem, specifically her spots. She'd squeezed the worst of them earlier and put on a spot cure thing to dry them out. The redness had died down, but she knew that she had more work ahead of her. She smoothed on some foundation before dotting concealer onto her spots and the dark circles under her eyes. Finally she dusted Rose Clair powder over her face and neck. The end result was a flat, matte mask that stopped like a tideline just below her neck. Majella didn't really understand how this look was better than her normal look. She found make-up distracting. Every time she saw someone cleastered in slap, she couldn't stop wondering what it was they were hiding. Majella turned her attention to her eyes. They were easy for she always repeated the same trick: black kohl pencil around the whole of her eyes (making the top line heavier than the bottom), then smokey quartz eyeshadow smudged all around that. She clamped her eyelash curlers onto her lashes before combing on mascara. Then she slicked some Born to Bling onto her lips, before blinking at herself in the mirror. Majella knew she was no Kate Moss, but that she'd do for pints in Aghybogey. She dropped the lip gloss into her handbag and hunted for her purse. Then she sat down on the bed and pulled her black PVC boots on. The zip was bust on the right leg – it only went halfway up, so she had to use a safety pin at the top. All this was hidden under her trousers and Majella hoped the boots would do another year if she was careful. She stood up, pulled on her coat and clomped out the bedroom door, feeling a little like a horse emerging from a stable. At the bottom of the stairs, she paused, and listened to her ma coughing as she watched a *Family Fortunes* rerun.

— Ah'm away out.

Her ma didn't answer. Majella opened the door and stepped into the chilly night outside.

9.11 p.m.
Items 14.7 and 14.9: Medical stuff: Procedures and devices

Majella sat at a table on her own, drinking a pint of Smithwicks. Her fags were tucked away safely in her bag. She doubted she'd need a smoke this evening. She never used to smoke outside of the chipper. But she had to admit that in the last two weeks there'd been more and more sneaky off-duty fags on top of the odd joint. She looked up at the bar where Mairead Carroll was sitting drinking a cider and blackcurrant. Majella hated cider and blackcurrant for the smell of it reminded her of her first smear test. Her first test had been the worst. She'd stressed about it for months beforehand. Aideen, being older, had already been for hers, and had reported back to Majella on the procedure over cider and blackcurrant one Sunday night. Her graphic descriptions had fuelled a fire of anxiety in Majella's belly. When Majella got her appointment card the following spring, she asked Aideen to instruct her on how to handle it.

Majella had tried to follow Aideen's advice. She'd planned her smear outfit: her new jeans, her long woolly jumper and a big pair of black cotton knickers. She had planned to stick one of those smelly panty liners she'd bought specially onto her knickers in case of the 'light bleeding' Aideen had mentioned. And she intended to shower just before she left the house so she wouldn't be what Aideen sneered at as a Sweaty Betty. But when she got home an hour before her test, she'd discovered that she'd forgotten her keys. When she'd rung the doorbell for her ma to open the door there'd been no answer. Upset, she'd battered at the door until Hazel Dolan had come out to say she'd seen her ma leave about ten minutes earlier, and she hadn't a baldy where she'd been headed. Hazel offered Majella a cup of tea, so Majella'd gone into hers and sat down in her two-day-old knickers, her manky joggers and her dirty oul fleece. Her ma didn't turn up before it was time for the appointment. Majella, like her da, could never be late for anything, so at half-past three she got to her feet, said cheerio to Hazel, and headed down to the doctors. The surgery was packed as usual with coughing weans, old people, and flushed, crying babies. It smelt of cheap air freshener defeated by the stench of diarrhoea. Majella signed in at the reception, then sat down, her belly and uteral muscles clenched tight. She had resigned herself to a long wait. She'd never had a doctor's appointment on time in her life, even if she was first on the books. She'd picked up a magazine but inside a few minutes she heard the receptionist call her name.

— Majella? Doctor O'Hanlon is free now.

Majella had jumped up, blushing, and trudged into O'Hanlon's office. O'Hanlon had been glancing through her notes, and then glanced up at Majella. Under O'Hanlon's gaze Majella thought it was important that she explained her situation.

— Ah locked meself out a mah house ann ah didn't have a chance tae shower or change mah pants.

Doctor O'Hanlon's expression stayed neutral. — Don't worry. If you just want to take your bottom half off and jump up there.

Doctor O'Hanlon returned her attention to Majella's notes, missing what Majella thought might be an expression of horror on her face. She'd stumbled towards the examination table but then stopped, not able to continue.

— Ah need the bogs.

O'Hanlon looked up again. She wasn't an easy woman to read, but Majella detected a whiff of pissed-offness in the air.

— Go on then. Quick!

Majella went quickly towards the door but O'Hanlon called her back.

— Majella? Could I have a urine sample please?

She held out a plastic container. Majella took it in her hand and almost ran out of the room and down the hallway into the toilet, which still stank of diarrhoea. She realised when the cold air of the toilet hit her just how sweaty she had become. The whole toilet was tiled – ceiling, floor and walls. It was the sort of room that was designed to be hosed down at the end of a working day. There was no lock, no toilet seat and no toilet roll. Majella checked her pockets. She had no tissues or shopping receipts. Majella looked around her. There were no hand towels and there were no curtains. And Majella had been instructed to pee in a test-tube. A few minutes later, Majella noted that she had indeed peed in the test-tube. She also peed over her hands, the bottle and the floor. She washed the test-tube and her hands, trying not to think of the damp spot spreading at the crotch of her two-day-old knickers. She opened the toilet door with wet hands and returned to O'Hanlon's office. She passed the sample to O'Hanlon, who accepted it wearing a pair of those rubber gloves that always made Majella feel as though she'd caught something nasty, or that she was something nasty.

— Right. Bottom half off and up you pop.

Majella wasn't sure what her bottom half was. Her joggers? Her joggers and pants? Her joggers and pants and skin and hair? She slowly took off her joggers, thinking about Aideen, who'd cried for an hour in her bedroom after her smear, then bled for a day. Majella stood miserably in the office wearing just her knickers and fleece. O'Hanlon glanced over at her.

— Pants too, Majella! Then up you pop!

Majella pulled off her knickers and balled them up. Then she tried to give herself a surreptitious rub between the legs with the balled-up knickers, before bundling them into her fleece pocket so that O'Hanlon wouldn't see the state of them. She turned around and saw O'Hanlon checking a big metal device. Majella wondered where that was supposed to fit. Then O'Hanlon pushed something and the device opened up like a metal umbrella. She caught Majella staring.

— Just hop up and spread your legs, there's a good girl.

Majella got slowly up onto the couch, trying to make her fleece cover as much of her arse and fanny as possible. Then she tried to get comfortable on the wide roll of thin toilet paper, but it had instantly stuck to her sweaty skin and torn, and now half of her arse was stuck to the plastic couch cover. Majella felt that there was something dreadful about being fully dressed from the waist up, and stark naked from your waist to your socks. Everything that was exposed felt shrivelled and loose, her pubic hair felt thin and balding. Hanlon came over.

— Just relax yourself there, Majella.

Majella stared at the ceiling, not breathing.

— Wider there please, Majella.

Majella forced her thighs apart.

— Now this might be a bit cold.

Majella wondered what 'this' was.

— If you're relaxed, this shouldn't hurt.

O'Hanlon's couch side manner had failed to relax Majella. It (whatever *it* was) was bloody freezing and fucking huge. And then O'Hanlon activated the umbrella button, causing Majella to spasm. But O'Hanlon was a pro, and had braced herself so that she forced Majella's thighs to remain at a 180 angle.

Scrape, scrape, SSSCcrape

Majella didn't hear the scrape: she felt it. O'Hanlon sighed.

— Oh dear. Not getting any results here.

She moved away from the examination table and Majella heard her clattering implements about on a tray.

— I'll just try this.

There was no more scraping. Now Majella could feel scratching. The ceiling suddenly seemed far away and the lights too bright as Majella shrank and shrank and shrank.

— All done!

Majella's knees twanged together as though elasticated.

— Now. That wasn't so bad was it?

Majella reckoned the question was most likely rhetorical, so she shook her head. Then she pulled her fleece down as far as it would go, her left hand scrabbling for her joggers. O'Hanlon was holding up something urine-coloured and plastic, which was covered in a bloody mucus.

— I wasn't getting any results with that, so I used this instead.

O'Hanlon then brandished something metal that she'd already wiped, but was still gooey. Majella was unsure how she was supposed to respond, so she aimed for a tone of generalised enthusiasm.

— Right. Right. Great stuff.

She tried not to calculate how many of the women she knew in Aghybogey might've had that reusable metal contraption pushed inside them. She waited until O'Hanlon had turned around to go back to her desk before trying to get up off the examination table. The toilet paper was stuck tight to her. O'Hanlon looked up briefly as Majella was pulling it off her arse and crumpling it up. Majella quickly pulled on her joggers and trainers, hoping O'Hanlon hadn't noticed that she didn't put her pants back on. Majella wasn't sure what happened next – Aideen's instructions hadn't covered the aftermath of the procedure.

— Can ah go?

— Oh yes certainly. Call back in about a month for your result.

— Grand. Thanks. Right. Bye.

Majella forced herself to move slowly to the door and to walk out of the surgery normally. Then she walked home at a normal pace, despite the gradual wettening of her joggers as blood began to trickle down from her scraped cervix. She was thankful that she was wearing navy joggers. When she got to her front door and rang the bell, her ma opened the door and started telling her about a great bargain in steak mince she'd just got off Feely's meats. Majella listened as she climbed the stairs, her fist clenching and unclenching around the knickers in her pocket.

9.42 p.m.
Item 1: Small talk, bullshit and gossip

Majella was enjoying watching the bubbles float from the bottom to the top of the glass on her fresh pint. One of her earliest and happiest memories was of watching the booze bubbles in one of her da's pints. She would've happily sat for hours between her parents watching the bubbles streaming upwards. Even now, when she was the right stage of drunk, she could still feel their fizzing, buzzing happiness.

— Well, Majella. How're ye holdin up?

Majella looked up and sighed. Charlotte Keenan had taken it on herself to come over to Majella, beaming one of her tight little smiles at her.

— Grand. Sure ah've only had a few.

Charlotte frowned. — I meant with yer granny ann . . . ann everything.

Majella shrugged and took a sip of her pint. — Sure, she's dead and buried now, so we'll just have tae get on with things.

Charlotte kept frowning. Majella looked around for Dinny, her husband, and spotted him sitting down near the door with a few of his cronies. Charlotte was on the vodka and Diet Coke, as usual. Majella took a swallow of her Smithwicks.

— Well I suppose they say life has to go on.

Majella didn't answer. She couldn't stand Charlotte. They'd been in the same class the whole way through school. Before Majella'd fallen in with Aideen, Charlotte had taken it upon herself to make Majella a personal project, doling out advice on personal hygiene, social conduct and family relationships. The advice in itself wasn't terrible – it was the way Charlotte did it that annoyed Majella. She'd gather an audience of their classmates, then repeat whatever fuck-up or mistake Majella'd made, before acting out the right way to behave, so everyone would have a laugh at how wrong Majella got stuff. Aideen had a quieter way of helping Majella. Aideen'd wait until Majella was in the toilet, or alone in the yard or down at the lockers, before she'd whisper a word of advice, or fix her hair, or roll down her socks to the right length for the fashion that was in that term.

— But how's yer poor mother doing with this and the arrest adding tae her troubles?

Majella felt a surge of anger so it took her a few seconds before she could shrug again. — She's the same as ever. Drinking her way tae a hole in the ground.

Charlotte looked horrified. — Och, now, Majella, don't be saying such a thing. That's shocking. Your mother has a good few years ahead of her yet. A good few.

Majella thought about all the years stretching ahead of her ma and ahead of herself and took a gulp of her pint. Charlotte was the same age as Majella, but she'd been born middle aged. She'd been married before she hit nineteen. Three weans she had now to Dinny. But, according to Marty, Dinny had a few more than three weans dotted around the country.

— Ann what about yer Auntie Marie? I heard it said that she wasn't right well there, over the weekend?

— Ah didn't know she was ailing.

Charlotte shifted uncomfortably. — Well. She's not ailing. Ah heard she was upset.

— She's just buried her mother. I've been told that's upsetting.

From the corner of her eye, Majella saw Charlotte frown. — Och, I know. Then I suppose there's youse falling out with her too?

Majella raised an eyebrow and sat back a bit, saying nothing.

Charlotte pressed on. — Suppose a woman of her age, on her own up that mountain, and her feeling the loss of her mother and the loss of a neighbour, and now maybe too the loss of the family home . . . maybe she's just feeling a wee bit down.

Majella made an effort to look Charlotte in the eye. — You're right. She's probably feeling down. But enough about me and mine. What about you? How's the weans?

Charlotte looked a wee bit irritated, but then switched from her concerned face to her proud Mammy face.

— Och sure I'm doing grand. And the weans are all great. Wee Dennis is loving school, so he is.

— Aye ah'm sure. And what about Dinny? Found any work yet, has he?

Charlotte's smile stayed painted on. — Och, no luck. But sure it's wild hard these days tae find steady work, y'know. You're dead lucky with the chipper ann that.

— Ah heard there's taxi-ing jobs goin in Bogey Taxis.

Charlotte bared her teeth in her smile, then took a sip of the vodka and Diet Coke Majella knew she'd be nursing for the rest of the night.

— Dinny's not keen on heading back tae the taxi-ing. Wild unsociable hours. And him a family man.

— Aye. Suppose you'd see next to nothing of him but half the town'd be chatting him in the taxi.

— Aye.

Majella kept her gaze fixed on Charlotte until she broke away, fingering her glass. Then she cleared her throat and took another tiny sip of her drink. Eye contact was a lot of work, but sometimes Majella felt it was worth the effort. She turned her gaze back to her pint and let the silence stretch out between them.

— Anyway. Ah'll let ye go. Tell Dinny ah was asking after him.

Charlotte got up, awkward with relief. — Right. Well. Mind yourself.

Majella watched the now much shorter path of bubbles stream to the top of her pint for a few moments, then she put the glass to her head and drained it.

9.50 p.m.
Item 3.4: Noise: Shite singing

Behind Majella an oul fucker at the bar started up singing. The people around him went quiet. Half of them were embarrassed, the other half sitting listening with big intense heads on them. He had a quavery voice and was half in and half out of tune. Majella hadn't a clue what he was singing, and neither did anyone else, for no one was making any attempt to join in. The Breen brothers at the end of the bar burst out laughing at some joke or other, and then Mairead Carroll started shushing them with furious hisses.

— Shuddup, will youse? Shuddup! Seamy's singing!

They pretended to ignore her, but quietened down while the old man stumbled on through the song. He lost the run of it before it was half over, got raging with himself and gave up.

— Ach, Seamy, go on ahead ann finish her off, go on.

— We were enjoying that, Seamy!

Majella had not been enjoying that, and was relieved when Seamy wouldn't be cajoled into starting up again and instead sank his head in his pint in a sulk. There was a scattering of half-hearted clapping, and then the Breen brothers starting howling at some clip on a mobile phone. Porn, Majella reckoned, and lifted her pint of Smithwicks. The last swallow was warm and flat, the glass smeared. She threw it back and felt for her purse. The bar seemed like miles away.

— Can ah get ye one, Jellah?

Majella looked up and saw Tommy Wheels.

— Ah dunno Tommy, can ye?

Tommy Wheels laughed, and so did Majella, for it was their regular joke.

— Pinta Smith-icks then?

— Pinta Smith-icks Tommy, thanks.

Majella smiled as she watched Tommy dander over to the bar. It was nice to see him, for he wasn't always about. But when he was, they'd have a pint, for Tommy and her went way back. Back to the days when they'd both had bikes and they'd ridden about the place in the summer time. They'd ride out to her granny's, criss-crossing the border, passing the barricades and skirting around craters. But bikes weren't really where it was at with Tommy – he'd been mad into the cars. He passed his driving test the week of his seventeeth birthday and he'd got himself a car. But not the same sort of a car as the other lads in the town – not a blacked-out, souped-up boy racer. No. Tommy'd went out and bought a fucked-up Ford Escort, in a shitty orange colour. Ran the wee fucker until it died up the M1 one December, leaving him and his mother stranded with the Christmas shopping until Majella's da had gone up to get them. They'd towed the wee car back and got her running again, but she was a dead loss for going places. Tommy'd sold her for scrap to some lad who'd given him fifty quid in notes. He was still car hunting when his wee Ford Escort got a star turn on the Five Live news, being blown up by the army at the border crossing in Pettigo. Tommy'd been lifted after that and questioned for two days up in Castlereagh. Before his bruises had faded, he'd bought the Toyota Carina II. There'd been nearly 300,000 miles on the clock before he started with her. The wee Carina had been Majella's favourite car. Tommy'd taken to calling on her in the evenings after she'd come home from school. And then that summer they'd jaunted all over the place. Bundoran for the slot machines. Donegal town for the pubs. Derry for the shopping. At nights they'd go up the border and sit in the darkness of the bombed-out roads. Not smoking. Not drinking. Tommy wasn't into any of that. Just the pair of them sitting and chatting.

— Pinta Smith-icks fer the lady.

Tommy placed a pint in front of Majella, in the exact centre of the beer mat. He was particular in ways that suited Majella.

— Thanks a million Tommy.

Tommy settled back into the seat and took a long swallow from his pint of Tennants. Majella didn't like Tennants.

— Ah dunno how ye can drink that mank.

— Och, sure it's all the same. In wan end, out the other.

Majella smiled.

— How've ye been keeping?

Majella shrugged. — Grand. All right.

— Didn't get tae chat ye after the funeral. But sure it was a big do.

— Aye. Didn't really chat many at it. Too many people there, if ye know what ah mean.

— Aye.

They sat in silence for a while. Majella remembered the day that Tommy had taken her up the border and they'd driven right into the forest. It had been haunted, or so it was said. The Brits had lost two men on patrol there one night, with five wounded. There'd been a closed inquiry into the incident, but stuff leaked out anyway. Stories about how the soldiers had seen things, got spooked, then started firing. Though the IRA had claimed the incident was a successful Republican assault, in the morgue the Brit coroner had dug only British bullets out of the soldiers' backs. Majella'd been staring out the windows the night they'd gone deep into that forest. It stretched for miles around them. After a long time, Tommy had spoken to her.

— Got something to show ye!

His eyes had been sparkling with good humour. Majella'd always liked Tommy's eyes, and in this dark his pupils were big, black pools.

— What've ye got?

— Come here over here tae me.

Majella remembered the way she'd sat still, her heart beating faster. — What?

— Come here ann lean over tae me here.

Majella'd leaned forward, tentatively.

He'd put his arm around her shoulder and pulled her closer to his chest. — Gimme your hand.

Majella'd pulled back. — Fuck off Tommy.

— Shut up you daftie! Give us yer hand. Go on!

Majella had hesitated.

— Please?

She leaned back in, put her right hand in his hand, her heart thumping. She could smell the aftershave on him and the much sexier tang of his sweat underneath.

— Right . . . houl on.

Tommy took her hand and guided it to the dashboard, where he pushed her finger on a button. The car roared into life and Majella had jumped back.

— Jesus Christ! What the fuck?

Tommy'd sat there laughing. Majella'd punched him a few times on the arm, and he'd curved his body away to protect himself, laughing until she'd laughed too.

— What are ye smiling about, Jellah?

Majella took a sip of her Smithwicks. — Och. Just thinking back til that night ye drove me up til the forest in yer oul Toyota Carina. D'ye mind her?

— Oh aye, oul Cassie. She was a deadly car.

— Aye. Ann you'd bust the ignition in her so ye had to rig her up with thon button. D'ye mind? Then ye made me press it ann scared the life half outta me?

Tommy started to laugh and had to put his pint back on the table. — Fuck aye. D'ye mind the Brits then! And mind how ah opened the boot?

— Ah'm hardly gonna forget. There's him all, 'Can I See Your iDentiFiCation Please Sir,' and 'Can You Step Out of the Car and Open the Boot For Me Please Sir,' and you saying, 'no need fer that,' ann then you pulling on that bit of rope ann the boot popping open scaring the life out a the Brits. There's them all cocked guns ann 'Out of the Car with Your Hands in The Air!'

Tommy bent over laughing beside Majella, and she shook with big silent laughs.

— Then the fuckers body searched me fer being so smart.

Majella remembered Tommy spread out against the army jeep, his coat in a heap in the ditch, one soldier with a gun to his head, another roughly searching his lean body while they questioned her.

— Them were the days. No craic like that now.

Majella didn't see much of Tommy these days. He'd got a new car. A Nissan Primera. Sometimes he'd wave out at her as he passed in the street, his snobby cunt of a girlfriend sailing by with her snootery nose in the air.

— Naw. No craic at all these days.

Tommy's phone vibrated on the table. He picked it up and checked the message. Then he sat back again, but turned towards her.

— Ah heard about Jimmy's arrest, Jellah.

Majella nodded, avoiding his eyes. She could find nothing to say.

— Ah was thinking that'll be rough on all of yeez, if he's charged.

Majella nodded again, tears prickling at her eyes like the bubbles in her pint.

— Him a neighbour. Ann a customer of yours this years.

— They haven't charged him with anythin as far as ah know. Ann the Daly brothers were lifted too.

Tommy tossed his head. — Sure they'd try to pin the rising of the sun on the Daly brothers if they could. And still have to let them walk loose at the end of the interrogation period.

Majella looked at her pint. Tommy laid his hand on Majella's arm. It'd been years since they'd touched.

— Look, ah know you're the independent sort. Ann ah know you're able for this. So ah'll get out of yer way. Just wanted ye to know ah was thinking of ye.

Majella gathered herself. — No bother, Tommy. Thanks fer the pint.

She raised what was left in her glass in Tommy's direction without meeting his gaze. She could picture his eyes.

— Ye're welcome.

Tommy stood up and Majella watched him head to the side door. She knew he'd look around before ducking out, so, at the last second, she glared at her mobile phone, frowning as if she had something to read.

11.11 p.m.
Item 47: Shiftiness and double dealing

Majella had been horsing the pints back and now she reckoned she was well oiled. She couldn't feel her feet, but she could still see the bar, which was a good enough state of drunkenness. She didn't mind the warm stink of beer, sick and pish seeping out from the rotting foam under the velour seats. She didn't mind the lights from the fruit machines or the music from the jukebox or the people moving around her. Majella glanced down at her Smithwicks, which was getting low. She wasn't looking forward to the effort of going to the bar, of focusing and holding herself up straight and talking slowly and deliberately, because while she liked the feeling of being drunk, she didn't like looking or sounding drunk.

— Can ah get you a drink there, Miss O'Neill?

Majella looked up, confused. She didn't recognise the voice. It was some bogger of a farmer by the looks of him. She wanted a drink, but she didn't want to have to listen to any oul shite.

— Looks like yer on the Smith-icks.

Majella hesitated, then nodded. She watched him dander over to the bar, nodding at a few heads on the way. She couldn't place him. He wasn't a chipper customer and he was no regular of the Bogey Inn either. She eyed him while he stood there chatting to Phelim, who poured her pint before setting out a wee Jameson's with a jug of water on the side. He was old enough to be wearing a suit and a flat cap. He paid with loose change from his trouser pocket, then picked the drinks up and went back to her table.

— D'ye mind if ah join ye?

Majella shrugged. It was no odds to her where he sat. He put his jug of water on the table, then sat down, holding his Jameson's in his hand. He didn't look too pished to Majella. Seemed sober enough.

— Wild weather we've been having.

Majella nodded. — Tis aye, but sure it could be worse.

She tried to swallow the last of her old pint but misjudged how much was left. There was too much for a mouthful, so she had to open her throat and let the beer flow down instead of just swallowing. She wasn't fond of doing that unless she wanted to scull a pint. Left her very gassy.

— They say it's snow we'll be having. Next weekend. maybe.

— We could be doing without the snow.

— We could.

They both sat on. Majella let a quiet burp rise out of her. Your man took a sip of his whiskey, then poured a wee taste of water in on top. Majella stared at her new pint. She realised she'd lost count of how many she'd had now. That wasn't good. She was way too pished for eleven o'clock. This was her one-in-the-morning feeling. Her I'm-ready-for-a-taxi feeling. It was all the blood loss that was doing it. She'd have to slow it down a bit.

— Well, sure at least it's wan more winter yer poor granny'll not have tae sit out in thon wee shack of a caravan.

Majella closed her eyes. Here we fucken go again, was all she could think before the world began to spin around her.

— Course we were always up there fer her, y'know. Calling in ann that. Ah know twas hard fer ye tae be up as much after yer daddy . . . after yer daddy went.

Majella opened her eyes. Closing them had been a mistake. Everything swirled around her in crazy dips and snaps and it took a few seconds for her to clamp her eye on the stuffed deer head on the far wall. She focused on it until the swinging slowed, then stopped.

— Aye. Twas hard, all right, with no car.

— Ye know she was nearly like family til us too.

Majella took a long look at your man. She could remember him now. She'd seen his face at the wake a good few times. He'd been in and out and always bringing stuff – tins of biscuits, bags of ham sandwiches. During the burial he'd been up at the front of the crowd at the grave, his dirty wee cap in hand. But she couldn't remember his fucken name.

— Ah hear ye came in tae the land.

Majella remembered his name. Maguire. The fucker who'd always been torturing her granny, looking to buy the land off her. Majella suddenly felt a wee bit more sober.

— Ah did, aye.

— That'd be the land ah've been renting off of yer granny fer a good few years now.

— It would. Ten acres, ah've been told.

— Aye. Ten acres. Not the best land ah've farmed in me life, but ah've farmed it a long time now. A long time.

Majella knew how long he'd been renting that land.

— Sixteen years.

— Would be sixteen years, right enough, aye. The guts a sixteen years.

Majella looked at the bar. Nobody caught her eye, but she knew they were being watched. Knew the whole bar would know why Mealy Maguire had come into the Bogey Inn the night.

— Aye. Ye got it after Bobby died.

— O Lord, aye. A wild loss of a good man. A wild loss. Still, he died fer the Cause.

Majella took a sip from her pint and said nothing.

Mealy nodded to himself. — No Better Cause.

Majella still said nothing. Mealy looked uncomfortable and reached for his whiskey. He took another swallow, left the glass down, then diluted the whiskey further with a small splash of the water.

— Had ye any notion what ye'd like tae do with the land?

Majella lifted her new pint and took a small, slow sip. — Dunno. Might take tae farming.

Mealy looked up at her, frowning, trying to suss her out. Majella had already stuck on her blank face.

— Farming?

— Ah could, aye. Majella warmed to her subject. — Ah could maybe get a dose of cattle or sheep ann have a go at living out there. Maybe put up some of them polytunnels for the mushrooms. Or ah could develop the land. Get planning permission ann build a lock of houses.

Mealy toyed with his glass. His frown had deepened. He looked up at Majella again.

— Would ye ever think a selling it, now? As farmland.

Majella held her silence.

— Just if ye were thinking of it, ah'd be interested. It's nearly like me own land now, after sixteen years on it. Ye get attached to land like that. Raising your cattle on it. Pulling the crops. Watching over it.

— Oh aye, ah'd say ye could now, get attached.

— Ye would aye.

There was another silence. Majella lifted her eyes towards the bar. A few heads ducked down as she looked up. She realised her family didn't have to be on the news to be a free show for them.

— What price would ye be thinking of?

— Oh, a price. A price. Ah wouldn't have wan on me now. Ah wouldn't know. What would ye be looking?

A ball of fire rose in Majella's gut, and she looked directly at Mealy. He'd been in the bar all night, she'd realised.

And he'd waited until she was at least seven pints in before coming over to touch her up about some land. She wasn't impressed.

— What would ah be looking? Well now. With that border road opened up ah'd say the price of land up Garvaghy's been rising. With a bit of peace money ah'd say there could be all sorts of improvements up there. If ah hold on fer even a year, ah'd probably see a right wee rise in me farm.

Mealy's face had hardened. — What price?

Majella's da hadn't been a farmer, not really. He'd been a factory man. A fixer. But he'd still passed on a few farming tips to Majella. One gem she'd never forgotten was that in bargaining she should never name her price first. First person to name their price has already lost the battle.

— Mr Maguire. You came over tae my table the night with a price in yer head. Ah think ye should name it ann be done with it.

Mealy took a reddener. Majella guessed he was raging. She knew she was being a cunt, but at the same time, what sort of a basturd was he to be coming over to her and her drunk and her granny not cold in the grave?

— Ah'd give you forty thousand for the whole ten acres.

Majella kept her face blank. — Would ye now? Forty thousand.

Mealy sat there, gripping his whiskey glass tight. — Cash it would be.

Mealy looked over at Majella, who was staying silent.

— Tis a handy wee amount a money, forty thousand.

Majella looked back at Mealy. — Tis aye. Ah could do something with forty thousand.

Mealy nodded encouragingly at her. Majella could nearly smell the hunger off him. — Young cuddy like you could do anything. Build a decent house near the town. Go travelling. Get a car.

Majella nodded slowly. — Ah could. But that's if ah took it off ye. Ann ah won't be takin yer forty thousand off ye. But thanks fer the drink.

Mealy's face deepened in colour and he lifted his whiskey to his head and fired the last of it down his throat. Majella could see the men shifting at the bar, looking at each other. Without looking at her Mealy growled. — Yer welcome.

He got up to leave, then stood for a moment, adjusting his cap.

— If ye change yer mind, Miss O'Neill, ye know where ah am.

Majella felt a grudging respect for his persistence. — Ah do, aye.

1.22 a.m.
Good list
Item 8: Cleaning

Majella could see Bridie McGlinchey wasn't in any form for taking shite. She'd started her clean-up behind the bar at half twelve. And as soon as one o'clock had chimed on the Guinness clock, she threw the bar lights off and headed away like a demon with the hoover. Majella watched her start at the far end of the room, rolling the hoover in tight lines up and down the floor. It wasn't long until she'd reached the bar. The noise of the hoover cleared a few of the more sensitive drinkers out. They sculled what was left of their drinks and hit the road. Majella sat on in her corner, warm and sleepy, watching as Bridie began to vacuum around the stragglers, bumping into feet, lifting handbags and stacking chairs as she went.

Majella thought that if Bridie had a big enough hoover she'd hoover them all up. It wasn't too long until she'd landed over at Majella. Bridie gave her a quick nod and hoovered around her. Majella felt the nozzle whack against her legs. She didn't feel like moving. She fancied sleeping there for the night.

Bridie moved away and finished up around the last of the tables. Then she switched the hoover off, and rewound the cord. It snapped tight inside the machine, and Bridie carried it back behind the bar. Then she started on clearing the tables. Even if a drink wasn't drunk, it was lifted and dumped. Majella stretched her hand out to lift the last of her Smithwicks. She picked up the glass, brought it to her lips, but then just let a rift out of her. She'd had enough she reckoned.

— Izzit not time a cuddy like you wuz in her bed?

Majella looked up. Terry Cavanagh was standing above her.

— Slate enuff, ah spose.

— Tis aye. Though ah could do wi a bittay a feed.

Majella blinked and thought of food. She put the last of her pint on the table. She'd hardly put it out of her hand before Bridie swiped it.

— Bitta food woulden hurt now.

— Naw. Ah have the van. D'ye wanta lift?

Majella blinked again. A bit of a feed and a lift home. She could do worse.

— Aye. Ah'd take a lift.

Majella felt a pressure on her bladder. Time for a pish. She heaved herself up out of the warm smelly cushions.

— Hafta pish first.

— No boller. Ah'll wait fer ye.

As Bridie lit on the empty table with a J-cloth and some scoosh, Majella stumbled across to the toilets.

1.32 a.m.
Good list
Item 1.3: Eating: Chinese food

Majella leaned up against Terry Cavanagh's blue van while he fumbled for his keys. She was stocious. She knew Terry was more than half-cut too. He'd be done if he was caught driving. But that was his problem. He finally found his van key and slotted it into the door lock. After climbing in, he leaned over and unlocked the passenger side for Majella. She opened the door and waited for a few moments while he knocked a clatter of cassettes, maps and old newspapers from the van seat to the floor, then she heaved herself in. She was shivering with cold.

— We'll soon get ye warmed up.

Majella shoved her hands under her oxters to get a bit of heat into them. Her breath steamed out hot and white, then clotted on the window. Terry was struggling to get the key into the ignition. When he finally succeeded, he started the engine and whacked on the heating. Cold air blasted out in Majella's eyes and she turned her face away.

— Turn that off me, will ye?

Terry rolled the fan away from Majella and directed it down to the floor.

— Ye hungry?

Majella nodded. She was fucken starving.

— Chipper or Chinese?

Majella thought he was daft for asking. — Chinese.

— All right.

The heating had cleared the mist of their breath from the windscreen, so Terry put the van into first gear and set off down the town. Majella laid her head back against the headrest. She was blootered. The orange streetlights of Aghybogey flickered in on top of her as they drove to the bottom of the town. Terry pulled the van up and dimmed the lights.

— Ah'll get the food. What are ye lookin?

— Chicken fried rice.

— Ah'll layve the engine on tae warm ye uppabit.

Terry got out of the van and walked slowly towards the brightly lit Chinese. It looked empty. Majella turned her face away. A faint heat was now blowing from the van heater. She turned the dial so it was directed at her feet. She hadn't been able to feel them for a long time now from the drink, but she knew they'd be freezing. Her arse was freezing too. It was never the warmest, but sitting on the icy-cold seats of the wee van had done it no favours. She turned on the radio and one of Terry's country and western cassettes kicked in. He'd wild taste in music, had Terry. Majella was just nodding off when he opened the van door and swung a bag of Chinese food across to her. Majella caught it and hugged the hot food to her chest, soaking up the heat of it. Terry pulled on his seat belt and put the van into first gear.

— Where d'ye want tae ate?

Majella shrugged. — Ah'm easy.

— What about the castle?

Majella shrugged again. — Grand.

Terry drove slowly towards the car park near the castle. After the archaeologists had fucked off back to Belfast, the council had tarmacked over a field to make parking for the tourists they'd been told would flock to Aghybogey as part of the Peace Dividend. But the car park was empty of tourists all day every day, and only got busy at night with locals eating takeaways and shagging. Used condoms had become a regular subject of complaint in the Local Letters section of the *Bogey News* from people who signed themselves as *Concerned Local Resident* or *Outraged from Riverview Park.* Terry drove into the darkest corner of the car park and switched off the lights. The van had warmed up by now and Majella had stopped shivering. She tore into the brown bag on her knee and pulled the lid off the first foil carton. The smell hit her before she could see what it was, and she knew it was her chicken fried rice. She lifted the carton out, and dug about at the bottom of the bag for a plastic fork and a handful of napkins, then she passed the rest of the food over to Terry.

— Fucken starven.

She pushed the fork deep into the rice and chicken and then brought it to her lips. She opened her gob and got the whole lot in without dropping even a grain of rice. The food was roasting so she took in a series of quick small breaths of cold air to cool it, then she closed her mouth and chewed. The flavours smeared across her tongue and the roof of her mouth. Small shreds of chicken mashed into the mushy rice. Fucken gorgeous, was all she could think. A second mouthful was on its way to her lips before she had swallowed the first. Majella wished she worked in the Chinese. After a few mouthfuls she turned to Terry.

— Whatchewget?

Terry's mouth was full and Majella took another mouthful as he worked his way through it.

— Sweet ann sour battered chicken ballz.

— Awwww luvlay.

— Want wan?

Majella hesitated, chewing her food.

— Sure gwan. Take wan. The sauce iz luvlay.

She swallowed her chicken fried rice and reached out and lifted a chicken ball in her hand. It was roasting hot, the oil sticking to her fingers. She dropped it.

— Fuckit.

She tried again, this time grabbing the thinnest end of the chicken ball. She got it and dunked it into the sweet and sour sauce. She took it quickly to her mouth and bit through the thick cushion of batter into the chicken chunk inside before the sauce could drip on her. She chewed slowly, enjoying the twang of the sauce on her tongue.

— Nice?

Majella grunted and nodded, her mouth full. She delved into her chicken fried rice again. It had cooled, so she lifted the foil dish under her chin and ate rapidly, spooning the rice and chicken into her mouth. After she swallowed it down, she sighed and took a long gulp from Terry's Coke can. Then she crushed her tin foil carton, and wiped her greasy fingers in a napkin before shoving the carton, napkin and fork into the plastic bag. Terry was still picking over his food. Majella felt full to bursting, so she opened her mouth and rifted. Immediately she felt better. She put her head back on the headrest and sighed again. She felt sleepy now. She was still langered, but a wee bit steadier than earlier on thanks to the cold air and the food. An old Meat Loaf song came on the radio. Majella leaned forward and turned it up. She watched as Terry took one last mouthful of food, before giving up and wiping his hands and mouth with a napkin. Then he thrust his leftover rice and fork into the bulging plastic bag, opened the van door and dropped the package outside. An icy breeze swept through the van and Majella shivered.

— Fucken freezen.

Terry closed the door and the light went out. But Majella could still see his face. He was smiling. — C'mere ann ah'll warm yup.

Majella let Terry pull her to him and turned her face close to his. He leaned in and started snogging her, his free hand moving in around her waist and up under her top. Majella could taste the sweet and sour on his tongue, the grease of the batter balls from his lips. He wasn't a bad oul snog, Terry. He'd a big cock as well. It was a shame he was so ugly. She pushed her hands up under his shirt, to his belly underneath, she felt the hairs snag in her nails as she ran her fingers over his skin. He had worked his way up to her diddies and Majella breathed heavily as he rubbed his rough hands over her skin. She took her hand back from under his shirt and moved to his thigh, rubbing slowly up and down, as close as she could to the bulge of his cock without actually touching it. Terry leaned in closer to her, breathing heavier, and began to kiss her neck, moving down to the crease of her boobs, where he buried his face. Then he came back up to her.

— Come on ann we'll get in the back.

Majella nodded. There was more space in the back of the van.

— Ah threw down an oul blanket there earlier.

As Majella climbed between the seats to the back of the van, Terry put his hands between her thighs. When she stepped forward her thighs rubbed around his hand, sending a tremble through her. Majella lay down on her side in the cold back of the van. She shivered until Terry lay down beside her and together they warmed the blanket. After a bit, Terry shifted his hips backwards and began to unbuckle his belt.

Then Majella remembered. — Ah fuck.

Terry stopped what he was doing.

— Wha?

— Ah'm on the rag.

— Eh?

— Ah'm on the rag. Fucken forgot.

Terry shrugged. — Ah don't mind playin on a flooded pitch.

Majella stored Terry's response in her brain for analysis later, and watched as he unbuttoned her trousers.

4.44 a.m.

Item 16.11: Booze: The truth coming out

Majella slammed the door of Terry's van closed. He waved at her, then drove off. It was raining. Majella checked her phone.

It was late. And her head was beginning to hurt. She began to walk down the path to her house, her feet sore in her boots. The wet patch on her trousers where Terry'd come felt icy cold in the wind. She tried to walk faster, but couldn't find the energy. By the time she came to the gate of her house, she was soaked. She fumbled with the catch on the gate. Her fingers were too cold to work properly. She finally opened it, and then reached in to her jacket pocket for her house key. She opened the door. The house was cold and dark, so she figured her ma'd made it to bed. She closed the door behind her and tramped down the hallway. She flicked on the light switch in the kitchen, and closed her eyes against the jerky light. When the bulb settled Majella looked around the dirty little kitchen. A cup of tay was needed. She turned on the kettle and took her mug from the cupboard, then dropped a tea bag into it. She stood there, staring at the grease-splashed tiles until the kettle boiled. When she was pouring the steaming water into her mug she noticed that the nail polish on her thumbnail had chipped. She frowned and put the kettle down to have a better look. There was a crack down the middle of the nail. The polish around it was brittle and when she put her other thumbnail under it flaked off. She stood there, working at the polish until the whole nail was bare. She stared at the one naked nail and suddenly a huge shudder went through her. She gasped for air and a noise like pain came out of her open mouth. She gasped again, the pain in her chest, the darkness in her head overwhelming her. She whined this time. She dropped to her knees in front of the kitchen cabinets, pressed her forehead against the cold Formica and took a third breath. Tears burst out from her burning eyes, scalding her cheeks. Majella squatted there, crippled, gulping in one ragged breath after another, letting the tears pour out of her, gasping for air. It was a long time before she could slow her breathing and control the sobs. The tears slowed. Something had shifted inside her. Something was different. She wiped the tears from her eyes, then stood up and threw her cold cup of tea in the sink before climbing the stairs to bed.

Majella locked her bedroom door, pulled her shoes off and climbed into bed fully dressed. She lay there, picturing her granny, her Uncle Bobby, and her da, and the land they'd clung to for generations. Land that was now hers. She pictured sly old J. R. Ewing smiling at her from under his Stetson, with a whiskey tumbler in his hand. She considered what J. R. would do. She thought of all the things he had taught her over the years: Never forgive. Never forget. To do unto others before they do you. To take advantage of every opportunity that presents itself. Lessons Majella had listened to, but never learned from. And then it clicked with Majella what she should do. She felt her eyes closing as a weight lifted off her chest. She needed a good sleep. For she'd a solicitor to talk to in the morning about the price of land.

Acknowledgements

Thanks to:

The whole team at John Murray Press, especially Becky Walsh, Alice Herbert, Joanna Kaliszewska, Jahan Hussain and Sara Marafini.

Mehdi, Rónán and Cillian, who gave me time to write and rewrite.

Charlie and Mary, Úna, Christine, Mickey, Deci and Pauline, who have loved me fiercely.

Tina, Sorsh, Roni, Pauline and Cinta for being there for me for forever.

Julie-Anne, Carey, Ruairi, Tom, and Brendan, who made Belfast a hard town to leave.

Aude Doody, Karen Virapen, Declan Gallen, Rowan O'Neill and Annie McCartney for reading the early manuscripts and providing critical feedback – the book would not be here without you.

Marianne Gunn O'Connor, who is never afraid to say 'no'.

Clare, who said it was OK to quit but is glad I didn't.

Russell, who told me to quit everything else and is glad I did.

Sylvia, who helped me find the key.

The staff of St Patrick's Primary School and St Eugene's High School, especially Maureen Kelly, Danny Glackin and Colette Rush.

Maria McManus and Patsy Horton for including me in the Irish Writers Centre initiative xBorders (supported by the Arts Council of Northern Ireland and the Arts Council of Ireland).

Catherine Dunne, Anthony Glavin and Anna Carey, who judged the Irish Novel Fair 2019, which was organised by the Irish Writers Centre.